# Kill the Gods

Being the third part of
Lake of Dragons

E. Michael Mettille

TMR Books
PO Box 510886
Milwaukee, WI 53203
www.themikereynolds.com



All images provided provided by Deposit Photos

Cover Artwork – © 2021 L.J. Anderson of Mayhem Cover Creations

Published by TMR Books 05/15/2021

ISBN 978-0-9975571-5-2

# DEDICATION

For Shelia…you know.

# CHAPTER 1
# DARKNESS

Pain can be a tricky thing, difficult to gauge. The same pain can be at one moment merely an annoyance detracting from one's ability to focus on the task at hand while in the next moment the only thing on which they can focus. The throbbing in Doentaat's leg when he woke in darkness so pitch blindness seemed the only possibility was the latter. Rather than pushing the pain away from his focus, the disorienting fear of being without sight and unaware of his surroundings only served to strengthen it. It pulsed like someone stood above him repeatedly striking the same spot on his thigh with a hammer. Attempting to sit up only made it worse, like a jagged spear tore through his flesh. The sound he made as he gave in to the pain and lay back was something to which a warrior of his stature would never admit. The Lake could have his soul if only his agony might cease.

As the dwarf king lay in darkness waiting for death to come and end his suffering, his focus shifted. It seemed accepting his eventual demise somewhat numbed him to the pain. Of course, the throbbing in his leg had not ceased. However, it slowly loosened its grip on his awareness, or he simply stopped caring about it. As his breathing grew steady and his heart rate slowed, the why seemed increasingly less important. His mind drifted to other things, and he followed.

Helpless to do much else besides lie on the hard ground and wait for death, his mind slipped to his argument with Bindaar. They had been in his chamber talking about the war ships anchoring up in

Biggon's Bay when the great horn of Havenstahl—one of the twin horns of Galgooth—blared. The sound sparked something in him, some hidden longing lying just beneath his awareness. That spark must have shown on his face.

"Don't even think about it," his old chum and most trusted general had told him. "The king's royal rump had best remain firmly planted in its throne. Leave the fighting to your solidas."

Whether it had been hubris or defiance—the king gives orders, he does not take them—his response had been less than agreeable. "This from the scrawny waste I molded into a proper dwarf. Anything good about you, you learned from me. Tell me you don't presume to stand in my own chambers and give me orders."

The memory of the look on his old friend's face hurt almost as bad as the throbbing in his leg. "No," he looked as if he might lose a tear, "I presume nothing, but reports of what came riding in on them ships have me worried for my king's…my friend's…safety. This ain't a pack of rogue grongs. They say giants fill them massive ships. My friend, you have risked your own skin to save mine more than once. I seek only to repay the favor in kind. But what do I know? The king does what the king wants."

Of course, he failed to heed the warning, and Bindaar stormed out of the room. That was the last they had spoken as chums. When the five battalions Alhouim sent to support Havenstahl in the battle at Fort Maomnosett formed up to march, he gave the orders, and Bindaar obeyed like the rest of his generals. He recalled that same look on his old friend's face—the frightened, sad, fury, fear that looked like tears waiting to spill onto rough cheeks—when the battalions split to take up their assigned positions, but he ignored it. Friend or no friend, there was not a dwarf alive who would give him orders.

The benefit of hindsight can help a dwarf make better decisions in the future, but it cannot undo foolish decisions once they have been made. Had he listened to his old friend's wise counsel, he would not be blind and lying helpless in… It suddenly occurred to him that his eyes had grown accustomed to the darkness surrounding him. He was not blind. The pain in his leg was still nagging him enough to stifle a chuckle at how easily he let himself fall to panic, but it did nothing to keep him from feeling a bit of shame. Luckily, nobody would ever know about the moment of weakness but him.

Doentaat had not been elevated to the status of king of Alhouim by his peers because he allowed things to be done to him. He was a dwarf of action. He did things. He controlled situations, and that was precisely what he intended to do with the one he was in, control it. The world around him was still very dark, like the late hours of a moonless night. However, he was not deep into a night of any kind. The light filtering through the canopy above him was faint, but it was there. It took mere moments for him to realize he was deep in a dense forest, and the last bits of light were fading from the western sky. Had he woken just a few hours earlier, the fear of potential blindness would never have entered his mind.

With blindness out of the way as a pressing matter, Doentaat could focus on what had quickly become his most pressing matter. Despite a great urge to ignore it, the throbbing pain in his leg demanded attention. Shifting focus back to it was like blowing on a smoldering fire. Intense and furious, it flared again. Though he was not blind, there was insufficient light to see the cause of his agony. Touching the spot certainly would do nothing to ease the pain at all. Simply moving felt like a spear was shoved through the spot. He did not want to imagine what touching it might do. Therefore, he did not imagine it very long. He gritted his teeth and got to it.

It was worse than he thought. His fingers slid slowly down his right leg toward the source of distress. His trousers were torn open, the edges crusty. Though the carnage remained hidden from sight, the spot was obviously saturated with blood. How long had he been unconscious? Considering there was no wetness, it had to be a while. It made no sense to put it off any longer. He had to assess the damage. He clenched his teeth together so tightly it hurt his jaw as he shoved his fingers into a deep, ragged gash. The spear was back, and this time it sliced through and twisted. It was difficult to tell whether it was bone or meat his fingers probed, but the cut was deep, wide, and full of gore. Through tightly clenched teeth, his howl sounded more like a war cry than a pitiable expression of pain. His hand shot to his dagger, quickly slipping it out of its scabbard. He desperately wanted to plunge it into his gut and twist, end his own suffering. That would be the coward's way out. King Doentaat was anything but a coward. The Lake had failed to claim him, and he had no intention of giving it an easy meal.

Doentaat had grown accustomed enough to the pain throbbing in his leg to finally notice the smell. He had spent enough time with healers working over wounded solidas to recognize the stench of infection hanging in the air. It fraternized with the smell of death. Where was Feingaal? Memories trickled in. Feingaal had been with him when they chased a mob of fleeing grongs into the woods south of the wide clearing in front of Fort Maomnosett. By the time they had realized their battalion was no longer tromping through the dark wood behind them, they were deep in it. Had it been blood lust, the glory of battle, or hatred for the vile, scaly bastards they pursued? In the end, it did not really matter. They barely had time to acknowledge they were lost in the forest when the amatilazo came. It was a large pack, at least thirty of the hungry beasts. He and Feingaal had put up a good fight, took better than half the pack before… What had happened? The last thing he remembered was slamming the back of his fist into the side of an amatilazo's face. He protected his neck, but the damned thing latched onto his thigh. After that, everything went black. Knowing the source of his wound did not diminish the pain at all, but at least he knew the reason for it.

If Feingaal were still alive, he would have to wait. Doentaat needed to dress his wound before he could be of any help to anyone. He slit the leather straps holding his chest plate in place. Then he cut a strip out of his shirt. The thing was dirty and covered in sweat, not the best option for covering a wound. Unfortunately, it was the only option he had just then. The mangled gash needed to be covered, and the bleeding stopped. Based on the condition of his trousers, he had already lost too much blood. He could not afford to give up another drop. He wrapped the strip of shirt around the wound covering it as best he could without being able to see it. Then he cut his belt and fashioned a tourniquet above it. Hagen would not be impressed with the work, but it was the best he could do with the tools available.

The dressing did nothing to ease the pain. Thankfully, Doentaat's focus had shifted from self-pity to duty. If Feingaal still lived, he had to find him. Before trying to move, he took note of his surroundings. A quick, wide sweep with both of his arms found something. He quickly ran his hand over the lump and realized it was a head. There was no hair, just leathery skin, and the ears were small and slightly pointed. It was not Feingaal. That dwarf had more hair than any dwarf Doentaat had ever seen, both on his head and his chin. No, this head belonged to an amatilazo. The body that had once extended from it was no longer attached, just a bunch of gore hanging from the spot where it should be connected. Based on the thing's proximity to his mangled, right leg, it had to be the one that got him. Feingaal must have taken the thing's head before it could finish him off.

Aside from the amatilazo's body and an axe—that must have been Feingaal's—there was nothing else within reach of Doentaat's outstretched arms but a tree behind his head. As horrible as the idea seemed, he had to move. He dug the bottom of his palms into the soft dirt beside him and struggled toward the tree. The pain had become a conquerable adversary. It could try to stop him, but he refused to be turned aside.

Moving was a struggle. He had no idea how much time had passed as he labored, but he eventually found himself sitting up against the trunk of a stout tree. After a bit more struggling and more grunting than he cared to admit, he was on his feet leaning against that tree. Now dizziness dropped in to dance with the pain. He must have lost a lot of blood. Where to begin his search? Though he could see the faint breath of light in the canopy above him, the ground was nothing more than darkness with none of the light above able to penetrate deep enough to reach the forest floor. He would have to feel his way.

Shuffling forward hurt, but not near as much as gaining his feet had. Luckily, it was a short journey before his foot encountered something other than soft, decaying leaves. Though It was dense and had a good bit of girth, it was not a rock. A rock would not have given at all when his foot struck it. Dropping back to his knees hurt at least as bad as standing. He pushed the pain aside once again and examined the mass. The hairy thing had to be Feingaal. As Doentaat ran his hands across his dead friend's body, he thanked Coeptus the wound in his leg paled in comparison to the gore he felt. The stout dwarf must have fallen protecting his king.

He knelt there in darkness above his dead companion long enough for a heavy sense of dread to settle into his chest like a weight crushing down on his ribcage. He had no idea what to do next. He had to move, but to where? Feeling his way through the darkness would be painfully slow and the direction near impossible to gauge. It was an unattractive option but, slim as it was, probably his only chance of survival. His dry throat and grumbling stomach assured him he needed both food and water. Would he survive the night if he waited out the sun? How much could even the light of a new day improve his odds of surviving a slow trek through the dark forest?

Doentaat had barely decided not to test whether the forest would grant him another day when he heard something other than the sound of his own breathing. Bodies moved through the forest, more than five as best he could tell. By the time he struggled back to his feet and turned toward the sound, he caught the faint flicker of torchlight through the darkness. It was closer than he expected. The group moved quietly toward him. He strained his eyes trying to make out who carried the torches, but the underbrush was too thick. A quiet grunt solved the mystery. They were grongs. Perhaps the Lake would have him before the light of a new day.

Quietly into the night is a place no self-respecting dwarf would go. If this would be his end, Doentaat would bring as many of them with him as he could. He gritted his teeth, pushed back the pain, and knelt back to the ground. After a bit of fumbling around over the mossy ground he came upon the axe he had found earlier. Gripping the handle, he shoved the pain deep into his gut and let it fuel his rage. The bloody axe in his hand and that fire in his belly were all he could depend on deep in the dark wood. Shuffling through darkness with only flickering torchlight in the distance to guide him, the ample trail he followed remained invisible. It was not until the grongs with their torches rounded a bend about twenty feet further up the path that he noticed the uniform lines of trees to either side of him and the unfortunate lack of cover before him. There were six in the approaching group, all armed for battle with bloody clubs and stained armor. They saw him as soon as he saw them. So much for the element of surprise. 'For the glory of Alhouim,' he thought as he readied his axe.

"Come then, you vile monsters," he shouted with as much fury as he could muster, "show me you ain't just sacks of scales and fear."

The pack seemed startled at first, but the shock wore off quickly. Grongs are opportunistic if nothing else, and Doentaat was obviously alone on the trail. Wildly swinging their clubs, grunting out war cries, and gnashing their teeth, they charged.

Adrenaline was just the thing the wounded dwarf king needed. It surged through his body, propelling him down the trail at something just short of a slow jog. The distance between him and the grongs shrunk quickly. A mere few moments passed before the blade of his axe tasted the scaled flesh of his first victim. The thing's oblong head had barely reached the apex of its flight before Doentaat's axe came down onto the skull of his next victim and cut clear down to the grong's collar bones. He roared into the beast's split face as he yanked his axe back out of it. The scaly bastard stood there blinking with eyes too far apart from each other for a few moments before falling dead in the dirt. The dwarf king nearly watched the result of his fury too long, ducking just in time to avoid a club swinging past the split face as it fell. By the time he stood back up, another club came sailing toward him from his other side. This time, he was a hair too slow to avoid the blow.

The club crashed into Doentaat's temple; a brilliant flash of light accompanied by an equally impressive blast of pain. Luckily, the stout dwarf had a thick skull which had collided with things far denser and harder than any grong club in its long career of encasing his brain. He rolled with the blow, regaining his feet after a short tumble. Despite a brief wave of dizziness, a dull throb was all that remained where the weapon had struck. He had precious little time to regain his wits before that same club flew at his head again along with two others. He ducked low and swung his axe. A grong's leg flew into the brush alongside the trail as a club pounded into the top of the raging dwarf's skull. It was a heavy blow. The world grew bright again. Even after it dimmed, white dots flashed all about Doentaat's blurring vision.

The last blow was a tough one. It dropped Doentaat squarely on his rump and sent a sharp jolt up his spine. As pain flared in his tailbone, an upside to all these new pains suddenly occurred to him. Since charging into battle against the small pack of grongs, he had completely forgotten the pain in his leg. The idea sprinted away as quickly as it had come. The grong whose leg he removed fell toward him. He raised his axe and the scaly thing crashed upon it. The beast was thick and heavy. Once the edge of the axe had penetrated its sternum, the other blade—the one facing Doentaat—nearly crashed through the dwarf's chest. He would rather be dead than locked in a macabre embrace with a dirty grong. Doentaat shifted and let that side of his axe pound into the trail. He rolled and tried to regain his feet, but the three remaining grongs were already swinging clubs at him.

The first few hits were rough, across his shoulder blades, then his right arm, and finally his chest. The bone in his arm was probably broken. There was no time to lament the injured limb as the clubs just kept coming. Savage and merciless, they beat him to the ground and kept pounding him deeper into the forest floor. Despite orange light flickering from a small, dead bush which had caught fire when one of the grongs had dropped their torch, the world grew darker again. After a while, the blows hardly hurt anymore. It became increasingly difficult to distinguish one blow from the next. The Lake was finally calling him to rest.

Consciousness was fleeing quickly when something caught Doentaat's eye. It probably caught his ear first, but it was difficult to pick individual sounds out of the dull ringing in his ears. Several of the blows had struck his head. Whether he heard it before he saw it made little difference. It was a horse with a rider who had orange hair, burnt like the sky at sunset, and the unmistakable glint of metal bathed in torchlight. A savior draped in the colors of Havenstahl galloped quickly toward him. Before the world went completely black, Doentaat hoped the fellow knew how to swing that sword and that he was not too late.

CHAPTER 2
KILL THE GODS

The tent was not much more than some fabric loosely strung between posts haphazardly pounded into the dirt on the wrong side of the broken bridge to Havenstahl. Daritus stood worrying over his map, wondering how much time they had before needing to defend their broken city from another attack. The map mocked him, his painted tokens occupying spaces with little meaning. It appeared a proper strategy to the three men in the tent with him, but he knew the reality of it. It was all a sham. He could lie to them but not himself. There was no plan. His forces were strewn about the valley, maybe in the Sobbing Forest, maybe on the other side of Alhouim, or maybe in one of one-hundred other places. The truth was, he had the loosest approximation of where roughly a quarter of his forces resided at that moment. The rest was anybody's guess.

The faces staring back at him across the map were worn, hungry, and far thinner than a grown man's face should be. It was a blessing he had not seen his own face in a time. He was certain his reflection would be terribly disappointing. He could not worry about that. Thankfully, his tent boasted no mirrors. Besides, there was work to be done, and the men who owned those far too thin faces needed him to lead them. He could scarcely believe anyone would follow him after the utter failure he authored at Fort Maomnosett, but there they were awaiting his direction.

All three of the men had once been riders of Druindahl back before the awakening when Maelich and Cialia scattered Kallum to the wind over the Forgotten Forest. They had followed him to Havenstahl when he came and vowed to protect their new city as their own. None of them could have imagined how their loyalty would be tested or just how great a sacrifice they would have to make. The nightmares they faced during the battle at Biggon's Bay to the attack on the city they swore to protect were like nothing any of them had ever seen. That is the thing about vows though, they must be kept.

"Jalicon," Daritus addressed the man to his right, "you ride for Ycantle, correct? Where do his numbers lie?"

"A handful better than one-hundred men answer Ycantle's call, my lord," Jalicon replied as he brushed his hair back from his face. Even carrying a good bit of dirt, it was dark, wavy, and luxurious, the same as his beard. The man did not look like he belonged anywhere near a battlefield. He was far too pretty. However, there were few men with which Daritus would rather ride into battle. He was damned handy with a blade.

Daritus nodded and then asked, "How many horses?"

"Only twenty-two," Jalicon frowned. Then he added, "We may be a small group, general, but we will march to battle in bare feet should the need arise."

"I am certain you would, old friend. I recall your force marched into the battle at Fort Maomnosett and fought with honor and fury," Daritus smiled. "Still, let us hope that need does not arise. Pass this message along to Ycantle for me. Send five men with horses ahead to Biggon's Bay. Have them take the main trail, not the northern pass. They are not to engage our enemy. I want a report of the giant's camp. The rest of your force will make camp at the edge of the wood. Take enough supplies for a full week. Send word if they appear ready to make war. I will send further instructions if I have not received a message from you within one week's time."

"Your will, my lord," Jalicon bowed and left the tent.

Daritus turned to the man directly across from him, "Marivel, where do Ygraml's numbers lie?"

"Fifty, my lord," Marivel replied. His voice carrying a gruffness that almost hurt the ears. He was not near so pretty as Jalicon—his dark hair scraggly and streaked with the same gray that adorned his weak excuse for a beard—but he was a titan on the battlefield.

"Fifty?" Daritus failed at hiding his shock.

"Fifty," Marivel replied, "me and forty-nine of the fiercest mounted men I have ever had the honor of riding alongside."

Daritus flashed a shallow smile. "I do not doubt that fierceness," he paused allowing his smile to wane, "Our forces have been scattered. We need a proper accounting of our strength. Split your numbers. Find our men. Search the valley and forests around the city."

"My general will be disappointed with that charge, my lord. Those fierce men would be best used for battle, not wandering aimlessly about searching for men who may or may not actually be lost," the young soldier frowned.

Many men charged with leading a force as massive and mighty as that which defended the greatest city of men might bristle at a challenge posed by a messenger, but Daritus was not most men. He welcomed, even encouraged, all in his ranks to voice their opinions. He was also not so far removed from the fury of battle to have forgotten that intense desire, that duty or how troubling his command was to Marivel. No warrior, especially one as fierce as the brute standing before him, wished to be reduced to a messenger, effectively a raven speaking his message rather than delivering it on a small bit of parchment tied to his leg, but that was Daritus' command. Instead of scolding the messenger, the accomplished general invited him to elaborate. "How many men currently ride or march under the banner of Havenstahl?" he asked plainly.

"Well," Marivel shrugged, "add my report to Jalicon's, and I know of a bit more than one-hundred-fifty men. However, I expect you know of thousands more."

"Do you recall the Battle at Biggon's Bay?"

"I was not among the men fighting that day, but I have heard stories," Marivel nodded.

Daritus nodded and asked, "Did any of those stories include an accounting of the number of men that battle claimed?"

"More than half…"

"Estimates place the number at about twenty thousand," the old general's tone grew grim. "I do not doubt the honor nor the ferocity of you or the men with whom you ride, but I must ask if you believe it would be wise for Ygraml to lead you and those men—as fierce as they are—in an assault on the ships anchored in the bay?"

"I do not," Marivel acknowledged as his gaze dropped to the floor with his right knee. "Thank you for the wise counsel as well as the command, my lord."

"Rise," Daritus scolded. "My men should stand tall beside me not kneel before me. Should our king or queen ever return, bow before them."

Marivel's cheeks reddened as he rose back to his feet, "Forgive me, my lord."

"Now go, find our men and bring them home," Daritus allowed his tone to mellow. Marivel had made it to the doorway before Daritus added, "New recruits are welcome. If any men remain in the villages with minds to find revenge, we will arm them and train them. The smiths are working day and night. We need men to wield those swords."

"Yes, we do," Marivel nodded as he left the tent.

Daritus' eyes followed Marivel as he left the tent. Once the man had gone, he turned his attention to the last warrior occupying the tent with him. Everything about Tarturan was big. He was near a giant, his massive head towering at least a foot over most men. That giant head sat atop a mountain of muscles clad in gaudy armor that made him appear even larger. He looked every bit the brute, and it was no façade. He could back it up. Daritus had watched him lift a wagon full of supplies out of the mud when they were young. It would have taken five strong men to do the same, but Tarturan did it with ease. If there were a force of men anchored in Biggon's Bay, Daritus would simply send the man to scare them away.

"Best not ask about the number remaining in my rank, my lord. We were camped in the fort. Most of them died when the first boulder struck. Only five of us remain," the musical tone of Tarturan's voice bore a stark contrast to his imposing stature.

"I know," Daritus nodded. "We all felt the loss. I am certain none as great as you."

The big man's head dipped. He stood like that for a moment in silence. His eyes were glistening by the time he raised them back up to Daritus. "That was the first time in my life I was afraid, the sounds of wood crashing and men screaming…" he trailed off.

Daritus remained silent, allowing the man a moment to reflect.

Tarturan pulled himself together and allowed a broad smile to slip onto his face. Raising his massive cheeks appeared a great effort. "That fear is gone. Now I am angry. Allow me to take my men to the shores of Biggon's Bay. We will wade out into the water and pull those ships down with our bare hands."

Daritus returned the smile, "Your vigor strengthens me, old friend, and I doubt not your desire. However, you are needed elsewhere. You are a great asset on any battlefield, but you are far more than a giant, scary sack of meat. You have a gift with words and a calming voice to propel them from your mouth. I need you to travel to Alhouim and gauge the status of the dwarf army. Fifty dwarves remain to aid in the rebuilding effort, but I need to know if we can still count on their axes when the inevitable next wave comes."

Tarturan's smile dipped, "I am as happy about that command as Marivel was about the one you gave him. My sword thirsts for blood. However, I cannot debate the wisdom of your request. As much as I would like nothing more than to shout at those ships and cut monsters down with the waves of the bay crashing against my legs, the effort would have little impact on the greater campaign. I will visit our friends in Alhouim and ensure they are with us when the fighting returns."

"Thank you, old friend. Safe travels," Daritus replied as Tarturan bowed and left the tent, ducking to make it through the exit.

Then Daritus was alone, a place he preferred not to be. Fear and doubt were poor companions. Sadly, they were the only ones left with him in the tent. Immediately after the battle at Fort Maomnosett—the crushing failure it was—he nearly lost hope. How could anyone follow him when he proved unable to protect the city with the greatest army on Ouloos? His plan had failed miserably. Was he even fit to lead? As the reality of the situation slowly set in, his perspective shifted. He was fit to lead. It was a good plan, a solid plan, and it still failed. There were gods on the battlefield that day. No plan would have succeeded. Was he merely shepherding a flock destined to be destroyed by a vengeful monster? How do you fight a god?

Absorbed in questions for which he had no answers—or he did have answers and just did not like them much—Daritus failed to notice the answer to one of them enter the tent. How do you fight a god? With the greatest power on Ouloos.

"Father?" Cialia's voice was the sweetest sound Daritus had heard in months.

Daritus' first genuine smile in more days than he could remember quickly spread across his face. "My precious daughter, my Dragon, your voice is like a feast laid before a starving man," he said as he raised his head up from the map at which he had been looking but not really seeing.

His happiness quickly faded when he saw his daughter. Her blonde hair was wild and free as always, and her soft, blue eyes peered peacefully at him from the smooth, angelic curves of her face. She was beautiful as ever, but something was wrong. She wore a simple, white robe in place of the rugged gear she donned when taking to the trail, and her swords were damnably absent. Of course, she did not need swords, but her twin blades had always been a part of her, each an extension of one of her arms. Cialia was a warrior. The woman standing before Daritus looked like something else.

"I missed you on the battlefield," he finally continued. "Word of the Dragon decimating monsters from across the Great Sea spread quickly. There is no telling how many more may have fallen had you not intervened. Why did you leave so quickly? I would have liked to speak with you then."

"That battle took its toll on me," Cialia replied with a joyless smile. "I felt such rage when I saw those monsters destroying so many innocent lives, but…"

"But what?" Daritus' voice was a bit louder than he intended.

Cialia shrugged, "I have had time to reflect. I fear my rage was misplaced."

Daritus squinted at his daughter. "Misplaced?" he asked. "Monsters, heartless, soulless beasts set upon the city you vowed to defend and killed innocents without mercy. Your rage was not misplaced, my dear. Your rage, your fury, was precisely where it needed to be. I only wish it had remained with us that day."

Her smile faded, "I understand your perspective, father. I do. I felt that way too, not long ago. But you are wrong. Your enemies are not heartless or soulless. Perhaps they do appear beasts to you, but that is only because they look different than you. They have fears and wants and desires just like you. How many giants and trogmortem and grongs did the valiant warriors of Havenstahl grind into the dirt? The blood of many dead men may soak your battlefields, but it mingles with the blood of other equally dead creatures."

The words stung. Failing to suppress a scowl, he replied, "Havenstahl did not seek this war. Those monsters brought it to our shores. The men of this city need a champion, someone strong enough to defend them against the nightmares they face." He shook his head in disgust before adding, "You were their champion, you and your missing brother. They have faith in you. Would you leave them alone and vulnerable to be slaughtered?"

"I am their champion," she raised her head high, "I am the champion of all the inhabitants of Ouloos. The journey has been long and meandering, but I have determined it is not my lot to judge or destroy any life. It is my role to defend it, all of it. You look to your gods and they to theirs. That swell in your breast as you march off to cut living things down in the name of a city you would have burned to the ground yourself less than ten summers ago, what do you suppose that is?"

"Duty," Daritus spat.

"Duty," Cialia shook her head. "Duty does not drive you to kill. It is your gods filling you up with false hatred for things you do not understand. They use you to play their games against each other. You faced them once. You told me about it when I was young, your fear and awe. You failed to mention anything of love when you spoke of them. Did you feel any from them?"

Daritus scratched his head and dropped his gaze back to his map, "What is your point, Cialia?"

"You have spent your life in service of creatures who care nothing for you. You destroy at their command. They use you. My father is a far wiser man than the simple soldier standing before me. What have your gods ever done to earn your service, love, or worship?" she asked.

He raised his head back up and replied, "They guide us and protect us."

Cialia raised her arms to her sides and glanced about the tent, "This is how they protect you, with war and death? They do not protect you. They inspire you to maim and kill. They reduce you to something no better than that which you hope to destroy. I will not join you on the battlefield. I will not take the life of any living thing, but I will defend Ouloos and all her children. I will eradicate the authors of all this violence and destruction. I will kill them all."

Cialia's words sunk into Daritus' mind and cut into his soul. The sweet face staring back at him was a contradiction of the beast hiding behind it. Words danced around his mind, answers to his daughter's nonsense. None of them made it to his lips. There was nothing left to say. The beast before him was not the girl he raised to defend Dragons and men from the terrible things that would destroy them.

"I hoped I could persuade you to seek peace with those you hope to destroy," Cialia finally broke the silence, "but you are far too deep in the fantasy they have created for you. I am going the kill the gods, all of them. Please think about what I have said. Search your heart. You battle and fight, kill and destroy, yet nothing ever changes. Do you think life should be an endless exercise in sadness and pain? Where is your joy, father?"

Daritus remained silent, nothing to offer his daughter but a blank, shocked gaze.

There was sadness in her smile when she continued, "I should go. There is much to do. I love you, father. I hope you can find better answers within yourself."

Cialia had made it to the edge of the tent before Daritus finally found words. "Wait," he began, continuing after she turned to face him, "Kallum and Brerto are evil. They have earned your wrath. However, Kaldumahn and Moshat protect us. If you refuse to defend the men of this world, you cannot take them from us."

"They are all evil, father, one no different from another," she frowned as she stepped out of the tent.

Then she was gone, and Daritus was left alone with his thoughts once again. Though he scarcely recognized the woman who had just left his tent, he knew his daughter well enough to know she would not cease until her task was complete. If a god could be killed, she would kill them all.

## CHAPTER 3
## THE BLUE PEOPLE

Heat rose from the dry ground as the sun mercilessly scorched the cracked land. The air felt thick and heavy, like it had mass and could be carried about. Maelich sat with Maulom and Ding just within the mouth of the cave the Shaiwah occupied. It was a comfortable spot, the cool air from deep within the cave mingling with the heat from outside. Maelich brushed his damp hair back from his face. He and Ymitoth had spent the morning training those Shaiwah who would become warriors, the protectors of their people. Ymitoth had traveled deeper into the cave to find some food while Maelich remained to nourish his mind with the help of Maulom. The man knew everything about the history of the Shaiwah and seemed wise on a great many other topics.

Both Maelich and Ding were quite dirty from a morning full of rigorous training. Maulom's appearance was a stark contradiction. His close-cropped white hair and beard seemed to glow, as did his impossibly clean white shirt and trousers. Maelich had only been with the Shaiwah a short time, but he could not recall the man ever looking any less than impeccable. How did one remain so clean in a land covered in dirt upon dirt?

As Maelich pondered the man's impossible cleanliness, Maulom spoke, "The Tahnka are a violent, destructive people. They take what they want and kill any who oppose them. They were not always such. It has taken centuries for them to become the monsters they are. Hundreds of summers past, the Shaiwah and the Tahnka were one people, the Ohna. They were peaceful, living off the land in a bountiful paradise far south of the cracked land. In those days, the Ohna had two great leaders, a brother and sister. Shaiwahka loved peace. He marveled at nature, the things growing up out of the soil and the creatures crawling across it. He loved all life. His sister, Tiakwah, loved life too. However, she wanted to control it, to learn its secrets and bend them to her will. She valued knowledge above all else, pouring herself into studies of how things came to be.

"Eventually, Tiakwah was drawn to a great power deep within a cave further south in the rainforest than anyone before or since has ever ventured. What she found in this cave—if there ever was a cave at all—is shrouded in myth. Some say it was a great wizard who taught her the secrets of creation and unlocked her great potential. Others say it was a god who did the same, a hidden god, not one of the ones we know. Still others believe she found a hidden path, a portal to the mysteries of the unknown. Whatever she found there, as the stories go, it bent her mind toward conquest. She returned with a desire to rule all, to bend nature to her will. Her people marveled at her great power. She built elaborate temples and developed weapons. She taught them to hunt and use the land to grow things that did not occur naturally. She completely changed the course of the Ohna.

"Shaiwahka watched his sister's power grow. At first, he thought he could help temper her desires and guide her to a balance with their surroundings. He quickly realized her ambition would not be tempered. The land changed, resources were drained as massive structures stretched up into the sky higher than the tallest trees of the forest, and several species of animals were hunted to near extinction. Finally, he could no longer stand by and watch his sister destroy the land he loved. He opposed her and was nearly killed for his efforts.

"Almost half the Ohna were peace-loving like Shaiwahka and followed him to the cracked land where he fled to escape his sister's wrath. For his bravery, they elevated him to king and began calling themselves the Shaiwah in honor of his name. Food was scarce. They learned to cultivate the land and grow things. They learned to trap. They lived in peace for a time. Tiakwah would not allow that peace to last.

"As Tiakwah conquered the land, building and displacing nature, she taught her people to fight. She took the tools she had given them for hunting and concocted weapons to kill men. She hunted the

Shaiwah to the ends of the cracked land. They have lived in fear ever since those dark days."

Ding had been distracted by some of the beads in his matted hair but perked up as Maulom finished. "Land fierce," he said. "No forgive."

Maelich smiled at Ding, pointed at the blue covering on the man's skin, and replied, "But you are a wise people. Look how you have learned to live in harmony with the land. You are safe from the sun within the cool confines of this cave, and you have devised a method for protecting yourself from it when away from the safety of darkness."

A bit of agitation crept into Ding's tone as he continued, "Berries good, protect from sun. But life hard. No food. Land kills. No fish. If fish, Tahnka kill. Only scaly things for food. We go home. Fight."

"Ding struggles with the common tongue. Very few venture into this desolate waste, but his words have meaning," Maulom interjected. "The Shaiwah live in constant fear. This land they occupy cannot sustain them. They are ready to take back their homes."

Maelich shook his head, "You said all these things happened hundreds of summers past. None of the Shaiwah have ever seen this place you describe. How can they call it home? What do they know of the place? How do you know it even still exists?"

"Shaiwah want home," Ding sighed as he kicked a stone and stormed off.

Maelich looked over at Maulom, "I did not mean to offend him."

"Ding will be fine," Maulom replied quietly, "but you have to understand what you mean to these people. They have been waiting centuries for you to arrive. Obviously, not the people occupying this cave right at this moment, but they have a history they all know. You are the savior they were promised, the savior who would lead them home, the savior who will teach them to defend against their enemies."

Maelich's gaze dipped toward the ground before he looked thoughtfully back at Maulom and asked, "Have any of the Shaiwah ever encountered the Tahnka? And please save the history lesson. I mean now, today. Have any of the people living in this cave today ever encountered these people they fear so much? Ymitoth and I journey to the river and back every day on our morning run. The Shaiwah brave enough to join us have as well. We have been all up and down the river and all the land in between here and there. Not once have we found any sign of men other than those living in this cave. Where are these nightmares they fear?"

The impeccable old man shrugged, "No. None of the Shaiwah living today have ever encountered the Tahnka."

Maelich stood, turned toward the mouth of the cave, and asked, "Then how can you know they even exist anymore? Where is this great threat?"

"You did not let me finish," Maulom replied, "None of the Shaiwah living today have ever seen a member of the Tahnka, but I have. I have journeyed as far south as the land goes, and I have seen their terrible structures, black stone scratching the sky. I have seen their weapons, unimaginable things. I have seen cylinders that blow holes in the ground, liquids that melt flesh from bones, and other horrible things of which I would rather not speak. The Tahnka are real. The threat is real. The Shaiwah need you to protect them and lead them home."

Maelich thought for a moment. He barely knew this man. What he did know, he was not sure he could trust. Ding was passionate. He obviously believed in these nightmares. Even if they were merely stories, the Shaiwah did occupy harsh lands. Knowing how to defend themselves certainly would not hurt them.

After a few moments of silence, Maelich finally replied, "Fine. I will continue to train the Shaiwah to fight, and I will lead them south once they are ready. Hopefully, this paradise you have promised them will be there to greet them when they arrive."

Maulom nodded, "I ask nothing more. Lead your people, Maelich. You will bring them something they have lacked their entire lives, hope."

# CHAPTER 4
# THE QUEEN RETURNS

Leisha's haggard form slumped in one of two chairs opposite the entrance to Druindahl's throne room. The seat had been hers for most of her life, crafted at her command. The great throne the men of Druindahl had offered her was far superior to it, gaudy and massive, crafted of skillfully carved wood and decorated with shimmering prang. The mistress of the Lake deserved no less. That chair gave voice to the first lesson she ever gave her people. No man stands above any other. All are equal. She ordered the thing destroyed along with its slightly less gaudy counterpart. The seat she occupied matched every other chair in the room exactly. She had not expected her rump to ever rest upon it again. Unfortunately, the peace promised by the prophecies about her children killing a violent god never really came to pass. Sure, Dragons returned to Lake—and the lost souls of hundreds of summers were finally able to make their way home—but Ouloos remained as violent and horrible as it had ever been. When would it end?

The world had become so complicated. Gods battled alongside men and monsters, everyone seemed to want to kill everyone else. Two kingdoms looked to her for leadership, and both had fallen far from their former greatness. Each day brought news of more violence and death. The eyes of her people—full of fear and hopelessness—looked to her for answers, for peace, for something more than the misery their lives had become. What could she offer them? How could she give them hope when she could scarcely secure any for herself?

The heavy door at the other end of the throne room groaned as it slowly opened. Leisha did not bother looking up. She had grown tired of looking upon all the beautiful contradictions adorning her city. They were all lies. Life was not beautiful. It was hard and painful, full of fear and violence and death. Besides, whoever owned the purposeful steps echoing back at her off the smooth, prang walls surrounding her probably brought more horrible news. She did not want any more news. If only she could have one day without news, one day of peace, that would be a good day.

"My queen," Boringas' voice was deep, full of purpose and honor.

The queen did not look up at him, "Please, Boringas, no more news. I wilt under the weight of it all."

Despite the queen's request, Boringas continued, "Forgive me, my queen, but Cialia has left the city."

"One day, Boringas, all I want is one day of peace," she sighed. "I imagine it will be a long time before I receive a gift so beautiful as that. In any event, I feared she might. Did she give you an idea of her purpose?"

"Only that she is bound for Havenstahl," the damnably dutiful soldier continued, "and no more souls would journey to the Lake for the entertainment of gods."

Leisha finally raised her head. Before she could respond to her general, she caught sight of her reflection in the polished prang of the throne room's wall. The thing looking back at her nearly startled her out of her chair. She rushed over to that shiny wall, placed both hands against it, and took in the sight. Her hair was ragged and disheveled, a twisted, ratty nest of dingy gray. Lines cut deep into her face, down her cheeks and across her brow. Her eyes sunk deep beneath that troubled brow and above dark bags. She could not remember the last time she saw her own reflection.

"Is this your queen or some witch from the dark wood of a sad forest?" she asked, still staring at a face she barely recognized.

"It is the face of my queen, I hope," Boringas's tone raised slightly, "if she still exists. I remember the strong, confident woman who led this place. She was full of hope and life. I admired her, both her beauty and her strength. She was a titan who did not need the assistance of a sword to see her will done. She was leader."

"She sounds wonderful," Leisha replied with a joyless chuckle. "If only she were real."

A bit of sternness crept into Boringas's tone, "Forgive the disrespect, my queen, but your people need you. I have sent out a call for new recruits, and Druindahl has answered. They want to serve. They want to see your will done. They want…"

Leisha spun toward him, gnarled up her hands into fists, and shouted, "What is my will?" before falling to her knees and sinking into sobs.

Boringas bowed his head and allowed her a few moments of tears before continuing, "You are the mother of gods, queen of Druindahl, and defender of Dragons. I hope your will is to stand up and lead your people, lift them out of darkness, and show them your vision of a peaceful world which you will help them create."

Leisha's sobbing ceased as she looked up at Boringas, "Is that what you see weeping here before you?"

"I do," Boringas proclaimed boldly. "No one can steal the faith you instilled in me, not even you. You made me believe this world could be more than blood and pain and sorrow. I have not stopped believing in that, and I have not stopped believing in you. Please, my queen, pick yourself up and be the person I know you to be. My sword and my life are yours to command."

Leisha looked deeply into Boringas's eyes, looking for hints of whether he genuinely believed all the words he gave her. His gaze never faltered. Her eyes once glistened with that same hope. He was correct, of course. The people she led had loved her, believed in her. She knew that. Where was that woman? She certainly was not in the tired, old face which had stared back from her reflection. Could she ever find her again? Could she live with herself if she did not try?

The floor was cool. It would be easy to lay down upon it and give in, forget everything and sleep until all the days that would ever be had come and gone. Easy had never been her way. When Kaldumahn, the great silver lion, had led her to the Lake and bid her bathe in its waters, she knew her path would be hard. For seventeen summers she had lived a simple life in a small village, and, according to this god, she would become the protector of Dragons. At that time in her life, she knew nothing of the world. She had no experience. The greatest decision she had made up to that point was whether to sweep the dust from the floor before or after she prepared the mid-day. Yet, she answered the call. After she had given birth to twins, champions of Ouloos, and vicious dead things came to steal them in the night, she did not give in. Even after those dead things stole one of them, her baby boy, something kept her from flinging herself from the highest cliff she could find. She became that woman Boringas had described. She persevered. She led.

Leisha slowly raised herself off the floor and gazed at her reflection. That was not her face staring back at her. She was not that broken woman. She wrangled her matted hair up with both her hands and tied it off at the back of her head. Then she ran her hands up both her cheeks and raised her head high. By the time she turned back toward Boringas, the tired old face in the reflection had been replaced by the countenance of a queen.

"You are wise beyond your years, Boringas," she said quietly, allowing the slightest of smiles to lift her cheeks. "Come, we have work to do."

Boringas flashed a wide smile, "The soldiers from Havenstahl who accompanied your caravan remain in the city. I would bid you allow them to remain with us and aid in our efforts. As I said, we have many recruits, but far too few experienced swords to train them. Cialia has gone to Havenstahl, so those swords will not be needed there."

"Yes," Leisha looked up toward the ceiling, "that is wise. They will remain. We will have to trust the safety of those remaining in Havenstahl to my daughter and husband." She paused, dropped her gaze back to Boringas, and asked, "How was Cialia when you saw her?"

Boringas shrugged, "She seemed well, sure of herself. Her spirits seemed higher than I have seen them since her return. However, she has changed."

"How so?" Leisha asked.

"Well," he scratched his head, "she left her swords behind and wore a simple, white robe. She looked more like she belonged in a cathedral than on a battlefield. I am sure you would agree, that does not sound like Cialia."

"No," she shook her head, "it certainly does not. As much as I would like to speak with her right now, I am glad to know she is in Havenstahl. We are safe here in our city in the trees. The same cannot be said for those who remained in that broken place."

"Yes, she is needed there," Boringas agreed, "and we are safe, for now. However, that safety is a fragile thing. We must prepare for the coming storm."

Leisha thought for a moment and then said, "I wish to address our soldiers, both seasoned and fresh-faced. Please prepare them. Give me a few hours to make myself presentable. This is not how I want them to see their queen."

"Your will, my queen," Boringas' smile seemed to eat up his face as he bowed deeply, turned, and hurried toward the door. Just before he left the room, he turned back to the queen and added, "Welcome back. You have been sorely missed."

CHAPTER 5
# THE NEXT ATTACK

Maomnosett Ott wore a deep scowl within the charred walls of a floating throne room. The great warship it sat upon had belonged to his son, Bok, failed conqueror of men and dwarves. The seat his rump warmed had been that same son's throne. Killed by a mere man, that dead giant had not deserved a throne. Kings occupy thrones. Bok had proven far meeker than his ambitions. Ouloos was blessed to be rid of the weak excuse for a giant.

As Ott sat damning his son's name, it became increasingly difficult to decide which was greater, his disappointment in Bok or the wounds he earned marching on the greatest city of men. The greatest city of men, that was a contradiction. Men had never done anything great. They were too small and inconsequential. Bok should have crushed them but proved unable. Ott would succeed where his son could not. He would take both Havenstahl and Alhouim, and giants would rule over men for the rest of eternity, as it should be.

The giant's gaze washed over the room. Impatient eyes stared back at him, waiting for a command from their king. Ohm, his last living son, sat next to him. Hopefully, he would prove mightier than his two brothers, both killed by men. Across from Ott, along the northern wall, sat Chi-Ta, king of the trogmortem, staring back at him with fierce, emerald eyes. To Chi-Ta's right, along the eastern wall, sat Slurg. Slurg was the choontah of the grongs. Loosely translated into the common tongue, choontah meant chief.

Chi-Ta pulled at his bulbous nose before breaking the silence with his deep, gravelly voice, "I yearn for the dryness of my home. The damp air of this place does not agree with me. How long do you intend to remain in this bay?"

Slurg nodded before offering an unintelligible grunt.

Ott's eyes narrowed to slits as he growled, "You pledged yourself and the trogmortem who follow you to my son in his campaign against Havenstahl and Alhouim. Brerto himself set that task before him. When he died before satisfying the desire of our god, that task was given to me. Go back on your pledge, Chi-Ta, and you need not worry of facing the wrath of the great tiger. You will face my wrath. I will make you hurt in ways you could not possibly imagine. You will beg me to let you die, but your pleas will be ignored. I will torment you until there is no life left in my body. I will make that my life's work."

Chi-Ta's gaze fell away from Ott's horrible stare. Though the giant was wounded and weakened from the battle of Fort Maomnosett, the trogmortem king dared not challenge his might. None sharing the room with the furious king of giants would. Of course, Ott was not really the king of all giants. Giant politics differed from those of men. Houses did not rule over one another. The head of each house was the king of their own kind. However, the other houses fell in line behind Ott after Brerto spoke to him. None were so bold as to challenge the one Brerto had chosen as his herald and tasked with such great purpose. For all intents and purposes, Ott was the king of giants.

The sound of the door to the room creaking open granted Chi-Ta a temporary reprieve from Ott's fury. The giant adjusted his gaze to his grandson, Bom, Bok's eldest son, another disappointment. Bom was slight by giant standards, and far too short. Standing at just over ten feet tall, he could not even boast being twice the height of a man. Violence seemed to trouble him too. Giants did not shudder at blood, they reveled in it. On top of that, he gave far too much care to his appearance, keeping his hair clean and brushed and his beard neatly trimmed. He looked more like a very tall man than a member of the proudest family of giants. Ott scowled at the young giant with whom he had nothing in common but a name.

"This is a conversation for warriors," Ott said quietly. "You were not invited. For what cause do you darken my door?"

Bom stood tall and flashed a pleasant smile to his grandfather, "I have come seeking your permission to lead a small group on a diplomatic journey to Havenstahl, grandfather."

"Diplomatic?" Ott spat. "Why on Ouloos would I allow a diplomatic mission to a city I intend to destroy. I have no use for men. I will take their lands and their resources. They will bow before me or die."

"Why?" Bom's tone quickly acquired a pleading quality. "Has the race of men ever slighted you or any of us? Our home is across the Great Sea. We have no need of these lands."

Ott clenched his teeth together so tightly the muscles in his jaw looked as if they might rip right through his cheeks as he growled, "Careful, boy. I loved my son, your father, despite his weakness. Never will I forgive his failure, but I did love him. Even still, the words you speak are blasphemies against the great tiger. I will not stand for that. Bind your tongue, or the fishes of this vast bay will feast on your shredded carcass."

Bom's smile faded, "Please, grandfather, hear me out. Maomnosett Ahm, my uncle, was a mighty ruler, a titan among giants."

"He was a titan among giants," Ott interrupted, "until he grew fat and lazy being catered to by lowly dwarves. And never forget, he was killed by a man just like your weakling father. How could it come to this, two of my sons killed by men and my grandson shrinking away from his duty? If the great tiger had not set me on my path, I would be certain he had abandoned me completely."

"I have never met the lad of the Lake, but by all accounts, he is a god among men. Your disappointment is misplaced. Ahm should never have been here in the first place, ruling over dwarves. Giants are free to do what they will. Men and dwarves should be the same. What gives us the right to impose our will and take…"

Ott had heard enough. In a blink, he was out of his throne and squeezing his grandson's neck in his steely grip. He pulled the young giant close to him and growled in his ear, "You exalt the man who killed your uncle to the status of god? Would you call him the great dragon? Do you fear his flame, you coward? I will eat the flesh from his bones and extinguish his flame. Men and dwarves exist only to serve us. I will take everything from them. Stand in my way and be trampled under my feet with them."

Ott squeezed harder. His massive hand fit easily around Bom's fair neck. Blood began to trickle from small cuts his fingernails made in his palm as he tried to crush his grandson's neck. The fear dancing about in Bom's eyes as they bugged from their sockets only served to stoke

Ott's rage. He squeezed even tighter. Another member of his family would die. This one would not expire at the hands of men. This one would die for his love of them.

"Your father should have listened to me," the furious giant growled in his grandson's face. "He brought you before me on the day you were born. The pride in his eyes sickened me as I gazed on the pathetic thing he held in his arms. I told him to cast you off the highest mountaintop. If he were alive to witness this treachery, he would lament the day he failed to heed my advice about you."

"Ott," Chi-Ta called out from behind him, "he is your blood. Would you kill your own blood for the sake of rage? He is young. Counsel him. Teach him truth. Do not take his life for foolishness."

Ott was stunned. Would there be no end to the treachery? His grip eased on Bom's neck as he turned his head and flashed an angry stare at the trogmortem king. Keeping his eyes on Chi-Ta, he gave Bom's neck one last squeeze before launching him into the wall. Perhaps the trogmortem king wanted to offer his neck in place of Bom's. The raging giant took a mere two steps toward Chi Ta before noticing the shock on his face. It was not the shock itself which stopped him. Facing down death is enough to shock any manner of beast. It was the fact that Chi-Ta's wide, terrified eyes were not fixed on him. They looked past him at something else.

When Ott turned to see what had so concerned the trogmortem king, shock found its way onto his face as well. The wall surrounding the doorway to the throne room had crumbled when Bom's body slammed into it. That was expected. Ott knew his own strength. What surprised the self-proclaimed giant king was the fact that a small group of giants and trogmortem were standing outside the room assisting his grandson. Lito-Bi, Chi-Ta's finest and most trusted warrior was among them.

"I am surrounded by traitors," Ott growled.

"This war is over," Lito-Bi spoke plainly, "at least it is for us."

Before Ott could respond, Chi-Ta admonished his soldier, "Measure your words. You serve at my pleasure, and I am in the service of Ott of the house Maomnosett. Do not share in Bom's treason."

Ott did not wait for Lito-Bi to respond. His fists clenched tight and his roar rattled the walls as he charged toward the group of traitors. He wanted to feel Bom's face crush beneath the weight of his fist. However, when he charged, Lito-Bi had shuffled the gasping giant behind him. Seeing the trogmortem traitor standing defiantly before him infuriated him even more, the hubris of this lowly soldier. No trogmortem stands before any giant. They bow and follow obediently, or they die. It appeared Lito-Bi had decided to end his time on Ouloos. Ott fired his right fist at the trogmortem warrior's head.

Lito-Bi was spry, a well-trained killing machine. Ott knew this. However, he was not so blind with rage that he failed to see the trepidation painted across the warrior's face. The trogmortem's instincts were sharp. That face had ducked low long before Ott's fist came close to it. Before the giant could follow the first shot with his left hand, lights flashed as pain rocked the bottom of his jaw. The blow slammed his mouth shut and sent a shockwave through his entire head. He barely had time to register that he had been hit with an uppercut when the lights flashed again. This time the pain radiated from his temple. Before he knew what had happened, Lito-Bi's foot hammered into his chest knocking the wind out of him and depositing him on the ground. The room swam around him, tilting one way and then the other. He barely noticed Chi-Ta charge past him as he focused on keeping the contents of his gut from pouring out of his mouth.

By the time Ott regained his feet, Chi-Ta was standing just outside the broken wall of the throne room shouting at nothing. The traitors had apparently fled. The shouts pouring from Chi-Ta as he stomped and waved his arms wildly did not register to Ott. He did not need to hear the curses, nor the volume with which they tore through the salty air. The trogmortem king's actions were enough to ensure Ott could still count on his loyalty. The only question that remained was whether they should give chase immediately to exact justice on the pack of traitors, or if they should wait to cut them down with the men and dwarves for which they had abandoned their cause. As much as Ott wanted to hunt them down and crush them all, he had no idea of the extent of any planning they may have done. The treachery was obviously deep. His grandson had an entire group of treasonous bastards at his back when he came calling. The possibility of a trap was undeniable.

"Calm yourself," he called out to Chi-Ta as he rose to his feet. "They are obviously gone."

Chi-Ta took a moment to compose himself before replying, "They are. They fled like cowards after Lito-Bi ambushed you. Give me leave to bring them to justice. I will take my best killers and hunt the traitors down."

Ott inhaled deeply, giving his heart a chance to slow, and said, "Patience. They will pay for their treachery in time. This was not a random act. They planned this assault carefully. We will not fall into any traps they may have laid for us. We will plan. We will measure our response. And we will crush them all."

# CHAPTER 6
## MAKING A WARRIOR

The trees glowed in the bright sunlight as they stretched toward a sky free from clouds. They looked more like the spires of an emerald castle than simple pines barely moved by the slightest approximation of a breeze. The clearing they surrounded had been growing steadily warmer as the sun slowly gained height. It was not quite directly overhead when Perrin finally paused in her sword training with Glord and brushed back the few wisps of hair that had escaped her ponytail.

"I can barely lift my sword," she remarked as she walked a slow circle and tried to get control of her breath. "Can we call it a day?"

"Aye, my queen," Glord chuckled, "I'd been ready to quit an hour ago. None can say you ain't taking this training seriously."

Perrin pawed at her blouse. The thing was loose, light, and typically comfortable. The thick sheen of sweat covering her body made it less so. It stuck to her in spots. She pulled at those spots and fanned them. If only there were a breeze. Of course, a cool breeze would not help her legs at all. Leather trousers might be durable and built for the trail, but they certainly were not crafted with comfort in mind.

"How do you men wear these horrible trousers every day for all your days?" she asked as she bent at the waist and gently patted the inside of her right thigh. "These awful things have the insides of my thighs all chaffed, red, and sore. I ain't never been much of a lady, but I'd trade these stiff, sweaty things for a loose dress in a blink."

This time Glord laughed outright. "Aye, my queen," he glanced around the clearing and continued, "Since none of them other blokes be around to hear this, I can tell you I'd be trading my trousers for a comfortable dress right now too." After a brief pause, he added, "It may not seem like it now, but you'll get used to that as the trail drags on. I won't try tricking you into thinking you'll ever call them comfortable, but they won't be cutting up your legs so much."

"Thank Coeptus for that," she smiled. After a few more moments of pawing at her sweat-drenched clothes, she asked, "Glord?"

"Aye, my queen?" Glord asked.

The humor left her voice, "Why do you keep calling me your queen? I ain't nobody's queen anymore, probably won't never be again."

Glord scratched his head and looked up toward the bright sky. "I can't see you no other way. I'd been a young lieutenant in Havenstahl's army when you came to us, all fresh-faced and bright-eyed. Of course, you were no queen then. No, then you'd been a cherub, not much more than a babe with no father or mother to look after you. Well, Ymitoth, may the Lake forever bless his soul, he'd been my general and only days returned from training your husband, the lad of the Lake himself. He minced no words with us when he told us about you. He told us all about what them monsters done to your family and how fresh them wounds were. You can ask any of them men serving with me then, we all vowed to take you as our own. I never had no daughters, or sons, for that matter. Maybe I saw you as that. Of course, as a soldier, there ain't no way I could give any child the kind of life Kendal and Haleen gave you. It's a shame what happen to them."

"Aye," Perrin's head dipped as she chewed her lower lip, "ain't a day goes by without them two being in my thoughts. I'd been so young when my mama and papa were taken, but I knew them. They'd been good. But what Kendal and Haleen done for me, I have no words. They never let me want for nothing, treated me just the same as if I'd been their own." Perrin's cheeks blushed slightly over her smile as she continued, "I do remember all the gifts you would bring me when you would come to the pub to visit. Papa built me the biggest toy chest in all of Havenstahl to house all the baubles and dolls and such." Her smile widened and she added, "Come to think of it, I might have been a bit spoiled by you and some of the other soldiers."

Glord blushed a bit too, as he replied, "Aye, I saw many a hardened man melt when seeing your face all bright with excitement at a gift they'd given you. Ain't a one of us would ever let you want for nothing." He grew a bit more somber before adding, "When them monsters took Ymitoth from us, it was a hard day. Truth be told, it was one of my hardest. You became my queen on that day. On that day, I vowed to follow where you led and let no peril befall you so long as a breath remained in my body."

"You are a good and noble man, Glord," Perrin smiled. "Ain't no man I'd trust more with my safety."

"Thank you, my queen," Glord returned the smile. "You can't possibly know how much your kind words mean to this old soldier. I only pray I deserve the compliment."

Perrin flopped down on the ground next to her horse sack and fished out a hunk of dried meat. She was only about three chews in before she chased it down with a big splash from her water skin. Sword training worked up a mighty appetite and an equally mighty thirst. Glord flopped down beside her and did the same. They both looked out into the trees as they ate.

Birds sang their songs and flitted from this tree to that and back again, as if trying to decide which spot was the best for belting out a melody. Meanwhile, furry critters scuttled about searching among the brush and dead leaves for the perfect morsel to chomp away on. A stag caught Perrin's attention. Filtered sunshine glinted off the fallon's rack as it scraped it against a tree to rub off the remaining velvet. The sheer serenity of it all nearly made her forget the horrors which had driven her to the trail in the first place. Of course, nothing ever could. The trail, her journey to find her lost son, precious Geillan, was all that mattered.

After swallowing down a mouthful of dried meat, Perrin broke the silence, "You know, this is my first real adventure. Been more than a few times I've forgotten my purpose and got all sucked up into it."

"Aye," Glord chuckled, "the call of the trail. It is something you can't understand until you've been on it. Every time she calls, it is to satisfy some goal, some great need. You ain't the first to be feeling that. It's a kind of freedom."

"How so?" Perrin asked.

"I ain't what you'd call a wise man, but I know more than most about the trail. Just look at all that surrounds you, the trees, the air, the way the sun glints off everything and pulls out the colors in all their glory. Listen to the songs the birds sing. They never sound so sweet trapped between four walls. Once you have been out in it like we are now, that is when you can understand the call," he paused as his gaze drifted deeper into the trees. "Now that you have been in it, surrounded by all this life, you'll be feeling that call for the rest of your days."

Perrin nodded, "You sound like a wise man to me. A couple weeks on the trail, and I can't picture myself surrounded by no walls any longer."

"And you sound like a proper adventurer," Glord remarked. "Based on where the stars are sitting in the night sky, I think you'll have once more what we have already seen before getting to that spot where the lad of the Lake crossed the Lost Forest."

"Aye, Cialia taught me much in her odd way," Perrin agreed. "It wasn't like no lesson I'd ever learned before. She placed her hands over my eyes, and I saw everything. There are thousands and thousands of Dragons, all mighty, terrible, and beautiful to behold. I can't wait to see that place with my own eyes."

Glord failed to suppress a nervous chuckle, "You can probably count me and the men a bit less eager to look upon that sight."

Perrin smirked, "Could it be the great and mighty Glord found something he fears?"

"Laugh all you want. For most of my life, Dragons were mighty and terrifying beasts that could burn all of Ouloos with their rage. Dragon's fire will melt the flesh from your bones before burning them to dust," Glord's reply was barely more than a mumble. "The story your husband showed us may have proved them tales to be as false as Darg's wooden teeth, but it didn't erase them from our memory. I never met a Dragon. How could I know what will happen when I do?"

"You ain't wrong about that," Perrin agreed. "Maelich told me Dragons are love, honest, pure, and unconditional. I can't trust that man in much else these days, but in that I do. Even if I didn't, I need them Dragons to help me find my lost babe."

"Aye, you do," Glord agreed before adding, "and I can't let you face no peril on your own. Scared as I might be, if them stories prove to be less than true, I'll protect you as best I can."

"Of that I have no doubt," Perrin smiled as she stood, stretched, and packed up her things for the short journey back to camp.

"Are you ready to get back to the trail?" Glord asked as he followed suit. "If we hit it hard until sunset, there is a small brook where we can water the horses and refill our water skins."

Perrin nodded her response before taking one last longing look into the peacefulness surrounding her. She had no idea how long it would be until she could feel as carefree as the birds singing from the branches of tall pines. Hopefully, when that day finally came, and her precious Geillan was back in her arms, he would still be small enough to sit in her lap and look out at a peaceful forest with her.

CHAPTER 7
# THE EMPTY THRONE

Bindaar stood alone in the courtyard of the palace at Alhouim. The place seemed a vast and lonely desert to the dwarf. Of course, that had probably been the intent when Ahm ordered the dwarves of Alhouim to tear down their castle and build his palace over its ruins. Everything about the place seemed geared to make dwarves feel even smaller. Never mind that giants logically require larger structures and wider expanses due to their massive dimensions. The fact mattered little to Bindaar. Everything that bastard, Ahm, had ever done was probably intended to make the dwarves feel miniscule and worthless.

Much had changed since the lad of the Lake strolled into that courtyard to relieve a giant of his massive, stupid head and free a city of subjugated dwarves, but even more had not. The massive thrones which sat atop the steps leading up into the palace and were big enough to hold Ahm and his wife's giant rumps had been replaced with seats of more modest dimensions for Doentaat and his wife Gleeanna, and additional floors had been added within the palace itself. No dwarf alive had any need for a twenty-five-foot ceiling. However, the very spot where Bindaar stood looking up at his missing friend's throne was the exact same spot he stood while Ahm passed judgement on him for shirking his responsibility in the mines and tromping off to the hillside to smoke a bit of fairy weed. That was so long ago.

Doentaat had turned out to be a great king, caring, honest, and fair. Bindaar knew he would. Just then, he wished he knew where that king could be. Five generals led dwarves into battle at Fort Maomnosett.

Despite his counseling, the king was one of those generals. Bindaar had wished his former housemate to remain safe in the castle while his generals conducted the work of pushing the invaders back to their boats. Unfortunately, if a more dutiful dwarf than Doentaat existed, Bindaar had never met the bloke. After the battle, that dutiful dwarf was nowhere to be found.

Bindaar had not heard Lentaak enter, so when the thin, sly dwarf said, "My lord, I bring word," he nearly jumped out of his boots.

"Aye, you sneaky bastard," Bindaar nearly shouted. "How do you get around without them damned boots making a sound?"

"Please forgive me, general," Lentaak bowed. "You know my father, may Coeptus rest his soul, had been quite an accomplished thief before Ahm ordered him strung up on the Sacred Pine. He taught me how to keep my steps quiet. I never unlearned the skill."

"Your father had been more than just a simple thief," Bindaar replied after composing himself. "We all did things we weren't proud of when Ahm was king here."

Bindaar patted Lentaak on the back before draping an arm across his shoulder and leading him toward the gates at the edge of the grand courtyard. "Let's step over to Boonda's Pub, and you can catch me up over a pint."

The road leading out of the palace was far too quiet. Normally, at this time of day they would be bustling with dwarves gossiping or shopping, grabbing a meal out for the mid-day, or maybe even challenging a chum to a feat of strength before heading back off to the mines. Too many of Alhouim's sons were off helping Havenstahl rebuild or searching the surrounding lands for those who had yet to report back in after the battle.

Boonda the bald—the youngest of three dwarves all bearing the same name, one the son of another and so on—perched atop a wobbly ladder touching up the paint on the wooden sign hanging in front of it. The entire sign was looking a bit worn and weathered. The happy dwarf clicking his heels at the center of the thing looked no worse for wear, but the ale splashing up from the pint he toted looked a bit more like foam than the healthy amber of a good ale. A stiff breeze picked up just as Boonda was stretching a bit too far and blew the hat right off his head exposing the bright pink bald spot right in the middle of his white hair. The hat swirled a bit as the teetering dwarf swiped at it and nearly fell from his perch.

"Blasted wind and bastard hat," the embarrassed dwarf grumbled as he helplessly watched the thing drop to the ground at Bindaar's feet.

Bindaar chuckled as he stooped the pick the tattered thing up off the dirt, "This battered old rag getting the best of you?"

"It ain't that hat what's got me all riled," Boonda snarled back, "Alenaat, that scrappy waste, was supposed to have this old sign all prettied up even before that horn of Havenstahl called all able bodies to help in fighting them giants."

Alenaat was a dwarf for which Bindaar had a bit of a soft spot. Scrappy waste was more than a fair description, too thin, too scruffy, and at least a week from his last bath no matter what day of the week you crossed his path. He reminded the old dwarf general of himself at a younger age, back before Doentaat was king and nothing more than his housemate. "Alenaat hadn't been on the battlefield with us fighting folk. That bloke couldn't lift a mighty dwarf axe past his belt," Bindaar shrugged. "Why ain't he up there in your stead?"

"Probably off smoking fairy weed and looking at clouds," Boonda growled as Bindaar and Lentaak passed by him and entered the pub.

Boonda's was the largest building in the city besides the palace. More like a hall than a pub, there was ample room for more than three hundred dwarves to drink, eat, arm wrestle, or dance a jig. Rows of long tables made from wooden slats, sturdy and stained with a deep glossy finish, stretched from the front to the back. A bar, equally dark and equally glossy, ran the length of the place on the right side. Fifty dwarves could sit shoulder to shoulder along the thing with room to spare between them. On this day, only one dwarf sat in front of it. He was the owner of the place, Boonda the bored, and he was face down, fast asleep on the bar. His son, Boonda the round, stood behind the bar chuckling and counting pub crisps as he stacked them up on his father's cheek.

"You are a far braver dwarf than me," Lentaak commented quietly.

"Aye," Bindaar agreed. "Your father might be the eldest of you three Boonda's, but he'd be the first one I'd be picking to my side if a fight were brewing. You'll have your ears boxed if he ever wakes from that nap."

"Twenty-six," Boonda chuckled through a sly grin. "Have you ever known my father to wake from any nap for any reason other than he's all done sleeping?"

"Might you see fit to break from torturing your father long enough to draw a couple pints for a couple of thirsty dwarves?" Bindaar asked as he and Lentaak took two stools a bit farther down the bar. Once seated, he looked over at Lentaak and said, "Alright then, let's have that update you promised."

Lentaak took a swig from the shiny cup Boonda had just set in front of him, wiped his mustache off on the back of his sleeve, and began, "Fifty or so of our best craftsmen be about the work of rebuilding the castle at Havenstahl."

"Fifty?" Bindaar's shocked tone—just shy of a shout—caused a stir in Boonda the bored, who grumbled an inaudible response, scratched his cheek, and promptly got back to snoring.

"Aw, piss off," Boonda the round complained as pub crisps scattered from his father's face. "Now I need to start all over."

Bindaar continued in a quieter tone, "Why so many for building when lost dwarves be littered all about the surrounding hills and valleys?"

"Ain't a one of them builders built for fighting or riding, strong arms but ain't none of them got no kind of stamina," Lentaak shrugged. "Helping get that castle back up suits them just fine. Sooner the better if you're asking me."

Bindaar thought on it for a bit while he took a long drink. After wiping a good bit of foam from his mustache he added, "Aye. The quicker they get that castle back together the less chance we have them giants will turn their vile gazes toward our palace. Go on."

"Another one hundred dwarves scour the pines on our hill and down in the river valley below," Lentaak continued. "They find a few injured here and there, but far too many dead. Two more groups of equal size search the forests to the north and south of the clearing in front of Fort Maomnosett, or what's left of it. Then we have five and twenty working with an equal force from Havenstahl. They monitor the comings and goings of them bastards still anchored at Biggon's Bay."

Bindaar had been leaning in as he sipped from his cup and listened. His left eye squinted a bit when Lentaak failed to continue. "Well, what more have you got?"

"Ain't no more," Lentaak shrugged, chugged the last of his pint, set it down on the bar, and waved Boonda over to pour him another.

Bindaar's gaze dropped to the floor, "Them ain't no kind of numbers."

"Many a stout dwarf found their way back to the Lake that day," Lentaak agreed. "How many more remain lost or still fighting is hard to know. The men of Havenstahl fared no better. A giant of a man," he paused trying to recall the name. After a moment, and a few more chugs off his pint, he continued, "Tarturan, that was it. Damn near scared the beard right off my chin. Thought him a giant as big as he was. Had five other men with him. They were all big, but this one was massive."

"Aye, I remember that one from the battlefield at Fort Maomnosett," Bindaar chuckled. "He stood out like a tall oak in a sea of maples in them columns. What did he want, supplies, pord, something else? Why didn't you bring him before me?"

After a long sigh, Lentaak scratched his head and said, "I'd been afraid of what you might say to him. He came calling for more dwarves to aid in defending Havenstahl."

"Every able-bodied dwarf is out to field aiding in their fight and protecting, or rebuilding, their city. Did you ask if the men of Havenstahl will be there when them bastards from across the Great Sea turn their wicked eyes on us and our castle?"

"I did," Lentaak nodded, "but I didn't yell, threaten, nor strike him. You might have done any or all of them things."

"Aye, that was wise," Bindaar grinned briefly. "That big one, he'd have been a tough tree to chop down."

Bindaar grew grim as the room shifted and dizziness swept through him. It was not the ale. He had only put one away at that point, and he could match any dwarf drink for drink. It was not even the sheer number of dwarves who had given everything at the battle of Maomnosett. He had yet to take any time to grieve, but he was on the field that day. The ridiculous ask from Havenstahl was enough to get his hackles up, but that was not it either. As much as he hated hearing Lentaak's report, it contained no real surprises. None of the things he said were the cause of the bile at the back of Bindaar's throat threatening to pour out over the highly polished bar. The empty throne, his missing chum, and his dearest friend, the king, had not been mentioned at all.

"You failed to mention anything of Doentaat," Bindaar's voice was barely more than a whisper.

Lentaak sighed, drank his freshly poured pint, and waved for another before answering just as quietly, "Ain't been no word of the king."

"That ain't no kind of answer," Bindaar began shaking his head. "You had best come up with something a just a wee better than that."

Boonda quietly set two fresh pints down before patting Bindaar on the hand and giving him a somber look.

"Is that pity, Boonda? Why look at me with them sad eyes like I suffer the loss of one dear to me?" Bindaar's tone echoed how offended he was at the thought.

Lentaak replied as Boonda failed to find the words. "Old friend," the solida began, "the time to consider what we might do if facts would have it our king found his way back to the Lake is upon us."

The tone of Bindaar's reply did not slowly mount to a loud crescendo. It began the same as it ended, as a shout. "A stronger, stouter dwarf than our king ain't never lived," he pounded his fist against the table before adding, "You've no cause for worrying over what we might do if my old friend is dead, because he ain't that. We all be bound for the Lake, but it ain't his time yet. And you'd best not go around suggesting anything different." His cheeks shook as he grabbed hold of Lentaak's shirt, and Boonda quickly scurried away.

"Forgive my foolish words, Bindaar," Lentaak remained calm as he gently placed his hand on Bindaar's. "I'm sure we'll get word of the king's whereabouts in short order."

Bindaar seemed to deflate like an empty waterskin as he released his grip on Lentaak's shirt. Though admitting the solida beside him gave sound advice was the last thing he wanted to do, each passing day made it difficult to think otherwise. The odds of Doentaat being found shrunk with each passing moment.

***

The pain had returned with a vengeance by the time Doentaat woke in the orange glow of a healthy fire. He would rather have held in the howl with which he greeted the waking world, but it got away from him before his wits had fully returned. The flickering flames cast eerie shadows all about the trees as his orange-haired savior worked feverishly over him to save his mangled leg.

"What in sweet dragon's tits are you doing to my leg?" Bindaar groaned.

"They call me Banch, my lord," the man replied without looking up. "Based on your markings and that mighty axe you wield; I assume you to be King Bindaar of Alhouim. I'm humbled to be at your service. You've had a rough go of it. I used the fire to stop the bleeding from your leg, but infection is setting in and moving fast up toward your heart."

"You'd best be telling me you ain't suggesting…" he trailed off before saying the words he did not want to hear.

Banch finally made eye contact. His green eyes glowed like emeralds beneath the flames of his orange hair as he replied, "Aye. You ain't making it back to Alhouim with that leg. If you're going, that leg is staying in this forest."

Doentaat laid his head back against the ground. The trees reached toward the star-speckled darkness above him. If only he could fly up into that darkness and escape the reality suffocating him in the orange dome of flickering fire light. This big orange-haired bastard wanted to have his leg off. The option seemed worse than the agonizing pain radiating from that spot. Unfortunately, there was no denying the young soldier's prognosis was correct. The leg would have to come off if he wanted to live.

"Fine," Doentaat's whisper was barely audible over the crackle of the fire.

"Forgive me, highness," Banch leaned closer, "What was that you said?"

This time the dwarf king shouted, "Have my damn leg if that's what you want, you grim bastard!"

Crestfallen, Banch replied, "It ain't my desire to have your leg. My only desire is to see the great king of Alhouim safely back to his throne."

Doentaat struggled up to a seated position and grabbed hold of Banch's shoulder to pull him close. A tear tickled his cheek as it slipped down his face to moisten his mustache. Normally, the thought of showing any kind of weakness in front of any man would seem a fate worse than death. Right at that moment, he did not care. He was quite fond of that damned leg, and the thought of losing it was sad, at least sad enough for one lousy tear.

"Forgive me," Doentaat had gained control of his tone, "You seem a fine man. This thing you want me to do, well it ain't wrong. I know that. It's just…" Doentaat trailed off as he turned his gaze toward the fire and stared for a moment before asking, "How good are you with that blade?"

"I ain't promising you won't feel it, but you will have no unnecessary pain," Banch replied earnestly. "The flame I'll kiss it with after, now that is…"

"I know," Doentaat interrupted. "Get to it."

Banch did just that. He sized up a girthy branch lying just outside the fire's glow. It would do. He dragged the heavy thing over to his injured new friend. The dwarf king lost another pitiable howl when Banch raised the wasted leg up onto the thing. He paused for a moment, waiting for another verbal assault. When it did not come, he grabbed a thick stick from a pile of firewood he had gathered and stuck one end deep into the hottest part of the fire. Then he disappeared behind a tree.

"Hey," Doentaat hollered, "you'd best not be leaving me out here. If that's your plan, you could have just let them damned, scaly bastards finish me off."

Banch quickly returned with a leather strap and a water skin. The latter he handed to Doentaat and said, "Here, take a good long pull off of that."

"I'd been hoping for something stronger than water," Doentaat grimaced.

"Aye, fairies tears," Banch replied, "It'll help to ease the pain."

Doentaat finally smiled despite his pain. "Ah, fairies' tears, much stronger than ale, mightier than wine, forget your fears with fairies' tears and all will be just fine," he finished with a wink. "An old barker came through my city some years ago selling this beautiful concoction. Lost me many a night to this beauty."

Banch chuckled as Doentaat took a good, long pull. "Just let me know when you're ready, highness."

Doentaat nearly drained the entire water skin before he decided to grit his teeth and get it done. He nodded to Banch as he handed over a significantly lighter container than he had received. Banch, in return, handed him the leather strap. The dwarf king bit down hard on the thing as he clenched his eyes tight and nodded again. Time slowed. His cheeks grew sore with the weight of his bite. A hint of oil entered his awareness. Whether it was a taste or a smell, he really could not tell. Just get on with it already.

Then the sound, sharpened steel slicing through still air a split second before the thump. His leg unceremoniously flopped to the ground. It must have been a clean cut. He had not felt a thing. Though he knew it was over—one big piece of him missing—his eyes refused to open. The sharp stabbing pain that remained seemed far too low, probably phantoms. How long would those last? His grandfather, Coeptus rest his soul, had complained regularly of itching in the leg he had lost to a mining accident many summers before Doentaat had even been born. Would his missing leg cause him grief for the rest of his days? The thought died a quick death when the burning came. It took all his attention. He did not want to open his eyes, but the pain seemed a million times worse than what the cut was meant to fix. He saw no joy on the face of his savior when his eyes did snap open, just a young soldier doing a job that needed doing. In that moment of blistering agony, Banch's motivation meant nothing.

"You cowardly bastard," Doentaat howled, the strap slipping from his mouth. "Get me while I'm down at my lowest, will you? I promise you this now, if ever we meet on a battlefield, my hungry axe will have both your damn legs off, you pretty son of whore!"

Banch's tone remained measured as he struggled to finish cauterizing the wound with the flaming brand, "It ain't no good to have you bleeding out all over this forest floor, highness. Once we get all this mess behind us, she'll be smarting for a time, but you won't die on account of infection. We'll get her bandaged up good, and you'll be on your way to healing."

Doentaat gave up complaining. The deed was done, and he was less one leg for it. He knew as well as the author of his pain that it was a necessary loss. Somehow acknowledging the necessity of the deed did nothing to make him feel any better about it. Nor did it dull the pain at all. However, as the moments shuffled by, he slowly got used to it. The initial shock of intense pain is always the worst. Luckily, the mind has a way of dealing with things once a tragedy has finished. He laid back and let the lad do his work. Before long, his lids grew heavy. Whether it was the pain, all the blood he had lost on the forest floor, or the fairies' tears, sleep seemed about the best option just then.

The sun was rising by the time Doentaat woke. The pain in his leg had diminished enough that he no longer wanted to kill every living soul in the forest. That was a start. He was deep into rubbing the sleep from his eyes when the most succulent scent he had smelled in ages drifted past his nose. His stomach grumbled in response. He could not remember the last time he had eaten. The past few days had been such a blur, and his damned leg had earned the lion's share of his attention. Food would be a delight. Locating the source of that wonderful smell suddenly became the most pressing matter in his life. He glanced over toward the fire. There it was, the ass end of a fallon stuck on a spit with that beautiful leg stealer slowly spinning it over the fire.

"If I could get up off of this ground, I'd kiss you square on the mouth," Doentaat boomed. "Where did you find such a beautiful hunk of meat?"

Banch chuckled and flashed a wide smile, "That is the best thing about this wood. It is teeming with fallon. If you have a bow and a bit of patience, there are feasts bounding all about among these trees."

"Ain't never been too fond of bows," Doentaat shrugged. "Mostly the women folk be doing all the hunting."

A sly grin slipped onto Banch's face despite the slight. It was not the first time his gruffness had been questioned because of his prowess with a bow. "Things are different for folks who hail from small villages. One can only eat what he kills living deep in the woods. A sword ain't much help for that. I learned to fire brands from a tightly strung bow long before I'd look anything but silly swinging a sword. I had never even held one before traveling to the great city to ride under the banner of Havenstahl during my sixteenth summer after my mother passed, Coeptus rest her soul. She's the one who taught me. You can thank her for this grand feast. It might be my father would have taught me different skills had he been around. On the other hand, it might be she would have put him right back in his place and taught me what she did anyhow. We can't know which would be true, but I can tell you what a mistake it would be to question her on it if she were here. Either way, it's lucky for you she did," he finished with a wink.

"Ain't truer words ever been spoken," Doentaat smiled. "She raised a good, solid man. Coeptus never saw fit to bless me with no sons. If ever they do, I pray they see fit to bring me one righteous and caring as you."

Banch's cheeks reddened a bit at the compliment. He slipped his dagger out of its scabbard, sliced a healthy slab off the dripping hunk of meat he had been slowly spinning over the fire, and handed it over to Doentaat.

The king of Alhouim attacked it like a ravenous beast. Juice saturated his beard as he made the kind of sounds typically heard from a bed chamber occupied by passionate lovers. The juicy morsel was more than just a necessary meal to keep his haggard carcass from the Lake. It was a little bit of light in the darkest chapter thus far in his life. If he could sit leaning up against that sturdy tree and gnawing on the delicious hunk of salvation in his hand for the rest of his days, he just might.

While Doentaat attacked his meat, Banch slipped around a tree. He returned wearing a wide smile and carrying a wooden contraption. The rectangular thing was roughly three feet by four, framed by four thick sticks tied together with twine. Two additional sticks ran diagonally from one corner to another, respectively. Two leather straps were attached at either end of the shorter side and ran the length of the longer dimension. Two more leather straps ran along the shorter dimension, one at the top and the other at the bottom.

When Doentaat finally noticed him over the dripping morsel he was taking down, he did not much like what he saw. "That best not be what I'm thinking it is, you grinning idiot," the dwarf grumbled around a mouthful of meat.

"There ain't no other way to get you out of this forest," Banch replied, his smile not fading in the least. He slipped his arms through the straps running down the longer dimension, pulled them tight and turned around to show the thing off. "We can strap you onto the back of this, and I can haul you out of here."

"Now listen here," Doentaat began, swallowing a big hunk of half-chewed meat before he continued, "I appreciate all what you've done for me, but I am the king of Alhouim, and a proud king at that. You ain't lugging me around like some kind of hairy baby."

Banch's smile faded a bit at the king's reply. Still, he pressed on, "You can't walk, highness. If I ain't carrying you out of this wood, how do you suppose you'll be getting back to your throne?"

Doentaat finished his hunk of meat, splashed a good long drink of water down behind it, and scratched his head. "Can't you just prop me up on that horse and walk me out of this damnable place?"

"Don't you think I thought about that?" Banch asked. "I did the best I could with that leg of yours, but I ain't no healer. By my best estimate, we have about two weeks before we see anything but trees if we walk. If I strap you to my back, we might be looking at two days, long days, but days not weeks. I am greatly worried you haven't much more than that before that leg starts causing you more than a bit of pain."

Doentaat's form deflated. As much as he despised the idea, Banch was right. His leg was good and red all the way from where the brute had taken it off up to his groin. Infection was moving through him. Before long, he would be mad with fever. Shortly after that he would be dead. It would take a proper healer to really fix him up. If only Hagen had happened upon them in the forest. Alas, fanciful dreams would do him no good.

"Think you can lift my fat rump up onto your back with that thing?" Doentaat asked, his voice barely more than a defeated whisper.

"You're a stout, strong dwarf, highness, but my legs and my back are strong too. I'll be hefting you up onto my back, and we'll be riding out of here," Banch's smile had returned.

Doentaat did not respond. He just nodded and waved for Banch to get on with it.

Banch obliged. Laying the contraption down next to the king he said, "Do you think you can wriggle yourself over onto this thing?"

"I make this vow to you right here and right now," Doentaat grumbled as he worked his way onto the contraption, "if you ever breathe a word to any soul about me doing any wriggling, or riding around on your back like a damned baby, I'll be taking one of your long legs for my wall."

"I'll take that secret to the grave, highness," Banch chuckled as he pulled the straps tight across Doentaat's chest and waist, and then helped the dwarf king up to a seated position.

Aside from a bunch of grunting and groaning, the two remained silent as Banch struggled to get the pack on his back. The effort of strapping a full-grown dwarf to his back seemed easy until he attempted to get his feet. Though Doentaat may have felt like a baby helplessly strapped to someone, Banch's legs would disagree. By the time the soldier was standing upright with the king of Alhouim on his back, his face was red and his breaths rapid and deep.

"Perhaps I should have handed you a smaller hunk of meat," Banch groaned.

Doentaat remained silent. His face just grew redder as he thought of all the ways he would punish his savior if he ever breathed a word of his unfortunate mode of travel to anyone.

# CHAPTER 8
# FEAR OF A LOOSE DRAGON

Moshat and Kaldumahn lounged upon thrones carved from stone and etched with elaborate designs. Of course, no chisel had ever touched the stone of those thrones. No man, nor dwarf, nor any other creature could manage the impossible shapes. Gods did not need the labor of men to craft their wares. The thrones sat at the center of an immense dome with impossibly smooth walls of the same stone and etched with designs equally impossible.

Both gods wore impeccable white robes, and both had hair and beards which matched them perfectly. All of it glowed like the brightest star in a black sky. Both gripped staffs—Kaldumahn on the right held his in his right hand, and Moshat opposite him held his in his left—which ended in images of dragons perching atop them like statues and glowing with the same perfect, white light. Both gods trembled and mumbled with their eyes shut tight as if they were deep in trances speaking incantations.

Kaldumahn's eyes snapped open first. They were at once beautiful and horrible, the deepest black pits where no color could escape. But that black was an illusion. Somehow, in that absence of any light or color was an impossible negative glow where all colors existed at once swirling and mixing in a never-ending dance.

"The Dragon is on the hunt, hungry for the souls of gods," Moshat proclaimed as his eyes snapped open exposing the same beautiful yet horrifying contradiction of colors.

Kaldumahn shook his head, "Gods do not have souls, brother. We have discussed this on more occasions than I would like to remember."

"Yes, brother, on this point we disagree," Moshat replied flatly. "However, now is not the time to debate this or that or attempt to sway one another to different ways of thinking about something of which we are both convinced."

"Agreed," Kaldumahn conceded. "Of which Dragon do you speak?"

"Cialia, of course," Moshat shrugged. "The lad of the Lake has hidden himself, neither Helias nor any of her sisters harbor anything besides love for all living things. None of them are a concern at this point. Geillan could be a force, but Kallum has taken..."

"The eagle I battled above the castle at Havenstahl was not Kallum," Kaldumahn interrupted.

"Indeed. That is what you said. However, you were outmatched and perhaps confused. Either way, the force you faced that day is a powerful adversary. Even still, I would contend that adversary is not our most pressing concern at this moment."

Kaldumahn snapped his fingers, "Finally, you have stumbled upon something on which we can agree. Cialia has proven herself to be the most dangerous of Dragons. Drawing half her heritage from the race of Dragons and half from the race of men, she harbors the greatest power in all of Ouloos and the will to use it."

"She wants to kill us and our brothers," Moshat agreed. "Perhaps, we should seek her out and lobby her to our way of thinking."

"I do not believe that to be possible," Kaldumahn contended. "Her desires do not match our own. We should focus the entirety of our intent on hiding from her fury. Perhaps, we should seek a truce with our brother, Brerto. Though I do not agree, he believes the eagle I faced over Havenstahl to be Kallum. His rage at being betrayed may be enough to convince him into an alliance, especially with Cialia hunting us as she seems to be."

"Coward," Moshat spat, unable to hide his disgust. "You would help that vile thing to save yourself?"

"I would not," Kaldumahn fired back. "However, I am not too proud to realize we are outmatched and will be destroyed if we face that supposed killer of gods."

Moshat calmed slightly, "None of our options are desirable, brother. Though it may be cowardice, bending our will toward hiding from her might seems our only option. How long do you suppose we can hide from her fury?"

The incomprehensible colors seemed to swirl faster in Kaldumahn's horrible gaze as he stared off at nothing, "It is impossible to know."

"Yes," Moshat nodded. "If the time comes when she fully realizes her power, nothing will be hidden from her sight."

"A truth," Kaldumahn agreed.

"A truth which raises the question, is it better to face her now while she wanders unaware of her full potential, or wait for her to find us once she has?" Moshat scratched his beard.

"A fool's errand," Kaldumahn scoffed. "Even now, as she remains blissfully unaware of her potential, we have no hope of defeating her. We wait. If she finds her true self, she destroys us. If she never does…"

"We hide in this hole until the end of time?" Moshat spat. "I cannot remain idle waiting for the inevitable end. If we wait, we must prepare, learn everything we can about her nature and intention. Then, when the time comes…"

"If the time comes," Kaldumahn interrupted.

"If the time comes," Moshat allowed, "we will be as prepared as we can be to face her fury."

# CHAPTER 9
## THE DRAGON AND THE TIGER

The great waste sprawled in all directions. Bodies at various stages of decomposition littered the blood-stained ground where a mighty forest once stood. Scavengers picked at the bodies which had yet to be cleaned of meat. The smell of the place was even worse than the sight of it, weeks of rot oozing into the soft earth. It all seemed so senseless to Bom.

Lito-Bi walked beside Bom ahead of a long, tight column of trogmortem, grongs, and a handful of giants. Noticing the despair in the giant's expression, he commented, "The aftermath is always worse than the fury of battle."

"It is far too easy to forget the things we battle are living creatures when viewing them through eyes red with rage while adrenaline courses through our veins," Bom agreed.

"Do you see that one?" the corners of Lito-Bi's mouth dipped to a frown as he pointed to a pile of slick bones. "He was my oldest friend, Harim-Ka, born just one day before me. So many adventures we shared growing up," he paused as the beginning of a tear formed at the corner of his eye. "Now he feeds the soil of a foreign land."

Bom saw no difference between the decomposing pile and any of the thousands of others in the vast field. "Forgive me. I know how this must sound, but how can you tell?" he finally asked.

"The leather sash draped across that ribcage. I gave him that when he passed the trial of stone and fire," Lito-Bi wiped his eyes.

No response was necessary from Bom. He simply nodded and

draped his arm across the trogmortem's shoulders, as they both bowed their heads toward the fallen warrior.

After a few moments of silent prayer, Lito-Bi raised his head and changed the subject. "It was a brave thing you did, standing up to your grandfather. I am not certain I would be as bold."

Bom allowed a shallow smile to turn up the corners of his mouth, "If I recall correctly, all I did was get thrown through a wall. It was you who brought the bravery to the party."

"I merely reacted," Lito-Bi disagreed. "It is easy to appear brave when instincts are controlling your actions. Given a moment to reflect, I may have behaved differently."

"You are a humble…" Bom's reply was lost beneath the fury of a growl loud enough to rumble the ground beneath his feet.

Hountmytall Moh, son of Mon, cried out, "The great tiger has come to judge us for our betrayal."

Brerto, the great, white tiger had indeed joined Bom's group in the great waste that day. The ground trembled under his paws as he sauntered toward them. His head towered even over Moh's brother Moy who at nearly twenty feet counted himself as the tallest living giant. All in the field fell to their knees and bowed their heads to the ground before the horrible tiger. The memory of watching the vengeful god indiscriminately kill every living thing he happened upon during the battle of Fort Maomnosett was fresh in all their minds.

"Maomnosett Bom, son of Bok, grandson of Ott, you taint the mighty name of your house with this ragged group of traitors," the great tiger growled with a voice both magnificent and horrifying.

Lito-Bi touched Bom's arm as the young giant rose to face his accuser. It was too late. Bom had already decided he would stand for what he believed in regardless of the peril. Lito-Bi's somber recollection of his fallen friend had further strengthened his resolve. "Please forgive the hubris, mighty Brerto, great tiger, god of my fathers, but I disagree. I believe my actions will elevate the name of my house," he replied with strength in his voice.

Brerto's humorless laugh belied the fury boiling beneath his fur. He roared, "All of you kneeling before me, take note. You commit blasphemy against my name and will suffer for eternity lest you repent. Turn away from this folly of a mission. Return to your ships and fall in line behind my chosen. Fail to heed my command, and I will torment your souls until the end of time."

The grongs in the group scattered. There was nothing shocking about that. It was surprising any of them joined the cause in the first place. If nothing else, grongs were opportunistic. Brokering a peace with Havenstahl provided little benefit to a nomadic group. The precious metals mined beneath Alhouim and promised them by Bom's grandfather did. The only other member of the group who left was Moh. That was a surprise. Bom had counted Moh a dear friend since they were children. Apparently, he could count on that deep friendship no more.

Bolstered by the sheer number of his group who remained, Bom stood taller against his god and loudly proclaimed, "The mission you have lain before your chosen is not ours. Strike me down if you must, but I cannot kill and maim innocent men and dwarves in the name of stealing from them. They pose no threat. We are the invaders."

"Petulant fool," the great tiger boomed as he raised his paw to crush the young giant, "you will regret this decision. Your soul will suffer for eternity, long after Ouloos is but a memory."

Brerto's paw moved an inch before he froze in place. Bom only had a moment to consider the terrifying beast—from the sneer upon his face to his mighty claws poised to strike—before a great wind sent him tumbling back into his group. The stiff current was accompanied by a blinding flash. By the time sight returned to Bom's eyes, they beheld something truly horrible. Cialia, bane of giants, stood before the great tiger where the defiant young giant had been.

"All living things on Ouloos fall under my protection," Cialia said calmly, but loud enough so all could hear. "They have nothing to fear from petty gods."

The tiger trembled, unable to move for what seemed eternity. Bom and his group raised up from their knees to witness the unthinkable, a god brought to heel. Cialia remained unmoved as the tiger's trembling steadily increased to the point of convulsion. Still, the paw failed to move in the slightest. The Dragon had the tiger completely in her control. Then a growl—terror, anguish, and rage all boiled into one emotion—erupted from the tiger's open mouth.

Another bright flash lit up the great waste. This one was not so brilliant as to induce temporary blindness, but more than one member of Bom's group found cause enough to shade their eyes. Once the light faded, the tiger was gone. Bom gasped. He had never seen the god outside of his animal form. The creature standing where the tiger had been looked like nothing more than an old man.

Though Brerto had abandoned his guise, his voice remained as powerful as ever, "Ah, Cialia, the twin. This is not your fight. These giants and trogmortem would destroy those you protect. Your talents would be best suited to helping those men of Havenstahl rebuild and prepare for the coming storm."

"Like all gods, you are a vile and treacherous deceiver who has long abandoned his role as teacher, nurturer, and guide to the Lake and Coeptus. You must pay for your failure," Cialia's tone remained flat as she accused the god. "I stand in judgement against you."

"You stand in judgement against me?" Brerto's words dripped with rage. "I am a god. I answer to none, not even Maelich, and he is the Dragon. You are nothing more than an afterthought."

Despite his anger, Brerto realized he was outmatched. Cialia had found her flame and proven to be a powerful adversary. That very flame began swirling around her. In a moment, she would burn him to dust. He had no choice but to retreat. His staff pulsated with white light as his eyes gently closed. When he slammed the staff against the ground, that light erupted with a concussion which blasted all but Cialia onto their backs, and he was gone.

Bom quickly scrambled to his feet. Despite his fear, he called out to the Dragon, "Cialia, the great tiger lied. We seek to help the men of Havenstahl rebuild and defend against the invaders from across the great sea."

Cialia turned toward the brave, young giant and shook her head, "You have nothing to fear from me. No giant does, not even your grandfather. The goal he seeks to fulfill is not his own. While he plots and schemes against the men of Havenstahl, my father plots and schemes against your kind. Neither is any better than the other, and both are driven by the whims of violent and jealous gods."

"Your father seems an honorable man. He fights to defend his land," Bom disagreed. "My grandfather came to conquer and steal land."

"Perhaps we can discuss the idea of laying claim to something which rightfully belongs to all creatures another time," Cialia allowed a shallow smile. "Even if you grant ownership of land, this is not my father's city. His home lies hundreds of miles from here. He fights for the desires of a god just the same as your grandfather. They have both been manipulated into a playing a game neither can win."

"You mean to kill the god," Lito-Bi piped in.

"Gods cannot be killed. I mean to scatter him to the wind and sentence him to a limbo where he can do no more harm to any of the creatures I protect," she corrected. "Now, I bid you farewell. It heartens me to know you seek peace with the men of Havenstahl. I pray the men of Havenstahl welcome the peace you promise," she added before vanishing in a flash as bright as that with which she arrived.

Overwhelmed, Lito-Bi grabbed a firm hold of Bom's shoulders and pulled him into a tight hug. "Glorious day," he shouted as he released his grip on the giant and turned toward the group following them. "The great Dragon herself has blessed our mission."

"Yes," Bom smiled wide, "she will bring peace to this place, and we will help."

## CHAPTER 10
## TEARS FOR THE DRAGON

Helias, terrifying and beautiful, perched atop the stony hill at the east end of the Lake of Dragons, the queen of Dragons, the first, sitting on her throne. She, like all Dragons, seemed a contradiction. The first creatures born of the Lake, the most powerful, were bound by love to never destroy. Their great power, their flame, was a threat never spoken. She looked out at her sisters, her loves. Thousands upon thousands of Dragons lounging or laughing or soaring to the great heights of a cloudless sky. There was no hurt, no pain, no suffering, only peace, until…

A great surge of emotion swept through Helias. Burning with the heat of Dragon's Fire, this mixture of feelings seemed to have mass. It was like anger and hatred, and more she could barely name, all wrapped into a desire to destroy. It was no idle thing. It felt like action. Helias cried out. Her wail born of the most pitiable suffering.

Two of her sisters, Delcinia and Lameah, rushed to her side. "What troubles you, love?" Delcinia asked.

"Yes, what horrible thing causes our sweet sister, love begotten of love, to cry out in such pitiable tones?" Lameah added.

Helias had fallen to sobs. Her sisters silently consoled her as she let the sadness seep from her eyes. When she had finally let enough of the horrible feeling out to speak, she said, "I fear our sweet sister, fair Cialia, in her fearless ambition is walking into a trap set by one so foul I dare not speak his name."

"Of course, she is," Delcinia's tone was sweet, almost musical.

"We all know our beautiful kin well enough to know there could be no alternate outcome for her," Lameah added in a tone just as sweet.

"But what if that vile monster is able to…" Helias trailed off as her tears gained control of her again.

"Love, fear is the only enemy who could ever defeat us," Lameah smiled. "For how long did we languish in that prison built for us by Kallum's ambition, separated from you and the perfection of our home? And yet, here we are beside you. Everything is as it should be."

"Yes," Delcinia agreed, "imagine if you had succumbed to your fears and attempted to rescue us. You would have left the protection of the Lake and been killed. All would be lost."

Helias finally gained control of her tears but remained unable to find peace. "Thank you for the wise counsel, my sweet sisters. It is not our role to interfere, but how can I sit idle. If this is not the most helpless feeling in all of creation, I do not know what horrible thing could be."

"Sweet love," Delcinia smiled, "worrying over an outcome will not change it."

"Cialia's path is her own," Lameah added.

"And we must let her travel that path and find herself," Helias finally agreed. "I know this. Thank you, my sweet sisters, for saving me from my tears. As always, you bless me with wise advice."

# CHAPTER 11
## REINFORCEMENTS

The map had been mocking Daritus for the better part of the morning, so he stopped looking at it. Word from the field was coming so infrequently the painted tokens here and there on the thing meant extraordinarily little. The truth was, he had barely an idea of what his forces were up to and where in Havenstahl they might be. The reconstruction effort of the castle was moving along nicely. That was the only thing of which he was truly certain, and that was only because his tent sat just across the great ravine from the castle.

Daritus was staring at a small slit in the tent when Spang entered, but his mind was not registering it. That was elsewhere, out in the field with his men. Wherever they might be.

"General," Spang's voice startled Havenstahl's greatest general.

Once Daritus overcame the surprise, he replied, "Hello, old friend. I hope you come bearing good news. It has been in short supply."

"It might be best to keep it to myself," Spang replied. "Perhaps we could speak about what we might call the book they will write about the greatest general in the history of the greatest city of men. Here are a couple titles I have been contemplating. I like the first one, *Daritus, Mighty Slayer of Giants*. The other is less appealing, *A Boy and His Map*. What do you think?"

"I am afraid I feel like the latter, and I cannot figure out how to feel like the former again," Daritus chuckled as he tapped his wasted shoulder. "How about we leave the books to men with a mind to write them, and you share whatever news you have, good or bad.”

"As you wish,” Spang replied, "but the story of a man defeating a giant in single combat is a campfire worthy tale if ever I have heard one. And, whether you feel like that man or not, that is your story.”

"It is,” Daritus agreed as his gaze found its way back to that slit in the tent. "I promise to work on remembering that if you give me some news.”

Spang smiled, "Right to business then. I encountered Ycantle's force on their way to Biggon's Bay. That beach is no place for any man currently. I instructed him to camp at the edge of what is left of the forest and protect the trail. He will send small forces to monitor the invaders' movements, but only engage if necessary. Ott's forces are growing once again as reinforcements arrive from across the Great Sea. We counted at least twenty more ships. This war is far from over. His forces which are already here have been raiding villages all up and down the coast. They now control everything from Castrine in the north to Gorban's Sound in the south. Meanwhile, a small group is moving through the great waste. They are flying a white flag, but we have yet to confirm their true motives.”

"That is dire news indeed,” Daritus' expression somehow became even more grim as he continued to stare at the slit. "What of our men? How many have reported? How many have we confirmed returned to the Lake?”

Spang scratched his head, "Those numbers are a bit more difficult to know for certain. We have a few thousand around the castle guarding what is left of it and aiding in the rebuilding effort, and I just finished speaking with a scout sent by Ygraml. There are slightly more than one thousand more who have been instructed to work their way back to the castle.”

"Of course,” Daritus agreed. "I receive regular reports about their progress. Please tell me something I do not already know,” he paused long enough to sigh and scratch his head. After a few moments of quiet contemplation while still staring at the same small slit which continued to hold his gaze, he proceeded in a more agreeable tone, "What about the fallen? Have we identified all who have journeyed home to the Lake?”

"I could scarcely venture a guess, but I am certain that number far surpasses the number still among the living,” Spang shrugged. After a few moments of silence, he followed Daritus' gaze and strolled over to the small slit in the tent which had the general's attention. After examining the thing for longer than a small slit in a tent truly deserves, he stuck his finger into it and tore the slit a few inches bigger. "There, now it is a proper hole," he proclaimed.

"Why on Ouloos would you do that?" Daritus shouted a bit louder than he intended.

Again, Spang shrugged, "Forgive me, general. That slit had gained so much of your attention I thought you were trying to see outside the tent. Now you can."

Daritus sighed and shook his head, "No, old friend, forgive me. I have been distracted. Perhaps, we should rally the men, and I can ride out with you to gather our lost."

"I would welcome the company, but no. You need to remain here. That shoulder needs more time to heal. I will do my best to get better information from the field. We are spread thin, but I know we have men yet unaccounted."

Before Daritus could answer, the flaps of the tent's entrance snapped open with Kantiim stalking in behind them. His armor did not shine. It bore the markings of more than one fierce battle. Somehow, his tattered condition made him look the titan all the more.

"Kantiim's force has returned, general," Spang smiled. "There is some news for you."

Daritus finally allowed himself a chuckle before addressing Kantiim, "Your face is truly a sight to behold. Do you have news from the front?"

"Not much is new," Kantiim replied. "We have been sweeping the forests around Elzkahon and gathering up troops as we find them, healing those with fight left in them, making those with no fight left comfortable until the Lake calls them home, and shaming those in hiding until they pick their swords back up and fall in line. Sadly, the latter counts most of what we have found."

"Do not forget those men have looked upon the eyes of a god," Spang replied flatly as he left the tent.

"What?" Kantiim asked, as he watched the old warrior leave. Then he looked over at Daritus and repeated the question, "What?"

Daritus stood and draped his good arm across Kantiim's shoulder. "You are a noble man, and a fierce soldier who has had the good fortune to survive many battles."

Kantiim nodded, "I appreciate the sentiment, but what does that have to do with deserters?"

"Do you recall the first time you witnessed the fury of a god on the battlefield?" Daritus asked.

"Of course, it was the battle at the forest's edge fighting against the great city we now defend," the old general replied flatly. "It was terrifying. I had hoped it would remain a once in a lifetime experience."

"As did I," Daritus smiled at his old friend. "Try to imagine if that had been your first battle. Do you suppose you would be as eager to get back to that battlefield?"

Kantiim's face twisted as if he were working through a doozy of a puzzle, but no words accompanied the various expressions.

"There is no need to answer, just think about it the next time you are…shaming a young soldier you find hiding in the woods, terrified by the sight of their bosom chums trampled under the feet of a vengeful god," Daritus added.

"You are a wise man," Kantiim finally said, though his expression failed to match the sentiment.

"Perhaps, a bit too soft?" Daritus chuckled.

"That is not what I said."

Daritus finally lost himself to a hearty laugh, "But it is what you meant. I know you too well, old friend. No matter. Just please do me that favor. Try to put yourself in that young man's war tattered boots as you make an example of him."

"I will," Kantiim promised.

Satisfied his general would do his best to execute the command, Daritus moved on to other matters, "Spang brought word of a small force of giants and trogmortem moving through the great waste toward the castle."

"Invaders?" Kantiim asked.

Daritus shook his head, "It does not seem so, or at least they want us to believe they are not. They march under a white flag. I would much prefer to find out if it is a ruse or if they can be trusted well before they get near the castle, or what is left of it."

"Say no more. I will lead a small force out to the bloody waste and have that question answered," Kantiim replied before Daritus could levy the command.

"Very good," Daritus smiled as his old friend moved to leave the tent. "One more thing. Have all who are unable to fight been evacuated?"

Kantiim nodded, "I expect them to be halfway to Druindahl by now. They have supplies and a solid escort. All remaining are able-bodied men who are ready to fight," he paused, smiled, and added, "or they will be once I finish convincing them of such."

The flaps of the entrance snapped back into place after Kantiim left. Daritus continued to stare at the spot for a good while after his old friend had gone. The slightest breeze toyed with the corners. It would have been unnoticeable had his eyes not been trained on the spot. As it were, the corner of each flap danced the tiniest waltz imaginable as the weak current barely moved each in opposite directions.

Daritus finally shook his head and turned his attention back to the map. A small force was moving through the great waste under a white flag. He dared not wish for peace, but the group was taking a major risk. Even if they had employed scouts who managed to remain unseen, he trusted his generals to hide their numbers. This group from Biggon's Bay could have no idea what kind of resistance they would face if their flag was a ruse.

He knelt and picked up a smooth stone out of the dirt beneath him. After rubbing it between his fingers for a few moments to dust it off, he placed it half-way between Fort Maomnosett and Biggon's Bay. The space appeared a forest with a trail running through it on his map. In reality, most of that forest had been mowed down prior to the Battle of Fort Maomnosett.

After staring at the unremarkable stone far longer than the thing deserved, he turned his attention to a wooden token carved in the shape of a fallon and painted blue sitting just south of the clearing in front of Fort Maomnosett. Sliding the thing over to the smooth stone he said, "Hopefully, I am not sending you into a trap, old friend."

## CHAPTER 12
## GRIZZLY MONGS

The sky remained bright above the trail, as thousands of tired, hungry souls moved slowly toward Druindahl. Black clouds on the horizon promised those bright skies would not last. The entire trip would take weeks Tarantian had said when they were packing up for the long trek. Apparently, the dark-haired titan—the only member of the company who could count himself a rider of Druindahl, and the military leader of the group—had overestimated the speed of a few hundred wagons loaded down with enough supplies for the thousands of beaten refugees making the journey. Word around the previous evening's fires suggested his estimate of the time remaining had not changed. They still had a few weeks ahead of them.

Chagon, a blonde-haired farmer, was among the tired mass trudging along the trail. He was young and burly. Had his father not taken ill and made his way to the Lake at the beginning of his sixteenth summer, the brawny lad would have petitioned to march under the banner of Havenstahl. Though he was only a short bit into his twenty-fourth summer, that felt like a lifetime ago. The idea had recently been rekindled when the monsters from across the Great Sea came to kill his mother, sisters, and brother and destroy his land. There was nothing left for him in that scarred waste. Given the current state of things, there were no guarantees he would ever make it back to the city he had called home for his entire life up to that point. Hopefully, he would love his new city as much as the one he had left. According to Tarantian, the queen was actively seeking new recruits. Coeptus willing, he would ride under the banner of Druindahl. Years tending fields had done nothing to improve Chagon's sword skills, but it had kept his shoulders and back broad and strong.

Chagon's stomach growled as he kicked a stone off the trail and stared out over the River Galgooth rushing along on his right side, "When all this is done, and the ranks of them riders of Druindahl swell with our numbers, I pray we ride back to Havenstahl to push them beasts all the way back across that Great Sea. Can you even imagine what a sight that would be, red flags flapping above us while the thunder of mighty drums keep us in step?"

He glanced over at Galind, a short horse hand with pale, stringy hair and a slight chin. They had only just met early in their journey together, but they quickly became friends. Some of the soldiers had taken to picking on the sickly young man, and Chagon had stuck up for him. Any one of them could have easily sent him to Lake one on one, but when he stood in front of Galind and made clear they would have to go through him first, they let the diminutive horse hand be. Perhaps they respected the courage it took for a simple farmer with no training to stand up to hardened soldiers with many battles under their belts. Whatever their reasons, Galind became his bosom chum.

"It seems you might be walking in your sleep," Chagon commented after Galind failed to respond.

"Please forgive me," Galind seemed startled as he shook his head. "I guess I'd been stuck in a waking dream."

"Sounds like you've got a case of the trail sleep," Chagon agreed. "We've been at it long enough."

Chagon reached into a horse sack he had draped over his shoulder and fished around until he found a nice hunk of dried meat. "Here, have a go at that. The sun has a good stretch of sky to cross before we'll be stopping to take any nourishment. Them trembling legs might fall out from under you at any moment."

"Aye," Galind accepted the gift, "they feel that way, and my back. Too many nights under the stars have it all twisted and gnarled up."

"You might be speaking for all of us," Chagon agreed. "Chew that down, and let's head up to the front to bother Tarantian. I wouldn't mind an update."

Galind nodded, and they quickened their pace. It was a short journey. The wagons were painfully slow, and Chagon preferred to remain near the front of the line. They passed the lead wagon and kept on toward three rough-looking men mounted upon sturdy horses. Chagon did not know the names of the riders to the left or right. They were riders from Havenstahl, rough ones. Both rode white steeds speckled with brown and dressed in blue, white, and shimmering prang, the colors of Havenstahl. Tarantian rode between them mounted on a mighty black steed, dressed in the colors of Druindahl, red, black, and shimmering prang.

Just as Chagon prepared to hail Tarantian—and hear the jibes from his two companions, one of whom was among the group Chagon stood up to on Galind's behalf—a horn blared. The horn blast was not necessary. The rider who blew the horn was only about one-hundred yards up the trail, his horse galloping fast. The three riders with him attacked the trail just as hard.

"Grizzly mongs," the horn blower yelled, his voice dripping with fear.

Tarantian raised an arm to stop the wagon train. Riders all up and down the length of it began halting wagons and pulling loose groups of travelers into tight columns. "How far off?" the question carried on a deep, rich baritone.

Wild with fear, the rider's eyes conveyed his message more clearly than any words could. "About a half a mile and closing fast," he shouted just the same.

"You led those monsters right to us," Tarantian hissed. Then he turned and shouted, "Get out of those wagons, and get off the trail. Riders, to me!"

Chaos settled into the group as travelers fleeing their wagons for the tall grass of the fields along either side of the road crossed paths with mounted soldiers pounding the hard-packed dirt of the trail. A young boy was trampled as soon as his feet hit the ground. The rider— ready for battle with eyes seeing only red—barely noticed. The young lad's mother saw it all. Though her pitiable cries were drowned out by the sound of hoof beats echoing off carriages, the anguish twisting up her face spoke loudly enough.

Chagon saw it all too: the boy, his mother, and the pain. This was his moment. Without a sword or horse, he would be wasted at the front. Perhaps there were other ways he could help. He made two steps toward the sad embrace—a young mother holding the battered carcass of her son—before another rider trampled her into the dead child.

"No," Chagon cried out, his tone dripping with misplaced rage.

He fell to his knees. Of course, the rider was blameless. It was an unfortunate accident. A small child fleeing toward safety and the shield who might defend him collided. It was no one's fault. The fact did nothing to ease the tragedy.

The world slowed around him. Riders charged toward the front and travelers—recent vagabonds displaced by the fury of gods—moved about the periphery in slow motion as he focused on the bloody mother crushed beneath the hooves of a charging horse. His mouth continued to move as his body tensed. A tear full of rage, sorrow, and anguish formed on his eyelid before trickling down his cheek. Would life ever again make sense? None of the victims dashed and broken on the trail, trampled by the very soldiers who would give their lives to defend them, had done anything to deserve their fates.

Time became an abstract thing, something just outside the limits of his awareness, as he stared at the bloody scene. He had no idea how long he had knelt there silently lamenting before Galind's voice raised up over the ruckus and dragged him from the trance. There were no words, just a howl dripping with pain or terror, or some other horrible thing Chagon was unable to define in that moment when it reached is ears. Could anything be worse than what he had just witnessed? The sad answer was yes.

It seemed a labor simply to move his head enough to see the slight, young horse hand who had recently become his most bosom of chums, the young lad whom he had decided it was his job to protect. By the time he had, that young man's arm was arcing over the top of a carriage. He had to close his eyes to keep them from becoming saturated in Galind's blood. He felt it on his face. It was warm, and there was too much of it. After wiping his face, he shaded his eyes to look and immediately wished he had not.

The terror in Galind's eyes was quite possibly the saddest thing Chagon had ever witnessed in his life, even sadder than watching a young mother trampled while mourning her dead son. Perhaps it was because of the affection he had developed sharing the trail with his new friend over the past few weeks, but it burned him to his soul. There was a helplessness in those wide, pleading eyes. Somehow, they seemed to accuse him. Something about the look said, "You were supposed to protect me." It was probably all in his head, but it did not make it any easier.

He was sure it was not fear holding him in place helplessly staring back into those terrified, accusing eyes, but something kept him there on his knees. Even when glistening fangs stretching out from a massive, shaggy face flashed and bit through Galind's neck, Chagon could not move. The accusing eyes were gone, and the innocent horse hand's screaming stopped. A moment later, Galind had been ripped in two and the beast had moved on.

Everything else blurred around Chagon's periphery. There were no sounds or smells. The gory pile of bloody, mangled flesh he stared at was all that remained of his only friend, and the only thing in his awareness. He suddenly felt exceedingly small, as helpless as that dead pile. Were he a soldier, armed and trained to fight, perhaps he could have been a true protector to the lad. But he was not that. He was a simple farmer, nothing more. Outside of his field, he was nothing. A scream formed in his throat. He could not hear anything above a loud ringing in his ears, but it must have been booming as much as it burned his throat.

Chagon remained there staring at the same spot and screaming a song he could not hear until something crashed into him toppling him to the ground. The ringing suddenly ceased. It was a sad thing. Each new sound was more horrible than the last. Bones popped, teeth gnashed sloppily, and beasts roared. The screams were the worst.

As disoriented as he was, Chagon's survival instincts finally kicked in. He looked down at the heavy thing which had knocked him from his trance. It was a soldier. One of the nameless riders who had accompanied Tarantian at the front of the wagon train. It was the one he had stood up to for Galind. The burly soldier had looked so frightening that day, rotten clenched teeth peeking out from his scowl under eyes that looked no more than a whisper from insanity. Lying there dead on the trail, he just looked like another sad and senseless loss, no better or worse than Galind or the poor mother with her child. One of those near crazy eyes was gone and his nose was off. Three claw marks ran from the top of his head and clean through his jaw. His insides stretched out from his torn open gut to about twelve feet behind him. Chagon heaved.

After spilling the contents of his own gut onto the trail next to the dead soldier—as scarce as food had been on the trail, it was not much more than a bit of bile—rage consumed him. It was not so much anger at the beasts attacking his caravan. Of course, they would be the ones to feel his wrath. Still, somewhere deep in his mind, beneath the pain, sorrow, terror, and rage, he knew they were just beasts motivated by hunger or other primal desires over which they had no control. It was Coeptus. Him or her or them, whatever that thing was, that is precisely who deserved his rage. He pulled the sword from the dead soldier's hand and turned toward the front.

Moments earlier, he would have run for his life. There had to be hundreds of them, massive, hairy beasts all fangs and claws and shaggy white fur climbing over each other and tearing into the hard-packed dirt of the trail. Most of the riders had abandoned their mounts and fought the beasts with their swords. The few who remained mounted charged with lances. A monster leapt up high in the air and swatted a rider down into his horse, crushing them both into the ground before biting a hole in the poor soldier from his shoulders to his waist. Two more riders found similar fates only moments later. It was a slaughter.

The sound Chagon made as he charged toward the melee was foreign to his ears. It sounded like it had come from someone else. He saw Tarantian kill one of the beasts he was battling at the front. The idea that a simple farm boy could become a soldier seemed less silly as he gripped the sword in his hand and pumped his legs to hurry toward a battle against terrifying, monstrous beasts next to a true hero.

Then another hero fell. One of the monsters slashed clean through the soldier's neck with claws that sliced meat more efficiently than any sword Chagon had ever seen. He barely had time to think he had never seen a head fly that far before when a massive arm smashed against the side of his head. The fur was course and thick. As he spun through the air, he locked eyes with Tarantian who had been spun round and dropped to his knees by a similar swat. That moment—as Chagon spun helpless and Tarantian stared back with something akin to fear in his eyes—seemed an eternity. That eternity ended as Chagon watched a massive, clawed fist smash the side of his hero's head and send him careening into the brush alongside the trail.

The ground was hard when Chagon finally slammed into it. The idea he might leap back to his feet and help the armed men fight the monsters tearing through their column lasted the briefest of moments. The hard reality of a large rock put an end to it when Chagon's head pounded against it. Consciousness fled quickly, but not quickly enough that he missed more sounds of wood smashing, people screaming, and flesh tearing. Of the things he saw, smelled, and felt on the trail that day, none of them were as bad as what he had heard. The sounds were the worst. If Coeptus had even the slightest bit of mercy, they would take the memories of those sounds from him.

# CHAPTER 13
# SLEEP

The top of Mount Alharin was a contradiction, a tranquil garden with a pond and greenspace to spare on the flattened peak of a stony mountain the top of which should be covered in a thick blanket of snow. Of course, this contradiction was an illusion. The fruits and the grass were real enough, but none of them belonged. They all thrived under a dome of protection cast by Brerto hundreds of summers prior that had stood the test of time. The god considered it his paradise. It was a paradise few besides Brerto had ever seen. When Cialia materialized at the mouth of the god's cave, she became only the second member of the race of men to behold the glorious site, her brother being the first.

Brerto was there just inside the cave's entrance. Eyes closed tight, he mumbled incantations under his breath while his staff glowed with the light of a thousand suns. Cialia thought of destroying him right then and there, exploding him to dust with a thought. She could do that, burn him from the inside out, and she would. But lessons are lost if not learned. There were accusations to be made, and she needed him to hear them. Whatever happened to his consciousness after she scattered him to the wind—Coeptus willing, he would suffer until the end of time—it was imperative her accusations remained on his mind at least as long as her flames consumed him.

"Never again, coward," she said, her tone even and cool as the flames she called to swirl around her cast an orange glow on her white robe.

Brerto's eyes—those beautiful and terrible things—snapped open as a smile spread across his face, "I have been waiting for this moment since your mother, that whore, slipped her vile body into the Lake and let it impregnate her. Of course, this is not the outcome for which I had hoped. Maelich should have killed Helias and ended this game." He paused for a moment before adding, "And you, the afterthought, a lost soul clinging to a great power, why do you persist? Why do you care? This story is not your own. No prophecies exist where you do anything of import. You are what you have always been, the savior's sister."

Cialia's tone remained flat and emotionless, "Your jibes hurt my brother. You and Kallum certainly know how to raise his ire. He is passionate. His emotions cloud his judgement. Those tactics do not affect me. I too am passionate, for my people. However, I am not driven by emotion. It is justice which drives me, compels me to hold you to account. You have mistreated my people and all creatures under my protection, and I have judged you. Now you will pay for their pain and suffering. Believe me, it will not be a fair trade. Complete fairness would require I spend eternity making you suffer as you have made all living things on Ouloos suffer. Sadly, I must administer your sentence quickly, as I have more gods to kill. You all are evil, and you all will die."

Brerto's laugh was deafening. It shook the earth, but it also shook the air. When it finally finished, he continued in a more measured tone, "And where is the missing dragon? His fragile mind broke far more completely than I expected when Kallum's priests took his son. I would love to take a walk through his consciousness right now. What a clouded disaster it must be."

Cialia set her jaw tight and replied flatly, "I am the Dragon, and my fire will be your end. I will erase you from the histories. None will ever again speak your foul name."

"You are no dragon," the god spat. "You are a little girl playing at simplicity in your plain smock as if you are above the desires of men, a shadow of the true power of this place, your brother. Of course, he understands his power. I trained him. You are nothing but raw angst personified in a terrified shell of a person who knows not her way and plays with forces she cannot comprehend."

Cialia's eyes glowed red as the flames swirling about her thickened and spun faster. She raised her hand with an accusing finger pointing at the god before her. The fear she hoped to see etched in the features of his face was absent. He looked satisfied, like he had expected this exact outcome. Just as she was about to release her flame and burn him to dust, he slammed his staff against the rocks. The world around her exploded in light.

Cialia's flame was never released as her body lifted from the ground. She floated there as the world moved in slow motion around her, rocks lifted from the ground as the mountaintop beneath her split open. Everything was bathed in light so bright she could barely make out shapes. Nothing around her had any tangible shape or form. Everything melted together until no distinct edges existed. Then everything went black.

***

Thousands of Dragons, some flying, some thinking, and some lounging in the perfection of the Lake all cried out with one voice. That voice carried sorrow and hurt and pain. None at the Lake that day was the individual owner of that pain, but all Dragons were one together. They all felt Cialia's pain, and their cries were for her.

"No," Helias gave voice to the feeling.

"Our sister is lost," Lameah cried.

"All hope is lost," Helias agreed as tears flowed freely from her perfect eyes. "Ouloos is lost."

CHAPTER 14
TRAINING

The sun blazed furious above the cracked land, blistering the dry dirt beneath. Columns of Shaiwah worked through sword techniques as Maelich barked commands. The trainees remained protected from the mighty sun's fury by the blue dye with which they coated their bodies. Maelich was less fortunate. He wore a cloth over his head like a hood to keep his skin from burning. The water he had soaked it with had long evaporated. Any moisture remaining was sweat which had boiled off his head.

Ymitoth stood beside him watching the technique of the students before them. Two stood out among the rest. "Hey there, Ding and Zig," he called out, "step to the front."

Ding looked proud. Zig looked like a tubber being led off to slaughter. But both men walked up to the front as instructed. Maelich flashed a reassuring smile at Zig hoping to ease his mind a bit. It did little to help the poor fellow who still looked like he wanted to run away.

"All of you, have a look at these two. They get it. Keep an eye on their technique," Ymitoth raised his voice so all could hear. Then he looked over at Zig, "Hey there, you can pair with me."

"Ding, on me," Maelich piped up.

The old soldier noticed the sour expression on Zig's face and took pity on him, "Hey, you're doing a fine job, Zig. You have nothing to fear. I want them other blokes learning how to swing them swords as good as you and Ding. Now, attack me."

The young Shaiwahnian soldier's expression lit up, all hints of fear leaving his blue painted face. He launched into an attack his mentor could be proud of. Ymitoth's smile grew just as wide as Zig's, as he worked hard to defend himself against the assault.

Maelich took a moment to look proudly on Zig's attack on Ymitoth before turning to Ding and saying, "Prepare to defend yourself."

Ding took a defensive stance and awaited the attack. Maelich obliged with a forehand slash followed by a backhand. He finished the attack with a straight thrust. Ding ducked beneath the forehand, blocked the backhand, sidestepped, and parried the thrust.

"Excellent," Maelich commended him. "Now, attack me. Hold nothing back."

Ding's technique was spectacular, even when Maelich replied to an attack with a counter. The new swordsman was using what he had been taught during a handful of weeks to improvise. Though none of them were enough to break through the defense of a seasoned warrior like Maelich, two or three of them tested his ability. The mentor was impressed.

"Hold," Maelich commanded before giving Ding a congratulatory slap on the back. "You are a natural fighter. Tell me you have had some sword training before I arrived."

Overwhelmed, Ding hugged Maelich, "No fight. Only fish. Father say, 'No two fish same, so no fish two fish same.' Like fight. No two fight same."

"That is very sound advice. No two fights will be the same. Some fighters are better at masking their techniques, but they all have their own style," Maelich smiled. Then he patted Ding's back a few more times and added, "You will be a titan on the battlefield."

Ding smiled, "I fish good. Maybe I fight good too." He stepped back and slashed a few times at the air, working through techniques. As he slashed the air, he asked, "What is battlefield like?"

"A battlefield can be many things. It really depends on the situation," Maelich scratched his chin. "Usually, when folks speak of the battlefield, they are talking about two armies lining up in columns and attacking each other. Battles like that can be wide and ranging. There may even be archers firing arrows or catapults firing rocks or great balls of fire. However, a battlefield is anywhere a battle takes place. You and I trading blades in the blazing sun with the cracked dirt beneath our feet is a kind of battlefield. Do you know what every battlefield has in common?"

"Glory and blood and death?" Ding scratched his head.

Maelich smiled, "Yes, most battlefields have at least two of those. Some have even more, heroes."

"What makes hero?" Ding asked earnestly.

"It is more than just how you fight or how many men you kill," Maelich grew nostalgic as he stared out at the cracked dirt surrounding them and far beyond the heat rising from it. "Facing down a horde of invaders or freeing a town from the rule of some heartless king, those are things people remember. Sometimes it is just a matter of protecting the people you care about from harm. When people remember things, they tell stories, and when people tell stories about you, you can become immortal. Of course, not immortal in that you physically live forever, but immortal in the sense that people still talk about you long after the Lake calls you home."

Ding stared off at the same cracked dirt Maelich stared at as he replied, "Me, hero. People remember."

"I believe you will be. Your name will live on for generations," Maelich smiled again at his pupil.

"The Shaiwah look ready to range out and take their land back from the red people," Maulom called out as he approached the two, his clothes as impossibly white as ever.

Maelich glanced over and shook his head, "A couple stand out." He nodded at Ding before adding, "I would walk into battle with Ding here, and Zig. Maybe a handful of others, but none of them are ready to face an army of seasoned soldiers. We have trained for barely a moon. They need more time."

"I have been watching their progress, and I believe they are ready to march," Maulom countered.

"Have you seen many battles?" Maelich laughed.

Ymitoth strolled up laughing just as hard and added, "You haven't a warrior's look about you. Them soft hands ain't never swung a sword."

If Maulom was offended, he hid it well, "You are both correct. I have never swung a blade. My mind and my tongue have always proved to be weapons enough for every conflict I have encountered. However, I would counter that fighting to stop someone from taking your life is far better training than playing at sword fighting with opponents who boast an equal lack of training."

"You'd be sending them off to slaughter," Ymitoth scoffed.

"I agree with Ymitoth," Maelich added. "A real fight only serves as good training if you survive."

"Do you remember your first real fight? Though I am certain at the time you felt completely prepared and ready to fight the world when you tasted your first real test against someone trying just as hard to kill you as you tried to kill them, do you still feel that way after all the years you have tucked under your belt?" Maulom asked Ymitoth.

"Ain't a soul really ready when first they fight," Ymitoth remarked. "That don't mean you ought to send them out unprepared. It would be one thing if them red folks were tearing across the cracked land and bringing war on us. But they ain't."

Maulom's eyes narrowed with intrigue, "What was that first battle? Did you seek out that fight, or did glory come calling for you?"

"It was duty that called me," Ymitoth answered flatly. "King Jorgon had brought all the great cities from Dargouth way up in the north to Belscythia down south on the banks of the Sea of Sadness under the banner of Havenstahl. By all accounts I ever heard, he'd been a fair king with the love of all the people who called him so. I know not what sin he might have committed against Kallum, but it must have been a horrible thing he did. Brought Kallum's wrath down upon him and his son. Kallum's priests slaughtered them all, King Jorgon, his wife, and their son, Prince Cardon. Well, with all them great cities, you can imagine there had been more than a few claims to the throne."

"A scandal surrounding the crown," Maulom's tone jumped near an octave in his excitement. "How diabolical."

"You can't tell me you ain't heard about the battle for the empty throne of Havenstahl," Ymitoth's eyebrows raised as the corners of his mouth dipped.

"Of course, I have, but a first-hand account of a story from an honorable man is far better than any story re-told over and over again by folks who missed out on all the intrigue and real emotion of actually being there. Did you have a claim to that throne?" Maulom stepped closer.

Ymitoth chuckled, "Me, sure, after my uncle, then his son, then my father. Truth be told, I have no desire to be resting my rump on no fancy throne to this very day. Right there, heading toward the end of my fifteenth summer, that thought was the farthest thing from my mind. My first battle was in defense of my uncle's claim to that throne. By all accounts I'd heard, his was the strongest. Many men died, and I was not among them. That day, standing right beside my father, I sent ten to the Lake with my sword. I still count that as one of my proudest days."

"That sounds like a day any man would be proud of, so why would you deny that feeling from these men standing before you?" Maulom smiled.

"Did you listen to his story?" Maelich asked. "He did not walk into battle with a hundred men with no experience under their belts. He went to war alongside hardened soldiers who knew how to make war against other hardened soldiers. What you are suggesting is not the same."

Ding had been growing exceedingly agitated as he listed to the three men discussing the fate of his people. Finally, he could hold his tongue no longer, "Ding fight. Ding ready. Shaiwah ready. We fight. Take land back."

Maelich nodded and glanced over at Ymitoth who returned a shrug. Ding and a few others may have been ready to fight alongside trained men, but the Shaiwah were not that. Even with Ymitoth and Maelich by their sides, they could not take on an army by themselves. As renowned and seasoned as both Maelich and Ymitoth were, two men could not protect an untrained army from a trained army no matter how good either of them may be with a sword. With Maulom feeding ideas into Ding's head, it would be near impossible to keep the Shaiwahnian warrior from believing he and his kin were ready.

Maelich finally looked at Ding and sighed, "You might be ready, and Zig, he can fight, but look around at the rest of your men. You are their leader. Would…"

"No," Ding interrupted, "Maelich lead Shaiwah. Maelich great. Protect Shaiwah."

Maelich shrugged as he glanced over at Ymitoth for help convincing the confident young soldier his people were not ready. The old soldier just shook his head. It was obvious Ding believed he and his men were ready to range out and battle their enemies. Belief is a tough thing to combat regardless how logical the argument and with how much evidence it is presented. Maelich finally shook his head, looked into Ding's fiery eyes, and said, "Soon."

The disgust on Ding's face at the perceived slight seemed to linger long after he stormed off. The young soldier had passion, fire in his belly. Maelich remembered when a similar flame burned in his own gut. It hurt to be the one to stifle that blaze, but it was his duty. Maulom cared enough to stay with the Shaiwah for who knows how many years, but it seemed he did not care enough to lobby hard for the idea they should be properly trained before marching against an army of experienced warriors. If Maelich failed to stand for them, who would?

Ymitoth draped his arm across Maelich's shoulder and said, "It ain't no easy thing being the voice of reason at times. That don't make you wrong."

"Wait too long, and you may lose them," Maulom contended.

Maelich's gaze followed Ding until he was lost in the darkness of the cave's mouth, "Maybe, but if I lead them to battle before they are ready, I will lose them just the same. You see? I lose either way."

# CHAPTER 15
# HER FIRST KILL

The water was brisk and refreshing. It had been days since Perrin and her group had seen water, and that had been barely a brook hardly deep enough for anything more than filling water skins and soaking cloths to mop down dirt-streaked skin. The water Perrin submerged herself in was a proper river. Its slow current was perfect for a bath, and she took advantage, scrubbing the dirt from her weary body.

Thick trees stretched from both banks of the river. Some were thin with tight branches that reached toward the sky. Others were squat with wide branches reaching out in all directions and dipping toward the water. Together with thick shrubs growing wild around their trunks, they provided ample cover for a peaceful soak.

A rustling in the shrubbery behind her caught her attention. Suddenly, those thick, protective shrubs seemed less like ample cover for her bath and more like a place for someone to hide while they watched her. Turning toward the sound, she quickly covered herself the best she could and dipped deeper into the water. Naked was such a vulnerable thing to be. It was worse when someone was watching. Even a thin robe would have felt like armor in that moment. As she stared into the darkness beneath the foliage, the water somehow grew less refreshing until it was downright cold. A shiver started at her shoulders and shook its way through her racing all the way to her feet.

More rustling from the very spot where she was looking forced a slight scream from her lips. "Who is hiding there?" she asked, her voice absent the authority she had hoped it would carry.

She screamed again—this time jumping clean out of the water before diving under it—when a fallon poked his head through the shrubbery to drink. When she finally popped her head back out of the water, she startled the young animal as much as he had startled her. It was a young buck to be sure. His antlers were not more than two-inch nubs. The frightened creature stomped and snorted his displeasure before charging back into the brush.

"No, no," Perrin called after the animal, "I didn't mean to cause you such a fright, but you near scared me out of my skin."

It was too late, the majestic young fallon had darted off. He would probably be a mile away or more by that point. She laughed at what a fright the beast had caused her when his head popped out of the leaves. It was too late for her too. The timid animal had scared her to her bones. The dark shadows under the shrubs yawned like the blackest cavern she could imagine hiding all manner of nightmare creatures to terrorize and torment her. The bath was over.

She remained tentative as she slowly waded over to the shore, every out of place sound sending shivers down her spine. The riverbank had seemed so far away when she started toward it. As it grew closer, she wished it were further away. Where had all those sounds been while she was calmly enjoying a bath in some crisp, refreshing water? Everything had been so peaceful. Now it seemed the critters living in that darkness were belting out a chorus at her.

Her finger had barely touched the slippery shore when two massive hands attached to thick, hairy arms reached out of the darkness to snatch her up by the forearms. Those hands squeezed so tight her wrists felt like they might break, but pain was not the cause of her scream. Sheer terror earned that sound. She immediately knew those bulky forearms did not belong to any of her men. There was a mark on the inside of the left one, a circle with a cross at its center. The brute grabbing her had been branded a thief by someone.

She struggled, pulling against the pain in her wrists and kicking her legs, but the soft, muddy riverbank offered no traction for her wet, bare feet. Thorns and branches cutting into her and scratching her skin hurt but barely registered as the strong hands dragged her helpless through the muck. It would be obvious to even the rudest dolt she had nothing of value on her person. Whomever owned the hands pulling her through the brambles was after something other than material goods.

When the brute had finally pulled her to a clearing opposite the shrubs running alongside the river, her back was a canvas of red, a masterpiece concocted by a madman. Every scratch throbbed somewhere in the periphery of her awareness. Those cuts would heal. Whatever else the beast took from her would heal eventually too, but that would be a longer road to recovery.

Perrin's wrists burned as the monster of a man squeezing them lifted her off the ground. His hair was a nest of black streaked with gray. His dark eyes moved over her body feasting on every inch. She screamed in his dirty face. He roared back at her with a toothless laugh, his tongue slithering all about his grimy lips. She barely noticed the two dirty grubs behind him laughing just as hard.

"Get her on the ground," one of them yelled.

Rage grew from somewhere in Perrin's belly. These three vile men—the one holding her six inches off the ground and his two giggling friends—were bent on stealing from her. Right at that moment, the fury boiling up in her belly completely chased her fear away. She kicked with both her legs and connected with something. There was no way to be sure if it were his round belly, his groin, or somewhere on his legs, but it doubled the big man over enough that her feet were back on the ground.

"I am Perrin, rightful queen of Havenstahl, wife of Maelich, the lad of the Lake, and I command you to…" her words trailed off as the grubby man still holding her wrists flung her against a tree.

Old oaks are sturdy and do not move for much. The one Perrin's head smacked against refused to budge. A bright flash, and then her world went fuzzy and dark. She felt hands on her. They grabbed at her and pulled at her legs. Then that fat, dirty face was directly in front of her. Everything else may have been blurry, but that horrible face was clear. Her hand lashed out like a snake. She dug her nails deep and dragged them down the side of it from cheek to jawline. The world exploded in another bright flash when the big fist pounded the side of her head. Her eyes grew heavy. Everything in her line of sight bobbed and shifted as if floating on choppy waters. It took everything she had to keep from passing out.

The man's voice did not fit his countenance as he squeaked, "Grab a hold of her legs. We'll be teaching this wench a lesson on how she ought to be treating nice fellows like us."

A moment later, she could not move. Strong hands squeezed, two a piece at each of her ankles. They dragged her down the tree until she was flat against the ground. Then they pulled away from each other, spreading her legs apart. That is when she saw it. A glint of silver as the brute above her fumbled with his trousers. She screamed out as she grabbed for the silvery thing, sliding a dagger out of its scabbard. It was more instinct guiding her than conscious thought. A split second later, the handle of a long knife was jutting from that bastard's throat, and he was choking on blood.

Perrin grabbed for the dagger again, pulling it out of the dying man's throat. Blood rained down on her, pumping from the gash she had left there. She watched intently as the life left his eyes. Normally the sight of blood would have her squeamish. Not on this day. On this day, she wanted to watch every expression on his foul, dirty face as he struggled through his last few moments. Then he was gone, falling on top of her. He was heavy and smelly, and she was fairly certain he shat himself as his soul left him. His stench only grew stronger.

The rough hands still tugging on her legs quickly snapped her attention back to the present. There were two more souls to send to the Lake. She had never killed a living thing, but the small bit of remorse haunting her psyche was no match for the adrenaline coursing steadily through her veins. Glord had told her the trail had its own justice even before they started this journey. She intended to deliver that justice with a bloody dagger stolen from a vile creature.

Glord's voice rang out. It filled the forest like a giant's roar when he shouted, "Men, to the queen."

Perrin was unable to see her men exacting the trail's justice in her stead, but it sounded like they handled their task at least as brutally as she had intended. There is something undeniable about the sound a sharp blade makes when it cuts through tender flesh and dense bone. It is quick, slowing only slightly when it reaches the harder parts. Then the gurgling and crying and bodies losing everything they have inside. All of it sounded a symphony to Perrin. The vile scrods deserved to feel all of it.

Her mind was no home for remorse when her men finally pulled the dead man off her. She spat on the bloated and bloody thing, even gave it a kick. She would have preferred to spend more time hurting the man. Even though he failed at taking what he wanted from her, he got more than she would have liked. Any innocence remaining in her after all she had seen was gone, replaced by a black pit in her soul. The vile scoundrel stole the last bit from her. She had no tears to shed for him or his foul companions.

"My queen," Glord's voice shattered her hateful contemplation of the dead things lying at her feet as he handed her clothes to her.

"Thank you, Glord," her voice sounded like someone else's in her ears. She did not bother covering herself as she took the clothes from him and began stepping into her trousers. There seemed no reason to cover herself anymore. Even though her men had done their best to avert their gazes from her body, she knew everyone in the clearing had seen all of her. The bastards had stolen that from her too.

"Men, I'll be taking the queen back to camp. Burn up these bodies…" Glord began.

"No," Perrin shouted, the volume of her voice far greater than she intended. She continued with a more reasonable tone, "Not one of these bastards deserves a proper funeral. Leave these monsters out for the beasts of the bush, and I'll make my own way back to camp."

CHAPTER 16
# THE KING SLEEPS

Traversing the forest when you are not on a trail is tough for any man on foot. It is near impossible for a man on horseback. Add to that a stout brawler riding your shoulders, and you can forget making good time. That was precisely the predicament Banch found himself in lugging the deceptively heavy king of Alhouim around on his back. He took a bit of solace in the knowledge his horse gave up on the mission much earlier than his shoulders had, but it made little difference. Either way, he was guiding his horse through the brush rather than charging through it mounted atop a sturdy steed. They had probably made a mile before the horse just stopped walking. That was the point Banch dismounted, dropped his baggage, tied said baggage to his horse, and began guiding the creature through the thick brush. Of course, the trail would have been a better option, but grongs were about. And who knows what else?

Clouds had rolled in and choked out the little bit of light the late afternoon sun provided. Banch had just about reached the point of calling the day's travel complete and making camp when a light rain started. Somehow the raindrops found the journey from high in the sky, through the thick canopy, and to the forest floor much more easily than the sun's rays had. That settled it. Wet wood was no good for a fire.

"There be grongs about," Doentaat mumbled as Banch struggled to pull him down from the horse, "be a good lad and fetch my axe. I've a mind to bloody some arses."

"I seek only to serve, highness," Banch replied quietly. He had no intention of putting any kind of weapon in his fading friend's hand. He knew it was the fever talking. The poor dwarf had been babbling for the last few hours. The infection was moving faster than he had hoped it would.

After getting Doentaat propped comfortably against a fallen tree, Banch got to work building a makeshift shelter with a couple of woolen blankets from his horse sacks. At least the dwarf would stay dry. That was the first order. Next, a warm fire would not slow the infection, but it would keep them both from freezing as the rain helped lower the already cool temperature of the forest.

Doentaat continued the kind of nonsense typical from someone deep in the throes of a fever dream. Banch ignored most of it until the dwarf king sat up, looked him square in the eyes, and said, "Banch, you're a brawny soldier, as honorable as I've met, but this mission is at its end. Leave me behind. The Lake calls to my soul. Ain't no sense in you joining me on that journey."

Banch gave the fire a few pokes, stoking the flame before grabbing his water skin and moving toward Doentaat. "Nonsense," he said flatly as he handed the water skin over to the king, "Have a pull off that. I'll be grabbing you some meat."

"Brawny, honorable, and thick-headed," Doentaat called after him. "How far have we made it toward our goal with you lugging my broken body through the thick brush?"

Banch ignored him as he fished around in his horse sack for some meat.

Doentaat's eyes narrowed, "Hey. I appreciate all what you've done for me, but I am still the king of Alhouim. Best not be ignoring me."

Banch handed the meat over, "Forgive me, highness, but that ain't a conversation we'll be having. After I deliver you back to your people, you can hang me from that Sacred Pine." He paused long enough grab a bite off the hunk of meat he had kept for himself before continuing around the mouthful, "But it is my intention to deliver you back to your people. They await their king, and I refuse to see them disappointed."

"Stubborn arse," Doentaat groaned before chomping into the meat Banch had handed him.

They both sat in silence as they finished their meals. It would be all the nourishment they would get that night. At the rate they were moving, Banch would have to keep the portions small. He would hunt during the wee hours of the morning, but as plentiful as fallon were in the forest—and as good with a bow as Banch was—a successful hunt was never a guarantee.

Anyone who has spent any time in the forest knows it has sounds. For most, they slip to the periphery of their awareness until they become white noise. For folks like Banch and Doentaat who have spent a good bit of time exploring vast, dark, wooded places that symphony never slips from their awareness. They can identify the cause of each individual sound. Leaves rustling against each other in the canopy motivated by a light breeze and creating their own melody with their dance, small birds chirping and flitting from branch to branch, furry critters burrowing or climbing, all those sounds were known to both the blokes sitting beneath a makeshift shelter under a light forest rain in the glow of a healthy fire. The sound of heavy feet and big bodies moving through the thick brush and the occasional grunt which suddenly joined the chorus were equally identifiable. Several large creatures approached. They were obviously bipedal based on the cadence of their steps. Based on their level of stealth they had to be grongs, fifty or more at that.

Doentaat shot a look at Banch and whispered, "Best be handing me over that axe."

Banch obliged by silently shuffling over to his horse and fetching the mighty weapon. When he returned and passed it to his wounded companion he said, "Stay hidden as best you can. Best leave this battle to me."

The grizzled old dwarf responded with a wink and a smile.

The sound suddenly stopped. The two trail weary travelers had been spotted. At least, the glow of their fire had. Banch remained crouched in front of Doentaat as he quietly slipped his sword from its scabbard.

The grongs began moving again, significantly quieter than they had been. However, a stealthy grong is not really a thing. Based on the sounds of their measured steps, Banch assumed them to be no more than ten feet from the clearing he occupied with Doentaat. The fight was close at hand. He raised his eyebrows and nodded at the dwarf king as he gripped the handle of his blade tighter.

Banch counted off the steps in his head…1…2…3… When he finally hit ten, they would be just outside the clearing. He waited two more seconds and howled a war cry that would make any warrior from any of the great cities proud. At that same moment, he stood, spun, and leapt over the fire toward the other side of the clearing. The first grong whose head poked out of the darkness and into the fire's orange glow lost his scaly brain case to the smooth stroke of Banch's blade.

A club swung toward Banch's face. He parried the blow and thrust into the darkness stabbing through another. Then they all came. Grongs flooded into the clearing. One tripped, shoved by the beast behind him. That one rolled through the fire, singeing the bony plates on his back, and dragging sizzling embers with him. All that one saw were Doentaat's eyes as the dwarf king stabbed him in the throat with his dagger.

The first kill of any battle is the soldier's thrill. Most will demure and act as if taking a life was a last resort, a duty they had no choice but perform to protect their kind. Liars, the lot of them. That first kill was the kick. It got the adrenaline pumping. Any pain, any woe, any trepidation fled with the soul of that first kill. That kick was exactly what Doentaat felt as he struggled to his knee, propping himself up on the stump of his other leg, and shouted, "Come on then, you vile bastards. Bring your scaly carcasses over to my axe so I might cleave you all in two."

On the other side of the fire, Banch moved like an artist with his blade, elegantly slicing through scaly grong flesh as he dodged and danced among the clubs swinging for his head. A full ten of the beasts had fallen to his sword when one of those clubs finally connected. His thigh throbbed. A moment later, the arm holding that club was flipping through the firelight. A moment after that, the thing's head was spinning through the fire light in the other direction. Stab, slice, kick, he worked his way through the crowd, counting them off as he sent them back to the Lake…13…14…15…

A few of the grongs took notice of the furious dwarf hobbling toward them on one knee and a bandaged stump. Pain shot up through Doentaat's thigh every time that stump slammed into the forest floor. It only made him angrier. He pushed it down into his gut to fester with the rest of his rage. He swung his axe at the first grong who got close and that grong had two stumps. The thing had but a moment to lament his lost limbs before Doentaat's axe cleaved him in two at the belly. The raging dwarf yanked his bloody axe back up and swung high at the waist of another grong.

The dwarf axe is a thing of legend, two matching razor-sharp blades perfectly balanced with one another, but a grong's pelvic bones are dense. Doentaat's axe made it about halfway through its victim before getting lodged deep in that bone. The stout dwarf gave his death bringer a hefty tug, spinning with the force of it and finishing the cut from the other side. The move destroyed his balance and sent him tumbling to the ground next to the beast he had just sliced in two. He growled at the thing as its eyes grayed over.

Before Doentaat had a chance to get back up to his knee and his stump, a grong club was sailing down on him. He held his axe before him to block the blow, but it never came. Instead, Banch's soaring body pounded into the beast and sent them both tumbling into the brush at the edge of the clearing. Three grunts from the grong and a furious war cry from Banch later, and the swordsman from Havenstahl was back on his feet.

Doentaat's eyes went wide when he saw the man's condition. His rusty hair was streaked with red, obviously the result of a couple good whacks from grong clubs. His face had more scratches and bruises than the dwarf could count. There were just too many of them damned grongs.

"Stay with me," Doentaat shouted at Banch.

Banch wobbled, swayed, and threw up. Then he roared up at the dark canopy, smiled—a couple of teeth Doentaat knew had been there earlier were gone—and shouted, "The Lake can have me, but not before all them scaly bastards make the trip first."

"Aye," Doentaat agreed, "let's send these…"

It made a strangely hollow sound, Doentaat's head, when the grong club crashed against the back of it. He could not tell which came first, that hollow sound or the bright flash which accompanied it. Either way, the rest of his glorious proclamation remained stuck in his throat as the world around him became purple and fuzzy. It was not cognizant thought or even a willful desire to survive that prompted his hand to drop his axe, grab hold of the arm attached to the next club that struck him, and shove his dagger into the body attached to that arm four times before he released his grip. Nearly blind with his head throbbing, Doentaat was working strictly on instinct.

He was faintly aware of Banch's voice. The words were unclear, but it was obvious the mighty warrior was growling his rage at their opponents. Body parts fell all about him. He could not tell if they were limbs, heads, tails, or something else entirely, but his companion raged on.

Then something big and heavy fell next him. The words were clear as any he had ever heard when Banch groaned, "Forgive me, highness. I ain't worth the fire it will take to burn up my bones. I failed you."

Then the clubs came. They hit him all about the body. He urged his hands to stab and grab and punch and claw, but they refused his commands. His fight was gone. This would be the end, his last battle... But then, the clubs stopped. Doentaat's eyes had swollen shut, and the ringing in his ears was so loud he could barely make out any competing sound. However, what he could hear sounded like confusion.

Then a voice called out above all the buzzing and ringing. It seemed far away but sounded like, "Alhouim, to the king."

Doentaat was as good as blind with his swollen eyes. However, as the ringing dulled, he could hear more and more. Those were dwarf axes cutting through scaly grongs. He heard another voice, "Aye, flee into them trees, you scaly bastards." Then another answered, "Cut them down. Don't let none get away."

Then he felt hands on him. He could not move to fight them off had he wanted to. Luckily, they seemed to be checking him for injuries rather than trying to cause more. Those fingers felt like daggers in some of the spots they touched, but he ached in so many places it was difficult to notice. He thought he may have groaned a few times but could not be sure of that either. Sleep seemed pretty close, or death. Which of them approached was impossible to discern.

Then he heard a voice he recognized as Glaadrian spoke loudly but calmly in his ear, "Thanks be to Coeptus we found you, my king. Bindaar be all in a tizzy since you've been lost to us. There are ten in our group, and we'll be dying or getting you home."

There was probably some water. Maybe a few other voices. Somebody may have bandaged or wrapped this or that. Everything grew increasingly fuzzy. It became difficult to separate physical feelings from thoughts or ideas. Then it was just dark.

# CHAPTER 17
# EAT THE GODS

The babe, Geillan, prince of Havenstahl, son of Maelich the Dragon, hovered between four obelisks. He lay there peacefully sleeping. The obelisks flashed, shifting between the blackest dark and brightest light so quickly both conditions seemed to exist side by side. As if there were only light and only dark at the same time, two equal and opposite conditions occupying all concurrently.

Ijilv stood next to the sleeping babe. His staff mimicked the flashing obelisks perfectly; at once completely dark and completely light. His wide eyes—horrible things, black as the pit of a cavern but somehow all colors at once, blazing brightly—stared at the ceiling of the room they occupied. The cold stone had been replaced with a flickering canvas, like a live painting moving from scene to scene as quickly as the room moved from the brightest light to the darkest dark.

The god hunted, scouring the living canvas for pieces of his scattered brother, Kallum. Gods, of course, cannot be killed. Unlike dwarves or men or giants, they are not meant to return to the Lake, the source. Their role is to guide, eternal fixtures in a plane of reality in which they stand both within and without. As Ijilv moved through the scenes playing out before him, he happened upon bits of his scattered brother sparkling bright against the backdrop surrounding them. When he found these, he plucked them from the scene and consumed them.

Then one scene caught his attention. It stood out from the rest. A sleeping Dragon lie before Brerto's cave. Of course, this was not an actual Dragon with scales and teeth and mighty wings. It was Cialia. Her presence in Brerto's paradise high atop the snowy peak at Alharin was intriguing. She could only have one cause to go calling after the old wizard on the big hill, as the men of Ouloos had called the god in bygone days.

Despite the distraction—the mystery of why Leisha's Dragon would be sleeping on the enemy's doorstep—Ijilv noticed a glimmering piece of Kallum resting on a tree near the cave's mouth. He snatched it from the scene and popped it in his mouth. It did not have a taste which could be described in relation to other tastes. It did not taste like a food or element or chemical concoction. It tasted like strength, primal power. This morsel was different than the others Ijilv had consumed. It was more complex and had a finality to it. He swallowed it down.

A flash, like a star exploding in the blackness of space, enveloped the room. It chased away the dark moments and made the light moments insignificant. But this light was not merely brilliant white. It was all colors at once in equal saturation. Gods are seldom surprised, shocked even less frequently, but right at that moment Ijilv found himself in unfamiliar territory. He was surprised. He was shocked. He was furious. He was sad. He was in love with Ouloos, with space, with the trees, with men and giants, with all living creatures, and he hated them just the same. He was terrified yet unafraid. He felt all emotions equal and simultaneously.

He laughed uncontrollably until his laughs melted into the most pitiable sobs. Ouloos could be damned, but then, he should save them all. Peace is what Ouloos needs, but they could do just fine with destruction. Every feeling, every emotion, and every thought was a contradiction. In a moment both instant and eternal, he felt everything.

Standing at the edge of oblivion, Ijilv slowly gained control. This was infinite power. He had to be stronger than it. He had to understand. He did understand. He had been preparing for this moment since the beginning of time, since he looked at his brothers…and that other one. Who was that other one, that memory, that thing he knew but could not know? No matter, at that moment when they all came to be, he looked at them. *I will rule you all.*

He inhaled long and deep through his nose and released the breath slowly. "The god is in me. We are one."

## CHAPTER 18
## THE BLACK HORSE

Twilight in the forest is darker than twilight in a field. There is an eeriness to it. Sounds seem louder in the darkness. They are probably no louder than the same sounds in the light, but they seem that way. They echo off the trees like shouts. That is what was so strange about the silent forest surrounding Maelich. The trees were there, the moss, the darkness, the leaves above moving against each other, but where were the sounds? It bothered him. The forest had distinct sounds, and he knew them all. Well, he knew them as well as any other traveler. There probably were sounds he had yet to hear in all his days, but he would not know that until he heard a new one.

The ground was soft beneath his feet as he stepped along the trail. At least, he thought it was a trail. The trees seemed a relatively uniform distance from each other, as if the separation were intentional. He could not see the trail itself, if it really were a trail, due to a thick fog hanging about the forest floor. It came all the way up to his waist. There was something familiar about the fog. What that familiar thing might be was elusive, but it felt like something he knew once.

Then a voice called out from the darkness, "Help me, Maelich."

The sound was faint. It was impossible to determine whether it was a close whisper or a far shout, but he followed it just the same. It led him into the trees. The ground beneath his feet felt the same as he left the trail and started off into the foliage along the trail. Perhaps it had not been a trail at all. Trails had a specific feel to them under travel-worn boots. The ground there was harder than the soft mulch lining it beneath the trees on either side. No two trails were the same, but they had similar characteristics. Perhaps the trail-like thing he had been on was just a line through the forest where the trees separated for some reason. As he thought the thought, it occurred to him that what he was thinking about certainly sounded like a trail.

"Help me, Maelich," the voice called out again.

The urgency in the pleas made his contemplations about what constituted a trail through the forest seem a silly conundrum. Whether what he had been on was a trail or something else did not matter. Whatever it had been, he was no longer on it. He slipped around trees with bark that seemed too smooth. Perhaps it was the dim light, but it was not like any bark he had ever seen or felt. The fog remained unchanged. It still clung about his waist and sprawled out forever in every direction. The weird thing about it was it remained stationary, unspoiled as he moved through it, like he was not even there.

Then the voice again, "Help me, Maelich." It was louder than the last time which had been louder than the first. Fog, trail, who cares? He continued deeper into the trees.

The voice kept beckoning, "Help me, Maelich. Help me, Maelich." It was louder each time, the tone growing more urgent with each subsequent plea.

He rounded a tree and happened upon a clearing. The fog was gone there. It still clung about his waist and surrounded the clearing, but the clearing itself was clear. A stone slab sat at its center. The thing was smooth except for etchings. It seemed to have some ceremonial significance. A body lay upon it, and bouquets of light purple flowers had been placed at each of its four corners. Maelich approached.

As he neared the altar, the features of the small shape lying on it became clearer. It was a dwarf. He was dressed like a king with a crown upon his head and red bows decorating the thick braids in his magnificent beard. As Maelich got closer, a name popped into his head, Doentaat. There was something familiar about the name and the face of the poor dwarf on the slab, but he could not place it. A reason for the recollection was absent. He was suddenly sad but could not understand why. Of course, death can always be sad, but that depends on your perspective. It is sad if you see it as the end of something. However, if you see it as a journey to the Lake, it could very well be a time for rejoice. Why did the idea of this Doentaat dying make him feel sad?

"You have lost a friend, Maelich," a woman's voice called out from behind him. He jumped a bit, startled. It was the same voice which had been calling for help, but he had not passed anyone on his way through the trees from the trail—if it were a trail at all—to the clearing which remained oddly absent of the thick fog which covered everything else.

He spun to see who owned the voice. A black horse stood before him. "Is it you who beckoned me from the trail?" he asked the horse.

"Yes, Maelich," the horse replied. "I called you here to see your friend off to the Lake."

"Friend?" Maelich asked. "The face stirs feelings in me, but I do not recall. Who is Doentaat?"

The horse smiled at him. It seemed strange for a horse to smile. It reminded him of something, but the memory was elusive. He only had a moment to trouble over it before she said, "He was your friend once. When you met him, he was just another dwarf living under the rule of a giant. You helped him, freed him really. Because of your good deeds, his people crowned him their king."

Maelich shook his head, "I have met a dwarf or two, but I do not recall knowing any well enough to consider them friend."

"If not your friend, how do you suppose you know his name?" the horse asked.

"I am not one for riddles, horse," Maelich grew irritated with the game. "If you have something you would like to tell me, please say it plainly, and we can both be on our way."

"I speak no riddles," the horse continued, "and I have no plainer way to state my message."

Maelich scratched his head, "How you state your message will not make any difference. The message itself is the riddle. It only just occurred to me, but the white horse…" he paused before correcting himself, "Maulom warned me about you."

"The white horse warned you about me? What did he say?" she seemed genuinely concerned.

"Beware the black horse," he replied flatly. "After speaking with you this short time, it seems good advice."

The horse nodded, "Perhaps on the surface, but how do you know he is trustworthy?"

"He told me things," Maelich shrugged.

"Things you knew?" she asked.

Maelich thought for a moment, "No, I suppose not. But he said they were things I had known."

"How is that different from what I told you? These things I have said are things you have known. You need to wake up, Maelich," the horse spoke softly.

The horse had a point. She was at least as frustrating to speak with as Maulom. Perhaps they were both the same. If it were a game they both played, why must they include him? He was deep in the midst of concocting his next reply when the earth began to quake. The black horse stomped about as Maelich did his best to keep from losing his feet.

"You are unwelcomed here," Maelich could not see Maulom among the trees, but the white horse's voice was unmistakable.

A moment later, the altar on which the old friend Maelich could not remember lay dead vanished in ball of bright light that expanded quickly before shrinking to a spec and disappearing. The white horse stood in its place. He reared back and kicked at the black horse. She responded in the same fashion. When their hooves connected, the ground beneath them split open and both were consumed in bright, white light.

A moment later, Maelich woke with a howl. Ymitoth sat directly above him shaking him. "You've been shouting in your sleep," Ymitoth said. "That horse has been in your dreams again."

Maelich sat up and wiped the dampness from his forehead, "He was, but this time there was another. It was a black horse, a mare. She spoke in the same confusing fashion as Maulom."

"Another horse? Is it the one Maulom warned you about?" Ymitoth asked.

"Yes," Maelich nodded. "The two battled when the white horse arrived. But not before she showed me a dead dwarf laid out on a stone altar. She said I knew him, called him Doentaat."

"Doentaat," Ymitoth repeated the name. His black, dead eyes failed to reflect any recognition, but his words did, "That sounds like a name I maybe knew one time, but I couldn't say from where."

"It was the same for me," Maelich stared toward the edge of the smooth stone wall beside him. Not much light made it that deep into the cave, but he focused on the dim glow at a point where the cave bent sharply away from its entrance. "There was something familiar about his face, and I knew the name. But I am certain I do not know him."

Before Ymitoth could respond, Maulom charged around the corner with his finger wagging. "Beware the black horse, Maelich," he began. "She is evil and wily. I have done my best to hide you from her and hold her back. Obviously, I failed."

Maelich's eyes narrowed, "It seems you know her well. She reminded me of you with her confusing talk, all the words she uses while saying very little."

"That hurts, Maelich," Maulom seemed a bit crestfallen. "I have been clear with you from the start."

"You say a whole lot of nothing, as far as I can see," Ymitoth always tended to be a bit more direct.

Maulom ignored the jibe, "The sun is up, and the men are ready to train. You worry about them and leave the black horse to me."

Maelich glanced over at Ymitoth who shrugged and said, "Ain't nothing better than clashing swords to clear away the ghost of a bad dream."

Maelich nodded his agreement as he rose to his feet and began gathering his equipment. However, he was not completely certain he was ready to chase the ghost of that dream away just yet. Despite Maulom's confident proclamations, Maelich still had no real proof anything the old man had told him since they had met was true. What if the black horse spoke truth? Why should he trust either of them? Ymitoth might not be the wisest, but he was the only one Maelich felt he could completely trust. Though he might not be quite ready to chase the ghosts away, clashing swords would definitely clear his head. A clear head seemed a great idea just then.

# CHAPTER 19
## NEW FRIENDS OR OLD ENEMIES

The forests around Mount Elzkahon—the peak on which the castle at Havenstahl had been built—were known far and wide as some of the most beautiful and peaceful examples of the brilliance of Coeptus' creation any traveler seeking to escape the crowded stone streets of the city, or even the hustle and bustle of the busy towns surrounding it, could find. You would be hard pressed to find a hunter who did not share the sentiment. But that was before invaders came from across the Great Sea to mow a large swath of those pristine forests down with massive contraptions built to eat the very trees. It was before thousands upon thousands were slaughtered in the waste those destructive machines left in their wake. Beneath the decomposing bodies which remained in that haunted place, what was left of the trees may have made for good kindling if not saturated in stale blood.

The bodies—still far too many to count—spread from that bloody waste deep into the forests remaining on any side of it. An honorable adversary would have allowed time for the dead to be removed and given proper ceremony. Giants were massive and horrible monsters, but they were wise, their minds far more sophisticated than those of men or dwarves. The fact did nothing to steer their actions toward peace or any form of spiritual enlightenment. Instead, it left them aloof and uncaring about trivial things like opposing beliefs or ceremonies. In fact, the only thing most giants cared about was ruling. Some of them so bold as to question whether they were even wiser and mightier than the gods themselves, or

Dragons. All Ouloos belonged to them, and they should be rightly worshipped by all other living things.

Maomnosett Bom did not share the beliefs of the majority of his kin. He was smaller than most giants, but still massive and powerful. He was wiser than most. The difference was, he did not believe his size, strength, or wisdom gave him the right to rule over others. All living creatures should be free to find their own destiny, untethered by the rule of any creature over them. Of course, concepts like king or general seemed silly. The necessity was obvious enough. Any time you put a large number of any type of creature together in one place, there must be some kind of rule or law to guide the mass. It just seemed so stifling to the spirit. Life must be experienced, and all should be free to experience it in their own way and in their own time.

These contrary ideals Bom held so dear were exactly what had put him in direct opposition to his grandfather and his goals. Standing up to Ott had been the hardest thing he had ever done. Despite these differing ideals, Bom was a giant to his soul. He had been raised by Bok, one of the fiercest giants who ever lived, to be a leader among his kind. Walking through the bloody waste among the decomposing carcasses—all testaments to his late father's passion to rule—it was clear to him why that life could never be his. All these souls sent back to the Lake for what? One side followed his father as he attempted to impose his will, and the other only wanted to live their lives the way they wanted to live them. For him, the white cloth tied to a thick stick he held aloft high above his head was the result. He could not stand by and watch his kin slaughter these men and dwarves. Nor did he wish for the desires of his kind—as misguided and wrong as he felt they were—to lead them to their deaths. Sadly, the latter group refused to be turned away.

As Bom led his small group through the gore, Kantiim led a smaller group through the trees just north of the bloody waste. He had nineteen mounted men with him riding two by ten through the trees. He did not know Bom as anything other than an invader, an invader with three giants and hundreds of trogmortem with him. Both the lack of thousands of grongs and the white flag the giant carried were strange, but Kantiim was not one to fall easily for a trick. Rash decisions without proper counsel were also not in his nature.

"Denigran, Ychorell, on me," Kantiim said quietly as he raised his fist up to halt the group.

The two he had called out would provide the unique perspectives he sought. Denigran had served as rider of Druindahl for ten years before making the trip to Havenstahl, and Ychorell had spent an equal amount of time riding under the banner of Havenstahl. Both were as skilled with their minds as they were with their swords. Once the two had moved up the trail next to him, he asked Ychorell, "Well, what do you make of that?"

"A white flag is a white flag. After strolling through all my fallen kin, I'd rather be cutting them bastards down, but we ought to find out what they want first," Ychorell shrugged.

Kantiim sighed long and deep as he peered through the trees at Bom's group. After a few moments of silent contemplation, he finally agreed, "Your heart sounds to be in about the same place as mine. Though I am not keen on our odds of winning that battle, I would like nothing more than to rally the men and cut them down. However, that damned white flag demands investigation."

"It could be trick," Denigran offered. "These monsters from across the Great Sea, none of them have been what I would consider to be honorable."

"Aye, pack of vile bastards," Ychorell added. "You can send me in first. If that white flag don't mean to them what a white flag means to us, I'll cut down as many as I can." He spit on the ground before adding, "And if that be the case, you'd best make sure you avenge me and get my body back from that bloody waste."

Kantiim considered Ychorell's words. They were full of venom and anger but carried a healthy measure of good sense. They were carrying a white flag, and that did mean something to the men of both Druindahl and Havenstahl—and any other city where honorable men dwell. "You are a brave man, Ychorell," he finally said. Then he fished a white undertunic from his horse sack. A bit dingy, it was probably closer to gray, but it would suit the purpose. He handed the thing to Ychorell and added, "Fly this over your head as you ride out."

Ychorell nodded his response and dismounted to grab a branch.

As Ychorell tied off his white flag, Denigran said, "Send me too. If their intentions are less than honorable, we will make a go of it. And my request is the same. Do not dare leave my body in that bloody mess."

"Thank you both. That will be our plan. The two of you will ride out under the white, and the rest of us will just breach the tree line.

That way they will see you have support but will be unable to gauge our numbers," Kantiim said.

Lito-Bi noticed the two riders emerge from the trees along the northside of the bloody waste first. One rode a horse dressed in flags of blue for the mighty fallon of Havenstahl. That one held a white garment tied to a stick. The other rode a horse adorned in the red flags of Druindahl. The trogmortem warrior touched Bom's arm lightly, "Our mission has been noticed. Two approach. One flies the colors of Havenstahl and a white flag to match our own. The other flies the Dragon's colors for Druindahl. I count eighteen more at the tree line. That may be the extent of their support, but we cannot know what lies beyond the trees."

Bom looked toward Ychorell and Denigran, then to the trees, and finally back at Lito-Bi. "You and I shall go meet them and pray Coeptus their white flag carries the same meaning as our own."

"We have nothing to fear from two men or twenty, or more if they have a trap for us waiting in the trees," Lito-Bi replied.

Bom sighed deeply and looked at the sky, "We do not, but I would prefer not to color this already horrid place with the blood of anymore men, trogmortem, or giants. For their sake and ours, I hope they truly come in peace." Then he turned to the rest of his group and added, "Hold here, friends. Lito-Bi and I will meet the delegation from Havenstahl. If they prove untrustworthy, please proceed with a measured response."

Stekka-Ha, regarded as the finest trogmortem warrior alive next to Lito-Bi, replied, "If they move to harm you, we will crush them, my friend."

"I know," Bom frowned.

Bom held his white flag high above his head as he and Lito-Bi carefully picked their steps to avoid the bloody carcasses littering the ground at their feet. The men looked serious. The white flag could very well be a trick. It was quite possible one thousand riders waited in the trees to descend on them and cut them down amongst the rotting dead. His soldiers would fight. They would kill many men, and many of them would die. All of it would mean nothing except more souls for the Lake. He hoped they desired anything but more death.

Once they were close enough to speak without shouting, Bom said, "I am Maomnosett Bom, son of Bok, grandson of Ott. I lead a small group of giants and trogmortem who wish to see no more death.

I beg you do not hold me responsible for the actions of my father and his father before him."

Ychorell shot a skeptical look at Denigran before replying, "What about the beast next to you?"

Lito-Bi bit his lip and replied in as measured a tone as he could muster, "My kind, we do not look like you, but we are not animals. I am tired of fighting for others' desires. I seek only peace. They call me Lito-Bi. I cannot tell you the name of the one who named me, as I never met him. My mother was Dana-Ra. She was strong. She taught me to be to be a warrior. I lost her to sickness and fight only to honor her name, not conquer kingdoms."

"I am certain my companion meant no disrespect," Denigran began, "but you and your kind are twice the size of the largest of men. On top of that, your hands and your teeth are weapons at least as effective as any sword or axe. Please forgive our trepidation, but the very ground on which you stand soaks with the blood of our kin."

"We have suffered great losses on both sides," Bom replied.

"An equal number of my kin lay strewn about this field," Lito-Bi added.

Ychorell finally piped in, "You may be right. Maybe we're all beasts then, but them dead men rotting in that field died defending their own when your kind tore their bodies up with fangs and claws. All of you are invaders here. If you want to talk of peace, we will listen. But there probably won't come a time when I count you as friend." After a few deep breaths, he added, "I am Ychorell, proud to ride for the mighty fallon of Havenstahl."

"They call me Denigran. I ride in support of Havenstahl under the banner of Druindahl, great protector of the Dragon. If you want to speak of peace, the leader of your group may accompany us into the trees to meet with our general," the dragon rider added.

Lito-Bi shook his head in frustration, "No. That is not fair, nor is it equal. How can we know you do not intend an ambush?"

"You cannot," Denigran shrugged.

Before the trogmortem warrior could say anymore, Bom interceded, "This group has no leader. We all are equal, but I will submit to your request in the name of brokering a peace with you. Looking at the devastation surrounding us, I understand why it would be difficult to see us as friends. However, my grandfather has not abandoned his desire to bring your kingdom to heel. We would be good friends to have."

"I do not like this," Lito-Bi scowled at Ychorell as he clenched his jaw tight.

"This is about trust," Bom smiled. "Try to see it from their perspective. We are the invaders. They cannot possibly be certain of our motives. All they can know is I could tear their bodies in half with my bare hands." He smiled at Ychorell before adding, "One giant against twenty men is a fair fight. Their horses will not help them in the trees."

Bom's last statement certainly sounded like a threat. Truthfully, Ychorell did feel threatened. However, faced with the same set of circumstances, he would probably respond the same. On top of that, the giant was submitting to their demands exactly as stated. Not that he or Denigran would have entertained any kind of negotiation of terms, the point was moot. He looked over at Denigran and nodded toward the trees.

"To the trees then," Denigran said to Bom.

"We will hold here," Lito-Bi said flatly as he watched Bom follow the two riders toward the tree line.

The small group had only made ten feet toward the forest when the riders lined up at the edge of the trees pulled back. Bom felt confident they would refrain from killing him outright. It would be foolish. If they had the numbers to go to battle right then, they could have done just that. Their horses would certainly be more effective in the open field than stifled by thick trees.

The riders of Havenstahl were off their horses with swords drawn when Denigran and Ychorell arrived. They formed a semi-circle behind Kantiim who sat upon a fallen tree. He hailed Bom as the two men guiding the giant dismounted and joined the group behind the old general, "You have nothing to fear from us, just precautions. Please," he pointed to a large boulder across from him, "have a seat."

"Your words offer very little in the way of comfort with all the swords aiming at me," Bom smiled.

Kantiim offered a humorless chuckle, "I have seen hundreds of men literally ripped to shreds by your kind. How many of us could you kill even with those swords?"

"Please do not try selling me an idea where men are helpless," Bom countered. "I watched a man kill my father, the terror himself, in single one-on-one combat."

"And that man nearly died for the effort," Kantiim kicked a small stone. "Let us move beyond this. You came flying a white flag. Where I come from that means some variation of peace. No harm will come to you provided you sit on that big rock and speak quietly with me about why you are here."

"Very well," Bom said as he sat down. "I was opposed to this campaign from the beginning, but honor is of great import to my father. His god, my god, laid a command upon him. He died for it, and my grandfather damned his memory for the same. That was the final straw for me. This is your land. We have no need for it. We have our own land. It is beautiful. Have you ever seen the sun set across the stony desert?"

"What is the stony desert?" Kantiim asked.

"It would probably seem desolate to you. This is beautiful land, lush and full of life. My home is not lush, but it is full of life. The mountains there are not covered with green. They are stony, and when the setting sun bathes them in all his glory..." he trailed off lost in a memory for a few moments before adding, "Well, it is breathtaking. Any words I could offer as a description would fail to convey the majesty of it. Perhaps one day, after all this fighting is done and my kind leaves this place, you could make the long voyage across the Great Sea and look upon it yourself."

"I would love to see it someday, but what does that have to do with your presence here?" the old general asked. "You appear to be marching on the broken castle I am defending.

"It should be very simple based on what I have told you," Bom shrugged. "I am done killing to steal land. This is not my fight. However, I cannot simply walk away. After looking across that bloody waste, all that senseless destruction, I have come up with a new cause, a cause I believe in for which I am willing to fight. You and your people deserve to live in peace. My grandfather would shatter that peace with war. I want to help you stop him. The group travelling with me shares my desire."

Denigran shot a look at Kantiim and shook his head.

Kantiim shared the sentiment conveyed by the gesture. "I have encountered many men far wiser than me during my lifetime, but I am by no means dim. It sounds to me like you are suggesting a willingness to kill your own kind, because you are tired of fighting. You seem quite wise yourself, probably far wiser than me. Would you accept such a tale from me were our numbers and situations reversed?"

"Not immediately to be sure," Bom smiled. "Consider this, however. With a brief whistle, I could call one-hundred fierce trogmortem to these woods to cut you down. I have not done that."

"Cutting down twenty men ain't getting you no closer to your goal of taking that castle," Ychorell contended.

"I had thought of that, how this must look," Bom frowned. "Earn your trust and convince you to welcome us into your keep while the rest of our force follows closely behind waiting for the signal to attack. All I have is my word."

"And I do not know you well enough to take you on that word," Kantiim spoke softly.

"You do not," the giant agreed.

Kantiim roughly scratched at his beard as he stood and looked up toward the canopy. Both Ychorell and the giant were completely correct. They were at an impasse. Three giants and one hundred trogmortem would be invaluable to help defend against the coming storm if they really could be counted as allies. Could they be trusted? That was the question. Answering incorrectly would be fatal. After a few moments of near silent contemplation—he barely noticed he was mumbling as he scratched and thought—he walked over to Bom and stood before the giant.

"Look in my eyes," he commanded.

Bom obliged. Kantiim failed to see any madness or malice in those eyes. The giant looked earnest. If he were lying, he was an expert.

Kantiim's head slowly began nodding as he quietly said, "Fine, your group will accompany us back to Havenstahl. I will bring you before my general, Daritus."

Recognition sparkled in Bom's eyes.

"Yes, the same man who killed your father," Kantiim continued. "Are you prepared to face him?"

"I am," the giant replied earnestly.

"I do not like this one bit," Denigran piped in.

"None of us do, not me, not you, and not our new supposed friend and ally," Kantiim glanced over at Denigran before locking his eyes back on Bom's. "You will make a vow to me on this day in front of these men, the forest, and whatever god to which you pray. You will fight to protect these lands against your own kind who seek to destroy them, and you will raise no hand in malice against any man under the protection of Havenstahl."

"I pledge this to you," Bom's eyes remained just as earnest.

Kantiim leaned in a bit closer until his nose was nearly touching the giant's, "Betray me, Maomnosett Bom, son of Bok, grandson of Ott, and I will kill you. My sword will find your throat."

Bom's expression did not change as he replied, "I believe you."

## CHAPTER 20
## THE FEATS OF OUR FATHERS

Heights were not something Daritus feared. However, the rickety thing fashioned from ropes and wooden planks he traversed hundreds of feet above the river Galgooth had him reconsidering. The great drawbridge was being rebuilt for at least the second time. Never did he imagine he would be overseeing the effort. He had been the cause of at least one rebuilding effort when Cialia rescued him from the pits of the very castle he sought to rebuild. So much had changed since then.

The men were doing good work and making good time. They had been at it for weeks and managed to remain well ahead of schedule. Proper work on the castle could not really begin until a solid solution for bringing in materials was constructed. Daritus surveyed the effort alongside Danick, an engineer from Druindahl who was heading up the effort. The man looked every bit the wayward soul, always carrying a good bit of grime on his ill-fitting, torn clothes, but Daritus considered him a genius. He had a way of seeing a problem from angles most folks simply could not perceive. Function was never sacrificed in favor of beauty, but the man had an uncanny way of considering both and somehow managing to leave neither out of any plan he had ever concocted.

"The old bridge was solid. I found the plans they used to construct it. Truly, there was not much for me to improve upon. Look there," Danick's eyes moved all over the structure as he spoke. It seemed a thousand ideas ran through his head.

Daritus pointed at a fallon's rack carved into the end of a plank—

matching etchings adorned every tenth plank—as he said, "The fallon racks, hand carved? Do those add some structural integrity?"

If Danick noticed the sarcasm, he did not let on, "No, no, no, those are for identity. Of course, that is not as important as function or structural integrity, but those are the little things folks remember. These men are making art. And they were not hand carved. Those were burned into the wood with brands crafted in the forge. It survived the destruction, as did many of the swordsmiths. Can you imagine the pathways of Druindahl without the images of Dragons etched all about them?"

"Fair enough," Daritus replied. "They do add a bit of character to this massive thing."

"They do," Danick agreed while pointing toward the main gate to the city, "but look there. That is where we really made some improvements."

"What am I looking at?" Daritus saw ropes and gears, all exposed as the coverings had yet to be installed. The genius of whatever Danick was excited about was completely lost on him.

The architect shrugged, "I suppose it does not look like much to the untrained eye, but you will never find a smoother operating drawbridge in all Ouloos. What they had was fine, completely functional. It was all based on a weight and pully system, but the gearing was all wrong. The way we fixed it up, one man could raise or lower this behemoth, and it will not crash to bits if someone defeats the brake."

"That is why you are in charge of this effort," Daritus smiled.

As the two men walked along the makeshift bridge, Daritus looked with awe on the massive stones used to construct the outer wall of the city growing less and less concerned about the wide-open space between him and the rushing river below. Danick took it all in stride. He had been planning and building his entire life.

"The ingenuity of men has always impressed me," Daritus marveled. "Our city in the trees, this massive castle…just look at the size of those stones. How did they even build something like this?"

"The same way we will," Danick remained unmoved. "I will tell you this. I am greatly impressed by the condition of the stones which were torn down. Some are crumbled, cracked, or useless, but many of them can be used as is. We will not require much from the quarry."

Daritus stopped and faced the builder, "Tell me this castle does not impress you in the least. I am in awe of this structure and the things men can make with their hands and their minds."

"It is an impressive thing, equal at least to anything I have ever seen," Danick conceded. "But these old eyes have seen quite a bit. This castle will be at least as spectacular once we have finished putting her back together."

Daritus had to grab a tighter hold of the rope railing he had been casually gripping as the bridge began swaying. Danick did not seem disturbed by it at all, but the great general of Havenstahl's army was suddenly aware again of the great distance between he and the river below. He turned to see a scout hurrying toward him. A few deep breaths kept him from screaming at the poor bloke and embarrassing himself.

"General, my commander, Tarturan, sends me with word from Alhouim and the surrounding forests," the scout called out. He had obviously just arrived; his face and clothes still carried a good bit of grime from the trail.

"Are they words I want to hear?" the general asked as Danick bowed and departed.

The bridge finally stopped shaking and swaying as the scout drew near enough to Daritus to have a conversation without shouting. The brave general—man amongst men and killer of giants—did his best not to let any of the relief he felt seep into his expression. He was just glad all that bucking and swaying had not motivated the contents of his guts out of his mouth and all over the damned rickety bridge serving as the only thing keeping him from plummeting to the rushing waters below.

"Some, yes. Others, probably not," the scout answered once he had caught his breath.

Daritus thought for a bit before saying, "I usually like to hear the good news first. I have just had a bunch of that. What is the news you are less excited to share?"

"The king of Alhouim remains missing. His absence has General Bindaar in a horrible state. He has been acting irrationally, and some of the other dwarf generals are concerned he may do something rash," the scout rattled everything off while standing firmly at attention.

Daritus took a breath and shook his head, "Take a moment, scout. What is your name?"

"My father named me Tiegran, sir," the scout rattled his response off in the same formal fashion.

The old general smiled warmly as he reached out and grasped the young soldier's forearm, "Tiegran, that is a solid name. My father named me Daritus. Unless we are formed up ready to march off to war, it would please me greatly if you would refer to me as such. Drop the general and the sir."

Tiegran blushed slightly as he gripped Daritus' forearm, smiled, and replied, "Thank you, sir. Forgive me, Daritus. You must understand what a thrill it is for a young recruit like me to meet you. You are a legend, the giant slayer. I would wager all the coin I call my own that you could not find a campfire where tales of you besting that monster, Bok, in the bloody waste were not leaving at least one man's lips."

Now the old general blushed. He fancied himself a humble man, but he could not help but feel a bit of awe when he thought about it. A man killed a giant, and he was that man. Despite feeling more than a bit boastful in his head, he replied quite humbly, "I did only my duty, as any other man serving to defend this castle would. The men raise my name to heights I do not deserve."

"Do you really believe that?" Tiegran laughed.

Daritus laughed just as hard as he gave the scout a firm pat on the shoulder, "It is bold of you to say so, but you are quite correct. You have seen right through me. I still cannot believe it was me, that I did that." He looked west toward that place where he bested a giant in battle and paused for a moment. Then he added with a sly grin, "Legend, you say?"

"Not just me," Tiegran gleamed, "all the men. Serving under the command of the mighty Daritus, protector of Dragons, slayer of giants, and unflinching leader of men, is an honor. It is like having a god on your side."

"Your words lift me up and humble me at the same time. I only hope I am half the leader they believe me to be." His smile faded as he changed the subject back to troubling news, "King Doentaat is lost and the general, Bindaar, is losing control. They were housemates before one became a king and the other his most trusted general. It must be difficult for him. We can only hope his fellow generals can keep him from making any foolish mistakes. Is that the extent of the troubling news, or do you have more disheartening tales to tell?"

"The rest of my stories should sound more pleasing to your ears," the scout smiled. "The dwarves of Alhouim find themselves in a similar state as Havenstahl but have vowed to aid in the further defense of our fair city should she fall under attack again."

"She will," Daritus replied grimly.

Tiegran nodded, "All the dwarves aiding in the rebuilding effort can remain as long as needed."

"I had hoped as much, but that is more heartening news," Daritus draped an arm across Tiegran's shoulder before adding, "Now, accompany me to the ale tent for a pint or two. We can talk of battle and glory and forget reality for a bit."

## CHAPTER 21
## FIFTEEN SUMMERS

The sun was hot that day. Sweat glistened from Cialia's brow as she attacked the training dummy with two unsharpened training blades. The planks above her provided ample shade but offered little relief from the sweltering heat. She ignored it. Her technique was crisp and elegant. No movements were wasted. Every step she took, and each flick of her wrist had purpose. If only the dummy could fight back. She was ready to test her talent against a real swordsman, a warrior. When that day came, she would be prepared.

Her father called out to her as he emerged from his forge, "Cialia, put away them blades and break for the mid-day."

Once a fearsome warrior in the king's army, Agrimon was widely considered the finest swordsmith in all the villages under the protection of Varisghoul. He walked with a considerable limp, and his right arm was mostly useless due to severe damage to his shoulder on that side. Despite those injuries, finding anyone courageous enough to fight the half lame smith would be more than a challenge. He would call it ancient history, but the cause of those injuries was the stuff of legend.

Sixteen summers prior, he had led twenty of Varisghoul's finest riders north to protect a caravan of supplies heading for Mount Grindelhorn. The ore mined from the peak produced the strongest weapons known to man, and the dwarves who worked those mines were considered the finest smiths on Ouloos. The myths would suggest the mountain itself was a star fallen from the heavens. Whether the peak had fallen from the stars or sprouted out of the ground made no difference to Agrimon. The grizzly mongs that attacked the caravan were a different story. The battle was brief. It would have been a slaughter, but Agrimon earned the legends told about him that day. When the initial assault had ended, sixteen of his men lay dead and the rest too wounded to fight. He protected those wounded men against the five remaining grizzly mongs and killed them all. By the time the last of the monsters fell, Agrimon's right shoulder was mangled and useless, and his left leg could no longer hold his weight. The men he saved that day told the tale to all who would listen, the story of Agrimon the titan facing down the horrible snow beasts of the northern pass.

Cialia knew all those stories. They were not frightening enough to prevent her ignoring her father's command, and she was not quite ready to stop beating on the defenseless training dummy. The thing spewed tiny stones out its top every time she struck it. She used two blades. Father had trained her that way since she was old enough to lift a sword. Of course, he fought with his left hand. After battling the grizzly mongs, his right arm was not good for anything but holding molten metal in place while smacking it with a hammer. That was precisely the reason Cialia had learned to use both. Every limb is a weapon. When one fails you, you should know how to use the rest of them.

"Cialia," father called out again, "heed my word or you won't train for a full week."

Cialia launched a vicious assault on the dummy, her last stand for the day. Then she hollered back, "Coming, father." Once she could tell he had moved on to their hut, she looked down at the blades in her hands and added, "If only I could skip the laundry and floors and feeding of pigs, I would swing the two of you until the moon chased the sun from the sky."

The blades clinked dully together as she tossed them at the wooden weapons rack next to her training area. The sound they made grabbed her attention. It was not out of place or anything. They sounded exactly like two hunks of metal clanging against each other should sound. As it hit her ears, she suddenly could not remember how she had gotten there. As the idea slithered around her mind, it occurred to her she remembered nothing prior to smacking the dummy with those blades. Everything was familiar, the dummy, the blades, her father, the hut they shared, but somehow, she felt she did not belong there. These were all her things, and her days had always been the same. Why did she feel like a visitor in somebody else's life? The uneasy feeling remained as she walked toward the hut. Nothing seemed out of place, but…

The hut Cialia shared with her father was simple, more hunting lodge than home. The walls were stone, solid but chipped with age. The back wall across from the entrance was mostly dedicated to a large hearth good for cooking and warming the small room. The brick around it was blackened with soot despite being scrubbed weekly by Cialia. Stacked bunks took up most of the wall running along the right side of the room. They awkwardly covered the window there, but father had always cared more about function than form. He was not one to worry over impressing anyone. The left side of the room had another window. This one offered a nice view of the road that followed a winding path to the river. A large wash basin rested beneath it. A simple table—wooden slats and four sturdy legs—sat in the center of the room.

By the time Cialia entered, Agrimon and Marielle were seated across from each other at the table. Marielle was a lovely woman, full-figured the men would say. She always looked like she was heading off to a ball with her fancy dresses, elaborate hairdos, and delicate hats. Cialia always assumed Marielle was sweet on her father—she ran a bakery a full village over but always seemed to be haunting Agrimon's hut with gifts and breads and sweets. That was fine with Cialia. She had never known her mother, and Marielle had no children of her own. The attention seemed lost on Agrimon. He obviously liked her company just fine, but his heart belonged to one he lost.

Something bubbled in the big kettle over the fire. Whatever was in there smelled salty and savory. Cialia's mouth watered at the aroma. Then the sweet cake at the center of the table caught her attention. Marielle had outdone herself. It was beautiful, decorated all fancy with flowers and bows made of frosting. As Cialia took it all in, she suddenly realized it was the anniversary of her birth, the end of her fifteenth summer. She only had a moment to trouble over why the thought had not occurred to her sooner when Marielle stood and embraced her.

"Oh, just look at you," Marielle gushed as she held Cialia at arm's length to admire her. "So tall and pretty. I bet you can't keep the boys away."

"They won't be hanging around my door if they know what's good for them," Agrimon chuckled.

"Oh, Agrimon," Marielle scolded, "what do you have against love?"

"Not one thing," Agrimon shrugged. "I know my daughter better than anyone. Unless they're aiming to trade blades with my beautiful little lass, she won't be interested."

"The trail is my only love," Cialia smiled.

"Never mind that," Marielle frowned. "You have plenty of time to figure out where your path leads. Today is a celebration. Fifteen summers, lass, you are a woman today."

Marielle could barely contain her excitement as she hurried across the room toward a large box sitting on the bottom bunk. Even rushed, the woman moved as if she were dancing, each step more elegant than the last. The box was wrapped in paper, pink, of course, and tied with a frilly, white bow. She could have dumped whatever the box held into a burlap sack as far as Cialia was concerned, but she loved Marielle. Her elegant movements and mannerisms, her warm smile, how excited she got about simple things like sharing a meal with friends, Marielle was a gem.

Cialia's smile grew so big it nearly ran out of face as she took the pretty box from Marielle. She tore into it, destroying the delicate bow and mangling the pretty wrapping. Her smile fled as she flipped the top of the box off. It was a dress, pink lace with white bows just like the cake. Despite a genuine effort to hide her disappointment, Marielle was not fooled.

"You hate it," the sweet woman's smile never faded.

"It isn't that," Cialia lied. "I was just hoping for something a bit more rugged. Father always says his days of adventuring are long over, but I intend to test that claim every chance I get."

"My feelings are not hurt in the least, lass," somehow Marielle's smile grew even warmer. "I am not so foolish to believe Agrimon the titan's daughter would swoon over some frilly thing. Keep this one for those dreadful times you must play the part of the sweet lass. I made you something else I think you might like a bit better."

Marielle danced back to the bunk and grabbed something off the top. Cialia remained skeptical. This one was not a bit less fancy than the first. She managed to keep those thoughts from showing on her face as she gave Marielle a wide smile and accepted the gift. She tore into with the same vigor as the first one. This time, there was no disappointed look. Her excitement was completely genuine.

"These are perfect," Cialia shouted as she held up brown, leather trousers and a white, fabric shirt. She nearly knocked Marielle over when she threw her arms around the woman.

Agrimon laughed, "You've outdone yourself this time, Marielle. Those are perfect for the trail. I fear her days haunting my hut are few."

"This must be just how it feels to have a daughter," a tear slipped down Marielle's cheek, but her smile never left.

Cialia squeezed just a bit tighter, "You have always been like that to me."

"The girl speaks true," Agrimon smiled from the table. "We'd be lost without you, Mari."

"As I would be lost without the two of you, Aggi," Marielle smiled back.

Cialia gave Marielle an odd look before shooting the same at her father, "Mari? Aggi? Father, please tell me you haven't gone cute. I could vomit."

Agrimon shrugged, "I ain't all grizzle and grime. Sweet Mari is my oldest, dearest friend. Never mind that. I've made you something too." He reached under the table and pulled out what looked like an oily pile of blankets.

The bundle beckoned. It looked like something he had found stuffed into a corner of his forge. The fact meant nothing. Agrimon may not have been all grizzle and grime, but there was certainly nothing frilly about him. The wrapping did not matter. Cialia could not wait to tear into the oily mess and find what treasure lay inside. "What is it?" she asked.

"Only one way to know," he chuckled. "Open it up and solve the mystery."

Cialia charged over to the table and began unraveling the thing. The wrapping was completely inconsistent, twisting one way and then the other. At one point, she realized she was wrapping the thing back up rather than unwrapping it. Somehow, the fact only caused her excitement to grow. There was something hard inside. She could not tell what as she padded at it while trying to unwind the mass of oily cloth. Then something sparkled from the dark fabric. It was red and shimmering. It grabbed the light from the fire and splashed it all over the walls of the hut. She gasped as she slowly slid the thing out of the bundle.

The sword was the most amazing piece of weaponry she had ever seen. The scabbard by itself was a work of art. Black leather with a prang tip and a prang collar, both shimmering near as bright as the red gem encrusted to the base of the handle. The handle was prang as well, but it was in the shape of a dragon. Outstretched wings served as the guard, and a dragon's head the pommel. The shimmering jewel sat in the dragon's open mouth, still splashing color all about the room. Between the two, the handle was wrapped in black leather that matched the scabbard perfectly.

"It is beautiful," she whispered.

"My best work," Agrimon replied softly. "Well, come on then. Free that magnificent thing from its cage. You can't see the true beauty of a proper sword without looking upon the blade."

Cialia obeyed her father and slowly slid the sword out of its scabbard. It seemed impossible, but the blade shined even brighter than the gem or the prang handle. She could barely look straight at it, like stealing a glance at the sun. She flicked her wrist a few times going through sword techniques her father had taught her over the years. The balance was unbelievable. It felt like an extension of her arm, just another part of her body.

"You won't find a stronger blade," Agrimon said as Cialia looked on the thing in amazement. "That metal came from that mountain the myths say fell from the heavens. I don't know about all that, but I do know you won't find better stock for forging blades. That sword has no equal in all Ouloos," he paused a moment before adding, "except its mate."

"Its what?" Cialia managed to pull her gaze away from the glorious thing.

"You didn't finish opening your gift," Agrimon grinned. "I didn't teach you to fight with two blades so you could only swing one."

Cialia slipped the sword in her hand back into its scabbard and renewed her search through the bundle of treasures. A few moments later, she held a sword that perfectly matched the first. Crying was not something she normally did. Right at that moment, there was nothing she could do to stop it. Father had always been very clear she could never be a soldier. No army anywhere would have her. Not because she lacked the skill, but because she was a girl. Men fight wars while their women feed them and raise their children. The gift she held in her hand proved he believed that nonsense about as much as she did.

"You look just like your mother right now," Agrimon lost a tear down his rough cheek.

Cialia put the sword down and sat beside her father. She laid her head on his shoulder and asked, "Are you okay?"

He absently wiped at his eyes and put on his best attempt at a smile, "Aye, today is at once my happiest and saddest. The gods saw fit to take the first love of my life and replace her with the next love of my life in the same moment. She would have loved you."

"I wish I could have met her," Cialia's gaze drifted toward the fire.

Marielle sat down at the table across from them. She remained quiet, letting the two process their grief as she sliced up the sweet cake for them. This day was always a tough one for both of them, full of mixed emotions, joy and laughter, sadness and tears.

"They call me the titan," Agrimon chuckled. "I tell you true, she was the titan. We only had a little better than a summer together, and I was broken for most of it, healing from the battle that left me unfit to fight. She took care of me and everything else. There was nothing she couldn't do. She was just like you."

CHAPTER 22
# A TREACHEROUS PATH

The brush was thick and the going slow. Cloudy skies made it near impossible to judge what time of day it might be. Chagon had been at it for days and had no idea where he was or in what direction he was heading. As long as it was away from the terror on the trail, he did not much care. He never wanted to see anything like that again. The sights were bad, broken wagons, bloody, smashed bodies with missing limbs and heads, and piles of things which should remain inside bodies not in the dirt. Somehow, the smell seemed even worse than all the gore. Stale blood had a smell, something metallic. Couple that with the odor of rot, and it got right in your mouth and saturated your sinuses. That is why the direction did not matter. Away was all he really cared about just then. Still, it would be a dream to find a settlement or even a friendly face who might want to share some grub.

He caught sight of a bit of smoke drifting up between the trees. It seemed close enough. Hopefully, it was a settlement. There was no way he could know for sure without investigating. The land surrounding him was completely foreign. The fateful journey to Druindahl marked his first adventure. Prior to fleeing from giants and monsters, the only reason he ever had to leave his farm was trading with folks in other nearby villages. Ouloos ended ten miles in any direction from his gate as far as he had been concerned for most of his life.

The prospect of human contact—and hopefully some food—had him so excited, he failed to notice the large clearing he strolled into. Chagon knew very little about travel but avoiding wide open spaces when you are hoping to avoid grizzly mongs—who seem very fond of traveling along the same trails men used—seemed pretty obvious. Sadly, he was a good many steps into the broad clearing before he even realized it.

"Hey there," a gruff voice beckoned from the darkness at the other edge of the tall grass in between thick banks of trees.

Chagon nearly jumped out of his skin as he crouched low. He felt kind of silly crouched there with nothing to hide behind. "I ain't about looking for no trouble, just lost, hungry, and happy to mind my own business."

"Chagon, is that you?" the voice asked. "I hoped I was not the only one to survive the attack, but it seemed everyone else was dead or fled."

The tension twisting up Chagon's spine eased a bit as he finally recognized the voice belonged to Tarantian. It took a minute to place. He did not sound good. "I ain't found none alive. Must have lost consciousness when my head hit the rock I'd been resting on when I woke. I'd still been a bit woozy, but there weren't no signs of life around them wagons." He peered into the brush and asked, "Where are you hiding in there?"

"I am leaning against a tree just outside the clearing. The going has been slow for me. I have been moving as quickly as I can, but I remain weak from the battle. All I remember is getting slashed across the chest. When I woke, I was in the thick brush alongside the trail. I burned the wound with a hot brand, but I fear infection had already taken hold. I sweat and I sweat, but I get mad bouts of chill. Huddling up with all my limbs close under my cloak is the only thing that keeps me from freezing."

Chagon followed Tarantian's voice while he spoke. The brush was thick, burs grabbed hold of his shirt as thorns scratched and poked. A branch caught hold of his hair. After a bit of crawling, grunting, and the occasional curse, he finally found Tarantian sheltered under the branches of a big pine.

The man looked dead. Chagon's smile faded when he caught sight of the soldier's condition. His skin was pale as a corpse—and an old one at that. There was so much sweat dripping off him, it looked like he had dumped water in his hair and the soaking mess was dripping down his face. The eyes were the worst. They seemed unable to focus on one thing, darting about wildly like the man was caught in a dream, but the lids were wide open.

Chagon quickly removed his cloak and wrapped it around his shivering friend. Those wild eyes finally focused on him. "Chagon," Tarantian whispered, "I knew it was you."

The fact a warrior as stout and mighty as Tarantian recognized his voice had Chagon's cheeks a bit blushed as he replied, "It's an honor to be remembered."

Tarantian shifted and groaned before adding, "You chattered incessantly on the trail. How could I forget you? I hear your voice in my sleep."

"Aye," Chagon's cheeks grew even redder, "I guess I'd been all full of questions. Think you can walk? I saw fires burning not but an hour from here."

"I saw them," Tarantian replied quietly. "That's where I was headed. Not sure what we will be walking into to. The smoke surprised me. That village was abandoned more than ten summers ago. Grongs and amatilazo frequent the area. The trappers who lived there got tired of being beaten or eaten and moved on."

"Maybe there is someone there who can share us some food and help get you back on your feet," Chagon brushed the soaking hair back from the sweating man's forehead.

The hour Chagon had estimated proved to be much longer. He was a brawny lad—and strong as a bull tubber—but Tarantian was brawny too. The wounded soldier struggled as much as he could through the thick brush, but he needed help and required rest often. By the time the forest gave way to kept grass, the night was young, but the sky was quite dark.

The town was well-lit with torches burning brightly on posts along the one road leading through the middle of the place. Big huts lined either side of the road; no better than four on one side and six on the other. There was one large building on the other side of the road. It looked the same as all the other huts, just stretched in both directions.

"Ain't but a few steps more," Chagon assured Tarantian.

A man carried a bundle over his shoulder toward the hut closest to them. He looked clean and fit. Hopefully, he was friendly too. Based on the weight of Tarantian on Chagon's shoulder, the weary soldier was ready to rest again, and both men were ready to devour anything at least closely resembling food.

The man with the bundle noticed their approach. He dropped the bundle and jogged toward them. "Hey there," he began, "you look like you could use some help."

"Aye," Chagon answered. "We'd been fleeing one city ravaged by war to another promising peace and safety. The trail proved to be less promising."

"Your friend looks to be five breaths from the lake at best," the man commented as he looked Tarantian over.

"Grizzly mongs," Tarantian's voice was weak. "They attacked our caravan. I burned the wound to stop the bleeding, but I fear infection's running through my body, fever and sweats."

The man was slight but seemed able. He draped Tarantian's free arm around his shoulders and helped Chagon carry the load. "Come," he said, "we'll take him to Theiron, the healer. He'll know just what to do with them fevers and sweats, trained by Hagen himself they say."

"That will be a great help," Chagon replied. "What do they call you, friend."

"Brinzo," the man replied. "spent most of my life working the docks down in Belscythia. Moved on after a time. Them wharf folk can't be trusted."

The going was easier for Chagon with Brinzo to share the load as they crossed the road toward the large building at the center of the small settlement. The torchlight from the road cast an eerie, orange glow on the place. Dim light escaped from the windows, a few candles at best. The building seemed empty, too quiet for anyone to be about inside. However, they had barely made the steps to jingle the bell next to the front door when it opened and two burly men in loose fitting cloaks stepped out. They took Tarantian from Chagon and Brinzo and carried him into the door. Chagon started up the steps, but the door slammed before he hit the second one.

"Ain't they got no questions for me?" Chagon turned, confusion twisting up his brow.

"Don't fret over your friend," Brinzo reassured him. "That Theiron and his helpers have some odd ways about them, but they'll get your mate back on his feet. Come, you can wait for your friend to heal at my home. We don't get much in the way of visitors being this far from the main road. It'll be a fine distraction to have some stories from the trail to pass the time."

Chagon followed Brinzo across the road toward his hut. He could not give a name to it, but there was an uneasiness creeping around his mind. The two blokes who took Tarantian away had not said a word. They treated his friend with care and all, but a few reassuring comments would have been nice. And the place was so dark. What could they be doing in there? Healers were eccentric to be sure, but something just felt wrong about the place.

Brinzo's hut was luxurious compared to anything Chagon had ever seen. It was a full three rooms. One of them even had a loft above it. The door opened into a small room with a good, sturdy chair and a small table that did not look useful for anything. It was too short to be used for eating. There seemed no viable reason for a table like that. The only thing it would be good for was setting something on if you did not want to hold it while sitting in the chair. There was art on the walls, skins of some sort unlike any animal Chagon had ever seen. They were stretched and decorated with paint like canvases, mostly scenery. One was a sunset, another a mountain underneath a stormy sky. One caught Chagon's attention. It was a man, his hand held aloft above his head holding a human skull. The detail of the piece was incredible. It looked like the man was speaking to the skull, and they both looked like they might jump right off the skin.

"My wife," Brinzo commented, "she loved to paint, said it was her way of keeping in touch with them who have passed on. If you aren't ever forgotten, you can't ever die." He pointed to the adjacent room and added, "That's where she did all that work. She's long left to be with them who went before, but I couldn't bring myself to change it. She haunts the place, and I'd have it no other way."

The room Brinzo pointed to was bigger than the one in which they stood. More art hung on the walls, and tarps covered the floor. An unfinished piece in the center of the room caught Chagon's attention. The skin was stretched out on an easel. A nude woman stood smiling. Her left arm had been severed, and she held it in her right hand offering it to an unfinished man standing before her.

"Them scenes look as real as your face standing before me," Chagon commented. He could not decide if he was more impressed or disgusted by the work.

"Aye," Brinzo agreed. "I wish I had a talent like that. She'd always say the dead spoke to her through them paintings. Can't think of much I wouldn't give to hear her sweet voice again." He gazed into the room where his wife had done her work and reflected a moment before adding, "I maybe can't paint no beautiful scenes like these, but I sure can whip up some grub. Come on, got a nice stew boiling in the pot. Brew my own ale too, like nothing you ever tasted."

Brinzo led Chagon past a ladder that led up to a loft into a room that seemed more familiar to him. Aside from the absence of a bunk, the room resembled his hut back home. There were paintings on the wall and some pots—those were painted to—on shelves that looked like they had no use but for showing off the art on them, but there was a wash basin, a hearth, and a sturdy table at the room's center. A heavy black kettle steamed over the fire in the hearth.

"This feels a bit more like home," Chagon commented as his tension eased a bit. "Ain't but one room in my hut. It ain't so fancy as this with paintings and decorated pots or nothing like that, but it had this same kind of feeling."

Brinzo smiled, "If it weren't for my wife's talent and desire to make everything pretty, this place would probably look a lot more like your home. She'd done all these things before passing on." He pointed to a chair, "Go ahead and have yourself a seat there. Let's get you fed."

Chagon's stomach grumbled as if on cue. His cheeks reddened as he smiled and obliged the suggestion while Brinzo went to a cupboard to grab a bowl. The smell of the stew got his mouth watering. That had to be onion and garlic. He wanted to grab the bowl and dump it down his throat as soon as it hit the table, but that would be impolite. Brinzo was a complete stranger but so warm and welcoming, Chagon did not want to appear unappreciative of the hospitality.

Brinzo must have noticed Chagon's struggle. "Go on then. I know you must be famished from the road. It won't be no slight to me if you dig in and have that hunger satisfied."

Chagon did as instructed. He did not go so far as to ignore the spoon he had been given, but he did begin shoveling stew into his face as fast as he could. Perhaps it was days of too little food and hardly any meat on the trail, but the stew may have been the best thing he had ever tasted. The meat was unfamiliar, but it was tender and not gamey. It had been onion and garlic he smelled, but there was something else with a zing he had never experienced. The meat soaked it all up and nearly melted in his mouth. The carrots and potatoes were like an extra bonus. By the time Brinzo set a mug in front of Chagon, the bowl was empty, and he was sopping up the juice with a hunk of bread.

"You sure were hungry," Brinzo chuckled. "There be plenty more if you'd like another helping."

"Please," Chagon handed the bowl over. "I hope you can forgive me for acting such the animal, but you are right about how famished the trail left me. And that stew ain't like nothing I ever tasted. That meat, it is so tender. What is that?"

"Only what the land provides," Brinzo smiled. "It is all in the preparation."

Chagon took a good long pull off the ale he had been given. It tasted like a standard ale on the surface, but it was strong. Sweetness lingered underneath the base, almost like wine but with a boozy finish. It went down a bit too easily, and Brinzo was refilling the cup a moment after he set a fresh bowl of stew in front of Chagon.

Three bowls of stew and four cups of Brinzo's homemade ale filled Chagon's belly by the time the room started getting swimmy. Though he felt good and drunk, the ale was delicious, and it had been quite a time since he had sat to enjoy some tasty food and drink. He sipped at his fifth cup while Brinzo watched him with increasing intensity.

"You are quite a meaty lad, aren't you?" Brinzo commented.

Chagon finished a sip of ale and chuckled awkwardly. When he realized Brinzo had not made the statement in jest, he replied, "I've been called a lot of things, brawny, stout, strong, but I ain't ever been referred to as meaty."

"But you are," Brinzo smiled as he rose and left the room.

The room dipped and swayed, spinning a bit in one direction before shifting to the other. Chagon looked at the cup in his hand. The ale was strong, but he had put twice that many down on more than one occasion without feeling like he was at sea on a rickety boat during a furious storm. He tried to stand, but his legs would not respond. It seemed he was stuck, as if something held him in the chair.

The walls around Chagon seemed to breathe. The room grew steadily darker as his eyes grew heavy. Everything was nearly black by the time Brinzo returned carrying a heavy set of shackles. "You could probably feed a whole village with the meat you're carrying around on them bones," was the last thing Chagon heard before consciousness fled.

***

Tarantian woke in darkness. He felt better than he had since waking after battling the grizzly mongs on the trail. The room slowly came into view as his eyes adjusted to the dim light. The great room surrounding him was full of cots. It was difficult to see much, but it seemed all the cots were occupied by folks in a similar condition to his. Some even looked dead. He had been so wild with fever and so close to unconsciousness, he failed to notice any of it when they had brought him into the place. He vaguely remembered wet cloths and an awful tasting liquid. There was nothing after that.

A sharp cracking sound grabbed his attention. He had butchered enough fallon to recognize the sound of meat being separated from the hard parts of an animal. As he strained through the darkness to see the man making all that noise, he quickly realized the thing being butchered was no animal. It was a human hand on the carving table not a hoof or talon.

It took every ounce of restraint Tarantian had to keep him from leaping off his cot and lunging at the butcher. The man's back was to him, but he was armed. Though Tarantian was no longer feeling dizzy and chilled or burning up with fever, he lacked sufficient energy to disarm a man that size. How far would he make it across the big room before the brute turned and cleaved him with the small axe he used to chop up that body? He had nearly convinced himself his training as a soldier was enough to get him through despite his weakened condition when he noticed a man shackled to the wall across from him. The man kept his head down to feign sleep, but he managed to make eye contact through the stringy hair dangling in front of his eyes. Those eyes said more than any words Tarantian had ever heard. He decided it best to wait it out, regain as much of his strength as they would allow, and not attack until the time was right.

## CHAPTER 23
## BEHOLD, DRAGONS

A great red streak travelled as far as the eye could see to the north and south. A dirt trail cut across its middle interrupting it. It marked where the Lost Forest—for centuries, a prison for fallen Dragons—had once stood. The trees had vanished when Maelich scattered Kallum to the wind and freed the Dragons, but the red streak remained as a reminder of the wickedness men did in the name of that god. The trail cutting through the red dirt could not have been more than a mile long.

Perrin's group approached the spot where the trees and grass on either side of the trail ceased in favor of burnt red dirt. They rode in two loose columns. Perrin and Glord led the group. Darg and Halogren followed them. Those two often paired up when traveling two by two. Both had dealt with odd looks and whispers from folks who did not know them for too long to recall. Darg had shifty eyes and dirty blonde hair. He also had a set of false teeth carved from wood that were a bit too big for his jaw. He had an unconscious habit of kicking them around his mouth. It was anything but a pretty sight. Halogren's face was covered in scars from a short imprisonment by a pack of exceptionally vicious grongs. Neither was pleasing to the eye. Spending life feeling like their backs were against the wall while the rest of the world actively worked against them had made both men fierce and untrusting.

The two behind them were about as much a contrast as one could imagine. Jorgon—named for a distant cousin who was also a beloved, then damned, former king of Havenstahl—was thin, almost pretty, with soft brown eyes, smooth skin, and a flowing blonde mane that would have most maidens jealous. It would be unwise to think him soft or weak. He was a terror on the battlefield, vicious and unyielding. Ycharaz rode next to him. He was thoughtful, probably the wisest of the group. Despite all the time he dedicated to learning and knowing as much about life on Ouloos and why things are the way they are, he still found time to be one of the best swords in Havenstahl's army.

Ganodin brought up the rear. He was near a giant and had grown accustomed to protecting whatever group with which he happened to ride. Unlike most in Havenstahl's army, the massive soldier fought with a double-bladed axe similar to that which dwarves favor. The only real difference between a dwarf axe and Ganodin's was the size. His was big enough to cleave a full-grown horse clear in half at the waist, and he was strong enough to make that cut. Though he was massive in stature, he was miniscule on conversation. The fact ensured that in any odd-numbered group, he would be the one to ride alone.

Glord raised his right arm to halt the group and said, "Here we are, men, the Lost Forest, or at least what is left of it. Ain't really a forest no more, nothing but dirt. Just the same, we'll be the first men to cross this place in centuries besides Maelich, and he is part Dragon."

Ycharaz urged his horse forward until he sat alongside Glord. He looked over the great red expanse before them and said, "Those are just the stories you have heard. You must dig deeper to have any truth."

"And how do you get at more truth than what everybody already knows?" Glord rolled his eyes.

"You must ask the questions and question the answers," Ycharaz smiled. "Have a go at that red dirt for instance. How do you suppose that dirt got all burnt like that?"

"Asking too many questions is a good way to get your head off in the village where I grew up," Darg shoved his top plate into his cheek before spitting it out the other side of his mouth.

"That loose grouping of crumbling shacks at the edge of the swamp that spawned you could hardly be called a village," Jorgon smirked.

Darg got his teeth back in alignment and smiled a chipped wooden grin back, "Talking about my home like that might be a good way to get your head off too."

Both men laughed before Ycharaz added, "Even still, my words are true. None of the books you've read or men who'd teach you anything around Havenstahl talk about it, but they aren't the only folks who know."

"And who fills your head with all them things none of us simple-minded fools know?" Halogren asked.

"Hagen," Ycharaz shrugged. "He is the wisest man I know. Libraries full of books he has too, the kind of books you have to keep hid."

"Ain't no point in worrying who knows more and who don't," Glord raised his voice.

"Forgive me, general," Ycharaz bowed his head dramatically, "but we are about to walk through a place haunted by tormented souls for hundreds or thousands of years. Might it not be wise to ask some questions about it, like what burnt that ground and made it all red?"

All heads snapped back in surprise as Ganodin's deep voice bellowed, "Dragons."

The rest of the group remained quiet waiting for the rest of Ganodin's thought. Once it was obvious the big man had nothing else to say, Ycharaz broke the silence, "See, that is a viable suggestion. Dragons are like living fire encased in flesh and bones. If that fire had been trapped in the trees that used to stand here, maybe it soaked all through the roots and into the dirt."

Glord shrugged. He, like the rest of the group save Ycharaz, could not have cared less why the dirt was red. "The only thing worrying me right now is what might be on the other side. I expected it would be a longer trek. I ain't ashamed to say I am a bit nervous."

"Aye, the way my husband told the story, I'd have thought that Lost Forest to be miles upon miles. You can see them odd trees on the other side from where we sit," Perrin finally commented.

"Maybe there is an enchantment on the place," Glord remarked quietly. "A short distance can take a long time if something pushes back against you as hard as you push forward."

"Permission to learn the answer for myself," Ycharaz winked at Glord as he gave his horse a kick and took off down the narrow trail running between the red dirt. Nothing happened. He did not burn or float or fall from his mount. The rest of the group watched him charge on down the trail as if it were any trail anywhere.

Perrin was the first to follow Ycharaz down the path. It was not the first time he proved braver or at least more inquisitive than the rest of the men in the group. The way he analyzed everything had her regularly reflecting on the fact she had spent her life taking everything at face value. Things had always been how they had always been. The more time she spent with Ycharaz and his never-ending quest to know more, she found herself no longer accepting *that is just the way things are* as an acceptable answer to any question.

The air of the trail seemed cooler on the path interrupting the great red scar left by the Lost Forest. It was not the result of a stiff northerly wind picking up and dragging cool air down from the barren lands where snow flows free during most of the year. In fact, there was nary a breeze. The air remained as still as it had been. However, it was cool enough to cause Perrin to pull her cloak up closer around her neck. There seemed a presence accompanying the coolness—or at least the memory of one—like the last bits of a horrible dream that remain in front of your eyes even after they have opened. In that brief moment of terror when the hideous thing which frightened you enough to wake you from a deep sleep remains superimposed against the backdrop of your waking life as if the terror had hunted you from that dream dimension into your own is a horror so dark nothing in the waking world could ever compare. Something vile like that lived there once, and the faint memory of it was enough to get Perrin's heart pumping a bit faster.

The rest of the group followed once it became clear neither Perrin nor Ycharaz had any intention of turning around. None of them were the least bit eager to meet a Dragon much less thousands of them. Their slow trot—barely faster than a walk—was evidence of that. It was nothing close to Ycharaz's wild charge down the path. Had Perrin's pace not steadily increased as she moved down the trail, it may have taken them days to make the journey. Duty prevailed—as it has a tendency to do—over the trepidation those grizzled warriors felt at the thought of facing Dragons.

Perrin remained unafraid. The faint memory of whatever terror lingered among the coolness of the trail was insufficient to cause her more than the slightest pause. Recent history had shown her too many horrors to fear the ground regardless of cool air or strange colored dirt, and the wisdom of Dragons was precisely what she sought. Had Maelich not told of the terrifying visions that took control of him when he travelled through that place, she may have been first down the trail. She gave her horse a light kick with her heels and made some time.

Glord and the rest of the men had pressed hard to gain back the ground they had lost on their queen—whether she called herself that or not, they still saw her as such—and had caught up to her by the time they made the other side of burnt, red ground. They found Ycharaz lounging under an odd tree eating something strange and unfamiliar. The bark of the tree seemed too smooth, and it had no branches just big, balmy leaves up at its top. The roundish thing Ycharaz slurped at could have been an apple, but it was more oblong, and the colors were all wrong. The red was lighter than an apple should be, and there was also a bit of green. That would not have been so strange except apples were usually red or green, maybe even yellow, but typically not all three.

"What's that you're shoving in your gob there?" Halogren asked.

"Delicious," Ycharaz grinned with juice dripping down his chin. He tossed one to Halogren and added, "Have a go at that. The skin is thick and kind of bitter, but beneath that is ripe and sweet and juicy. It's like nothing I ever tasted. Careful how deep you bite into the flesh. The pit runs from top to bottom."

"Fool," Glord shook his head. "You know nothing about this place. What if that's poison you're slurping right into your belly?"

Ycharaz shrugged and tossed another toward his general, "How do I know what's good and what ain't without having a taste? Give it a bite. That ain't no poison."

Before long, the entire group had dismounted and began exploring the foreign world they had discovered. The foliage resembled familiar things. Trees like the one Ycharaz lounged beneath sprouted in random patches nothing like a proper forest. Flowers—deep purples, bright yellows, mellow oranges—grew just as haphazardly as the trees. Some of their petals were pointy and straight, while others were long and droopy. Vines bearing some kind of fruit snaked around all of it.

Perrin happened upon a group of smaller trees. These looked like proper trees, similar to the apple trees that grew around old man Kelsho's hut back in the village where she was born. However, the pointy yellow orbs growing on these trees were not apples. She plucked one and bit into its skin. It was firm and sour. It certainly did not taste like something one should eat. She dug her thumbnail in until she reached the juicy meat within and peeled a hunk of that skin off. It tasted nothing like the sweet fruit Ycharaz had discovered. It was sour. Her eyes squinted and it felt like her entire face was tightening up toward her mouth. It was horrible and wonderful at the same time.

When the feeling finally passed and she could speak again, she hollered, "Glord, try this one. Tell me if it tastes horrible or wonderful. I can't tell."

Glord bit into the thing when Perrin tossed it to him. "Yes," he agreed while making a similar face. "It is both horrible and wonderful."

The group explored the area for a bit, finding more things to bite into. There were orange balls with a skin like the yellow things, but the meat inside was sweet. There were bigger yellow balls. They had skins too, but the meat inside was pink. Those were not as sour as the yellow ones, but nowhere near as sweet as the orange ones. Then Darg found something different. It was small, brown, and fuzzy. He did not bother trying to bite into that one without peeling it first. It was green on the inside with little black seeds all about its middle. He shrugged and gave it a taste. It was a bit tart, but pleasantly sweet.

Jorgon flopped down next to Ycharaz and sighed, "I could stay here in this very spot for the rest of my days."

"It is perfect," Perrin agreed as she walked up to the two. "Sadly, the mission calls. It is time we found them Dragons."

"You heard the boss, lads," Glord called out around a mouth of some sweet, white mush he found hidden in a long, dense, yellow wrapper. "Let's move out."

There was a bit of grumbling, but the men gathered themselves up and wrangled their horses. No proper trails cut through the foreign, magical place, so riding was out of the question. None of them cared much. The air was warm, but a wonderful breeze kept it comfortable. Not to mention the fragrant odors it carried. It was perfect for a stroll.

After a good bit of silence Ganodin smiled broadly and exclaimed, "I feel good."

Ycharaz waited a few moments for the rest of the big man's statement before replying, "If you ever find any who might accuse you of being any less than painfully concise, send them my way. I'll set them straight."

Everyone in the group laughed except Halogren and Ganodin. Ganodin frowned at the jest, and Halogren stuck up for him, "I feel good too."

"Aye," Jorgon added once he finished chuckling, "this place is amazing. Why does nobody ever visit?"

"Dragons," Glord replied. "It might be Maelich opened our eyes to all them lies we've been taught about them massive beasts, but that doesn't make them any less frightening if you ask me. Dragon's fire will melt the meat right off your bones before crumbling them to dust."

"Ain't a Dragon who would," Perrin contended. "They are love. And that ain't just the word of my husband. Cialia said the same. Ain't no malice or fury sufficient in no Dragon to free their flame." Then she looked back at Jorgon and added, "This place is hidden to the eyes of men. You have to look at things a certain way to see it. Cialia taught me how to see things that way."

"Then how are we seeing it now? How did we find the trail?" Ycharaz asked. "Cialia ain't taught me nothing."

"Because you accompany me?" Perrin shrugged.

"I suppose we'll never…" Darg stopped dead in his tracks and dropped to his knees. Tears filled his eyes before pouring over his lids. "Dragons," he whispered before sobbing like a starving babe.

There they were, Dragons, thousands of them, majestic, beautiful, and terrifying. Some flew so high they could barely be seen only to swoop back toward the ground faster than any bird of prey. Others lounged about the random clumps of trees. They were so massive it seemed impossible none in the group had noticed them until just then. The sky was full of them, all swimming the air above a lake that seemed a mystery all on its own—a perfect circle of water surrounded by another perfect circle of sand. Nature's beauty typically comes complete with imperfections. The Lake had none. A stony hill jutted up at the far end. The circle of sand ended there, and a Dragon perched atop it overlooking everything like a queen upon her throne.

The group of adventurers surrounded Darg and stopped. There were no more words. Perrin fell to her knees beside Darg and wept along with him. Jorgon did the same. Glord and Halogren drew their swords and stood ready to face the terrifying beasts. Ycharaz stood with them, but his sword remained safely in its scabbard as he drank in the amazing sights. Ganodin's eyes grew wide with terror, and he ran the other way as fast as he could.

The big man got to huffing and puffing rather quickly. He ran as hard as he could for one hundred yards until a voice in his head stopped him in his tracks. "Ganodin," the sweet voice sang to him, "what is it you fear?"

Ganodin fell to the ground and curled up into a tight ball. "Please don't burn me alive," he cried out.

"I love you, Ganodin," the voice reassured. "I could never hurt you."

"You could burn the meat right off my bones and crumble me to dust for the wind to sweep me away," his voice cracked as he cried.

"No, I could not. I told you, great Ganodin of Havenstahl, I love you as I love all things. That love is unconditional. It prevents me from releasing my Flame. I am Lameah. Come to me. Let go of your fear, look in my eyes, and see the love they hold for you," the delicate voice pleaded.

It could have been a trick. Ganodin knew nothing about Dragons except what he had been told. For most of his life, all he knew of Dragons were horrible, terrifying tales of vicious beasts burning men alive and feasting on their roasted carcasses. Still, the voice was sweet, much too sweet for a ferocious beast. Maelich's tales were quite different than the nightmare stories he had been taught. The great savior was another about whom he knew very little. Could the lad of the Lake be trusted any more than Dragons?

Ganodin lay there curled against the soft ground trembling a bit longer before he mustered the courage to open his eyes. The moment he did, he wished he had not. The giant, scaly face before him was nearly three times his size, all scales, horns, and teeth. He would easily fit inside the thing's mouth. He wondered if the beast would even need to bother chewing on him, or if she could swallow him down whole. He could not decide which would be worse.

Lameah turned her head so Ganodin could look in her eye, "Look deep, Ganodin. See the love I described lingering within me."

The frightened soldier had no choice but oblige. The eye was so close he could have stabbed it with his dagger, but he suddenly lacked the desire. There was love deep in that smoldering red eye. It was something unseen, as if it were a portal to feelings rather than sights an eye could see and interpret. The love Ganodin felt just then was precisely as Lameah had proclaimed. It seemed eternal and complete, like no force existed which could diminish its strength in the slightest. Unconditional love.

Fear fled, chased away by an emotion much stronger. The love he felt—unconditional and true—was accompanied by trust, a faith so complete no other feeling could shake it. He loved the Dragon as much as she loved him. Like a child loves and trusts a parent, these feelings were all wrapped up in a deep sense of security. In that moment, he feared nothing. He rested his head against the massive face before him, wrapped his arms as far around it as he could, and quietly said, "Thank you."

Ganodin turned from the Dragon and walked toward the Lake. The sun warmed his face as he turned his chin toward the sky. As he approached his group, he touched each on the shoulder. Glord and Halogren were the first he encountered. "Stow your steel," he said softly, "You have no need for it." Then to Perrin, "Raise your head and behold the glory of this place." Finally, to Darg, Jorgon, and Ycharaz, "Love is all around us, and we are worthy. Lameah told me so." Then he continued toward the Lake with Dragons lumbering all about the ground around him and swimming the skies above.

# CHAPTER 24
# GODS, PRISONERS, AND WITCHES

The cell was cramped with walls so near they seemed to close in on each other. Those walls were made of odd-shaped stone held together with mortar. The stone itself was so wet it seemed to ooze moisture, glistening like tile after a good polishing but without the shine. There were no bars on the thing just an opening to a hall that was equally dingy and damp. Kallum woke in that dark and damp place. His head drooped down to his chest. Dirty hair clung to his cheeks. He saw it in the periphery of his vision and could almost feel the grime against his skin.

Memories flooded in, the hawk, the Dragon, and the lad of the Lake. He had groomed that traitor from birth to be his champion not completely aware of the depths of his failure until the wicked thing plunged his sword all ablaze in Dragon's flame deep into his heart. But that was it, the last thing he remembered before waking in a common thief's cell.

He tried rising to his feet, another failure. His wrists were bound tight with iron cuffs and chained against the wall. That explained the lack of bars. He willed himself free of his bonds, but nothing happened. Glancing down at his clothing only furthered his frustration. His glowing white robe had been replaced with a rough, gray frock. When he found the vermin who dared treat him so callously there would be a reckoning to be certain.

"You look horrible, brother," Ijilv suddenly stood before him bearing the grandeur he had expected for himself. His robe glowed with perfect, white light brighter than a thousand suns. His hair and beard, both perfect and straight, glowed with that same light. And the eyes of a god posed their various contradictions, the absence of light but swirling with all colors at once, both terrible and beautiful to behold.

"I will hunt you to the corners of Ouloos and scatter you to the wind, vile betrayer," Kallum's voice in his own ears served only to deepen his despair. The melodic booming quality it held before he faced Maelich over the Forgotten Forest had fled in favor of a gravelly and rough thing which sounded more fit for a ragged beggar than the king of gods.

Ijilv laughed deep and hearty far longer than the joke deserved if there were a joke at all. Once he had finished the jest he replied, "You will do nothing without my command."

Kallum scowled as he glanced up at his bindings, "The possibility of this crude confinement hindering me is precisely zero. I will free myself from this prison and destroy you with my glory."

"You have no power here, brother," Ijilv approached the bound god and crouched before him. Cradling his brother's face in his hands he added, "You are within me. We are one. You were mighty before the Dragon bested you. Now you are merely a dream haunting my conscious mind, and I have your strength."

Kallum wrenched his head away from Ijilv's embrace, "Impossible. I have always been the strongest of us. This condition is temporary. My will is greater than yours."

"You were powerful, and your will was great," Ijilv stood and crossed back to the hallway, "And now it all belongs to me. Struggle against your bonds, curse me, threaten me with every vile horror you can imagine. None of it will matter. You belong to me now. We are one. You will…" Ijilv was suddenly distracted.

Kallum managed a dry smile, "What troubles you, brother? Do you not believe your own boasts?"

Ijilv gave his brother a wink, "I must attend to other pressing matters. Much has happened since Maelich scattered you to the wind. Cialia has found her flame and vowed to kill all us gods, the castle at Havenstahl has fallen, I used the visage of your priests to destroy Maelich's supposed father and break his fragile mind, and I used those same priests to steal his son. The infant Dragon's power, like yours, belongs to me."

"Lies," Kallum's eyes were suddenly keen. "You have never been so ambitious, hiding out here at the edge of nothing in a broken tower abandoned by a failed magician."

"If only you were as wise as you were strong. Where you see nothing, I see everything," the god smirked and was gone.

Ijilv materialized in a small, circular room atop a tower taller than anything else ever made by men. It had once belonged to men as his brother had alluded, but that was before Kallum had spoken the words, "No more magic," and the elemental mysteries were lost to those who believed it.

Four obelisks surrounded a sleeping young man. A glowing orb hovered above each of the four pillars. Each transitioned from the darkest black to the brightest white so quickly the two conditions seemed to travel simultaneously down a parallel path rather than exist during separate intervals, one replacing the other and so on. Geillan, the young man hovering between the obelisks, had been a babe only weeks prior. Every day he grew, and every day his will became stronger. With each passing moment, it became increasingly more difficult for Ijilv to maintain control of the sleeping creature.

"Soon, my child," Ijilv smiled, "soon I will unleash you on this world and all will burn in the brilliance of your flame." He closed his eyes and addressed the presence which had drawn him away from his brother's cell, "Why are you here?"

Moluam stepped out from behind one of the obelisks near Geillan's head. Her hair was a mass of luxurious black waves. The face peeking out from those random curls carried the wisdom of a thousand generations without losing the soft, innocent beauty of youth. The gown she wore was as black as her hair and seemed to move under its own will. She looked at the sleeping young man and commented, "He is growing so fast. How much longer can you control him?"

"Time works differently here. That is what drew me to this place," Ijilv commented. "You need not worry about the boy's size nor his strength. I have consumed the god. Kallum is with me and under my command. My strength has doubled since last we spoke, and soon it will grow again. Cialia battles with Brerto as we speak. Soon he will be one with me as well."

"I pray you are correct," she replied without much confidence.

"I am," Ijilv grew bored with the conversation. "You have yet to explain your presence in this place."

"I have found the lost Dragon," she touched Geillan's face as she spoke. His skin grew brighter where her fingers connected with it. "Maulom interfered. It seems he is filling Maelich's fragile head with nonsense."

The god moved around the room until he stood next to her looking down on Geillan. Then he said, "Maulom has his role, and you have yours. That is how it has always been. Why should this mission be any different? He will drive Maelich on toward his inevitable meeting with the fabled red people, and you will help him understand his pain. He will feel the pain of all the faces you show him in time, but now is not that time. You and Maulom must continue your game, your forever dance. The lad of the Lake must be completely broken when he faces my Dragon, his son."

"I hope for all our sakes this game you are playing ends the way you expect. It seems not all the players are playing by the same rules," Moluam replied.

"There have been surprises to be sure," Ijilv nodded, "but everything is proceeding as it should. Keep to your task. Men and dwarves and giants and all the other creatures who inhabit this place will continue to kill each other. When they do it to the ones he cares about, you show them to him."

CHAPTER 25
# BEYOND CONTROL

Hiding, sitting idle, and waiting for others to act is something most despise. It is worse for a god. Unfortunately for Moshat and Kaldumahn, hiding away on their thrones protected behind multiple levels of enchantment to keep out the prying eyes of even the most powerful of creatures had become their lot. Cialia was a force of nature, and she had made it her mission to kill the gods.

Kaldumahn looked to his brother and said, "The loose Dragon battles the great tiger, and our brother is winning."

"But for how long?" Moshat asked as he absently toyed with his white beard. "He has her trapped in a spell. Will he maintain the illusion until the end of time? We should attack him now while Cialia has his attention. Together we could destroy him."

"Folly," Kaldumahn scoffed. "Once that Dragon is loose from Brerto's spell, she will turn her rage on us. I would never presume to speak for you, but I certainly would prefer not to be scattered to the wind as was our brother, Kallum."

Moshat shook his head in disgust, "Your cowardice stinks like flesh rotting in the sun."

Kaldumahn was undaunted by the barb but changed the subject just the same. "What about the new eagle I faced over the castle at Havenstahl?" he asked.

"If you are truly convinced it was not Kallum you faced in the skies over that broken place, it could only be Ijilv," Moshat shrugged.

"As much as I wish I could disagree, I fear your words ring true,"

Kaldumahn smoothed a hand over his white beard. "If it is, he is even more powerful than Kallum."

Moshat considered the idea for a moment as he looked out over the smooth stone surrounding them. When he and his brother had envisioned the place, it was a stronghold, a fortress. Hiding from their enemies made it feel more like a prison. Neither dare leave for fear of the great powers stalking Ouloos. "Should we confront him?" he finally asked.

"Could we defeat him even together?" Kaldumahn provided no answer.

"We cannot know that until we face him," Moshat replied soberly. "I would prefer that to cowering in a hole."

"Whether we could defeat our brother means very little. We cannot find him. That tower he likes to haunt at the edge of Ouloos and time has vanished. I have looked everywhere for him. All my attempts have failed. He and his tower are nowhere," Kaldumahn shifted in his throne so he faced his brother.

"Show me," Moshat replied.

Instantly, the two gods stood at the edge of a constantly shifting landscape. A black expanse stretched before them interrupted only by stars, moons, and shifting lights. The spot where they stood was the exact spot where the tower at the edge of time had stood for centuries. Now it was gone.

"He hides as we do," Moshat sighed.

"He does," Kaldumahn agreed, "and we should scurry back off to our pit."

Moshat looked out at the cosmos, the vast expanse stretching for eternity before them. It was different there than west of the Lake where stars and planets traveled set paths across the black sky. The scene before him was chaotic, celestial bodies forming out of nothing while others evaporated or blinked out of existence. Those which remained for any amount of time followed no obvious rules. They zigged this way before spinning that. Some slammed into others and pushed them off course. It was a macabre dance orchestrated by an insane choreographer.

"I feel sick looking at this chaos," the god whispered.

"Nonsense, we do not feel things like that," Kaldumahn argued.

Moshat closed his eyes, "What you say is true. However, what I feel in this very moment staring at the violent fury before my eyes is precisely what I have heard men describe as sick. We have no control of the events unfolding."

"We do not," Kaldumahn agreed. "However, we must remain vigilant. Never forget the vow we made to each other. No matter what events unfolded or what dramas Ouloos or our brothers created to torment each other or us, we would not intervene in the course of the physical unless our brothers did the same."

"And what does Ijilv do right at this moment?" Moshat slapped his hand against his forehead. "The time for heartfelt declarations has long since passed, brother. Havenstahl has fallen. Giants threaten that great city from the west while grizzly mongs and other even more horrible things threaten from the north and the south. Maelich is lost. Ijilv has dropped his disguise and proclaimed himself our enemy. The child who is key to all of this is lost beyond our reach. Now is the time to act."

"That sounds like fear. We are gods, brother. We do not fear. The Dragons are safe, guiding souls home to the Lake. Ijilv occupies himself with Brerto while that pathetic worm occupies Cialia. I agree we should not sit idle but attacking the Dragon or our brothers would be folly. The cities of Havenstahl and Druindahl still worship us. They are key to our strength. We must bolster the forces of Havenstahl and prepare them for the coming storm. I have seen a great army marching from the south. Armies of men from the great coastal cities all march together to aid in the defense of the greatest city of men. They need our strength," Kaldumahn placed his hand on his brother's shoulder as he finished.

Moshat sighed long and deep. He did not like it one bit but said, "Fine, brother, we will try it your way. You will travel to Druindahl and test their readiness, while I venture to Havenstahl to reinvigorate their resolve. But if we fail…" he trailed off.

"We will not," Kaldumahn's tone carried as much confidence as he could muster just then. "We cannot."

## CHAPTER 26
## RAGE AND SADNESS

The sacred pine soared up toward fluffy clouds lazily strolling across a blue sky. It still had scars from the shackles Ahm used to torture subjects who failed to follow his rule. Removing the metal straps, chains, and the spindle to pull a dwarf body across the massive tree had been Doentaat's first act as king after Maelich had cut down the cruel giant, Ahm. Bindaar touched one of those scars. That had been the lowest point in his life, the moment he realized what a waste he had become. In some strange way, it had also been his highest point. No dwarf had ever regarded him as anything more than a useless waste of space. The only one who had ever shown him any kind of love had been Doentaat, and that was clearly due to pity not any kind of admiration or respect. That changed while the heavy chains that left the scars on the massive tree had tugged his arms and legs out near to the point of dislocation. It may have been pity in the eyes staring upon him that day, but it looked close enough to caring that it changed the way he saw himself. When Maelich came to set him free, to set Alhouim free, that was the stiff kick in the rump he needed.

Bindaar strained his neck to look up through the branches. The top was too high for him to see from where he stood. It was the tallest tree on Mount Elbahor. No one had ever measured it, but it had to be at least four hundred feet tall. Dwarf myths say the tree was planted as a gift to the fairies who lived on the mountain before dwarves came to carve it up and free the precious pord it housed deep in its bowels. The dwarf is never named in the story, only ever referred to as the first one.

It was a great story to tell young dwarves around a fire, but Bindaar never really believed it. Fairies were made up, some fanciful dream of a dwarf high on fairy weed more likely than not, and if the first one had been a real dwarf someone would remember his name.

"They should be here any moment," Lentaak's voice startled Bindaar out of his reminiscing.

"Damn your quiet feet," Bindaar jumped.

Lentaak failed to hide his smirk, "Forgive me, general. I sent word to Ghordaan to prepare a bed for the king."

Bindaar's eyebrows dipped so deep they nearly reached his nose, "I told you to call for Hagen."

"As I did, but Hagen is out to field assisting as many as he can. The injured are strewn about the hills and forests. His tents overflow with the injured," Lentaak shrugged.

"We should count ourselves lucky Ghordaan is with us and not out to field with Hagen," he sighed. "The report Daanlioc gave before losing his consciousness to fever was grim. Three besides him and a dying king is not what I wanted to hear."

Before Lentaak could attempt any reassuring words, he noticed a small group approaching on the road. "There," he pointed.

Three dwarves slowly trudged up the hill toward the tree. With brown tunics ratty and torn and blood-stained beards equally disheveled, the group appeared to have lost everything they had to the trail. Even the sturdy pony looked less than a whisper from the Lake. Bindaar gave the briefest moment of concern for their condition. The body strapped to the light brown pony was what really concerned him. He knew it was his king and former housemate fastened there, and the body was completely still. They were still a good way down the trail making it difficult to ascertain anything about Doentaat's condition, but Bindaar suddenly felt sick in his stomach and tasted bile at the back of his throat. He ran toward them.

As Bindaar neared the group, Glaadrian jogged up to meet him. The concerned look, outstretched arms, and reassuring nonsense the dwarf babbled on with only served to increase his fear. None of what Glaadrian was saying registered in his head. The words did not matter anyway. He knew his oldest, dearest friend was dead as soon as he had made eye contact with Glaadrian. By the time the two met in the trail, the sick feeling in Bindaar's stomach proved stronger than his will. He spilled the contents of his gut out onto the dirt splattering Glaadrian's boots as well as his own.

"Bindaar, calm down please," Glaadrian's voice sounded as if it were coming from inside his own head which had suddenly began throbbing. His eyes burned like he had stared at the sun for hours, and the tears came. He did not care who saw it. He wept, and he howled. He pounded his fists into the dirt and screamed. Glaadrian had kept talking, but Bindaar logged none of the information the sound carried to his ears. It was all just noise.

Then he felt a hand on his shoulder. It was a gentle touch, but it burned him to his very soul. Condolences were the last thing he wanted. What good were they? He wanted revenge. He wanted to chop down giants, stab trogmortem, and rip grongs limb from limb. They would all die.

He grabbed hold of Glaadrian's arm, dragged the dwarf close enough the tips of their noses touched, and growled, "We will kill them. We will kill them all."

The raging dwarf rose back to his feet dragging Glaadrian with him. Then he tossed the solida into the trunk of a thick pine. More gentle hands, more consolation, and Lentaak's voice soothing and reassuring in his ear. He spun, grabbed him by the collar, and pounded his forehead into the poor dwarf's nose. Everything was red as he charged toward the two dwarves accompanying the pony—a sorry mount for a dead king.

Muljaak was the first. Despite being a full head taller than Bindaar and stout enough to cradle the dwarf general in his arms like a baby, he raised his hands in submission and backed away from Bindaar's rage. Whether or not Muljaak wanted to fight was immaterial. Bindaar did. He charged the big dwarf and rammed him in the gut with the top of his head. The attack left him woozy, but it sent Muljaak tumbling down the hill. Chialdaan tried to help but earned only fists for his effort. Bindaar left him with a black eye and a sore jaw.

Everything remained red before Bindaar's eyes. Logic had fled. All he wanted was to hurt something, anything. In some hidden place in the darkest, deepest depths of his mind, he probably realized he would come to regret the abusive behavior once his wits returned. The idea was completely inaccessible in that moment. All he knew just then was rage, furious, stomping, spitting rage. And then he saw Doentaat. The swollen, bruised, and battered thing barely resembled the face of his old friend, but he knew it was him. A pitiable cry roared from his mouth as his eyes leaked water and globs of snot dripped from his nose. He cut the ropes holding the king in place and dragged him down from his mount.

"I told you," he shouted at Doentaat's dead face. "I told you to stay here, stay in the castle and let your generals do the work of pushing the monsters back to the sea."

Nothing else mattered in that moment. The king was dead. Doentaat was dead. It did not matter how much Bindaar shouted, how many tears he cried, or how many times he pounded his dead friend in the chest. He would still be dead. He remained there, crying, shouting, and pounding his fists until he ran out of energy. Then he just laid his head down on Doentaat's chest and cried.

He should have taken time to think. He should have met with the other generals and planned a proper response. He should have sought advice. He did none of those things. Instead, he stood up, wiped his eyes, and growled to the sad group who he had just abused, "Round up all available solidas and prepare them for battle. We march at dawn." His eyes became slits as a sneer crept onto his face, "Do any of you have anything to say about that?"

None did but Glaadrian. "No prisoners. No mercy. We kill them all," he growled through a deep scowl.

## CHAPTER 27
## SOUND THE ALARM

The sky above Tiegran was a thick bank of gray as he sat on a log scraping mud off the bottom of one of his boots. The ground was already good and soggy from rains the prior evening, and the air smelled like more was on the way. A slight rumbling distracted Tiegran from his work. He would have thought it was thunder, but the ground trembled enough to wobble the thick log beneath his rump. It was a subtle vibration but undeniable. There were only two things he could think of that could make the ground vibrate like that, a herd of wild tubber—there were no wild tubber for miles and miles in any direction—or giants.

Tiegran barely had time to panic over the idea giants were marching on the castle when Tarturan ran by him, sword drawn and shouted, "Giants march on Havenstahl. To the castle, men. Form up on the high ground."

More men ran by shouting similar things. Some looked ready for war. Others looked ready to cry. As Tiegran struggled back into his boot, he decided he was the former. Standing shoulder to shoulder with Daritus the giant slayer, he would chase glory until he found it on the battlefield, or the quest led him to the Lake. Whichever ended up his destination, he would fight with everything he had until he arrived. Hopefully, someone would tell stories about him in the orange glow of a healthy fire someday.

By the time Tiegran made it up near the main gate, hundreds of men had already formed into tight columns in front of it. Daritus ranged up and down the ranks shouting out the glory of Druindahl and Havenstahl. Even limping the man appeared invincible.

Tarturan grabbed a hold of Tiegran's arm and tugged him into the formation shouting, "You are with me. We fight until we have no fight left."

The columns grew as men poured in from every direction. By the time the steady current of bodies rushing up the hill or from the castle or the trees surrounding the road up to the main gate slowed, more than three thousand men stood ready to fight with at least one hundred more on horseback. Some were grizzled men with years of battle reflecting in their hardened stares. Others were green, new recruits with fear in their eyes and innocence in their hearts. Tiegran thought back to his first battle. It had not been that long ago, and he remembered the feeling all too well, the fear in the eyes of those green recruits. It was nothing like what he felt standing in front of the gate at Havenstahl next to Tarturan. A chill of excitement shot up his spine. *I have goosebumps.* He nearly laughed out loud.

He looked over at Tarturan whose smile was just as big and shouted, "For Havenstahl!"

It nearly brought tears to his eyes when the group of soldiers formed up with him replied, "For Havenstahl!"

"For Druindahl," he shouted back at them.

"For Druindahl," they answered.

Tarturan let out a war cry as his heavy hand gave Tiegran's shoulders a stiff pat. The crowd responded in kind. Tiegran hoped the giants could hear them. He hoped they knew Havenstahl would never surrender. As long as one man drew breath, they would fight until the Lake called them home.

Tiegran finally caught Daritus' eye through the crowed. The general, the legend, gave him a wide smile and nodded. Tiegran shouted with all his might, "For Ouloos!"

The crowd answered, "For Ouloos!"

Then Daritus called the command, "Charge!"

A small group of giants had just rounded the bend onto the road into Havenstahl as three thousand screaming warriors began their charge down the hill. Behind them, the mounted men waited. Once the two forces engaged, they would circle up the invaders and cut them down.

At the bottom of the hill, there was no screaming, no charging, and no clashing of blades on shields. There was a bit of fear. Bom shot Kantiim a pleading look, "Is this a trap? I trusted you."

"Betrayed," Lito-Bi commented.

"No," Kantiim reassured him, "this is no trap. They do not know of our truce. Remain here. I will ride up and meet them."

Kantiim's words did little to calm the group with the rumble of thousands of feet stampeding down the hill toward them, and the clang of swords being slammed against shields. At least they hadn't time to bring out the drums.

"What choice have we?" Bom asked.

"Please," Kantiim pleaded. "Though it seems otherwise, you have nothing to fear. Hold your white flag high, and I will stop the charge."

Once Kantiim dug his heels into his horse's sides and got the beast moving up the hill, he quickly realized how little he believed his own words. The mass of bodies charging toward him was terrifying, and they were his men. If they were enemies, he may have fled in the other direction. As it was, he shouted, "Halt." Despite boasting a booming voice perfectly adapted for barking orders on the battlefield, the command was lost beneath the sound of the charging horde.

"Halt," he shouted again and again, but still they charged.

Finally, he halted himself and held his sword high above his head. The group slowed. He shouted, "Halt," again. They did not oblige his command, but they did slow further.

Then, finally, a glimmer of hope. He heard Daritus' voice raised above the rest, "Kantiim, dare you stand against Havenstahl?"

"I would die first," Kantiim shouted. "Stand down, old friend. The small force from Biggon's Bay comes under a white flag seeking peace. I promised them as much."

Daritus called out, "Hold," to the men at his back and approached Kantiim. "And you trust them despite their vile conduct in all the battles they have waged against us since they arrived on our shores? They have no honor. Our dead lay festering, decomposing in fields of carnage, and you lead them right to our gate?"

Kantiim dismounted and walked up to meet him. "I do," he replied as the two neared each other. Noticing Daritus had yet to stow his blade, he asked, "Shall I prepare to defend myself? Would you cut me down for accepting refugees fleeing a violent death, or attempting to broker a peace with a potentially valuable ally who could tip the horribly uneven scales of this war back toward our favor?"

Madness danced about Daritus' eyes as he circled Kantiim treating him more like an adversary than an old friend and faithful general, "That depends on your reasoning for guiding a pack of filth from across the Great Sea to our gates under your protection."

"You are one of my oldest and dearest friends. I would never draw my sword against you except to defend myself from the fury of your blade. Please do not force me to do that. The prospect of battle may have your blood boiling, but your fight with Bok in the great waste left you unfit for battle. You cannot beat me, and our men cannot see you fail. Our numbers are far too small to allow them to lose their belief that a slayer of giants is the man leading them into battle," Kantiim grew increasingly tired of the treatment.

After a few deep breaths, the wildness began to leave Daritus' eyes. Within a few moments he stopped circling. A few moments after that, he finally stowed his blade and said, "Fine, tell me why you believe we should trust these monsters."

"Why not call the men to hold and come see for yourself?" Kantiim shrugged.

"Men, hold," Daritus shouted up the hill. Then he turned back to Kantiim and said, "Lead the way."

Packed in the middle of three thousand men wild with adrenaline and ready to cut down anything that got in their way, Tiegran slowly deflated. "Why would we hold?" he asked Tarturan.

"The white flag they fly might have something to do with it," Tarturan shrugged.

The answer failed to satisfy the young soldier. White flag or not, he had witnessed too much blood and too much suffering to accept any kind of peace. He was camped just outside Fort Maomnosett when the boulders crashed through the walls and crumbled the thing to dust. He lost many friends that day, friends crushed in a cowardly attack with no chance to defend themselves. The bastards at the bottom of the hill had a debt to pay. Tiegran intended to collect.

Tiegran worked his way through the formation until he stood alone in front of it. He stopped there for a moment watching his general, the legend, the giant slayer walking toward those monsters who killed so many of his kin with his sword stowed. A tear teetered on his eyelid for a moment before rushing down his face. He licked it away when it hit his lip. Something deep in the saltiness of it tasted like betrayal. It was more than he could stand.

He barely heard the words, "Tiegran, stand down," leave Tarturan's lips as he sprinted down the hill with his sword raised. Those had probably been Tarturan's fingers trying to grab his sleeve, but he paid them no mind. He was not sure in that moment exactly what he was going to do. Attacking his general would be treason. Disobeying a direct order would also be treason. He was fairly certain the latter was his plan, so what was the difference?

Tiegran had nearly reached Kantiim and Daritus when he heard the sound coming from his own mouth. It was an unconscious thing. Something hovering between battle cry and pitiable wail. If sorrow, anger, and betrayal all smashed together had a sound, that was what poured from his mouth. By that point, the young soldier had decided he would not attack his own, regardless of their betrayal. His plan was to run right past them and attack the invaders. When Kantiim spun and drew his blade, Tiegran knew that plan would fail.

"You were commanded to hold, soldier," Kantiim growled.

Daritus recognized the young warrior, "Tiegran, what is the meaning of this assault?"

Two generals known far and wide as titans on the battlefield stood with swords at the ready. Right at that moment, Tiegran's hurt and rage and woe and feelings he had no names for dimmed enough for him to recognize the folly of his actions. His feet slipped as he tried to stop himself. The wet ground would not allow it. Just before he was close enough for Kantiim to have his head off with a clean swing of his blade, his face was squishing into the wet ground. It did not spend much time there. A moment later, he was effortlessly lifted from the ground. The sloppy muck of the road was a full six inches beneath his feet when he finally released his grip on his sword.

"What in Dragon's Fire has gotten into you?" Tarturan's voice still sounded sweet even as it shouted into his ear.

"I cannot stand by and watch these monsters spoil the dirt my friends died defending," Tiegran replied, his voice barely more than a choked whisper as his collar dug into his throat.

"Let him down," Daritus commanded before Tarturan could shout anything else into his ear.

"How could you?" Tiegran hissed. The words had barely passed his lips when Tarturan's massive hand connected with the back of his head. The man hit like a bull tubber charging with a full head of steam.

"Tarturan," Daritus scolded, "that is enough. Let his voice be heard."

"Raising a sword against your commander is treason," Tarturan argued.

"It is," Daritus agreed. "I would like to hear him answer for it. How will he do that if you knock the wits out of him?" He turned to Tiegran and added, "Well, now is your chance. Let your accusations be heard."

Tiegran shot Tarturan a look as he fixed his collar. Then he looked at his general and prepared to spew forth a big pile of venom on him. However, when he opened his mouth, the words refused to come. The thoughts were in his mind. The pain squeezed his heart. Articulating these things, that was tricky. He struggled to define exactly what he felt in that moment. The best he could come up with was, "You broke my heart."

Daritus gave him a dry smile. "I understand your pain. Do you suppose I feel differently? The beasts standing at the bottom of this hill showed my men no mercy, no honor," he paused and pounded his chest, "My men, mine. Men who look at me with admiration in their eyes like you did. How do you think that feels? This man," he pointed at Kantiim, "is more than just a general in my army. He is a friend, a trusted confidant. I have never known a man who provides wiser counsel. When this man whom I love and trust with my life stands before me ready to trade blades over any topic, I am nothing more than a fool if I fail to at least listen. Believe me, there is nothing I want more than to charge down this hill and cut those bastards down right where they stand, smear their vile blood all over the soggy soil. But…" he trailed off as he looked first down the hill, then at Kantiim, and finally back to Tiegran before he finished, "they ride under a white flag. That means something to me. It means something to any honorable man."

"So, their vile acts against our city, your men, remain unpunished," Tiegran spat.

Daritus sighed, "The fact they come to us seeking peace gives me hope they already punish themselves. Fleeing your post is as treasonous as raising a sword against your general, and most are far less forgiving than the one standing before you. It is a bold thing they did, and I want to hear why."

Tiegran remained unmoved, "We should grind them into the dirt beneath our feet."

"We could do that," Daritus nodded. "We could ignore that white flag and destroy them. It would feel good. The men would revel in the victory. We would celebrate over their rotting corpses," he paused to look down at the group of invaders, "but we would be no better than them. You would soar high for a time, but eventually you would recognize how empty it was. They have already surrendered. We have the high ground. We outnumber them nearly five to one. Is that the kind of vengeance you seek? It is not the kind of vengeance I seek. I forgot that for a moment," he glanced over at Kantiim before adding, "Luckily, an old friend reminded me. That does nothing to dim the pain I feel over what we have lost, nor does it dampen the rage I feel about what they did. Are you willing to take a chance with me and listen to what they have to say?"

Tiegran scratched his head. He honestly was not sure how he felt about it. Every shred of his being boiled with the urge to charge down the hill and kill them all, alone if necessary. He would fight with everything he had until he was dead, or they were all dead. And yet, Daritus' words made sense. The group had surrendered. Was he no better than the monsters who cowardly attacked in the dead of night? After a few moments of wrestling with the competing ideas in his head, he finally agreed, "I do not like this one bit. No, I hate it, but I am willing to listen. I wish not to be as low as the monsters we face."

The tension among Bom's group was thick by the time the four men approached. Kantiim's men felt it just as strong. There were only nineteen of them. If the fragile calm among the giants and trogmortem they accompanied broke, they would all most certainly die. They would be avenged swiftly. However, the truth about avenging is it really only helps those doing the avenging toward closure on what they lost. The dead remain dead, completely unaware of the effort.

Bom looked over at Ychorell and asked, "What do you make of this?"

"Best I can tell, them men had a mind to charge down this hill and cut the lot of you down, but Kantiim swayed them off that idea," Ychorell replied.

Lito-Bi added, "Though we seek peace, we will fight if the need arises."

"I would expect nothing less," even seated high upon his horse, Denigran had to look up to wink at the massive trogmortem. "If I know my general as much as I believe I do, the decision as to whether this day ends in battle is completely up to you."

"If your words are true, there will be no battle," Stekka-Ha interjected.

"Welcome to Havenstahl," Daritus' said as he approached. "I am Daritus of Druindahl. I lead the armies of both fair cities. Please forgive the poor reception, but giants approaching the city I defend has recently become reason enough to sound alarms."

"Daritus the giant slayer," Bom's tone was flat as he sized the small man up. "I would not believe it true had I not witnessed it with my own eyes, but you killed my father."

"Have you come to challenge me in the name of honor?" Daritus asked soberly.

Bom chuckled dryly, "No. You met my father on the battlefield. It was a fair fight, and you bested him. On that day, with sorrow and rage fresh in my heart, I would have crushed you. Today, I carry no ill feelings. On the contrary, what I am feeling might be considered admiration. My father was a terror. I cannot say for certain I would have been so bold as to stand against him as you did."

Daritus shrugged, "You might if it meant the safety of your kind. Speaking of which, my good friend speaks of truces and peace, but I have always been a bit skeptical. Why should I trust you?"

Bom dropped to one knee and bowed his head, "I pledge my might and my wits to Havenstahl. I am at your command. My grandfather seeks to destroy your fair city, take your land, and move on to take Alhouim back believing it to be his rightful city of Maomnosett. All who accompany me are tired of fighting to steal land." He paused and raised his head to look Daritus in the eye, "I wish to see your people free from this terror. I oppose my grandfather and his ideals."

"The aid is welcome," Daritus scratched his head, "but what do you expect in return? We have very little to give right now. As you can see, most of our resources are pouring into reconstructing our city."

"Nothing," Bom replied flatly. "After we have turned back those who have invaded your lands, we ask only for safe passage back to the bay and enough ships to take us home."

Kantiim nodded when Daritus glanced back at him. The gesture carried more meaning than anyone who saw it understood. The damage even a few giants and a few hundred trogmortem could cause within the city gates was monumental. However, they desperately needed the assistance.

"Rise," Daritus finally said. He failed to realize he probably should have waited to give the command until after delivering his next line. When Bom stood, Daritus' head stood nearly level with the giant's belly button. That didn't stop him, "If you betray us, or give me any reason to regret this agreement, we will cut you down."

"It is my goal to earn your trust," Bom nodded.

Daritus looked over at Tiegran, "Are you satisfied with this arrangement, or have you anything to add."

Fear had finally gained equal footing with the rage Tiegran felt. Though he had seen several giants roaming the battlefield that day in front of Fort Maomnosett, he had not been near enough to any of them to fight or even get a fair estimation of their size. The monster looming above Daritus was the smallest of his group, and still towered over even massive Tarturan. He pushed that fear deep into his gut, raised his head high and confidently proclaimed, "If your words turn out to be untrue, it will be my sword you die upon."

The words sounded laughable to Tiegran as they left his mouth, but the giant did not even crack a smile. He simply nodded and said, "If I betray your trust, the sentence will be earned."

# CHAPTER 28

# BEWARE THE BLACK HORSE

The cave was cool and damp, a stark contrast to the hot dry air outside of it. Torches blazing along the rocky walls had shadows dancing all up and down them. Maelich sat near a modest fire turning a spit with a hunk of meat dribbling and spitting juice down into the flame. He had grown accustomed to the meat. It was bland, not bad, but nothing like tubber. Ding called the animal chukwoka, but Maelich thought they resembled grongs. Chukwoka were smaller, had long tails, no scales, and walked around on four legs. Beyond that they were nearly identical.

"Ding asked after you," Maulom broke the silence and startled Maelich out of his thoughts. "They see less and less of you."

Maelich smiled, "Ymitoth is a much better trainer than I, far more patient."

"You seem troubled," Maulom sat down on a rock across the fire from Maelich. The flickering flames cast eerie shadows about his face and gave his white hair an orange glow. He filled two cups from a jug and offered one to Maelich, "Here, give this a try. It is just ready to drink. It will nicely accompany your meat."

Maelich accepted the cup and gave it a sip. It had a berry flavor with a bit of a boozy finish, "That is nice. What is it?"

"My own recipe. I call it flower of the sunburnt soul. Something like the ale you are accustomed to in the north, but I brew it with berries. Not much grows out here, but these exceptionally hearty berries grow in thick shrubs near the river. They are the very same berries the Shaiwah use to paint their bodies and protect them from the blistering sun," Maulom took a good long drink and then asked, "Now, tell me what is it that troubles you?"

Maelich set his cup down and pulled the meat from his spit. It was hot on his fingers. He had taken to cooking the meat a little long after getting a sour stomach from a batch he failed to heat sufficiently. He placed the meat on a fired clay dish and set it to the side to cool. Then he took another sip of Maulom's flower of the sunburnt soul and said, "Nothing I can really give a name to, visions mostly, stirrings, like the beginning of an idea that has yet to fully form."

"That black horse put those things in your head," Maulom scoffed.

Maelich shrugged, "That is when these feelings, or whatever they are, began. The thing troubling me so is they feel like they belong, like they have always been, not something that was shoved in there by some other being. They feel like memories begging to be recalled."

"Forget all that," Maulom waved the idea off as if he were swatting a pest. "That black horse is nothing but a witch. These feelings you are having are merely ghosts of ideas seeping up from kernels she has planted in your subconscious. They brew there, leaking their essence and making you believe they belong to you."

"You seem to know much about how the conscious mind and the subconscious mind work together. I do not. All I am certain of is the face she showed me looked familiar to me. I cannot explain why, but I even had a name to go with that familiar face. It felt like home. If what you say is true, how could these kernels you suggest have time to leak their anything into my conscious mind if she only appeared to me just then?" Maelich remained skeptical.

Maulom flashed a condescending smile, "Time moves differently in the subconscious. A lifetime to the conscious mind can be less than a moment in the subconscious, and the exact reverse is equally true. Though tethered, the two are as different as the darkest night and the brightest day."

Maelich's focus shifted to the chukwoka which had finally cooled enough to eat. He bit a chunk off and chased it with some of Maulom's home brew. It was a nice accompaniment. The berry on the front side somehow brought a bit of flavor out of the bland meat.

After a few moments of silence interrupted only by the sounds of Maelich eating, Maulom finally picked the conversation back up, "Do not fret over the black horse or the things she put in your head. Leave her to me. You need to focus on your people. Ymitoth may be more proficient at training men to be soldiers, but you are their leader, Maelich. They need to see you among them, toiling beside them in the hot sun. It lifts their spirits."

Maelich finished slurping all the meat off the bone he had been chewing from and drained his cup. He tossed the bone into the fire and held his cup out to Maulom for a refill. Maulom obliged the silent request. After another healthy drink, Maelich finally replied, "Wise counsel. I will spend the day training with them tomorrow."

"Very well," Maulom smiled. "Your presence shall raise them up from the dust beneath their feet to the cloudless skies above them. Now, we need to discuss crossing the cracked land. The time has come."

The fire blazed with fresh life as Maelich poked at the smoldering embers with a stick. Shadows retreated deeper into the cave in the face of the flickering flames. Once satisfied with the blaze, Maelich looked back at Maulom and said, "They are not ready."

"Though I understand your concern, on that point we disagree. I believe they are more than prepared, and you may continue training them during our journey," Maulom countered. After draining and refilling his cup he added, "There is another concern you must consider."

"What is that?" Maelich asked.

"It is an omen," the old man smiled. "Walk with me."

Maelich followed the old man out of the cave. He still found it peculiar how clean he was able to keep his bright white clothing. The land surrounding them within the caves and for miles in every direction surrounding the stony peaks was dirt upon dirt. Maulom's impeccable clothing, his close-cropped white hair and beard, even the odd white coverings he wore upon his feet, all of it was impossibly clean.

The cracked, sandy ground was blinding compared to the darkness of the cave. Maelich had to shade his eyes. The heat was overbearing. It was like a weight sitting on his chest, a heavy thing that made it hard to breathe. As Maelich's eyes slowly grew accustomed to the brightness of the world around him, Maulom tapped his shoulder and pointed toward the clear blue sky.

"Look there, Maelich," the old man said. "That is a total eclipse."

"That is our signal to begin," Maelich recalled from the story painted along the walls of the cave.

"Precisely," Maulom agreed. "The Shaiwah must depart to reclaim their stolen lands with the light of a new day, and you must lead them."

Maelich watched Maulom as he walked off toward a group of Shaiwah working through sword techniques. Ding was leading the group. He had proven a quick study and earned Ymitoth's favor. He became so proficient that the grizzled old soldier from Havenstahl trusted him to assist in training the others. A wide smile spread across Maelich's face. He knew how much the honor meant to Ding.

"With the light of a new day, then?" Ymitoth's sudden presence startled Maelich enough to make him jump.

"You nearly scared my soul right to the Lake," Maelich put his hand on his chest and felt his heart racing beneath it. "Why are you sneaking around."

Ymitoth shrugged, "I ain't sneaking anywhere. You've been distracted. What drags your attention away from the duty of training them men?"

"Many things," Maelich conceded. "The black horse in my dream, that face she showed me, Maulom and his confusing ways, I am unsure what to make of anything anymore. Maulom knows the black horse. He said she is a witch."

Ymitoth scratched his head, gazed at Maelich with black, dead eyes, and said, "I ain't a wise man, but if that black horse is a witch, what does that make him? Ain't it he met you in your dreams just the same as her?"

Maelich did not respond. He simply nodded and walked back into the cool dark of the cave. Ymitoth's point was well taken. Maulom was at least as great a mystery as the black horse. Hopefully, getting back to the trail would get his mind off them both.

# CHAPTER 29

# WHERE THE MAPS DON'T GO

Time is imaginary, a method for gauging the movement of celestial bodies through the heavens while tracking movement through the physical in a linear fashion, or at least a fluid concept impacted by an endless flood of factors. A year is an eternity to a child but a blink of an eye to an old man. Anticipation can make a day drag while deep engagement will send it sailing by. A few days lazing about the Lake surrounded by Dragons, serenity, and a peace so immersive and complete things like fear or concern shrink, shuffled to the farthest, darkest spaces of consciousness they cannot help but be ignored without actively being sought out for contemplation had Perrin nearly forgetting her mission. She might have forgotten completely had a quiet anxiousness not whispered, "Where is Geillan?" from somewhere in the back of her mind. Suddenly, the few days she had spent surrounded by the tranquility of the Lake seemed an eternity and her mission once again as urgent as it had been prior to meeting Dragons.

Perrin had been softly dragging her hand across Lameah's scales. They felt different than she expected. Instead of the rough scrape suggested by their appearance, they were smooth, almost soft to the touch. Once the quiet anxiousness whispering from deep in the back of her consciousness had fully grabbed hold of her attention and become a thing she could no longer ignore, she stopped petting Lameah's arm, looked up at the Dragon, and nearly shouted, "How can I lounge in comfort and peace while my baby boy is locked away somewhere? I must speak with Helias immediately."

Lameah's smile was sweet as she replied, "Of course, my dear. Your mission is urgent, and you will not be swayed from your great purpose. I sense all of that from you. She is there as always, beautiful in the rays of the rising sun."

Perrin stood and stretched to gently kiss the Dragon's face. She felt so much love in her heart it was nearly overwhelming. She wanted to hold Lameah and all the Dragons close, never letting them go. Nothing had ever made her feel that way before, not Maelich, not even sweet Geillan. Of course, Dragons were born of love. They were love. It oozed from their scales, surrounded everything and overwhelmed callous things like malice, fear, hate, and all negativity. "Thank you, sweet sister," Perrin finally said. "May I call you sister?"

"Of course," a tear rimmed Lameah's eyelid before moistening her cheek, "we are all your sisters. As all things, you are one with us and always have a home within our hearts."

It was difficult to comprehend why anyone would leave a place so perfect, how anyone who had felt what she was feeling just then could bring themselves to abandoned it, but Geillan, her perfect babe, needed to be found. She could never have complete joy, never fully submit to the peace surrounding her as long as that voice, that anxiousness, beckoned from the back of her mind. She looked to Helias, the great mother, love begotten of love, queen of Dragons and began the short journey.

The spot Perrin had been lounging with Lameah was a few hundred yards from the Lake. It was not long before her toes were sinking into the cool sand. Something compelled her to remove her boots and feel everything she could about the place. The Lake had always been a legend. Of course, Maelich had told her everything about it, and Cialia had recounted the same, but until she saw it for herself, experienced all the things those two had described, her perception of the place was built from the experiences of others. Her ideas up to that point had been borrowed. Now they were her own. She would probably never make it back there. She needed to experience all of it herself to form memories strong enough to never fade.

Across the Lake, Helias perched atop a stony peak. Larger and even more magnificent than all her sisters, the queen of Dragons was a sight. Beholding her was like looking into the blazing sun. Perrin only managed a few moments before her eyes quickly darted away. There was no pain, more of an emotion. Witnessing such monumental glory made her feel small and unworthy. The great mother was perfection, the first born from the Lake. Everything which came after was somehow less. Of course, Helias would say the feeling was nonsense, all were connected to Coeptus and equal in all ways. In that moment of wonderful torture, Perrin knew that was humility on Helias' part. She was perfection.

The Lake offered no respite. An enigma which would take one hundred lifetimes to truly understand, it was at least as difficult to behold as the Dragon. As Perrin walked through the cool sand, the perfect circle of impossibly still water spoke to her, not in words but colors and emotions. Though she could not understand the words, somehow the meaning came through. Things Maelich had told her which had made no sense at the time became suddenly accessible. The Lake connected Ouloos to Coeptus and thus Coeptus to all things, a portal to eternity, a river flowing in both directions to and from the source of all knowing.

Mesmerized by the Lake and all its knowledge, Perrin had barely noticed her movements around it. As she learned—grasping but not truly understanding—acceptance of a concept beyond comprehension slowly became something closer to knowing. She saw glowing lights hovering close to the ground. The first one stirred fear and sadness, deep but brief. Those initial feelings were quickly replaced with joy, a blissful perfection. Though she could not possibly know the light was a soul—the essence of something which had once lived and felt things, experienced life—somehow, she did. That soul had finished its journey through the physical and returned to the Lake full of the experience of a lifetime. That first one drifted out to the center of the Lake and sunk within it. A dim glow emanated from the still waters, even and perfect until that same light shot up into the heavens. Joyous tears ran down her face quicker than she could wipe them away had she wanted to. But she did not. They felt too good, like pure happiness rained down her face. After that first one, more came. It seemed her eyes were opened to the perfection of the Lake and its never-ending cycle of life. Finished life full of knowledge and feelings carried their energy home, while new life—empty and ready to feel joy and fear and rage and love—returned to begin a new journey.

And then Helias was directly before her. The stony peak the great Dragon rode like a throne stretched up before Perrin. She looked past the cave mouth which opened where the sand she strolled upon terminated up to the great mother. The Dragon remained glorious to behold, but Perrin no longer felt the need to look away. She could witness that perfection, feel the unconditional love, the pure bliss that is the queen of Dragons.

"My love," Helias' voice was a full chorus, the most beautiful song ever sung, "you burn with purpose. Why? Of course, I know why. Your desire cries out from your very soul. My question is, why do you think you burn with such purpose?"

"It is a burning desire, a need. There ain't no other thing that matters more to me in all of Ouloos, my baby, my sweet Geillan," Perrin's fear and awe shrunk as her sense of purpose grew. "You say you know my desire. If that is true, why ask the question?"

Helias' smile was like a soft blanket for weary bones. "What you say is true. Though I wish you felt differently, you understand your purpose and are certain of it. I will show you the path, point you toward your goal, but you must know sadness and pain are all you will find. Your goal will remain unfulfilled."

"I know you are wise, but I ain't certain of what you say," Perrin remained unmoved by the warning. "My whole life others have been telling me what to think and what I ought to do, what is right and what is wrong. It is far past time I began figuring these things out for myself. This is my journey. Geillan is my goal. Whatever end I find will be my own."

"I know, my love," she said. "I want to show you something."

The world surrounding Perrin suddenly changed. It was no gradual shift. At one moment, the Lake sat beside her in all its perfection with magnificent Dragons swimming the clear, blue skies, and the next, Helias remained upon her stony throne, but everything else was different. The sky above was no longer the clear blue it had been. It was all colors, every conceivable shade of orange, pink, yellow, purple, red, and more. Some of the colors seemed to belong in a sky, but not all at once, and never in the swirling combinations which stretched as far as Perrin could see. Things resembling clouds darted rather than drifted. They were not fluffy like the soft, white clouds which would laze about the towers at Havenstahl. These were sharp, like jagged gems with boundaries constantly moving and barely discernable against the sky which mocked their colors. Beneath the inconsistent sky sat an equally inconsistent ground. Colors swirled and morphed in the same fashion as the expanse above, but the terrain seemed constantly moving. Mountains fell to valleys as rivers flowed with wild rapids only to vanish, replaced by flowing waves of grass or trees or some other formation which was almost familiar but not quite right.

"There ain't one thing that makes any sense there," Perrin gasped.

"Precisely, my dear. What you see is the exact opposite of the lands where you were raised. They are ruled by order. Your destination lies on the other side of this place and is ruled by chaos," the song like quality of Helias' voice bore an undeniable contrast to the terror melting and morphing before Perrin's eyes.

"How could there be such a place just beyond this Lake and its complete perfection?" Perrin's voice was barely more than a whisper.

Helias song continued, "The Lake is perfection. The meeting of two equal and opposite concepts. You look out at this ever-changing landscape and see horror. From your perspective it is that. However, the feelings this place sparks in you are caused by things you have learned. Had you been born to the chaos, lived and breathed among it as you have in the orderly lands which you were raised, you would see something different. You would see unlimited potential. With no stifling rules to dictate how things must be, there is no limit to what is possible. And if you looked upon this place and saw those things, you would look at the place where you learned what life means and see nothing but a stifling prison. The unchanging and uniform patterns of that place would terrify you at least as much as the complete disorder you look upon now.

"In truth, one condition cannot exist without the other. The Lake— which is perfection as you have undoubtedly felt while surrounded by it—is a perfect balance between the two. Unconditional love, Perrin. We are all born from it. Dragons remain. All other creatures are drawn to one or the other."

"I am frightened to my very soul," Perrin looked earnestly at Helias, "but I remain unmoved. I will conquer this wild place you have shown me, and I will rescue my sweet Geillan."

Helias' smile never wavered, but somehow it slightly shifted from complete joy to a knowing sadness. "I know, my love. I know," she replied. "I must tell you one more thing. I should not interfere. Your path and your decision are yours. However, you have a caring soul, and I will hurt deeply when you feel this pain. I will not hurt for me, but for you. This scar will remain until the Lake calls you home. Of course, the choices you make will affect the outcome. If you follow this path, you will find your precious Geillan. However, everyone who accompanies you will find the Lake before you do."

The words stung at first, but they were not surprising. On some level, Perrin already knew the outcome. There had never been a doubt in her mind she would find Geillan. He was the only reason she had to exist. There was no other option. Though she had never actively thought about it, she knew none of the brave men accompanying her would survive the journey. When Helias gave voice to the idea, Perrin realized it had been there. They all knew the adventure was a perilous one, but she knew they would all die.

When Perrin finally woke from the vision, Glord stood beside her. He was barefoot in the sand and looking up at the magnificent Dragon. She addressed him with the glorious song of her voice, "Welcome, Glord, protector of the rightful queen of Havenstahl. You are an honorable soldier, a fierce warrior who would die before abandoning his duty. It is an honor to meet you."

Glord had never heard a sound so sweet as the Dragon's song. The immersive bliss he felt just then was beyond any emotion he had ever experienced. It was uncontainable and poured forth from his eyes in a torrent of tears. He fell to his knees before Helias and wept, "I don't deserve the honor of your praise."

"Of course, you do, my love," Helias' smile remained unwavering. "We are all bound together in Coeptus as are all things. You are me. I am you. We are love. Rise, dutiful knight."

"You and the men must return to Havenstahl," Perrin blurted as Glord obliged Helias' command.

"Forgive me, highness, but that ain't a command I am willing to obey," Glord bowed deep before his queen.

Perrin smiled and gently placed her hand on Glord's cheek. "There ain't nothing to forgive," she began. "You have been a faithful protector and mentor. You have prepared me for this journey, and it is a journey I must finish on my own. The Great Mother showed me a vision of the place where my path leads, and I can't ask any of you to continue with me on this quest. Any who do will be long dead before we reach our goal."

"You know I never had no daughters," Glord took both Perrin's hands in his own. "If I did, the last thing I would do is leave them alone when they need me the most. What you ask of me is akin to asking me to leave my own daughter to fend for herself against a pack of wild mountain scarra. That ain't a thing I would ever do. Your path is mine, and the rest of the men will tell you the same. All of us knew what this journey meant, even from the start. We march off into dark, unknown lands to challenge a god for your son's life. The vow we made was to give our lives for his. I beg you, please don't command me to walk away. You will force me to betray you, because that is a thing I cannot do."

Perrin failed to contain her tears as she threw her arms around Glord's neck and kissed his cheek. "It is a terrible shame you never had no daughters. I can't think of a better father than the man standing before me."

Helias lost a tear, "I will lose many more tears for you all when the Lake calls you home."

# CHAPTER 30
# THE HARVEST

Three days on the trail had been a welcomed adventure for Cialia. If it were just the two of them on swift horses, they could have made the journey in a day. It would have been a long one, beginning in the wee hours as the sun is only beginning to paint the dark eastern sky with color until just after dusk. However, it was not just the two of them on swift horses. Father supplied the king's army with weapons. Their cart lumbering over the deep, hardened ruts of the trail was loaded down with them. Though it was just the two of them, even the swiftest horse is less so when tugging a heavy load.

Cialia had almost convinced Marielle to accompany them for the great harvest, but she had her own wares to peddle and a good bit of baking left to do. The harvest celebration was her busiest time of the year. The fact was only slightly disappointing. Father was different on the trail, easier, treating Cialia more like a fellow adventurer than a daughter. Back at their hut, Cialia was responsible for all the chores typically reserved for women, washing dirty trousers and soiled kettles, sweeping floors, feeding chickens and pigs, and preparing all the meals. The trail was different. In the wee hours of their first morning, she had slipped away with her bow and bagged a stout fallon. Roasting meat over an open blaze on the trail is different than boiling stew in a kettle over a small flame in a hearth. She had not minded preparing that meal one bit.

Sitting in the glow of a healthy fire listening to father's stories was probably her favorite part. He would occasionally spin a yarn sitting at the table over a cup of ale back at their hut, but the trail brought something out of him. He looked different, like he had been trapped in a cage and someone left the door open. The shackled bird he resembled shuffling from his hut to his forge and back again looked nothing like the magnificent animal soaring down the trail alongside her. Sitting beside the fire after a long day of travel bathed in the flickering orange glow of a proper fire, he looked every bit the hero she learned about through the stories folks would tell her about him.

He had a story for her that first night. After filling up on a good, thick slab of the fallon she had roasted up, he leaned back against a fallen tree and said, "Did I ever tell you about the only time I was ever truly afraid?"

"The grizzly mongs?" she had asked. That was the most terrifying tale she had ever heard about him. She had never seen one herself, but the descriptions painted a frightening enough picture she hoped she never did.

"No," he chuckled. "They were terrifying to be sure, but I'd been running on rage and adrenaline. My men needed me. There was no time for fear. No, the only time I ever truly felt afraid was after my fighting days had long passed. I had woken in the middle of the night. The hut was always drafty and creaky, old bones, but on this night, everything was louder than normal. I quickly realized all that noise was caused by the wide-open door of our hut. Mind you, that didn't frighten me at all. My soldiering days may have been over, but I've still enough fight in me to send a thief back to the Lake on the end of my blade. I became afraid when it occurred to me what an open door might mean when the only person sharing the hut with me was a lass of just under three summers. That was the moment I noticed you were gone. That was the moment I became truly afraid.

"I jumped out of my cot and ran out in my nightshirt. When I heard growling and rustling brush about fifty yards off from our hut, well, that fear turned to terror. I just knew it was full grown scarra ripping my little girl to shreds. I shrunk inside, could have laid down right there in the road and died. I didn't even want to look. My heart was pounding so hard and fast I could hear it in my ears. The growling just kept getting louder. That was the moment I realized I had forgotten to grab my sword. Barefoot and bare-assed were bad enough. Half-lame, I'm pretty useless battling beasts without my blade. It was too late to worry about that. I took a deep breath and pushed my way through the shrubs into a clearing. All the way through I knew I was going to find a beast chewing at my dead child and I'd have to fight the monster for your carcass. That moment, just before I poked my head out into the clearing where all the growling was coming from, was the only time in my life I have ever been truly afraid."

He left it there like that, unfinished. It was a technique Cialia had become accustomed to from him. He would build up the tension, charge steadily toward the climax, and then stop, sip his ale, and act like the tale was complete. She let him drag his game out long enough to take a nice long drink, and then she dutifully asked, "Well, what happened? What did you see?"

He gave her the same satisfied smile he always did when she begged him to finish the story. They both knew she was patronizing him but neither cared. It was part of the game, part of the story, and part of the fun. "What did I see?" he asked. "Do you really want to know? I don't know. Might be it's too much for you. I told you how afraid I was."

"Stop torturing me," she laughed. "Spill it."

"Okay, okay," he laughed back at her before finishing the tale. "So, there I am pushing through the brush in nothing but my nightshirt, getting ready to battle a beast for my daughter's bones, and what do I find? My own sweet little girl barefoot in her nightgown with her chubby little arm stretched out to pet the *woof.* That's what you called scrods back then, probably on the count of the sound they make. I doubt you remember, but we would sit out on the porch when you were small like that. You would sit on my lap and we'd look at the moon. I'd ask you, what do we say to the moon, Cialia? And you would look up at the moon and say, ow, ow, owooo. Then we'd both do it. We'd throw our heads back and howl at the moon. Then you'd tell me, that's what the woofs say. Well, that beast in that clearing wasn't no scarra. It was just a scrod. By the time I'd made it through the brush, you were petting him, and he was licking your face. You looked up at me with those sweet, innocent eyes and those chubby cheeks and said, woof, Papa."

"Starless," she replied quietly. "That was Starless, wasn't it?"

"Aye, that's what you called him," Agrimon agreed. "It was a sad day when we lost him, but that's a tale for a different time."

"I cannot see him in my head," the idea had suddenly occurred to her. "I remember the name, but I cannot see his face. How old was I when he died?"

Agrimon scratched his head, "Well, it wasn't more than a summer ago. It was a tough time for you. Maybe you blacked it out of your head."

Cialia had left it alone at the time, but it wasn't the only thing she should remember but could not picture. Her memories seemed like unfinished paintings. The essence was there, but the details were missing or didn't add up. When they rounded the bend onto the busy road leading up to the great city at the top of the mountain with its towers scraping the sky and glowing orange in a setting sun, and father said, "There she is, Varisghoul, the great city of the north," she had to pick the conversation back up again.

"I know the name, father, but it sounds wrong to my ears," she complained. "Why are all these things familiar to me but feel unreal. It feels like I'm walking through someone else's life."

Agrimon gave her an odd look, "There ain't another name I know for the place. It was Varisghoul when I rode under its banner. It was Varisghoul when my father did, and his father before him. You've been acting strange since we celebrated the end of your fifteenth summer. Maybe we take some time out to visit old Hagen and have him look you over."

Hagen, that was a name with a face that sparked some real memories. However, they were not memories from her hut in Brickley's Bend. They were from a different place, a city in the trees somewhere, and a city on a mountain just like Varisghoul. But it was not called that. It was Havenstahl. She stretched toward that word, that idea. It seemed just out of reach.

"What on Ouloos has happened here?" father's voice distracted her from her search.

The edge of the city was always a bustling clutter of commotion, but what they rumbled into on their heavy cart was different. It was not the bustle of folks bringing their wares to barter or sell. People were fleeing. Some charged up the hill toward the city proper with its high walls and lofty spires. Others fled past them away from the city. Still others fled into their huts, slamming doors and shuttering windows.

"Hey there," Agrimon hailed a man rushing to his hut whose face flushed red with agitation. "What is all this ruckus?"

The man slowed enough to turn and shout back, "The prince,

Cardon has been taken by the great wizard who sits atop the mount of fire."

"Merkhal?" Agrimon's face twisted in confusion, "What would that old wizard want with the king's fair son?"

There was another name which sounded familiar, but this one lacked even the essence of a memory to go with it. It felt like something she had heard once in a story. All her memories felt like that. Things she recalled from descriptions rather than the residue of experiences. All the commotion kept her from exploring the idea any further. As much as she wanted to dive deep and examine these false feeling memories, try to find an answer to whom they may belong, a missing prince was too compelling a story to ignore. The king's men would be mounting up to march off to war against this wizard. She dared not wish the king would be in such a state as to allow a girl to march under his banner, but the idea refused to leave her mind. She would pledge her blades. The king could take them or leave them.

The massive drawbridge spanning the deep chasm between the southern gate and the entrance to the city proper was down, but the heavy iron gate allowing passage to the bridge was closed up tight. They should have been thrown wide for the harvest celebration with traffic moving in both directions across the heavy bridge. Instead, four guards in full dress stood before the gate turning all away. Their shiny prang helms dazzled in the sun.

"None in or out," one of the guards hollered to Agrimon as he and Cialia approached. His tone was deep and dripped the kind of authority which is rarely questioned.

Agrimon stopped the cart, "I'm loaded down with weapons for the king's army. If the rumors spreading through the town are to be believed, it may be wise to see me through."

Another of the guards leaned over to the first and whispered, "That's the swordsmith, Agrimon, from Brickley's Bend."

"The titan?" the first guard whispered a bit too loudly.

"One and the same," Cialia answered. Agrimon touched her arm and shook his head slightly. She shrugged and smiled as the four guards hurried to open the gate, "Only fair they know to whom they speak."

Chaos danced all about the stone streets of the city, as people ran this way and that carrying this thing or the other. None of it appeared useful to Cialia. Father had taught her early, and repeated the lesson often, precisely zero problems were ever solved by panicking. The only goal the folks zigging and zagging through crowds pushing against each other were accomplishing was slowing she and her father down. Sit tight and wait for someone with a clear head to solve your problems.

The city center was the spot where King Carowell should have been addressing throngs of people gathered from far and wide in celebration of a bountiful harvest. People should have been packed in tight around the fountain watching soldiers parade around in formation showing off their crackerjack timing and extensive training. Those same soldiers should have been engaging in mock battles and feats of strength while the boisterous mob cheered them on. The boisterous mob was missing. The vast courtyard surrounding the fountain sat mostly empty. The soldiers were there, dressed for war and flying the colors of their houses, but none of them looked prepared to storm a wizard's keep in honor of their king's good name. Most of them did their best to avoid the pleading eyes of their sobbing king as he begged for a champion.

The king's crown was off. His bald, normally pink head was red with frustration. Though his arms suggested at one time in his life he was formidable, the rest of his body suggested too many years spent on lavish pursuits. His gayly colored tights strained to cover his bare ass as he crawled from one champion to another with his belly nearly dragging across the ground below him.

"Please," he sobbed as he hugged the legs of a large man in gaudy plate armor buffed to shine without blemish, "help me rescue my son from that monster."

The man ignored his grace's pleas, turning away from the king he was sworn to protect. The scene disgusted Cialia, a king groveling at the feet of men dolled up for parade with brightly colored plumes decorating their helms and matching fabrics flowing from their pauldrons. Not one of them looked like they could defend a sweet cake from a pack of hungry children much less rescue a prince from the clutches of some magical being.

She looked at her father and said, "No."

"The king needs a champion," Agrimon said soberly without looking at her.

"This is not right," she shook her head. "That is no king, and those are not soldiers. This cannot be real."

"Of course, it is," he finally looked over at her. "You see it with your own eyes as I do with mine."

She scanned her father's face, looking for some clue he truly believed the words leaving his mouth. He looked blank to her just then, as fake as the crying king and his supposed champions. This was not her life. Despite the feeling she moved through scenes in some kind of dream rather than living and breathing in a world that was real, she simply could not sit and watch the pathetic drama unfolding before her. "I will be your champion," she finally called out.

The laughter of the men in their pretty armor echoed off the stony walls surrounding the courtyard. The sound swirled around her like a mocking tornado. The king did not laugh with the rest. He looked up at her, his pink cheeks shaking under his tears, and said, "You jest. It is unwise to tease his highness."

Father touched her arm, "Cialia, no."

It was too late. She was off the cart confidently stalking toward the prostrate king. "I see no other champions in this place, only frightened men decorated for parade not battle. I will challenge your wizard and collect your son."

"Petulant child," the big man with the shiny armor lumbered toward her. "Merkhal will suck your bones from your body with a breath and leave your flesh in a slimy pile."

Cialia smiled as she ducked under the backhand he tried to bruise her cheek with. It surely would have hurt had it connected. His gauntlets had thick nubs over the knuckles. He swung three more times. She danced away, gauging his movements and dodging around his attacks.

"I see why you fear this Merkhal," she chided. "He must be formidable to stroll into a heavily guarded city and steal its prince. You are unable to even strike a defenseless girl."

He finally drew his sword as two more lumbering giants of men approached and did the same. Their armor and swords were too fancy for fighting. They looked all a show. Cialia did not bother pulling her blades. She stood relaxed, waiting for the first the attack.

Before that attack could come, the king finally found his feet and gained a bit of control over his voice. "Enough," he shouted. His fat, pink cheeks shook as spittle flew from his lips. "None of you are willing to band together to challenge Merkhal for my son's life, but you will band together to challenge a wee girl for a slight?" Then he looked to Cialia and said, "What is your name, girl?"

"I am Cialia of Brickley's Bend, daughter of Agrimon the titan," she knew the words, but they sounded wrong coming out of her mouth. Her father was Agrimon. She lived with him in Brickley's Bend. Why did it feel like she was introducing someone else?

The king cast a disgusted glare about the courtyard at his brave soldiers before looking back to Cialia, "I pray Kallum you are as mighty as you are brave. I fear none will accompany you on your mission. You will face the horrible wizard on his mountain of fire alone."

"My daughter will not be alone," Agrimon piped up. "I may only have this one good arm, but I will accompany her on this campaign.

All traces of the king's tears had vanished as he proclaimed, "You should depart straight away, Cialia of Brickley's Bend, daughter of Agrimon the titan. You shall be given the swiftest horses in our stables to speed you on your journey."

She turned and shot her father a smile. He had always assured her she would never ride under the banner of any king. Not because she was incapable, but because men fight wars. No king would have her. The smile he gave back to her was his acknowledgement of how wrong he had been.

By the time she turned her gaze back to the king, he was gone. Everyone was gone. The courtyard was empty, and father was suddenly standing next to her. Somehow, he had managed to get off the cart and cover the distance between them in the time it took her to turn her head. On top of that, the cart he had been sitting upon was gone as well.

"No," she shook her head. "None of this is possible. Where has everyone gone? Where has our cart gone?"

"What are you talking about?" he asked. "The mission lies before us. This is everything you have ever wanted, a mission, adventure, the wide-open trail. Let's get those horses the king promised and be gone from this place."

Then it suddenly occurred to her, "He knows we are coming. We have only just accepted the mission, and already the battle has begun. He toys with my mind." She looked around the courtyard and up to the sky then shouted, "I will not be swayed, wizard. You will face me."

# CHAPTER 31
## A MIGHTY ALLIANCE

The walls of the tent rippled under a stiff southerly wind. The posts swayed from the force. Daritus quickly glanced around the room fully expecting the entire structure would blow away and leave him sitting in a field. A heavy gust snapped the flaps covering the entrance back and blew his map against the back wall spilling his painted tokens all about the grassy floor. He hurried over to grab the thing before it ripped or managed to escape the tent.

As he rolled the thing and fastened it with a thread, he looked over at the group sharing the tent with him. Bom and Lito-Bi sat upon the ground. Kantiim occupied a simple wooden chair. He would have sat in the grass with the guests, but they would not have it. "You would offer your seat if it could hold my weight. There is no sense in having an empty chair with three fools on the ground," Bom had said.

After collecting his map and tokens, Daritus looked to Bom and asked, "Have all in your group been provided with proper shelter and nourishment?"

"They have," Bom smiled. "The men of Havenstahl have been quite accommodating. They have even given us leave to hunt the surrounding forests with them and share their yields."

"Quite accommodating may be a slight exaggeration," Lito-Bi grumbled.

"How so," Daritus' eyes narrowed. He had been quite explicit that Bom and his group should be treated as guests.

"There have been a few skirmishes that…" Lito-Bi began.

"That ended without incident," Bom finished the statement. "Do not forget we are the invaders here, old friend. Do you remember when first we met?"

"I vouched for you," the big trogmortem countered.

"Yes, you did, but only after I had wrestled with your kin nearly all afternoon," the giant smiled wide. "If you recall, I held no grudge. I was the invader that day, and we are invaders now. Friendship among former enemies takes time."

"I appreciate your good nature," Kantiim interjected. "I expect at least as much from my men. Please inform me of any further altercations."

"Easy, old friend," though Daritus' tone was friendly enough, it was direct. He looked at Bom as he finished, "It is not unwise to be wary of friends who have yet to prove their loyalty."

Lito-Bi uttered a wry chuckle as he shook his head and mumbled, "I warned you of this. We should have stolen a ship and sailed home."

"We are here in a foreign land so drastically different than our own home. Do you not wish to explore it, to learn everything about this place and the various beliefs and cultures of the men and dwarves who occupy it? Even learning the differences between the grongs who live with us across the Great Sea and the grongs who live here. They are the same, but so completely different at the same time," Bom's tone had a pleading quality.

Daritus was intrigued, "Grongs live across the Great Sea? I assumed you had enlisted them from our lands as part of your campaign."

"I said the same when we arrived. I had no idea," Bom laughed. Then he looked earnestly at Daritus, "I want to learn all I can about this place and your culture. You speak well and seem wise. If you had the chance to visit my home and learn about us, would you not take that chance?" Then he looked at Lito-Bi and added, "I have also heard of a place far to the east where trogmortem live. Would you not want to meet your kin and learn about how they live?"

Lito-Bi waved the idea off, "All trogmortem came from Tal when he conquered the bintoosha in the vast desert of the setting sun. There are no trogmortem in this place."

Bom's form deflated as he sighed, "I know the myths, stories told from one generation to another by folks who have never seen anything outside of the lands on which they dwell. What if there were trogmortem in this land? Would you not want to meet them and know them?"

The trogmortem offered a slight nod and shrug.

Daritus scratched his chin, "You are very convincing, but words are easy. Actions are far more difficult to fake."

"I vow to you now on the house of Maomnosett, we will help you rebuild your city and defend it against my grandfather's army from across the Great Sea," Bom rose to his knee and placed his right hand over his heart. "I realize that name carries little meaning to you, but you must understand the honor of my house means everything to me. I will not betray you or your trust."

"Take this bargain, Daritus. We need their help. They have been with us for days. None have gone unaccounted for. They are with us," Kantiim added.

"You have been here for days, and I see truth in your eyes," Daritus finally conceded.

Daritus rose and moved to a table in the corner of the tent. The wind still whipped, but the table was heavy and the jug sitting upon it full. He poured out four cups and shared them around. The cups were a bit small for his guests, but they did not seem to mind. He raised his glass and said, "To a mighty alliance with new friends."

Tiegran ran into the tent as the four drank down their toast. His eyes were wild as he breathlessly shouted, "Forgive the intrusion, general, but Alhouim marches on Biggon's Bay."

Tarturan entered right on Tiegran's heels, "The lad speaks truth. Ychorell happened upon the full force of Alhouim's army pounding boots through the bloody waste. The general, Bindaar, would not be swayed. He says the bastards from across the Great Sea will pay for King Doentaat's death."

Daritus' form deflated as he slumped down into his chair. His head shook slowly as he cradled it in his hand, "I did not hear the horn of Alhouim."

"They never blew it," Tarturan replied.

"Take one thousand men and support their attack," Daritus' voice had fallen to barely more than a hoarse whisper.

"I fear the fighting will be finished before we arrive. They should be on the beach by now, and the sun will be long set before we see a grain of sand," the big soldier shrugged.

"If there is anything to be done, do it. But do not spare any lives if the cause is already lost," the words sickened him as they came from his mouth, but they had already lost too many men to engage in battles spawned solely by bouts of rage. Then he turned to Bom and said, "You say you want to earn my trust and wish to send the invaders you came with back across the Great Sea. Helping our friends from Alhouim would go a long way toward that goal."

Bom glanced at Lito-Bi. The fierce trogmortem offered only a frown and a slight nod as his response. Then the giant looked back to Daritus, "We enjoy the prospect of losing more of our kin as much as you, but we will do this thing. This man, Tarturan, will lead the assault. We will follow him. If he gives the command to attack, we will fight by his side. If he calls the retreat, we will heed his call."

"I could ask for nothing more than that," Daritus offered a joyless smile. "Believe me, if I could get hands on my dwarf friend right now, I would do my best to smack the ridiculous idea from his head."

## CHAPTER 32
## STORM THE BEACH

A few days of rain had done nothing to improve the stench hovering about the bloody waste. Nor did it clean away the gore from grass or stump or bits of shredded tree. Scavengers supped on carcasses left behind to rot in the elements. Several attempts had been made to reclaim the dead from the grim reminder of how little honor could be found amongst the invaders from across the sea. Every effort ended in a battle, more death, and more carcasses for the pile. Five thousand dwarves stomped through the field, breathing in foul death, and crushing decomposing bodies deeper into the soggy ground.

"Cut them giants down," a voice from the crowd raised up over the sound of ten thousand boots pounding into wet death. "Aye," another answered, "fill the bay with the blood of giants. Let the fishes feast on their bones."

Bindaar led the charge. Normally, he would march alongside long, even columns of dwarves stomping feet in time with drums of war. There were no drums, and the mob trudging through the bloody waste behind him was anything but normal. This was not a mission. It was strictly revenge, unquieted rage. When those ships had anchored in the bay, the goal was simply to convince the invading force to leave their shores and return home. That idea had been long forgotten. The only goal which remained was killing every living thing on the beach or in the ships.

"Hold," Bindaar shouted when he saw the first grong step out of the trees bordering the south side of the clearing. The control he held over the dwarves marching behind him was a thin veil holding back the vicious jaws of a hungry beast. Had the dwarf general so much as twitched, the dwarves gripping their axes aching to taste the blood of grongs and trogmortem and even giants would have descended on the tree line like a mountain scarra running down a rabbit. Bindaar felt the same, but he was not so blinded by rage that he missed the folly dripping from the idea. Grongs never traveled alone.

A moment after the first stepped from the cover of trees and raised his club high, thousands more charged out from the darkness. They poured from the forest like flies from a carcass and formed up in a loose mob. Grongs were ferocious, but they lacked order, swarming enemies rather than marching on them. Once it seemed all who would be joining the battle had made their way into the ocean of death between the trees, Bindaar raised his axe high.

No words left the dwarf's mouth. There was no need for them. All the dwarves following him knew what that raised axe meant. When he swung it down, they erupted, a charging horde. The sounds pouring from the lips of dwarves racing through a field of their own dead was a terrifying symphony of sorrow, rage, and despair. Their song filled up the clearing like a flood, spilling over the tops of trees and startling birds from their nests. It was time for revenge. It was time to kill.

The mob of grongs responded, shouting and howling, waving their heavy clubs, and charging toward the dwarves. It was a short journey. The two groups collided. Bindaar's axe tasted the first grong's blood, slicing through the beast's thick neck and tossing its head through the air. He howled at the headless body as it fell at his feet spilling blood all over his boots. He stomped on its chest as he swung his mighty axe again. An arm flew south, and a leg flew north. Every time he swung his axe a body part flew. His vision narrowed. He imagined every grong face he saw was the one who swung the club that ended his friend.

A dull thud against the furious dwarf's thigh snapped him out of his tunnel vision. The deep and guttural growl that poured from his mouth was not pain. It was rage. Had he taken a moment to give his emotions conscious thought it would have seemed impossible for him to grow angrier than he had been, but he was. He did not swing his axe at the grong holding the club that swung low and struck his thigh. He slammed his forehead into the beast's snout, smashed his elbow into the side of the thing's head, and kicked him in square in the chest. It was only after the burly monster was stumbling backward that he swung his axe and removed the thing's head.

Hundreds of grongs fell to the mighty axes of dwarves, but dwarves fell too, pummeled by the heavy clubs of ferocious grongs. One dwarf lost was too many as far as Bindaar was concerned, but it was payment for a debt owed, a debt which could only be satisfied with blood. The dwarves raged on. By the time the resolve of the grongs battling the raging dwarves began to crack, more than one hundred dwarves had fallen. However, the sight of grongs splitting from their loose formation and fleeing to the trees earned loud cheers from bloody dwarves eager to hunt them down and cleave limbs from their bodies.

The celebration was short. Though more than half the grongs remaining on the battlefield were running in any direction where dwarves with their mighty axes did not stand, something one hundred times more horrible than the fiercest grong had entered the fray. At least three hundred trogmortem raced up from the beach. As if those monstrous beasts were not bad enough, a handful of giants charged along with them.

"No dwarf leaves this field unless their destination is the Lake," Bindaar shouted as his axe tasted the flesh of another grong. "For Doentaat! For Alhouim!"

The command was unnecessary. Not one dwarf considered leaving that battlefield. It would have been a wise choice, but the mission had nothing to do with wisdom. It was about revenge. It was about sending as many of the vile invaders from across the Great Sea to the Lake as possible.

Then Bindaar saw his goal. Laenkishot Kon lumbered among the throng of giants and trogmortem racing toward his pack of deadly dwarves. If he could kill that one giant, everyone on that field would know it was not a feat too great. Once the dwarf general set eyes on that prize, no other soul on the battlefield mattered. That lumbering giant would fall to his bloody axe. Daritus, a man, no more special than any other man had done it. Men are no better than dwarves, and a finer weapon than the dwarf axe does not exist. If that leader of men could fell a giant on his own, why could Bindaar not do the same? After all, the group he led into the battle of Fort Maomnosett had killed three giants.

The battle raged on around him, but he only saw his goal. The first swing of his mighty axe failed to earn even a nick on the giant's thick ankle. He swung it again and again at the same spot. After five solid strikes, he finally earned a trickle of blood. It would prove to be the last thing he ever did in the living world. It was only the giant's fingers that connected with him when the monster backhanded him, but that was enough to send him sailing twenty feet through the air. He had barely landed on the soft ground before the giant's knee pounded him deeper into the mud. Consciousness had all but fled when the massive knee raised off him. It was instinct which lifted the axe in front of him to defend against the next blow, but it made no difference. When Laenkishot Kon's massive fist slammed down him, the slight cut the axe made on the giant's knuckle was of little consequence, and one more dwarf soul made its journey back to the Lake.

Lentaak saw his general fall under the pummeling fist of a massive giant. He did not need to see the eyes of his old friend gray over to know he had lost another of his kin. It was difficult to differentiate between the various emotions he felt just then. Everything was red and black. It was the most pitiable sorrow, the deepest angst, the most furious rage, hopelessness, and countless other feelings all wrapped into one desperate emotion. Despite their desire, the dwarves of Alhouim would not win the day. They charged on a superior force with no plan, and they failed.

"Retreat," the words hurt as they left his mouth, but there could not have been more than two hundred dwarves left standing when he did.

Retreat was a foreign concept to the stout dwarves of Alhouim, but his group obeyed. They had been drunk with rage when first their feet touched the bloody waste, but watching your kin die by your side with giants and trogmortem tossing bodies like fairy weed buds into the trees is a sobering experience. Every dwarf still standing fled south toward the tree line. Half made it. The rest found peace after a bloody and violent end.

***

Alhouim sat unguarded. All her defenders waged war against grongs and trogmortem and even horrible giants in the bloody waste. Only the elderly and young remained. Maomnosett Ott led no more than a few hundred grongs and took the city easily. The few dwarves with courage or hatred enough to resist died quickly. It took only a handful of gruesome deaths for those with less resolve to forget the effort. For some, a life without freedom is no life at all. For others, any life is better than none. The latter fell in line, and Ott took the throne. Alhouim died a quiet death while Maomnosett was reborn.

CHAPTER 33
ESCAPE

It was difficult to gauge how much time had passed since Tarantian first woke in the dim light of the large sick room he occupied. There was little difference between day and night. Bodies came and went. Some seemed alive, others did not. Some were in beds like his, others shackled to the walls surrounding those beds. Occasionally, one would cry out and big men would come to remove them. A man calling himself Theiron would come occasionally, look him over, and administer a foul-smelling liquid. Other times, the butcher would be at the table in the corner chopping up meat, chopping up men. Tarantian did his best to feign sleep when that one was about his work.

On this particular occasion, the room was exceptionally dark. Everyone else seemed asleep, and the butcher was not at his post. Despite a throbbing in his head making it extremely difficult to focus, it seemed to be as good a time as any to escape the place and avoid ending up on the butcher's block. Chagon was probably already dead. He had been healthy when they arrived. Based on the attention Theiron had been paying to the meat on his bones, the old healer was only helping him to get him healthy enough to feed the village.

Tarantian slipped silently out of the bed. The dusty wood planks of the floor were cool on his bare feet as he crouched low and scanned the room. One of the bodies on a bed across from him farted and mumbled something before rolling onto its side and settling into some loud snoring. The rest of the room remained completely still.

Two doors led out of the place. Though he only remembered bits and pieces of entering the vast room, he knew the door to his right led out into the street. He had no idea what lay on the other side of the building, but he hoped it were a better path to freedom than a well-lit road. He decided to take the door to his left, despite the fact it was right next to the table where that awful butcher chopped up men by dim candlelight.

He moved slowly, quietly across the floor, crouching as low as he could and pausing to scan the room at the end of every bed. Everything remained quiet except the occasional creaky board. Each time he found one, he stopped to scan the room. The short journey seemed to last forever, but he finally made it to the door. He grabbed the handle to turn it but paused. After all the care he had taken to make the exit, charging into a crowd of folks who just might want to eat him would be a horrible failure.

Instead of turning the handle quickly and charging out into the unknown, he slowly stood until he could see out the small window. A thick shade covered it. He pulled it back to expose the smallest sliver of glass. There was a small porch on the other side of the door. It looked nearly identical to the one in the front of the building, but there was no well-lit road beyond it, just a short dark field bordered by the security of a thick bank of trees. The pounding in his head was an inconvenience, but he was certain he could make the trees.

"What on Ouloos are you doing out of your sick bed?" Theiron's voice was musical, almost like he sung words rather than speaking them.

Tarantian's heart would have sank into his boots had he been wearing any. Where had that sneaky old bastard been hiding? He had been so careful not to make a sound. None of the other patients—or victims more like it—had made a peep besides the snoring farter. The sinking feeling gripping his spine threatened to knock him to the ground until it occurred to him that even with a throbbing headache splitting his head in two, he was a soldier who had probably taken as many lives as the old healer behind him had healed for the butcher. Though an inconvenience, the old man was an obstacle he could conquer.

"Some folks, like me, are good at sending souls off to the Lake," his voice carried the calm sureness of one who completely believed what he was saying as he turned toward the man, even if it was a lie. "Other folks, like you, are good at stealing souls from the Lake. You are very good at what you do, and I am feeling much better. I would like to leave this place and get back to the trail."

Theiron's smile was warm and genuine as he said, "I appreciate the compliment, but you cannot leave. The people of this town need to eat, and you must repay our hospitality."

"Please let me go on my way," Tarantian dropped the authority from his tone. "I would much prefer to not kill you, but I intend to leave this place."

The healer laughed hearty and deep, "I have little to fear from you. I know your condition better than you do. That pounding in your head," he paused, "it hurts, does it not? Of course, it does. It has your vision all blurry and your balance off kilter. You are not leaving this place. Return to your bed. Your end will be painless, and you can rest knowing you provided nourishment and will live on as a member of our tribe. You will die an honorable man."

The vile wretch was correct. The room was fuzzy for Tarantian, his head throbbed like a spear would slam out of his forehead at any moment, and the muscles in his legs cried out an agonizing song as they trembled under his weight. None of that mattered. If he were to be someone's meal, it would not be an easy one. He charged.

Theiron was quicker than he looked. The shoulder Tarantian had intended to plant into the healer's gut missed. All he managed was a loose arm around the old man's hip. It failed to take him down, but he was able to grab a firm hold of his robe. The momentum was enough to send both of them tumbling across the floor. By the time they stopped rolling, Tarantian's back was against the dusty planks of the floor, and Theiron held a small wooden club aloft above his head.

The club raced toward Tarantian's face. Luckily, instinct was his friend just then. His legs shot out and pushed the old man back. By the time they were both back on their feet, the club was sailing toward his face again. The old man's forearm felt stronger than he expected when he blocked the blow. Whether it was the cause of Tarantian's condition or the old man's might, he would not be an easy win. Tarantian swung a stony fist at the old man's face. It missed. Not only was he deceptively strong, but he was wily too.

It quickly became clear to Tarantian that he would not be able to charge through his opponent like a raging tubber. He inhaled a deep breath through his nose and released it through his mouth. By the time the last bit of air had passed his lips, his heartrate had begun to slow, and his focus had grown razor sharp. He raised his hands up before his face and prepared to defend himself.

The hand-to-hand battle stance earned another hearty laugh from the old healer, "Do you suppose I would release a vicious mountain scarra in my home? I have healed your wounds, fought off the infection which would have killed you had I not intervened, but I have not restored you to your former glory. I have given you many elixirs. Some saved your life, and others dampened your strength. You could not defeat a child with your fists right now."

It all began to make sense. The healer was not strong nor fast, Tarantian was just groggy and weakened. He did not care. He was a big man, stronger than most, but he had sent more than one warrior who was bigger and stronger than him to the Lake. His timing had to be perfect, and his technique impeccable. He waved the old man to attack.

Theiron's wicked smile plumped up his cheeks as he feigned a strike at Tarantian's head. The arm the soldier shot up to block the attack was a ruse. When the old man followed up with a low strike toward his ribs, Tarantian took the blow and captured the old man's arm under his own. He would not be able to hold the arm there for long, so he wasted no time. The old man's nose exploded in a spray of blood when Tarantian's forehead smashed into it. Twisted and broken, the skin on its bridge had split into a deep gash. Tarantian pounded his head into the same spot again. Theiron's cheeks cracked under the weight of the attack. With the old man's arm still trapped in his left armpit, Tarantian threw his right elbow at his jaw. Only after that blow did he release the healer's arm. By that point, the club was easy to snatch away. Once he had a firm grip on it, he pushed the old man down and pummeled his head with it until he stopped struggling.

Theiron was still twitching when Tarantian got off him, but his soul was already on its way to the Lake. The commotion had woken some of the other victims in their beds and shackled to the walls. A certain groaning from across the room caught his attention. The voice was familiar. He raced over to the slumping form. It was difficult to make out his companion's features in the dim light, but there could be no doubt it was Chagon hanging from those bonds.

"I thought you dead," Tarantian whispered as he removed a gag from Chagon's mouth.

There was little strength behind Chagon's words as he replied, "I fear I'd be not long for this world had you not found me. That old healer has the key to these bonds. Free me, and let's be gone from this horrible place."

Other would-be victims began slithering from their beds. Whether crawling, limping, or walking upright, most headed directly for the door. Tarantian worked his way through the suddenly crowded darkness until he made it back to Theiron's still corpse. It took a few moments of rifling through the deceased healer's robe before he found a small key. Time suddenly seemed an enemy as both doors of the building hung wide with folks trying to escape becoming dinner for the village. All those bodies moving through the streets were sure to attract attention.

Tarantian raced back to Chagon and asked, "Can you walk?" as he freed him from his bonds.

"Well enough to get out of this horrid place," Chagon replied quietly.

"Hey," a raspy voice called out in the darkness. "Would you leave us here to die?"

The man hanging from shackles next to where Chagon had been bound was the source of the query. *Yes, I would.* That was the first thought to cross the soldier's mind, but it was not his final answer. It seemed another time, but when he had accepted the crest of Havenstahl he vowed to defend all who call the great city home. Though this village was a bit off the beaten path, it fell under the protection of that great city. It fell under his protection. As Tarantian thought about it, it did not matter to him where the man was from. Whether he hailed from the city itself or one of her villages, or from somewhere across the Great Sea, he was a man who needed defending.

"Wait here," he said to Chagon. Then he worked his way around the room freeing all those shackled from their bonds.

The first one followed along as he freed the others, thanking him profusely as they worked their way around the room. He remained by Tarantian's side right up until a deep voice called out from the back of the building, "And where do you think you're getting off to?"

"Sorry, friend," was all the man said. Then he was gone, racing as fast as he could out the front door.

Tarantian spun to face the owner of that voice. He knew it was the butcher before he laid eyes on the brute. He shot a look at Chagon to keep him seated on the bed where he had left him, and then focused his attention on the vile thing who cut flesh from his own kind to feed his own kind. The man was big and thick through the arms and shoulders. A small part of Tarantian wanted to grab Chagon and run away from the fight. In his current state, he had barely managed to beat an old man. The brawny fellow barring the door might represent his last battle. But there was a bigger part of him that simply could not do that. He had no idea how many men that bastard had butchered, but he decided right then there would be no more.

He still gripped the bloody club he had used to beat the healer to death. Though the small thing felt good in his hand, it offered little reassurance considering the man he would be brawling with clutched a cleaver in his own, the same cleaver he had used to separate the meat from the bones of who knows how many men. Hopefully, Chagon would not be captured by the same duty which kept him from fleeing. If he could keep the butcher busy long enough, perhaps the green farm boy could escape and let someone know about the horrible place where men eat men.

And then the butcher was gone. It all happened so fast it barely registered. A massive, hairy arm ending in a horrible claw dug into the big man's face and dragged him back out through the door. Three deep breaths were all it took to expel the shock of what Tarantian had just seen and allow his brain to register signals from his other senses. Growling, screaming, bones breaking or popping from sockets, and sloppy sounds that could only be a beast eating flesh filled the dark room. The grizzly mongs had found the quiet village.

Tarantian crouched low and made his way to the bed where Chagon still sat. "We cannot stay here, but it is unsafe to leave," he whispered.

"There is a stairway in the back corner," Chagon whispered back. "I do not know where it leads, but I saw the butcher taking..." his eyes grew misty as he paused, "parts down there."

"That sounds far better than what is going on outside of this place," Tarantian decided. "Show me where."

Chagon led the way toward the stairway he described. It was little more than an opening in the floor with wooden stairs leading down. There was a wooden door at the bottom. It opened easily. The room on the other side of that door was even darker than the room upstairs. Tarantian did not need light to know what horror they had walked into. He remembered the smell. It was like yesterday's battlefield when you go to retrieve your dead. Flesh rots quickly in the blazing sun. It probably rots more slowly in a cool room under the earth, but the smell is the same.

"Get on the ground," Tarantian commanded. "Bury yourself in the dead. They will cover our scent." The instruction sounded even worse to his ears than it had in his head, but grizzly mongs were hunters not scavengers. Those beasts would not eat the rotting flesh of corpses. If Tarantian and Chagon hoped to survive, they would need to blend in with the dead.

Besides the smell—which was overbearing—burrowing into a pile of carcasses is mostly just a psychological challenge. They were dry and cool for the most part. It was knowing they hid beneath a pile of meatless corpses that was the real problem. They did not feel any different than the bones of other animals, aside from maybe their shapes and sizes. The fact was small consolation. Both the men hiding beneath that pile of death knew what hid them. Luckily, the sounds of live things being cut down and devoured by vicious beasts above their heads was even more horrible and terrifying than lying under a blanket of bones and dead flesh.

# CHAPTER 34
# THE VOYEUR

The garden atop Alharin was as lush as ever when Ijilv materialized near the calm pond. He offered a casual glance to the fishes swimming the clear waters. Some were too big. They seemed out of place with their silver scales flashing in the bright sun. The others, orange ones and white ones, some spotted, some blue, they seemed to fit, but, truthfully, none of them belonged. Everything on Brerto's mountaintop paradise was a foreign visitor from somewhere else the god had willed to be there, a mishmash of things from places on Ouloos he loved. Ijilv enjoyed the illusion, inhaling the sweet perfume of flowers wafting across a gentle breeze and basking in the warmth of the afternoon sun.

The god from the east, the great hawk as he was known, strolled slowly through Brerto's garden. There was no need to rush. Things moved along as they should, and he had spent precious few moments away from the darkness of his hidden tower at the edge of time and reason. He certainly had a few moments to spare enjoying the fruits of his brother's effort.

That brother, Brerto, stood just inside the entrance of his cave. His eyes were tightly closed. The tension dug deep lines into the flawless skin of his face. His staff glowed as bright as a thousand suns. The reason for all that effort lay before him, Cialia, the Dragon, self-proclaimed bane of the gods. She was a power beyond reason or understanding. The control Brerto held over her was dangerously thin. Ijilv watched in silence, smiling at the struggle.

"What are you waiting for?" Kallum's voice rang out in Ijilv's head.

Ijilv's smile only grew, "For the Dragon to complete her journey, of course. There is no doubt I could scatter our brother to the wind if I so desired, but why expend our energy? The Dragon will do that for us. Then we will gather him up, and he will be one with us, even more powerful than we are at this moment."

"That stinks of cowardice," Kallum scoffed.

Ijilv chuckled at the jibe. "You were always powerful but rash, my beloved brother. That is why the lad of Lake defeated you so easily. Of course, the Dragon is far more powerful than any of us, but you fell far too easily. If you had even the slightest hint of patience, you would be free to terrorize those who worshipped you rather than trapped, helpless within me."

"Beloved," Kallum spat. "If I were truly your beloved, you would have stood beside me rather than cowering in wait to shackle me when I was unable to defend."

A god's eyes snapped open—horrible and beautiful—and cast a negative glow against the bright light of his staff. "You invade the sanctity of my garden," he said to Ijilv.

"I do," Ijilv agreed. "Kallum, our mighty brother, is with me. His strength is mine, and soon yours will be as well. We will all be together, a power like none other on Ouloos or any plane of reality."

A seeming impossibility, the glowing of Brerto's staff grew even brighter. "You will find I am not easy to subdue."

Before Brerto could do anything to defend against his brother, Ijilv boomed, "SITTU AHU!"

The glow of the god's staff did not dim, but his horrible eyes slammed shut.

"What did you do to him?" Kallum asked.

"A simple spell," Ijilv's tone was relaxed once again. "I commanded him to rest."

"Magic?" Kallum hissed. "I ended magic after Merkhal's failure. It no longer exists."

Ijilv shook his head, "What you call magic is nothing more than bending the rules of reality and morphing them to fit your will through our eternal connection to all things through Coeptus. You did not end that connection or any being's ability to access it. You simply convinced yourself, our brothers, and all who worshipped one or another of you they no longer could."

Then Ijilv, smug in his control over his brothers, sauntered casually over to Brerto. He put his mouth close to his brother's perfect ear and whispered, "The Dragon will defeat your illusion. She will triumph and scatter you to the wind. You will be mine." Then he looked down at Cialia, "What illusion has he concocted for you? What terrors play out in your mind?" Turning his head back to his brother, he added, "I want to play this game with you. Let me in your head, brother. Let me play with your illusion."

# CHAPTER 35
## THE MIGHTY HAWK

The trail is both loyal companion—a close friend who is always there regardless the length of time between visits—and brutal challenge. The reason for the journey is irrelevant. Whether warrior, adventurer, explorer, or vagabond, each has a unique and personal relationship with both its blessings and challenges. The freedom and fresh air are intoxicating, magical things which can only be enjoyed by venturing from the security of one's home. However, hunger is a regular companion. Only what has been packed or killed can be eaten, and no matter how lumpy or rough the cot, it will typically offer a better night's sleep than the hard ground. At the beginning of a journey, the allure of the trail may be enough to lift the spirts or turn up the corners of the mouth into an exhilarated smile. As the adventure drags from days to weeks, the excitement can fade. The comforts of home typically taken for granted become things missed, things desired. Sleep comes less easily, and the slumber a traveler gets becomes less and less rejuvenating. Dreams are more vivid in the great unknown.

After weeks chasing an unknown destination through lands with sparse wildlife worthy of being a meal, Cialia had not quite reached the point where home became more attractive than the trail, but it loomed closer than she cared to admit. Each mile looked exactly like the prior, and every clearing where she and her father made camp appeared the same as the night before. The journey was taking its toll. Father's stories grew vaguer with fewer details or twists, the sparse meat offered up by the land grew bland, and the ground seemed rougher with each passing night.

This particular morning had been like each since the journey began. The only difference being the types and number of trees lining either side of the trail or what was going on in the sky. On rainy days everything got wet and the horses struggled through the muck. On sunny days the damp leaves glistened, and the canopy had a magical glow. Right after a shower when fat raindrops still clinging to the leaves above would grab the light and twist it into rainbow colors was probably Cialia's favorite time. Even that grew less exciting. Both glorious blades father had crafted for her sat unchallenged in her scabbards dully flapping against her horse's flanks as they trotted down the trail.

Father did not seem to care much. He would whistle or hum, shout out what type of bird was flying by, or wonder aloud about the age of this tree or that. Cialia was tired of it. She grew increasingly depressed with each passing mile. If father had not made an absolute nuisance of himself that morning, she might have remained wrapped in her cloak leaning against the tree that had served as her bed for the evening until she died of starvation.

She was just about to complain out loud when she saw a banner flapping in the breeze. The standard bearer remained out of sight as they mounted a slight hill, but someone had to be carrying it. Simple human contact was not much of an adventure, but it would be nice to share words with another human besides her father. Not that he was poor company, but he had been her only company for weeks. She longed for the sound of a different voice or an idea from a perspective other than one she expected. Either would be a grand diversion.

The banner itself was black with a red sigil she did not recognize, a coiled snake grasping something in its fangs. Perhaps whoever rode under that banner would have an interesting tale to tell about the lands from which they hailed. "Riders approach," she smiled at her father and gave her horse a nudge to quicken his step.

"Cialia, wait," the reply was too late. She was already charging up the trail.

As she crested the hill, the prospect of light banter to pass the time seemed unlikely. The line of men marching along the trail two by two stretched as far as she could see, and the faces those men wore far less than welcoming. Father had always told her not to judge a man based on the way he looked or the condition of his goods, but on his character alone. However, when he finally caught up to her on the hill, he had different words, "These are not friendly men. We should get as far from the trail as we can until they pass."

It was difficult to disagree with the sentiment. The dirty, scowling men marching up the trail wore matted furs and the skulls of some unfamiliar animal in place of helms, and they carried their swords in their hands like they were ready to battle. Despite these things, Cialia was just about to challenge her father on how easily he had forgotten his own lesson when the leader of the approaching horde noticed the two of them. The guttural howl he let loose seemed a sound an animal would make rather than a man. The rest of the group answered with the same sound, and they charged.

The beastly war cry filled the forest like the loudest crack of thunder, rolling across the trail rather than the sky. Coupled with the sound of all those feet pounding into the dirt, it certainly seemed a good reason to flee. Cialia might have considered that an option had the group not already been so close to them. Their horses would never move quickly enough through the trees to escape the savage men. She had no sooner decided to stand and fight when father said, "Too late," slipped off his horse and drew his sword. She did the same. The horses charged off into the trees, and the two weary travelers prepared to fight the charging mass.

Agrimon drew first blood. His blade slipped through the bannerman's neck and sent his head careening wide-eyed into the trees. Even half-lame he was a titan. Cialia claimed the second life that would die on the trail that day. She blocked an overhead slash with the blade in her left hand and cleaved the man's head off with the blade in her right hand.

The beastly men kept howling and charging and swinging their blades, and the two travelers kept cutting them down. The bodies piled up until the raging mob had to climb over their own dead to reach Cialia and Agrimon. The sound of swords clashing echoed off the trees. It mingled with the howling, the grunting, and the sound of cold, oily metal slicing through meat and bone in a grotesque chorus of death.

Then Agrimon fell to one knee. A massive man with legs like the trunks of thick trees and big swollen arms dove down on him from the top of the pile of his dead kin and slashed down with his sword. The swordsmith blocked the blow and saved his skull from being cracked in two, but the force of it drove him to the ground. The next blow would have killed him if not for Cialia. When she saw her father fall, she stabbed the man before her in the throat with one blade and spun to cleave off the head of the monster about to slay her father.

She stood above him battling, but their numbers were too great. Her blades slashed faster and faster, but the monsters just kept coming. They pushed her back. By the time Agrimon had regained his feet, five men were slashing at him in unison. There were just too many of them. A blade sliced through his right arm at the shoulder. He growled at the man who took his limb and stabbed the bastard in the heart.

Cialia battled with even greater vigor, slashing and cutting, but she could not get to him. She screamed as she fought even harder, but the effort failed to stop the next blade from thrusting into her father's gut or the following from punching through his heart. The final blow took his head off. It did not fly through the air spinning toward the trees or into the crowd but flopped unceremoniously to the dirt and stared at Cialia.

She wanted to fall to her knees and cry, to gather up the pieces of her father and hold them close, but first she needed revenge. Tears streamed down her face as an agonizing song of pain roared from her mouth carrying spittle, tears, and snot with it. She would kill them all.

Then a sound more terrible than Cialia's pitiable song or the beastly war cry of the vile, dirty, and dishonorable men she battled filled the suddenly heavy air of the forest. All not lying dead on the trail paused to see what horrible thing could make a sound so beautiful and terrifying.

The great hawk soared above the canopy. The size of thing was hard to make out through the trees, but it seemed impossible. The body was longer than five horses standing snout to tail, and the wingspan was more than one hundred feet. No words came from the small battlefield, just gasping and a few cries that sounded more like fear than war rage. The thing flew high up into the sky before diving down toward the canopy. Just before it hit the highest branches of the tallest trees, a light so bright every living soul who saw it had to slam their eyes shut to keep them from being burned out of their heads filled the sky.

Everything was silent by the time Cialia opened her eyes. A few moments passed before she could make out shapes again, like the bright circle one sees after looking directly at the sun. When she finally could see something other than that bright flash, all her attackers were gone. No dead bodies remained except her father, but he was whole. None of it made any sense. She watched his head and arm removed from his body. It was as if the battle never happened, but father was still dead.

An old man stood next to father's body. His eyes grabbed her attention. They were black, like two small abysses sucking away all light, but were all colors at once, blending and cracking like a kaleidoscope spinning faster than anything could. His hair and beard were both downy white waves, but they were too white, glowing like a source of light rather than an object reflecting the sun's rays. His robe was the same. He carried a staff in his hand. The end of it formed a delicate, chaotic mass of thin barbs arching around each other that glowed with the same perfect light as the rest of him.

Before Cialia could process enough of what she was seeing to come up with any words, the old man spoke to her, "Cialia, great champion of… What did he come up with? Oh yes, Varisghoul. You have been blessed with a great purpose, or so you believe."

Cialia remained mostly speechless as tears for her father continued to stream down her cheeks. "But…" was all she could come up with.

"My name is Ijilv. That is not important, but you should know to whom you are speaking," he offered her a friendly smile. "This trail seems never ending. Does it not?"

"Merkhal lives atop a mountain of fire far too the east across the cracked land," the words came from her lips, but they sounded as if they belonged to someone else.

"That sounds quite far indeed. Do you believe it is a place you will ever find?"

Cialia was not sure but did her best to sound like she was, "Of course. I have made a vow, and I intend to make good on that promise."

"Does any of this feel real?" Ijilv's smile never faded as he asked the question. "I know you believe in your mission, this adventure, but I wonder how certain you are of it. I wonder if there are times when it feels you are an actor playing at adventure in someone else's story. I must go. Before I do, I will offer this advice. You will never find your true destination until you wake up."

"Please do not speak to me in riddles. I just watched my father cut down by vicious beasts of men," Cialia complained. "I am obviously awake, as I am speaking with you now. Did you come to visit me in my dreams?"

Ijilv ignored the question, "You must seek advice from the girl who knows everything. She is connected to all things."

"I already have a mission…" the words were lost as the old man vanished.

Cialia was alone in a field of unkept grass with her father's corpse. Trees and trail had vanished with the old man. The shifting scenery slipped to a place in the periphery of her awareness. What did it matter where she stood? Father was dead. She knelt beside him in flowing waves of impossible green and wept. Her body convulsed as she finally laid her head down on his chest and let the sorrow consume her.

She remained there for a good long while. How long was impossible to know. Time means very little when consumed with things such as deep sorrow, rage, or blissful joy. She was in the moment just then. The sun could rise and set day after day. Stars could be born and burn out. She would be there weeping over the only person in the world she had ever loved. But then…

Confusion gripped her. She could not remember where she was, how she got there, or why she wept so strong. She raised her head and looked at the man she wept over. The dead face staring back at her was as unfamiliar as the dry, cracked earth surrounding the two of them. Her tears ceased. Of course, she felt pity for the poor, dead man left to rot beneath the blazing sun, but every soul returned to the Lake at some point. Could she shed tears for them all?

A cave sat directly in front of her. It had not been there before. Or had it? She could not remember. She looked back at the dead thing in her arms. It shifted slightly causing her to jump. Dead things should not move. Before fear could tickle her spine with icy fingers, the body crumbled to dust. After the last speck drifted into the air from her hand, she completely forgot why she crouched there in the soft, mucky earth. Her wet knee was almost enough to grab her attention, to sway her focus from the dim light glowing in the cave which may or may not have been there only moments prior. It was almost enough to make her question where the trees had gone—then the grass, then the cracked earth, then what? That dim light was just bright enough to keep all those questions at bay. She stood and walked toward it.

An eerie dark filled the forest, not like night, but something different. The dark seemed an illusion, like light playing at darkness. A quick glance would fail to see the trick, but a focused observation could expose the ruse. The thick fog hugging the ground up to Maelich's waist was the same. It kept him from seeing the soft forest floor beneath his feet, but it was a fakery. He knew the place too well. The forest probably had no floor.

"Maelich, help!" the passionate voice dripped urgency.

Another trick. Whether it was the black horse or the white horse attempting to rule his subconscious did not matter. He refused to let them.

His feet slowly lifted from the soft ground which may or may not be hiding under a thick blanket of fog which did not behave at all like fog and probably was not even there. After a deep breath, he closed his eyes and the fog truly was no longer there. The mystery of the soft ground was solved. It was there. He sent it spinning. *This is my dream.*

The voice beckoned with more urgency, "Maelich, help!"

He ignored the plea. Another ploy, another trick, another game he refused to play. Instead, he floated higher, above the canopy and into the open air. Speed steadily increasing, he rushed past clouds, dim in the dark sky, toward a moon growing just as steadily. The dark spots on the glowing surface become craters and ridges. The glow dimmed until it was nothing more than a dusty surface, a gray desert. He raced past planets and stars faster and faster until his flight abruptly ceased.

The sensation should have been jarring, like a horse at full gallop suddenly stopping, but it was not. It felt like everything else had been moving and he had been stationary.

The planets and stars were gone. He was back in the forest. The fog had returned. "Get out of my head," he complained.

The black horse stood before him with fear in her eyes, "Maelich, you must see what I have come to show you."

His hand snatched out to grab her mane as quick as a snake striking its prey, but she was gone. In her place stood an altar in the glow of a bright light with no source. A dwarf decorated for the pyre rested on the altar. He seemed peaceful despite the great dwarf axe gripped by his hands and resting on his chest.

"Bindaar, old friend," Maelich whispered. "Why do I know your name? Why do I call you old friend when I do not recognize your face? You appear a warrior with your mighty axe, so I assume us to be kindred spirits. But I do not know you."

He touched the dwarf's face expecting it to be cold, but it felt like nothing. "I know you are not really here. Neither am I, not really. Why are you here in my dream? I wish I could feel deep sorrow. I wish I could mourn for you. I feel we were friends, maybe in another life. If that is true, it is a shame I cannot honor your memory with heartfelt sorrow for the loss of you."

"He was your friend, Maelich," the black horse called out from beyond the alter. "You saved his life once. It changed him. You may have meant more to him than he did you, but you cared for him."

"I have had enough of meeting you like this," Maelich scowled. He failed to notice when he began to walk right through where the altar had been, but it was gone.

"Please, Maelich," the horse begged, as he stalked toward her.

"You and Maulom are the same. I want more than riddles or mere pieces of stories. Give me something tangible that means something to me," he growled as his pace increased, each step more purposeful than the last.

"Wake," she cried as his hand slashed out toward her.

The world went black for a moment before his eyes snapped open. His clothes stuck to him and his beddings were soaked. Ymitoth worried over him, eyeing him suspiciously with those black, dead eyes which used to startle him so. "You've been dreaming again. It's got you sweating like you're burning up with the fever."

"It was the black horse again," Maelich replied breathlessly. "She showed me another dead dwarf. His name was Bindaar. His face was unfamiliar, but I knew his name just like the last one."

"Bindaar," Ymitoth repeated the name. "It sounds familiar, but I can't see a face to put with the name."

The flaps of the small tent snapped open and Maulom strolled in. Despite days on the dustiest trail Maelich had ever seen, the man's impeccable white clothes remained unblemished. Everyone else looked as if they wore rusty, brown clothes. His lips parted between his perfectly trimmed beard and mustache as if to speak, but Maelich cut him off.

"The black horse was in my dream again," he said, his tone sharp. "She reminds me too much of you. It seems the two of you work together to keep me befuddled within my own head."

"Nonsense," Maulom waved the idea off. "She is a witch filling your head with lies. Have no fear. I have been searching for her. When I find her, I will send her off to never trouble your slumber again."

Maelich was unconvinced, "You cannot discount the similarities. You both come to me in dreams. You both speak to me in riddles. You both seem bound to control me by invading my unconscious mind. Do you deny it?"

"I do deny it," Maulom rolled his eyes. "She and I are as different as night and day. I led you to your destiny, and she seeks to sway you from it. Surely, you must recognize the difference."

"I do not," Maelich began, but before he could add anything else, Ding charged into the tent bursting with excitement.

"Fires burn, south," he could barely get the words out.

"It is time," Maulom smiled.

Concern spread across Maelich's face, "I hope they are ready. If these Tahnka are as fierce and formidable as you have described, our first fight, the Shaiwah's first fight, will be no easy victory."

"Aye," Ymitoth agreed, "no easy task at all."

Ding remained confident, "Shaiwah ready. Shaiwah fight. Tahnka die."

Maelich hoped Ding and the rest of his kin were as ready as the excited young warrior suggested they were. He was less so, but nothing could be known before the first test. He and Ymitoth had already strategized about how the Shaiwah's first battle would go. They had trained the eager soldiers as best they could with the time given to complete the task. The ones who proved the most proficient with their swords became leaders to the ones who proved less so.

All the thoughts of war and worrying about how his band of new warriors who would taste their first battle with the light of a new day completely dragged his attention away from concerns about horses haunting his dreams.

# CHAPTER 37
# THE WARRIOR

The land changed quickly as Perrin's small group travelled away from the Lake, and not just the land, but everything. The shifts were slight, gradual, but undeniable. The vegetation had changed first. None in the group found that terribly odd. The fauna around the Lake had been so different than what any of them were accustomed to that leaving those wonderfully odd trees, flowers, and plants only made the land around the place seem even more enchanted. The trees and shrubs they encountered a mere few miles from it seemed more familiar. They looked like pines, oaks, maples, and a variety of other trees common in Havenstahl and the surrounding lands, but they were different somehow. After a few more miles, they seemed less like different trees and more like the same trees but unfinished. The grass on the ground changed in similar fashion. As they progressed it looked less like common grass and more like something else entirely. The sky seemed the biggest riddle. When they had looked out across the place where the maps don't go while standing in the sweet perfection of the land around the Lake, blue skies stretched on forever. However, as they got deeper into this foreign land the sky changed. Directly overhead it remained blue, but in the distance, it was different, splashed with colors which did not belong in a sky outside of sunset, or even at all in some cases. Silver and green, the darkest blue and most delicate orange, even deep black and complete white, and more all mingled together, swirling and changing in patterns which were not really patterns at all. They were more like random happenings. At one moment this color existing in this shape, and in the next it was a different color in a different shape.

A few days had passed before the land became hilly. Their path followed up hills or around them and down into valleys. None of it seemed strange until Glord realized they should have been traveling up a pretty steep incline for the better part of a day, but it had leveled off and began to lead them down into a valley instead.

"I am no expert on this terrain, but we should be heading up a good-sized hill right now," he said.

"This land is inconsistent," Ycharaz agreed with amazement in his voice.

Perrin remained unsurprised. "It will only get worse," she replied. "The Great Mother showed me a chaotic place. It resembled our surroundings but lacked any order at all. These gradual shifts we have been seeing will steadily become more consistent until the very ground we stand upon will shift and change constantly."

A bit of irritation slipped into Ycharaz's tone as he replied, "You might have shared that with us before we left that perfect place."

"Would it have made a difference to you?" Glord snapped.

"I suppose not," Ycharaz shrugged as he glanced around, "but it would have been nice to know what to expect."

Perrin could not blame him. It was a shame to leave that place, but Geillan was more valuable than any amount of peace or comfort. She would eat dirt and sleep on spikes for the rest of her days if it meant saving her son from those vile demons—emissaries of a violent god—who stole him away from her. "I should have told all of you what Helias had showed me," she sighed.

Glord's eyes narrowed as he looked at Ycharaz and replied to Perrin, "It would have made no difference."

"None at all," Ycharaz smirked and nudged his horse forward.

As one day drifted into another, it became increasingly difficult to discern the difference between them. At times, the night sky was brighter than noon on a cloudless day, while at others, day was as dark as a starless night. The land and skies around them continued to change as if contradicting themselves. Rushing rivers with rapids violent enough to be heard a mile off became trickling creeks before they arrived, or the opposite. One morning they woke in a field of orange-yellow grass as thick as small tree branches. That same spot had been heavily wooded with plenty of cover when they had made camp the prior evening.

High cliffs began rumbling up from nothing and inching toward the sky as the trail dipped downward. The cliffs seemed rocky despite being light blue with green sparkles catching the red sunlight and casting orange shadows. By the time they stopped growing, the walls on either side of the trail towered at least two-hundred feet above them. Wide-eyed, Perrin took it all in until she saw movement. Dark shapes scurried about the rocks above. "We are not alone," she whispered to Glord.

"The queen is correct," Darg piped up. "I spied them creeping around either side of the trail a few miles back, even before the cliffs they scurry upon grew up out of nothing."

"They pose little threat to us high among the cliffs," Glord said as he surveyed the canyon walls, "but be prepared."

A scowl spread across Ganodin's face as he looked up and boomed, "I will split any man or beast who wishes to challenge my queen in half. Best keep your distance or the name Ganodin will become well known in these lands."

"My queen, I know nothing of the beasts who dwell in these lands, but I make this vow. That beautiful blade you carry will have no cause to taste their blood. None will get close to you," the sing song quality of Jorgon's voice made the promise seem a farce, but he meant every word.

Darg's right cheek swelled as he sucked on his teeth. He shifted them back into place and boomed, "All your blades will remain starved for blood as I slay all these beasts before any of you have a chance to draw them."

Ycharaz nudged his horse close enough to Perrin's that the two animals bumped hips. Perrin shot him a look. He returned the look with a wink, "They all speak gibberish. I will be the one to slay your enemies, my queen."

Halogren looked back and scowled, twisting the scars around his mouth into a grotesque horror, "You will all be boasting of your greatness all the way back to the Lake if you fail to stay sharp."

Perrin remained silent, scanning the tops of the cliffs. It was difficult to gauge the strength of the force tracking them. Shapes would move close to the edge and then push off disguising their numbers. Her best estimate put them at around one hundred strong. Her men could boast of their prowess with blades and vow to kill any creature who looked at her cross, but they would need her as much as she needed them. As she glanced around at her escort, she made a vow to herself to fight beside them not cower behind them.

The cliffs beside Perrin's group began shrinking away as the sky above changed. It looked burnt and ashy, twisting like the remnants of a spent fire swirling in a cyclone. The path beneath them changed as if in response to the burning sky. Dry and cracked like a desert, it blazed bright yellow. The cracks moved constantly, flashing a glistening green as they zigged and zagged. Black things began springing up randomly across the cracked, yellow ground. They resembled shrubs but appeared prickly and dangerous.

"They have our flanks. Charge," Glord shouted the command as he drove his heels into his horse's sides.

The cloud of dust the horses kicked up as they charged across the cracked dirt was milky white with the faintest blue glitter haunting about it like a formless ghost. "This place is alive," Perrin gasped.

They charged half a mile before Glord called them to halt and form up. By the time they had circled round to face their pursuers, the dust hiding them from sight had settled. At least one hundred creatures resembling men but in proportions that made no sense charged toward them. Their heads and torsos were too small and their arms and legs too big. They wore furry animal hides that seemed wholly inappropriate considering the warmth of the surrounding lands. The weapons they waved above their heads were black and pitted. The beasts they rode were proportionally similar to horses, but bigger with fur that looked painted. Some were red, some blue, others striped of various colors, none of which made sense for any beast. They all had hooked tusks curving up from either side of their foaming snouts.

"Not one step further," Glord's command dripped with all the authority of a general of Havenstahl's army. If the approaching hoard heard it over the hollow slapping sound their horses' hooves made pounding into the cracked dirt beneath them, they showed no sign.

The smile which spread across Ycharaz's face as he watched the group of not quite men riding their not quite horses completely ignore his general's command oozed joyous insanity. He looked around his small group and laughed, "Show these beasts no mercy. A pound of tubber says I slay more of these monsters than any one of you."

"I will take that bet," Perrin's eyes narrowed as she drew her sword and drove her heals into her horse.

Perrin's horse had made it to a full gallop before Glord was able to call out, "Charge."

The ground between the two forces no longer resembled any kind of ground. The stuff their horses raced across looked like a cloudless, midnight sky with stars and moons and comets. Each hoof pounding the sky beneath them kicked up stardust instead of dirt. The sky above turned to a grassy field.

Darg may not have been the best sword in the group, but he was by far the best pure rider. By the time the two forces collided, he was ten lengths ahead of anyone else. A moment before he crashed into that line, he jumped up onto his horse's back. Another moment later, he leapt onto the rider immediately left of the space his horse slipped through between two riders. Not more than a second after that, he stood tall on a tusked, horse-like monster holding the severed head of the creature who had been riding it. He killed five more like that, leaping from horse-like beast to horse-like beast and decapitating its rider, before one of the monsters finally tackled him out of the air.

There was precious little time for Darg to consider his opponent after tumbling across the starscape beneath them. The thing looked like a man with wonky proportions. It had long, hairless legs. Those odd legs terminated at a waist which sat midway between Darg's own waist and his sternum, but its torso was so short the two were nearly identical in height. Its skin was the palest purple with large, reddish veins showing through more clearly than they should. Its face was hairless—not even eyebrows—but resembled a man' face, only roughly half the size of a normal one. The small ridge above two slits where a nose should have been—under eyes twice the size of an average man's—was the only thing which really kept the thing from looking like anything other than an odd-shaped man.

The not quite man swung his black, stony looking sword at Darg's head. The wily soldier spun beneath the attack and cut through those long legs right below its crotch. He continued spinning with the velocity of his strike and a tiny head was spinning through the air. "That makes seven," he called out to Ycharaz who was slicing through the gullet of another while speeding by on his horse.

"I count ten," Ycharaz shouted back over his head as he halted his horse to stab another through the throat. "Make that eleven," he shouted as he charged over the falling carcass.

Ganodin was off his horse. He stumbled backward, losing ground against three as he blocked attacks with his mighty axe. His foot slipped on a comet and he tumbled onto his back. He brought his axe up in front of him to block a black blade arcing toward his face, but the blow never connected. Instead, the arm which had been swinging that blade landed harmlessly next to him. A moment later, a severed head landed on his other side, while another bounced off the blade of his axe. Then Perrin's bright face peered down at him with a wide smile. "That makes six for me," she said before spinning to parry a blow.

A moment later, Ganodin was back on his feet. He worked his way over to Perrin and spun to defend her back. "My queen," he called out, "I had intended to protect you from our foes, and instead you have saved me. Grant me the great honor of guarding your back."

"You protect mine, and I will protect yours," Perrin yelled back. "We will show these beasts why all should fear the fiercest of Havenstahl."

The two battled like that, back-to-back, cutting down the manlike things attacking them. Perrin had a warrior's instinct. Glord had trained her, but her movements were like art, painting the star-streaked ground with the deep auburn blood of her enemies. She barely registered Glord's voice shouting above the fray, "Men, to the queen." Moments later, all in her group formed up in a circle, battling enemies on all sides.

Jorgon called out, "My queen, if this battle proves to be my last, I am honored to have fought alongside the fiercest queen Havenstahl has ever known."

"I am not a proper queen," Perrin shouted out as she ran a man thing through the heart, "but I have a command for you. None of you have my leave to die on this day. This land may not be ours, but this battle is. Paint the stars beneath our feet with the blood of my enemies."

All the adrenaline, all the hubris, all the feelings of glory rushing through the veins of Perrin's small group would not be enough to win the day. Their enemies boasted numbers too great to overcome. They continued to battle, slowly losing ground until their circle had shrunk to the point back touched back and elbow touched elbow. There was no more ground to give, but their enemies kept coming. The slightest bit of doubt slipped into Perrin's awareness. It was barely a tickle in her consciousness, but it was there. The black blade arced toward her face. She raised her sword up to block the blow, but its force was great enough to knock her down to one knee. The next one might cut into her soft flesh.

Before that finishing blow could come, a horn blared. The sound was melodic and deep, like a mountain scarra howling for her pups to return. Perrin looked into the eyes of the man thing looming over her. Was it fear she saw in those pink eyes? And then hoofbeats. She took advantage of the distraction to impale her attacker through the throat. He gurgled something inaudible as his sword hit the ground and he helplessly tried to keep the blood in his body.

The beasts were suddenly retreating, racing back to where the cliffs had been. Horses—real horses, not those tusked monsters the man things rode—raced around them chasing away and battling with the beasts. Once all remaining alive in the horde who had attacked Perrin's group were racing away as fast as they could, the calvary who had chased them off ceased their pursuit.

"Men, hold," Perrin said quietly, as she made eye contact with each of her men. "Let us find out if these riders are friend or foe."

"I pity them if they prove foe," Darg chuckled before sucking hard on his teeth.

The riders circled around Perrin's group. The move was unsurprising. Perrin would have commanded her men to do the same if addressing an invading force, even one so small as hers. The men circling her group were different than the man things they had just battled with. These looked like any other man from any of the great cities. Before Glord could open his mouth, Perrin addressed them, "I am Perrin, rightful queen of Havenstahl. My son has been stolen by a horrible and vile god. I mean to challenge this wicked creature for my son's life. I ask safe passage through this place and promise no mercy if you choose to hinder my mission."

One of the men leapt down from his horse. He had short, auburn hair that danced awkwardly in the light breeze. His face was clean with no beard to hide his cleft chin, and his dark eyes were easy to look at. "My queen," he said, as he bowed almost deep enough to be satirical and disrespectful, "Dirk, at your service. You are more than welcomed in these lands and can expect no challenge from me or my men." Once he had finished his dramatic bow, he smiled and added, "Forgive the blush in my cheeks, highness. A beauty such as that which my eyes behold is quite rare in these lands."

The compliment crossed a line with Glord. "Mind your tongue, lad.

My fair queen is spoken for. The blush in your cheeks will melt right off your skull. Though I may be willing to forgive the folly, it could be her husband would be less forgiving. Perhaps you have not heard of Maelich of Havenstahl."

"The lad of the Lake? The Dragon?" Dirk smiled wide. "Who has not heard of him. He saved us all, did he not? And your queen is the wife of this great power? I feel honored to be in your presence, highness. You might well be queen of us all," he paused as he scratched his head. "It begs the question, though. If your husband is the greatest power this world has ever known, why do you travel treacherous, foreign lands to rescue his son. Could he not simply will his son free of his bonds?"

"Mocking my queen is only a good idea if you are not fond of your tongue," Ycharaz snapped.

"Thank you, my loyal friends, but I am perfectly capable of speaking for myself," Perrin gently scolded her men. "My husband's whereabouts are not your concern, and my mission is my own. If you have a mind to interfere with my quest, my faithful men will cut you down. If you care to help, the assistance is welcome. If neither of those are true, stand aside and let us pass."

"Forgive me, highness," Dirk bowed again. This time the gesture lacked any sarcasm, "You are safe in these lands. None under my command will hinder you in any way. I invite you to be our guest. Come, rest, replenish your supplies, and start your journey anew refreshed and ready to attack the trail. Our queen may have some good advice to assist you in your goal."

"Words," Glord scoffed. "What do we know of you? Nothing. How does my queen know you can be trusted?"

"My word is all I have. Warrior to warrior, I promise to defend your queen as vigorously as you would," Dirk replied plainly.

Glord's scowl was all the response he intended to give. Perrin touched his arm, "My loyal general, my protector, we need supplies. Let us be mindful of the risks but see where this road leads."

The courtyard in front of the palace at Alhouim bustled as grongs grunted at dwarves chained together in single file. The dwarves shuffled along in teary silence, none daring to look at anything but the ground before them. A few had made the mistake of glancing around at something other than the dirt before their boots earlier in the day. Grong clubs made examples out of them, and the rest learned quickly. Dragging along dead kin chained fast by wrist and ankle is a lesson not soon forgotten.

Trogmortem milled about with the grongs. None of them served any purpose that day aside from terrorizing their victims with ugly sneers and violent growls. One dwarf trying desperately to remain unnoticed by the massive trogmortem looming over him made the mistake of jumping slightly when the monster howled down at him. One small bite later, his head was sliding down the trogmortem's throat, and his soul was drifting back to the Lake.

There were giants in the courtyard that day too. Not more than a handful, six including Ott. They remained aloof. None of them cared much about taking Alhouim back from the dwarves and re-establishing Maomnosett. Most would have preferred to return home across the Great Sea, but not Ott. Maomnosett Ahm's father wanted revenge. His desire had nothing to do with honoring his son. That pathetic worm had been felled by a mere lad. The fact that particular lad was special—born of the Lake and all that—meant little to the fierce giant. The only crime for which Ott held the dwarves of Alhouim to account was dishonoring his name. There was no worse crime than that, and every dwarf would understand the folly of their ways.

Ott sat upon one son's throne in the exact spot his other son's throne had sat. Both had fallen to mere men. The former bested by a general of Havenstahl, and the latter felled by the lad of the Lake. Taken together the two amounted to nothing more than a sad legacy of failure. Worse than that, Ahm's sons had followed their father to the Lake in a failed attempt to redeem his honor by taking back his city, and Bok's son had defected like a coward spouting nonsense of equality with lowly men and dwarves. Ott would restore his name, mend his tarnished legacy on the backs of the vile dwarves who had betrayed his son and supported a bastard born of a Lake.

The throne the new king of Maomnosett sat upon was a work of art. Bok may have been a failure, but the throne he had designed for his conquest of Havenstahl and Alhouim was magnificent. The massive thing was carved out of solid brindlewood—brindle trees are monstrous, the tops of the tallest soar more than four hundred feet above the ground—and etched with glorious renderings of mighty giants trampling men and beasts beneath their feet.

The remnants of the former dwarf king's throne, along with his wife's, lay splintered about the new king's feet. When Ott saw how the dwarves of Alhouim had treated Ahm's former throne, he thought it only fitting to respond in kind. When he had first walked into that courtyard and saw his son's body cast in Prang and hanging from the wall immediately behind where his throne had sat—his missing head, stolen by the lad of the Lake, had been replaced with the head of a tubber and the broken remnants of his throne fastened to the wall surrounding the grotesque statue—it was more than he could stand. Had it merely represented a slight against his son, Ott may have ignored it. However, it was more than that to him. To the new King Maomnosett, the callous treatment of his son's corpse represented another slight against his great name.

Chi-Ta, leader of the trogmortem, approached. Slurg, the grong's choontah, accompanied him, dragging a teary-eyed and defiant Gleeanna along by a thick rope fastened around her neck. The queen of Alhouim struggled against her bonds and shot deadly glares at her captors. She saved her fiercest look for the vile beast who had captured her city, broken her throne, and chained her subjects like beasts being prepped for slaughter. Though it was not Ott who had killed her husband, good Doentaat, she laid the blame of his death at the giant's feet along with the rest.

Ott's voice was deep and terrible, "You have a fiery spirit. Perhaps your dead king would stand in chains beside you if he harbored a similar blaze in his heart."

"Coward," she spat. "Loose these bonds, and I'll show you just how fiery is my spirit, you vile thing."

The giant's humorless chuckle sounded like rocks being ground up in metal gears, "I never met Doentaat, but I imagine him to be a titan among dwarves. He would have to be to suffer the likes of you. If my own wife acted in such a disrespectful manner, I would leave her body out to decay in the blazing sun while the crows had their fill." He flashed a patronizing smile and added, "I wonder. Did he ever show you the back of his hand, or was he weak?"

Gleeanna's face twisted into something dark and terrifying as she lost more ground against the tears she so desperately tried to hold back. "If he were here," the words were difficult to understand as they sloshed out of her mouth amid throaty sobs.

"If he were here, what?" Ott's laughter filled the courtyard. "Would he defend your honor and challenge me? I wish he could have stayed alive long enough for me to kill him myself, highness. I would have made a show for you. What would you have done, standing there helpless, watching your husband's life bleed from his body as his eyes grayed over? Would you cry? Would you stomp your feet like a helpless child angry at their parent's demand but helpless to control their own destiny?"

It happened so fast, Slurg had no time to react. Before the grong choontah knew what was happening, Gleeanna's foot was stomping on his, and her forehead was pounding into his snout. The shock was great enough to loosen his grip on the rope in his clawed hand leaving Alhouim's former queen bound but almost free. She charged headlong toward Ott. Three steps were all she made before her head was off her body and bleeding all over Chi-Ta's hand.

Ott's face drooped into something close to sadness, "Chi-Ta, why would you do that? Why would you steal from me the satisfaction of sending that wily sprite back to the Lake?"

"Forgive me, highness," Chi-Ta dropped his gaze away from the giant's as he dropped Gleeanna's head to the dirt. "I reacted."

Before Ott could press the conversation further, the remaining dwarves in the courtyard raised such a ruckus any words which passed his lips would have remained unheard. He set his jaw tight and nodded toward the ruckus. Neither the trogmortem king nor the choontah of the grongs had to think too hard about what the gesture meant. Both moved toward the bound mob of angry dwarves and began barking commands to their respective troops. Several intimidating howls, a few slaps from the backs of massive trogmortem hands, a few strikes from heavy grong clubs, and two dead dwarves later, the roiling mob began to calm.

Ott's voice boomed throughout the courtyard, "You will be freed from your bonds, allowed to move about my city and resume your lives. Tomorrow is a new day. You will go back to the mines. Your lives will be no different than they were provided you obey my law. Look to your former queen," he paused as the crowd quieted completely. The few moments which passed seemed to drag on for days before he added, "Any dwarf who dare challenge the rule of my city, the rule of Maomnosett, will find a similar fate."

Alenaat was among the group tethered together with chains. The shock of seeing his queen's head plucked from her body like the head of dandelion and then carelessly tossed to the ground to roll in the dirt was more than he could stand. The queen had pretty, amber eyes. After her head had stopped rolling, those wide eyes—frozen in shock, rage, and sorrow—stared at Alenaat. There were few in Alhouim the young dwarf could consider friend, but the queen had always been kind and treated him like more than the waste everyone thought he was. He had never stood up for anything in his life, but right in that moment he had no other choice. Tears filled his eyes as he shouted, "Coward." His voice rang out through the courtyard.

All eyes turned to see him, body shaking, tears pouring down his face, his skin red with rage. Boonda the bald was bound to Alenaat. He touched the young dwarf's arm gently and shook his head, desperately trying to stifle any additional words from pouring out of the angry fool's mouth, but it was too late. Alenaat would have his say regardless the outcome.

"You sit there above us looking down like we ain't nothing more than beasts slithering across the dirt on our bellies, like you are so much better than us lowly things," his tears dried as furious rage chased away sorrow and helplessness, "but you ain't no better. Look at you, sitting there smugly watching your beasts spilling blood on stolen land. This is our land. That queen you so carelessly killed had been true and fair, full of life and love for all her people."

Ott's eyes narrowed, but Slurg interrupted before he could respond. "Big pine. Good spot for this one."

"Go on," though it was difficult for Ott to disguise his irritation at the interruption, the choontah had his attention.

"Pine sacred," Slurg continued. "Ahm hang dwarves."

After a few moments of reflection, Ott recalled a visit his son had made shortly after taking the city so many years prior. "Yes, the sacred pine. Ahm told me of that. He took that token of dwarf heritage and turned it into a punishment for unruly dwarves. What a wonderful idea. Apparently, my failure of a son was not all bad after all," he chuckled dryly before adding, "Hang him from that pine and leave him until the creeping things of the forest are fed and full from his decaying flesh."

No one else in the crowd could overcome the shock or find courage enough to shout out in Alenaat's support, but he harbored them no ill will. After a lifetime of not doing much of anything to help any but himself, it was better for him they remained quietly agitated. The gasps he heard were enough. He needed this moment to be his. It was his time to care about something, to stand up for something, to be more than what they thought of him.

The determined dwarf remained calmly defiant as four grongs came up to free him from his chains and dragged him before the king. He lost no more tears, though his eyes sparkled with confidence. He looked up at the false king, the vile usurper, and boomed, "You can hang me from the Sacred Pine, desecrate that holy ground with my blood, send my soul back to the Lake, but you can't kill Alhouim. My kin will see me strapped dead to that pine, and there will come a reckoning. Be it today, tomorrow, or years from now, you will pay for your crimes against us."

Ott chuckled dryly. A small part of him admired the dwarf's boldness. "Not on this day," he smiled. "Take him away."

The rest of the courtyard remained silent as Ott watched the four grongs drag the defiant dwarf back through a sea of sad-eyed dwarves. Despite the dire warning, Ott knew the lesson he was giving would not soon be forgotten by any in attendance. He had broken their spirit, and they would obey.

After the gates closed behind the small group bound for the Sacred Pine, Ott turned his mind to more pressing matters. "Chi-Ta, have any of your scouts returned with word of viable routes to attack Havenstahl?"

"None very promising," Chi-Ta shook his head. "The northern gate of the city sits atop a sheer cliff with nothing more than a small trail doubling back and forth up its face. Perhaps a small force would have success given the element of surprise but attacking with any kind of numbers would prove foolhardy. The main road up to the southern gate is the only path allowing attack in any kind of numbers, and that path boasts a drawbridge spanning a deep cavern. Slurg may have a better report. Many in his command know these lands well."

Slurg's head began shaking before Chi-Ta had even finished speaking, "Diversion at main gate. Attack north gate."

"Wise words," Chi-Ta nodded toward Slurg. "We could send a large force around Mount Elzkahon, bang the drums and attract attention. That should pull their forces to the main gate to defend. Meanwhile, we could send a small, elite force to traverse that trail and infiltrate the city through the back gate. We could easily scale those walls. We will need some form of signal to coordinate the effort."

"The men of Havenstahl will provide that signal," Ott smiled. "They will blow their horns and sound their alarms, call their wayward forces home. Move forward with that plan. We need time to regroup in this place. I want a plan to execute an attack by the time that is done."

Ott watched Chi-Ta and Slurg depart after offering customary bows. His command would keep them busy. The truth was his next steps were not clear. Taking back Maomnosett had been his goal all along. Havenstahl had only ever been a stop along the way toward that goal for him. Brerto wanted it conquered and broken. They had certainly broken the great city with the help of Kallum, but it remained unconquered. Both gods had remained unseen since the battle at Fort Maomnosett. If Brerto wanted the city so badly, why had he failed to return? Havenstahl posed no threat to his throne. Why bother?

# CHAPTER 39
# PATIENCE

Geillan slept soundly suspended between four obelisks flashing with bright light so rapidly the room seemed at once bathed in light and shrouded in complete darkness. No longer a babe nor even a small lad, he had grown to near a man. Ijilv gently traced his fingernail along the young man's flawless skin and whispered, "Soon you will wake and burn Ouloos to oblivion, my sleeping Dragon. Nothing in this land will withstand your might. You will redeem this vile creation with fire."

"You would unleash this abomination on Ouloos to destroy everything we have built?" Kallum's voice echoed in Ijilv's head.

"Do not forget, you are a guest here. You should only speak when spoken to," Ijilv chuckled. "However, I will entertain you only because it torments you so. You built nothing. You took a perfect thing and bent it to your will, tainted it toward your desire, and now you can watch me undo the damage you have done."

"Guest?" Kallum scoffed. "I am a prisoner in your head, a plaything for your ego. Toy with me at your peril, brother. I will find a way to free myself from these bonds, and you will crumble before my glory."

Ijilv laughed as he continued to caress Geillan's cheek. How many years had he waited for this moment, for this time when he could bring his mighty brother so low and knock him from his pedestal? "I had hoped for rage and threats, dear brother, and you do not disappoint. You are one with me now. Never again will you exist outside of me. For all your posturing and threats, you are nothing more than words.

Thank you for this gift."

Ijilv waited for a response, but none came. Kallum's pain was not the goal, merely a satisfying result of the acts required to achieve that goal. Of all his brothers, the great eagle was by far the most pompous, ceaselessly seeking to elevate himself above the rest. Being trapped under the control of one of his kin was the worst fate for him, even worse than being scattered. At least then he was unaware.

"Maelich grows increasingly difficult to contain," Moluam's voice distracted Ijilv out of his revelry. "He is learning how to control his subconscious. I fear he may destroy me within his mind. Please, let me wake him."

"Nonsense," he offered the slightest of smiles. "You must remain brave and vigilant. You know what is at stake. Now is not the time to make rash decisions based on fear. The work we are doing is too important, and it requires patience. See your mission through. Guide the lad of the Lake to his destination."

"He is a Dragon," her voice quivered slightly. "He could burn me out of existence."

"It is a dangerous game you play with him," Ijilv agreed, "but it is a game you must control. His mind is cracked and scarred. He is deep in this delusion he has concocted for himself. That delusion was born out of the darkest places in his psyche, fueled by anguish and pain."

"But we meet in his head," the control Moluam had over her tone cracked. "He is learning to control his unconscious thoughts much more quickly than he is remembering. I want to show him Ymitoth."

Ijilv's eyes went wild with color as his voice raised loud enough to shake the very bricks of the circular room surrounding them, "You will do no such thing. I forbid it. It is far too soon. Waking him so abruptly might break him completely. We need him strong when he wakes, deeply hurt, but strong."

She quickly averted her eyes from his horrible gaze as she relented, "I sense you may feel differently if it were you meeting the lad of the Lake in his own mind, but it is wise counsel. Though my fears have not diminished, I will stay the course."

"Perhaps visit him without showing him a dead friend. Convince him you are a guide to more than heartbreak," the volume of his voice had dropped as quickly as it had grown.

Moluam gave him no more words. She simply bowed her head and vanished. He would have preferred more time to convince her, to steel her will against the fear. It may not have done any good. She was wise to fear Maelich. The time would come when he finally broke free from his illusion. A poor reaction on that day could crack Ouloos to its very core.

"I feel a great swell of pity for you if he reacts unexpectedly, brother," Kallum chided.

"You are aware only of the thoughts I allow you to be," Ijilv scowled.

# CHAPTER 40
# REVENGE

It is difficult to gauge the passing of time without the benefit of daylight. In that dark, cool place surrounded by the rotten stench of death, it was near impossible. Tarantian had snuck up the stairs only twice since he and Chagon had hidden away among the bones of dead men who had been the meals of a small, horrible village peopled with vile men who eat their own. The first time had been during the daylight hours after waking from his first sleep. He had only made it halfway up before the sounds of beasts scared him back down into the safety of the horrid tomb. It may not have been grizzly mongs grunting and growling, but he had still been weak enough at that point to not take the risk. The second time was during the night after two more sleeps. That time he ventured all the way to the back door. That time he saw a grizzly mong roaming alone along the tree line. It may have been it was the only one remaining, but again, he was not quite ready to test how much of his might had returned. It had been four solid sleeps since then, and he was ready to take another chance.

Tarantian touched Chagon's arm as he whispered, "I'll be checking them stairs again."

Chagon managed to keep from crying out, but he jumped nearly out of his skin. "Do that again and my heart might explode right out of my chest," his frightened tone was a bit louder than he intended. After a few moments, he continued in a quieter tone, "I hope them beasts are gone. If I have to choke down another raw rat, I might just kill myself down here among the dead."

"I am ready," Tarantian assured him. "Them rats might be raw, foul, and awful, but my strength is returning. I am ready to fight if need be."

"Good, I'm coming with you," Chagon whispered as he scrambled off his back to a seated position. He nearly lost himself when the bone he pushed on for leverage shifted on the pile beneath it. "I am full ready to be gone from this place too, and I'll be fighting any beast barring my way."

The door creaked as Tarantian gently pulled it open. It was a quiet sound. If not for the stark silence surrounding them, it would have been imperceptible. With no other sound to mask it, he may as well have been blaring a horn to announce his presence to every soul within a mile of the place.

Each of the fourteen steps it took to get from that pit of decaying death to the butcher's block above creaked like the door. The entire journey took near half an hour, but it felt like days. After the first step had settled, Tarantian looked back at Chagon and said, "One step at a time. Step when I step and listen before taking the next."

Chagon nodded and did as he had been told. The step would creak and groan, calling out through the quiet darkness like an alarm. Then they would wait and listen. A few moments would pass with no sounds to disturb the stillness, Tarantian would nod, and they would take the next in unison. As they approached the floor above, they both crouched low to avoid being seen until they were ready to jump out.

There were three steps left when Tarantian turned to Chagon and put a finger to his lip to quiet his companion. Then he took three deep, though quiet, breaths and gathered himself before slowly standing. The room was still as a corpse. All the killing and eating the grizzly mongs had done must have happened outside of the hall. The only body in the place was Theiron's. His corpse had not been touched. Grizzly mongs are hunters. Dead things hold no interest for them.

Tarantian cocked his head to the side and listened. A horny witch called out in the night. They were big birds, but nothing to be frightened of. It was probably calling out before swooping down on a rat scurrying across the forest floor. Hopefully, that bird would enjoy its meal more than he had enjoyed the handful of rats he had eaten while hiding away in that pile of bones.

He had been crouched there so long his thighs burned and shook. Finally, Chagon gave him a nudge and whispered, "I ain't heard nothing. You think it's safe?"

Is it safe? That was the question. Tarantian was not sure. The entire time he was crouching and listening, suffering through the burning in his thighs, he had been trying to convince those legs to stand, to take the next step. Had he been alone, he may have crouched there forever. It certainly was not that he expected Chagon to be much help in a battle. There was a good chance the farm boy would be more hindrance than help. However, his presence there gave the soldier the reason he needed to press on. Duty is a powerful elixir against fear. "Sounds that way," he finally whispered back before standing upright, sweeping the room one more time with his eyes, and adding, "Slowly. No need to go rushing to our doom like a couple fools. We will check the back first."

The last three steps were slow, but not nearly as slow as the first eleven had been. It was only a short five to the open door at the back of the big room. Tarantian approached tentatively, crouching deep again as he neared the opening. The dark bank of trees with their leaves carelessly tossing about in a light breeze looked far more welcoming than a dark and scary forest should.

He turned back toward Chagon and whispered, "It is clear."

"Let's go," Chagon whispered back. "We'll charge them trees and be gone from this horrible place."

"Hold," Tarantian put his hand up. "We need supplies. I refuse to take any meat from this wicked place, but bread, any nuts or fruits or berries we might find, I will take those. And water. We will not get far in the darkness without nourishment," he paused long enough Chagon thought he was finished before adding, "And my sword. I need my sword. You should find a weapon too."

They slipped out the door and worked their way right along the backs of the huts. They found enough fresh fruits and bread to take them three days into their journey before reaching the last hut at the edge of the town, but no weapons.

"I am not keen on traveling these woods unarmed," Tarantian complained as he pushed the back door to the last hut open, "and we will not get far if we are unable to hunt. It will take weeks to get back to Havenstahl on foot, and that is only if we move quickly with all the hours of..." he stopped short.

The moonlight which made it through the thin slit in the thick drapes covering the one window in the small, single-roomed hut was scarcely a dim glow. However, that dim glow glinted marvelously off the sharp blade it kissed. That glint was all Tarantian needed to recognize his sword. That beautiful hunk of deadly metal was the sweetest sight he had seen in longer than he could remember.

"This looks to be an armory," Chagon blurted as he pushed past Tarantian into the small hut.

The farm boy was correct. So rapt in the glorious sight of his own blade, Tarantian had failed to notice it was mounted to the wall between two blades of similar caliber. *How many warriors had fallen victim to the man eaters of this wicked place?* Judging by the quantity of weapons stored there, the number had to be great. The pieces mounted along the walls were all of the finest craftsmanship, blades and axes which must have been wielded by warriors of true note. The floor of the place was piled with pieces of lower quality, but still adequate to take into battle. The village could have armed a small army.

Tarantian quickly made his way to the wall and retrieved his blade, an exceptional piece next to it, and two glorious daggers. He handed the new sword to Chagon and asked, "Know how to use this?"

Chagon nodded, "I'd be far more effective with a rake or hoe, but I've no problem with swinging this thing around if need be."

"That is a fine blade," Tarantian commented as Chagon fastened the belt it hung from around his waist. "Treat that beauty like a lover. And you'd best be jealous about it. Never let her out of your sight."

"Will you be training me in the ways of the warrior," a bit of excitement slipped into Chagon's tone.

"I will," he promised. "After all you have seen that farm will no longer suit you. It will be like a prison." He glanced around the room one more time and looked down at his clothes, "There is no armor in this place. These nightshirts will do us little good in the dense wood. We need to find more durable garb. Come, let us check the huts across the road."

The building immediately across from the armory was stocked with leather trousers, shirts of mail, armored plates, heavy tunics, gauntlets, and other pieces of armor neither man had seen before. Tarantian found his entire set. He left the chest plate and helm behind—they would be too much of a burden traveling through thick woods—but he took the rest. Chagon managed to find a similar set that fit his burly size. He found one piece especially intriguing. It was a riveted mail and plate coat. He had never seen any soldier of

Havenstahl wear anything like it.

"Well, do I look like a warrior?" Chagon beamed as he turned toward Tarantian.

Tarantian examined the coat. "That is fine craftsmanship. I have never seen the like. These markings, like the great eagle, but not quite. I cannot say where they might be from. I can tell you this. That mail will be quite heavy tromping through the woods."

Chagon's smile never waned as he nodded his head, "Aye, it will. But this is the one. The sun glinting off this coat will blind my enemies in my glory."

Tarantian was deep into a chuckle before realizing it was the first moment of joy, regardless how brief, he'd had since leaving Havenstahl for a destination he would never reach. "Fine then," he finally said. "Wear that heavy thing, but it had better not slow you down."

"It won't," Chagon's excited reply seemed more fitting for a young lad leaving on his first hunt than a man finding a nice coat.

After getting all their clothes fastened up and weapons properly strapped on, the two men departed the small hut. They had grown less and less cautious as it became clear nothing remained alive in the village but them. On top of that, despite feeding on a diet of raw rats for probably a week and a half, the groggy weakness had left, and Tarantian was feeling quite able. If any souls remained roaming about the deserted trail who wished to get between him and his goal, he was ready to send them to the Lake with the rest of their foul tribe. He marched right back across the road without hesitation.

Chagon, on the other hand, turned left. There was one more hut he wanted to check. What he hoped to gain was elusive for him, but something in him needed to go back to the place where that man had treated him so kindly only to betray his trust. Perhaps it was closure he sought, seeing that vile wretch dead upon the floor with his entrails spilling out from his gut and the meat picked clean from his bones.

"The straight route is always the best route," Tarantian called out.

"I know," Chagon stopped, but his gaze remained locked on the hut further down the road, "but there is something I need to see."

"Your host?" Tarantian shook his head. "To what end?"

"Aye, Brinzo. I need to know," Chagon's voice dropped as he looked at the ground and kicked a stone.

Tarantian walked over, stood next to the farm boy, and gazed over at the place which had made such an impression on the young man.

"Are you certain?" he asked after a few moments of silence.

Chagon nodded without dropping his gaze from that terrible place.

"And what if he is not dead? Will you send him to the Lake?" Tarantian's eyes scanned Chagon's face as he asked the question.

"Aye," Chagon replied confidently. "You think the fate ain't deserved by that horrid creature?"

"Well deserved," Tarantian shrugged. "I only wonder which of us will carry out the sentence." He paused for a moment, his eyes still scanning the young man's face, before asking, "Have you ever taken a life? I mean a man's life not a beast. The two acts are not the same."

"Once," the answer surprised Tarantian.

"You killed a man?" he could not help the skepticism in his brow as it furled up.

"Farragon was his name," Chagon's eyes remained locked on Brinzo's hut. "My sister, Mianna, was the sweetest girl you ever could meet. She had only seen twelve summers when it happened…" his voice trailed off.

"Farragon, what did he do to her?" Tarantian knew the answer before Chagon gave it voice.

A tear perched atop Chagon's lower eyelid as he whispered, "He took her innocence, but it wasn't only that. He did things to her. Made it so she could never have no babies." That tear dribbled quickly down his cheek.

"How old were you when it happened?"

"It was the end of my fifteenth summer, the celebration," Chagon cleared his throat and found more power to put behind his voice. "Farragon was a man, lived down the road. He'd been kind to me. I even looked up to him. My father had let me tip back a few ales. Ain't nobody even noticed Farragon and Mianna had gone with all the revelry. My father found them the next day."

"And he did not kill the man?" the idea was difficult to grasp for the dutiful soldier.

Another tear made its way down Chagon's cheek, "No. He just sent the scrod away. Mianna refused to speak for a long time after that, so she wouldn't say nothing about her bruises or swollen face. When I asked my father about it, he told me when girls go chasing men all full of the ale them girls get what they deserve. She had dishonored our house and would be leaving the next morning to stay with our aunt for the rest of her days."

"Her own father said those vile things?" Tarantian's head shook slowly as he tried to process the horrible tale the farm boy told. "What did you do to him?"

"My father? Nothing," a few more tears dribbled down Chagon's face. "The thought crossed my mind more than a few times, but I was afraid of that man until the day he died. Farragon, that wretch, was a different story. I found him that same afternoon at the pub telling his chums about what he'd done to my sister as they laughed and egged him on. My eyes went red. I didn't even think about what I would do. I walked right up to him, slipped a dagger belonging to the man seated next to him out of its scabbard, and jammed it right into his throat. A couple members of the royal guard were there having a few pints. They weren't dressed up in all their armor, but they dragged me out before Farragon's chums could have a go at me for what I'd done to their friend."

"Did they throw you in the dungeon?"

"No. One of them said he'd been listening to Farragon's vile account and been a shallow breath from running him through himself. They sent me home," Chagon set his jaw tight as he finished.

"It was right what you did," Tarantian decided, "as is what you plan to do."

The hut was dark when Chagon pushed the door open. At least one grizzly mong had been through the place. Tables were toppled, the walls were scarred with claw marks, and the horrible paintings decorating the place were torn up and tossed about. But there were no bodies. Perhaps one of the monsters had dragged him away to finish him up. He was just about to leave when he heard breathing from the loft above the kitchen. The ladder had been smashed, but somebody remained alive up there.

"Brinzo?" Chagon called. "Brinzo, are you up there?"

A moment later, the terrified man poked his head out from the darkness of the loft. "Thank Coeptus for this good fortune. I thought you to be one of them vile beasts," he said before slipping over the side of loft and hanging from his hands. He remained there for another moment before dropping lightly to the floor. He fell to his knees before Chagon and wrapped his arms around the farm boy's legs.

Chagon gripped the handle of his new sword. It would be easy to slip it out and slide it into the cowering cannibal right behind his collarbone. That would never do. He needed the wicked creature to know. He needed to accuse him. "You would have eaten me, picked the meat from my bones with the rest of your wicked tribe," he said instead.

The man's pleading eyes filled with tears as he looked up at his accuser, "Forgive me, please. I ain't wanted to do it. Theiron forced us all to do these things. You are a kind soul. Let me go in peace and you won't never see me again."

"Come with me," Chagon's tone lacked any emotion.

Brinzo followed Chagon to the road where Tarantian waited. "This wicked thing who eats his own kind yet lives?" Tarantian asked.

"Aye," Chagon replied flatly as he drew his sword and continued past Tarantian to the center of the road. There he turned back toward Brinzo and continued, "I could have sent you back to the Lake as you cowered about my feet, but then I'd be as horrid as you. No, I'll give you the chance you never gave me." He turned toward Tarantian and asked, "Honorable soldier, would you allow this wicked thing the use of your blade to defend himself?"

It seemed impossible, but Brinzo's eyes grew even larger as Tarantian placed the heavy sword in his hand. "And what if I kill him?" he asked the massive soldier. "Will you just kill me then?"

Tarantian looked back at Chagon and shrugged. The farm boy shook his head and replied, "No. If you can defeat me, you are free to go."

"It seems you are lucky to have wronged one far more honorable than you," Tarantian opened his arms as if to invite Brinzo to attack Chagon.

Chagon worked through a couple moves he had picked up watching the soldiers practice their sword techniques along the road from Havenstahl to Druindahl. They were less than crisp, but the sword felt good in his hands. After a few moments of slicing through the still air while watching Brinzo's eyes dart all about like a tubber primed for the slaughter, he finally assumed a defensive stance and waved for his opponent to attack.

"Keep that elbow up," Tarantian coached.

A mere five seconds passed before Brinzo raised Tarantian's sword high above his head, but it seemed an eternity. By the time Brinzo began his charge, the handle was behind his head and the blade pointed toward the dirt behind him. It took three long strides to close the distance between the two, and the blade came slashing down at Chagon's face.

The attack was easy to avoid. Chagon was slightly disappointed as he stepped to his left and stabbed toward Brinzo's throat. He had hoped for more from his first real sword fight. It seemed sad the battle would end minus the sound of swords clashing. Then his opponent surprised him by jumping back quickly enough to save his neck and swinging wildly toward Chagon's waist. It was instinct more than skill or training that saved Chagon's gut from being split as he spun his blade down to block the blow. A second later would have been too late.

A furious howl erupted from Brinzo's mouth as he unleashed a barrage of attacks. They were random and uncoordinated but came rapidly enough to force Chagon to retreat and defend without opportunity to respond with attacks of his own.

Tarantian coached as he watched his new pupil fail miserably against a meek amateur, "Bend them knees, lad. Lower your center of gravity. Counter them attacks. Move your body. He charges like an animal. Use that momentum against him."

It did not show in Chagon's expression, but he was listening. He allowed his knees to relax and began bouncing on the balls of his feet. He kept track of where his opponent's attack began and where it ended to better gauge his response. He dodged and twisted his body instead of just blocking strikes and retreating. After roughly thirty seconds of bending, twisting, and parrying attacks, he made his move. Brinzo only employed three different attacks. One began from far above his head and slashed down, like his initial attack. Another was an awkward backhand which slashed from high on his left side to low on his right. The last was a straight lunge aimed for Chagon's heart. Each of the attacks came in the same order every time.

Once Chagon had studied his opponent long enough to develop a proper response, he unleashed it. First the overhead slash came, then the backhand, and finally the stabbing thrust. However, this time when the stabbing thrust came, he did not parry the blow. Instead, he stepped left and slashed toward Brinzo's throat with a backhand.

Brinzo's body fell to its knees before falling flat onto its chest while his head arced through the air. The lips moved around soundless words and the wide eyes darted about even after his head thudded dully against the dirt. The sound that roared past Chagon's lips when those eyes finally stopped rolling about in their sockets was foreign to his ears. He had never roared so mighty in his life. It was his first battle cry.

As the farm boy turned warrior worked to bring his breathing under control, Tarantian walked over, glanced down at the young man's work, and asked, "How do you feel?"

Chagon did not immediately respond. The only other man he ever killed had not truly been a battle. What he did may have been honorable, but his methods had been anything but. This was a true battle, a fair battle. He was a swordsman who had bested another swordsman in one-on-one combat. The fact neither of the combatants were true swordsmen did not matter a lick. Once he had firm control of his voice and his tongue, he replied, "I feel like a warrior, a swordsman. You'll teach me to wield this blade properly, and I'll do it with honor."

Tarantian allowed the slightest of smiles to crack his grim expression, "That might be, but we need to work on your technique." Both men laughed far harder than the joke deserved. They needed it. Their time in that horrible place had been joyless. Once the laugh was finished, Tarantian retrieved his sword, draped his arm across Chagon's shoulders, and said, "Come, let us get as much distance as we can between us and this place."

"Can you make me good enough to ride under the banner of Druindahl, as a defender of Dragons?" Chagon's boyish grin made him look as green as the farm boy he was.

"When I finish with you, any city would be proud to have you riding beneath their banner," he smiled right back before adding, "but we are not headed for Druindahl."

"What," the smile fled from Chagon's face. "Why not?"

"The grizzly mongs were headed toward Havenstahl," he shrugged. "It is our duty to warn them if we can."

# CHAPTER 41
## THE MOTHER OF GODS

The forest glowed in filtered sunshine streaming through a canopy of green glowing like gold in the light. A handful of experienced soldiers marched up and down columns of young recruits. The oldest of these recruits had seen thirty summers, but he was the exception. Most had yet to see their twentieth, and far too many were not far enough removed from their twelfth—which the youngest had celebrated only days prior. Boringas led his queen among the columns, as he updated her on the progress he and his men had made in filling out their ranks.

"They are all so small," Leisha remarked as she looked over the sweaty lads working through sword techniques. "More than half look lighter than their swords."

"Most of Druindahl's men are warriors, even those who double as baker or smith," Boringas shrugged. "Cialia's rage burned most of them to ash. These young lads before you are what remains."

The comment stung, but she could not argue against truth. Though she had come to grips with what her daughter had done, the wound it left had yet to heal. The closest she could come was acknowledging Cialia's reasoning had been just. However, she would probably never forgive her technique.

As Leisha resumed the internal debate she had been having with herself ever since she learned of the horrible thing her daughter had authored, she noticed a young lad who stood out from the rest. He moved like he had had training, not like the training the recruits in the forest were getting that day, but real training with a dedicated mentor.

He looked familiar. She could not place from where, but she knew his face somehow.

"That boy," she nudged Boringas and pointed. "He looks familiar. Who is he?"

Boringas' face reddened slightly, "You remember my father?"

"I do. He was not an honorable man," she failed to hide a sour look as she replied. "You were quite young when he left your mother to raise you on her own. You followed my husband around like a lost scrod."

"Your husband is an honorable man," Boringas smiled, "like a father to me. If not for him, I would not be who I am today."

The queen gently touched his cheek and offered a smile warm and genuine, "You have grown into an honorable man."

The compliment darkened the warrior's cheeks all the more, "Well, it turns out my mother was not the only one my father loved briefly and abandoned. As fate would have it, I have many brothers. They hail from far and wide. Most find me while searching for my father. Some stay. I train the ones who do. That one is named Sozmet. He hails from Belscythia. After my father left, his mother sold him for some bread and a frilly dress. He ran away and wound up here."

"That is beyond honor, sweet Boringas," Leisha glowed. "You are a good man."

"I would make a good husband," he quickly countered.

Leisha chuckled, "You would make a fine husband, and I would bless Coeptus every morning when the sun rose and each night when the dark chased it away if I could call you son. However, we both know that day will never come. My daughter…"

"The Dragon," he interrupted.

"That she is," the queen nodded, "and she will never give up the life of a warrior. As much as I wish it were not so, she will never submit to marriage and be your wife."

There was no humor in Boringas' chuckle, "No. No she will not. She will forever own my heart but never accept it."

The forest air suddenly grew heavier. A stiff wind picked up, the kind of gust which heralds the coming of a furious storm. Though a storm seemed the least likely cause of the heavy breeze. Based on the amount of light penetrating the thick canopy above, there could not be more than a random cloud lazing about here or there in the sky above. An odd smell accompanied the wind whipping through the trees. It was foreign and primal.

Boringas breathed deep through his nose. "What is that smell?" he asked.

"Power," Leisha's smile fled as she looked in the direction of the stiff gale.

A voice from the crowd called out a command, "Men, defend." Some of the lads training to be soldiers still had a way to go before calling themselves soldier, but they all understood the command as well as the proper response. They seemed a well-oiled fighting force rather than a pack of green recruits as they formed up in columns between the queen and whatever danger approached from the trees.

"Very good," Leisha commented quietly. "However, I fear they are terribly outmatched." She raised her voice and called out a command of her own, "At ease, men. Kneel."

Before Boringas could offer a shocked expression at the way his queen had assumed command of his men, even before the words finished leaving Leisha's lips, the great lion loomed above them. His head easily sat twenty feet above the forest floor with his silver main flowing behind it and glowing from within. Mighty claws dug into the dirt and glinted like metal in the filtered sunshine. He gazed down at the crowd bowing before him with eyes as horrible as they were beautiful, as full of color as they were black and empty, as impossible as they were incomprehensible.

"Men, kneel," Boringas called out to the handful of recruits who had missed the queen's command due to shock.

Once all before him had fallen to their knees and bowed their heads into the dirt, the great lion, Kaldumahn, graced them with the glory of his voice, "Mistress of the Lake, queen of Druindahl, defender of Dragons, mother of gods, and my chosen, I bless thee." As the final word left his mouth, the monstrous, silver lion vanished. At the very same moment, the god assumed the guise of a man—his eyes as beautiful and horrible but his hair and robe as white as fresh snow—and stood before her.

Leisha kept her head bowed as she addressed him, "My lord, Kaldumahn, great silver lion who stalks the skies, though we are not worthy, you bless us with your perfection. You bless us with your presence. You bless us with the glory of your voice."

"Rise," the god commanded her. "I seek a private audience."

Leisha did as commanded. However, she kept her eyes down.

Beholding a god was at once wonderful and terrifying. She recalled the first time he had come to her. It had been the same, only in a dream. He arrived as the silver lion, giant, terrible, and perfect but quickly morphed into a form resembling the man standing before her. Of course, he had been no man all those summers prior, nor was he a man just then. No man could emit perfect light, brighter than the sun like that, and no man had eyes which posed such contradictions being both beautiful and horrible, and both empty and full of life at the same time.

Leisha paused for a moment, searching for the perfect words. When words worthy a god's ears failed to come, she spoke plainly and hoped for his forgiveness. "Of course," she said. "Please accompany me to the throne room. It is but a short journey up that…"

Kaldumahn interrupted Leisha's words by slamming his staff into the dirt. The bright flash which followed forced any open eyes in the forest closed with its brilliance. When Leisha dared to open hers again, she was in her throne room, comfortably seated on her throne. Kaldumahn sat on the throne beside her.

"You may dispense with pleasantries from this point on," he spoke plainly. "We have little time."

"You honor me," she replied. "The last time you spoke to me, my children had just bested your brother over the Forgotten Forest and scattered him to the wind."

"I recall," he nodded.

An awkward smile slipped onto her face, "You told me I had raised noble children, true Dragons. You commended me for raising champions. You claimed Ouloos owed me a debt. I wonder," she paused as her smile fled, "what do you think of me now?"

"A god's mind seldom changes. You have raised champions, and Ouloos is forever in your debt," his voice remained flat and plain. "Never forget, you are my chosen."

"And the fact my daughter desires to kill all the gods?" Leisha managed to keep the fear coursing through her veins from slipping into her voice. "She believes you and your brothers to be the authors of all the challenges Ouloos faces claiming herself a champion of all creatures. She views you as enemies."

"You have seen her?" the slight crack in the god's perfect tone was nearly imperceptible.

"No," Leisha shook her head, "but news travels quickly, even here at the edge of the known world."

Kaldumahn smiled briefly as he stroked his beard. The gesture would not have been the least bit noteworthy had it not been committed by a god. Twice he had come to her. Both times he had remained magnificent, beautiful, and terrifying but flat and emotionless. During both prior encounters, his voice boomed like a song both glorious and horrible. On this day, it was quiet, even humble. Taking that with the simple gesture—only awkward because he was a god—and Leisha knew he was afraid. It was the reason he did not demand she kneel and bow and cower before him. He needed her help.

As if to validate her assumptions, the god confirmed as much, "She does. I would ask your assistance in dissuading her from that desire."

"I will try if given the chance," Leisha shrugged. "However, it seems she is quite sure of her mission."

"She is, but you are persuasive," the god contended. "Convince her Moshat and I are friends to men and dwarves and Dragons."

"What about giants or trogmortem or grongs," despite all her senses begging her to speak as if she were on her knees bowing before him rather than seated next to him, something deep in her soul would not allow it. "My daughter, my Dragon, counts herself champion of all. If you would seek to destroy any under her protection, you may as well destroy all."

Kaldumahn cast a casual glance around the room, "These etchings, the story they tell, do you believe it?"

"With all my heart," she smiled.

He returned the gesture and asked, "Why?"

It was a strange question. The people of Druindahl had told the tale since before the city had been built. It was the truth behind Kallum's twisted lie artfully crafted in perfect imagery. Of course, the images glinting from the shimmering walls of her throne room did not represent the entire story. Maelich had opened the eyes of all to the truth of Coeptus when he scattered the wicked god. However, adding more to the story did not erase those true parts already known.

Finally, Leisha confidently replied, "The stories recorded in those images were passed on from generation to generation until finally being recorded along these walls. All in Druindahl know these things to be true."

"Faith is important," Kaldumahn nodded. "Giants, trogmortem, and grongs—along with beings and creatures you have never seen nor imagined—have stories just like these, passed on from father to son or mother to daughter for just as long and in the same fashion. Your son has written a different story, shared it across the land until he left us. His story is just like these," he paused and pointed at one of the images carved in the shimmering glow of the wall. It appeared an apparition floating amid the glory of a setting sun, "Do you see that Dragon soaring free and belching fire?"

"I realize no Dragon has or ever would release their flame. They are love, unconditional and forgiving. That flame is recorded in those images merely to express the great power they possess. It does not diminish the validity of the story the image tells," Leisha frowned.

"Of course not," Kaldumahn waved his hand as if swatting the idea away. "However, Kallum used similar images to stoke fear in the hearts of men, to rally them in a campaign to kill all Dragons. He told them a story, they shared it among themselves, and they believed."

The queen shifted uncomfortably in her chair, "I know the history. Is this a lesson? We seem to have drifted far from our original topic."

"On the contrary," the god smiled wider. "We are right here in the middle of it. Your daughter is locked in battle with Brerto. She is trapped in a spell he began working on before she was even born. Knowing she desires to kill my kind, now would be the perfect time to attack her, to cut her down and save my brothers."

She nearly failed at hiding her fear as she snapped, "Have you sought an audience with me to threaten my daughter?"

The room filled with light. The flash was brief but blinding, erasing all other images for its duration. When it subsided, nothing in the room had changed. However, Kaldumahn no longer sat beside Leisha. They stood in the center of the room facing each other. He held her hands in his and said, "I threaten nothing. Cialia will defeat my brother. She will scatter him to the wind with the glory of Dragon's fire. His subjects will be free. I will give them a new story. They will worship me as Druindahl always has, and I will be their light. Giants and trogmortem, and even grongs will live in peace with men and dwarves. All the creatures of Ouloos will be one together with Coeptus seeking solace in the glorious light of Kaldumahn and Moshat. Through us, they will know eternal peace."

Leisha's eyes narrowed, "Is it belief in my daughter which gives you pause from taking her life while she remains preoccupied, or is it the fact you believe she is powerful enough to destroy your common enemy when you are not?"

Again, the room filled with light glorious, pure, and impossibly bright. It erased all lines and shapes. All spatial references to give Leisha's eyes any visual clues to depth or distance melted away until she cowered in an empty field of white. Though she could not remember physically bowing or falling to her knees, she bowed deep against a floor she could feel but not see. Her eyes, full of horror, stared at the place where a god had stood speaking to her as if they were equal. As she stared at that spot, unremarkable compared to any spot surrounding her, his features slowly materialized from the nothing. They remained washed out like a watercolor painting faded from too much time in the blazing sun, but they were there. His eyes seemed to float amid that glowing perfection, two pits of total darkness, the absence of light. All colors swirled in them. Though an impossible contradiction, there they were.

Then the sound came, a roar so deep and guttural it shook her insides until they felt like they might burst and spill out upon the floor. A screech so high-pitched and loud it left her ears ringing and her head throbbing accompanied the horrible rumble. Other sounds danced between the two contrasts like a chorus of accusations. The song continued until death seemed a sweet relief.

She dropped her head into hands folded against the ground and cried out, "Please."

Kaldumahn's voice boomed, glorious and terrifying, "I came to you bearing a gift, and you have spat upon the gesture. You are my chosen, but do not humor yourself into believing we are equal. If you refuse my request, I will levy a command. You will dissuade your daughter from her vile campaign. You kneel before me at this very moment praying for death. I promise you this is but a taste of the horrors you will encounter. Fail me, and I will cause you pain your simple mind could not possibly imagine. After I feel you have suffered enough to atone for your defiance, I will cease your torture. Only then will I give you reprieve from the pain and rip your soul from your body. But you will not find peace with Coeptus. Your soul will not journey to the Lake to be one with them. I will cast you to oblivion. You will be alone and cold, but most importantly, aware for all eternity. You will never know peace."

"Forgive me," she cried out. "I am willful and stubborn. I am beneath you. You are generous in your grace. Your will be done. Please, give me peace."

"Do as I have commanded, and I will grant the peace you seek. Your husband lives. He is rightful and true. Mighty Moshat, my brother, the great and terrible bear who lumbers across the north wood, has gone to him offering guidance for the city he protects. A mighty force from all the great cities of men travels to Havenstahl from the southeast. They will defend and rebuild the city. Havenstahl and Druindahl will find their former glory through the grace of the lion and the bear. You will control your Dragon, and she will be their protector."

Leisha remained there on the floor cowering with her head buried in her hands and her eyes clenched tightly shut for several moments after the god stopped speaking. Only after that silence did she dare open them again. When she finally did, the light was gone along with Kaldumahn. He had only come to her twice prior. During neither of those encounters had he showed that aspect of himself. He came wrapped in glory, love, and generosity. She felt none of those things from the monster who had just spoken to her. Perhaps Cialia was right about the gods. Perhaps they were all violent, childish things who cared nothing for the insignificant creatures who worshipped them. She buried the thought deep for fear he might find it in her mind and exact the tortures he promised.

# CHAPTER 42
## SWORDS OF LIGHT

It was impossible for Cialia to determine her surroundings. She imagined rocky walls stretching up from a stony path, but she could not see them. Perhaps stalactites stretched down from a ceiling high above toward stalagmites reaching up to greet them from the floor, or perhaps not. Perhaps pools of clear water surrounded her, teeming with unknown life existing for hundreds of years but hidden from record. Perhaps streams flowed connecting these pools hiding unknown mysteries in their depths. All those things could be true, but she would never know. She had not stepped in any water, so she had no evidence to prove or disprove the existence of any of it. The only thing she could be sure of was the dim light she had been following for... How long had it been?

Time was another thing impossible to gauge in the darkness. Whether she had been walking for hours or days was a question which would remain unanswered. She had not slept. That was a clue. It seemed she had covered a great distance, but the light had not changed. It seemed no closer or brighter than when she first saw it glowing deep within the cave.

The great hawk entered her mind. He seemed wise. He certainly posed some interesting questions. However, she did not know anything about him or his goals. It suddenly occurred to her the mission belonged to him. Her mission remained trapped at the top of a mountain of fire while she burrowed deep underground seeking a girl who allegedly knows everything. Could any creature or being truly know everything? The question seemed far less important than the reason Cialia sought an audience with her. She could just turn around.

"Your true goal lies before you, Cialia," though she could not see the hawk or the glowing old man he became, his voice was unmistakable, melodic yet booming.

She had questions for him, but her voice remained trapped in her throat. None of the answers to the questions she had posed when first they met seemed useful as any more than riddles. She had no time for riddles. Two missions lay before her. When the dim light she had been following for hours or days or longer finally began to grow, she decided to finish the one she was on.

It only took a few moments for Cialia to realize the light itself was not growing. She was getting nearer to it. The realization caused her pace to quicken. Before long she found herself jogging toward it. Brief whistles began filling the air, rapid and short. Perhaps they were the sounds of some animal she had never seen. She drew her swords as her pace quickened further to an all-out run until she saw a doorway in the distance, the source of the dim light she had been following. Though she could not see anything inside the room, she suddenly recognized the whistling sounds. They were the sound of sharpened metal slicing through still air. Someone trained with swords.

The whistling sounds grew louder as Cialia approached the doorway. A heavy wooden door hung open as if an invitation. She accepted. The room itself was a massive empty circle with no windows. Both the floor and walls stretching up from it further than she could see in the darkness were crafted of rough stones of odd shapes. There appeared to be no mortar holding them together, but the pieces fit perfectly like a puzzle sprung from an insane mind. Those impossible stones would have been worth examining had something even stranger not entered the room through an identical door immediately across from the place where she had entered at precisely the same moment. It was someone who looked just like her in every way from each strand of hair to every stitch of clothing. She even held her swords the same way Cialia held her own.

"State your name and tell me why you wear my face," as the words left Cialia's lips she realized the doppelganger replied with the exact same words at the exact same time.

"I do not have time for this," Cialia complained at the same time as her twin.

Both shook their heads in unison and approached each other, "If you stand as an obstacle to my goal, you will be removed."

When they were within five feet of one another, they both stopped and looked each other over. After a few moments of quiet examination, Cialia and the doppelganger both said, "Stand aside or prepare to defend yourself."

Neither moved. After several moments had passed, and Cialia decided she had given her adversary ample time to avoid conflict, she raised her swords and struck an offensive stance. Her twin mimicked her exactly. She stood the same and held her swords in exactly the same fashion. She even wore the same expression. Cialia took a deep breath and attacked.

Swords clashed so rapidly it quickly became impossible to distinguish between the ringing of sword kissing sword and the echoes of those sounds reverberating back off the walls. The two combatants matched each other perfectly in every way. Each attack earned an equal defense and counter. Neither proved able to gain an upper hand.

The battle raged for hours. Both Cialia and her opponent were unwilling to give up any ground, and neither proved able to gain any. They remained there in the center of the room surrounded by the ringing sounds of their battle matching each other blow for blow.

Frustration began to set in. Her journey could not end locked in a never-ending battle with herself. That gave her an idea. It was risky. However, as the battle raged on, she grew more and more confident the stalemate would never finish. She felt none of the exhaustion the duel should have easily earned her. It seemed likely her opponent remained equally fresh. On top of that, the doppelganger had proved her equal in every way.

Cialia unleashed a vicious barrage, both blades arcing toward her opponent from impossible angles. They were all easily dodged, blocked, or parried. She expected it. The series of movements was only intended to give her enough time to disengage without getting nicked on her way out. It worked. Before her opponent could respond with a similar attack, Cialia retreated several steps. The doppelganger copied the move precisely with equal timing. Once at a safe distance, Cialia tossed her blades aside. Again, her opponent copied the move exactly.

"I have figured you out," they both said in unison before charging toward one another.

Cialia never slowed nor braced herself for impact, but she fully expected to feel something when she slammed into her opponent. Her momentum was stopped abruptly, as if some unseen hand had grabbed hold of her, but she felt nothing. The doppelganger simply vanished within her, and she was alone.

A wind picked up, swirling clockwise around the room. She could not see it, but it howled like a mighty gale tearing across an open field. After a few moments, all four swords were lifting off the ground to chase each other around the room. Before long, her blades caught those of her opponent and absorbed them in a flash of light so bright it forced her eyes shut. When she opened them again, her swords were back in her hands glowing like the sun had been trapped within them.

She remained there for a good while glancing around the room and trying to make sense of what had just happened. As she glanced around the empty space reflecting on the battle, it became increasingly apparent her opponent had been herself. She got in her own way often enough that the symbolism was obvious. However, the idea was impossible. She had studied every book she could get her hands on and knew enough about the world to know one person cannot exist in two places at the same time no matter their proximity to each other. The laws of nature forbid it, but she could not deny the truth of it.

Perhaps she was dead. The idea seemed unlikely. Surely, she would remember dying if she had. Even if the memories were not vivid images of what happened to her, or even lingering feelings, perceptions, or emotions, there would be something. Of course, she could not truly know if she were dead or not. Some of the books she had read spoke with great certainty about an afterlife, a place where the soul goes to spend eternity in bliss or damnation. Though the accounts were all similar, no two were the same. For a logical mind like Cialia's, it made them all seem less than reliable if not flat out lies. As far as she was concerned, they were all just fanciful tales. None of the authors of those tales had any experience being dead.

As she stood there contemplating whether she was dead, the hawk's words stormed back into her head. He told her to wake up. Those had not been his exact words, but that was the essence of it. He seemed wise. What if she were not dead but dreaming? Would any of it matter? Someone once told her if you die in a dream you die for real. Could that be true? If she tested the theory, she may never know. That would probably depend as much on the virility of the stories she had read about what happens when someone returns to the Lake as on the answer to the question of whether or not she was awake or dreaming. If it were true, and she was dreaming, she would die just the same as if she were awake. Either way, she would never know. And so, the circle ended. She would not test any theory. She had one mission to finish before getting back to the one she had started.

The door through which she had entered the room was closed, but the one before her still hung wide. She could not be certain it was the correct path as she walked through that door, but she had decided it was the path she would take.

# CHAPTER 43
# ALHOUIM HAS FALLEN

The hall was a giant, empty thing. Crests from the great cities adorned the walls, massive, wooden, and painted with the colors of the city they represented. Some were cracked or chipped. Others lie broken on the floor. Daritus paid them no mind. He did not care about the great fish of Belscythia, or the furious scarra of Gandystrint. Nor was he nostalgic about dignitaries from those cities lining up at tables to feast and pay tribute to the mighty fallon of Havenstahl. When those haughty, righteous men packed up a month's worth of supplies to drive their horses and servants across vast swaths of unforgiving land filled with nightmare creatures and the vilest of men, none of those cities were friends to the city the weary general missed so much nor the Dragons he protected. No, none of that history mattered to him just then. As had regularly been the case since word of massive warships docking in Biggon's Bay had reached his ears, he was worrying over a map.

The battle at Fort Maomnosett had been well planned. Everything should have worked perfectly, and it probably would have had gods not decided to interfere. Despite all his planning and worrying, that battle ended in disaster for Havenstahl along with the men and dwarves who sought to protect her. Truthfully, it had not ended any better for the invaders from across the Great Sea. Everyone lost that battle. The city of Alhouim had fared better. However, a rash response to their king's death earned them a fate even worse. Maomnosett was reborn as Alhouim quietly ended.

The difference between that campaign and the current mission was the plan. He did not really have one. Of course, he gave commands, directed this one to do that or that one to do this, but most of them were responses to news about this or that. Rebuilding Havenstahl was a goal. It was under way. Defending it was a different thing entirely. Ott had taken Alhouim, now Maomnosett, and was in the process of moving troops and supplies from the ships docked in the bay to his reclaimed city. Any fighting dwarves not identified as dead or imprisoned remained unaccounted for like too many of his men. How would he find all his scattered forces and bring them home? How would he defend his broken castle?

Thankfully, Kantiim entered the room to distract him from his fruitless worrying. Daritus did not bother looking up. He recognized the confident gait of his favorite general and dearest of friends as the clicks of the grizzled veteran's boots echoed from the smooth bricks of the floor to the smooth bricks of the walls. "You are pale," he commented dryly as he crossed the room. "When is the last time your skin saw the sun?"

"It has probably been too long," Daritus finally looked up. "Save the lecture. We still have much to do. I assume you have an update. Let us have it."

Kantiim frowned at the unsatisfactory answer but obliged the command nonetheless, "The going is slow, but it is coming together. The main walls around the city are finished and reinforced, stronger than ever. The king's tower, tallest spire in the city, should be complete by the time we lose the sun today. The rest of the city will finish in due time."

"You may have saved the king's tower for last as empty as it shall remain," he grumbled. "Solid outer walls will help us defend those who remain. I worry over the north gate since Alhouim has fallen."

"Only a fool would attempt it," Spang's voice filled the hall as he entered accompanied by Bom.

"The gate has been fortified, the trail washed away, and traps have been laid all up and down the steep incline," Kantiim agreed. "Any giants who survive the climb will be greeted with boiling oil and angry spears. Do not fret over the north gate."

"That is heartening news," the broken general nodded. He nearly allowed a smile to his face before turning his attention to Spang and asking, "What is the state of our enemy?"

"Bom has a report," the former leader of the Dragon's Flame glanced up at the giant who bowed to one knee before Daritus.

Daritus stopped just shy of rolling his eyes at the gesture. "Rise," he commanded. "You have been welcomed here. I am not royalty in this place, just another general bumbling about trying to keep my men's souls in their bodies and out of the Lake."

"Thank you," Bom stood and gave the general a warm smile. "The dwarves have failed."

"Yes, I had heard as much," Daritus agreed. "Alhouim has fallen, reborn as Maomnosett. I had promised our friends Havenstahl would answer their call as they had answered ours. Where was our response?"

The giant's smile faded, "The one they call Bindaar was determined to have his revenge. By the time we arrived, he had already been defeated. There were few still living. We did our best to aid their escape, but we lacked the numbers to win the day."

Daritus set his jaw tight and glared at Bom. Without taking his eyes off the giant, he grabbed three tokens off his map and hurled them at the wall. One of them cracked on impact, splitting in two before the four pieces clattered to the floor.

"It is unfair to place blame at our new friend's feet," Kantiim interjected.

"Had he acted differently, you would be complaining of how many more men we lost," Spang agreed. "He made the correct choice."

Daritus kept his eyes locked on Bom's as he agreed, "I know. The fact does not make the news any easier to accept. Damn Bindaar and his rage." He looked over at Kantiim, and then at Spang before adding, "I may have done the same thing if someone brought me the corpse of either of you."

"There is more," Bom interrupted.

This time, Daritus did roll his eyes, "Could it be any worse?"

"Sadly, yes," Bom shrugged. "More reinforcements have arrived from across the Great Sea. If a giant remains in my homeland, I will count it a surprise. Supplies move from the shores to Alhouim."

"Maomnosett," Daritus corrected him. "Alhouim is dead once again."

"We could frustrate their supply route over the northern pass," Bom added.

"I fear the potential losses we could sustain would fail to justify the impact that might have," Daritus shook his head.

"Agreed," Spang piped in.

"We should bring all our forces back to the castle and regroup," Kantiim agreed.

"Make it so," Daritus nodded.

The room suddenly filled with light so bright it reminded Daritus of a dream he had years prior. Kaldumahn had come to him in a dream as the great silver lion blazing like the sun and astride the Dragon. Before any of his companions registered what was happening, Daritus gave a loud command, "Kneel."

All four men knelt and bowed until their foreheads pressed against the cool brick of the floor. Even with his eyes clinched up tight, Daritus could tell how bright the light was filling the room. Everything looked red through his closed lids.

"Rise," the voice boomed. It was definitely a god. No man could boast such clear perfection in their tone while achieving such volume. It sounded as if a chorus of voices sang the words rather than one perfect being spoke them.

The giant obliged the command. The three men quickly followed suit. Both Kantiim and Spang gasped when they saw the man walking with Hagen. Of course, it was no man accompanying the old healer. Daritus recognized the god as Moshat, Kaldumahn's contemporary. The last time he had seen the god in the guise of an old man clad in a glowing white robe and emitting light like a star was after his first meeting with the lad of the Lake. The two gods had admonished him and cast him into darkness surrounded by amatilazo as penance for his sins. Hopefully, this meeting would prove less painful.

"Are you a wizard?" Bom was the first to break the silence.

"Blasphemy," Hagen complained.

Moshat smiled as his dark eyes posed various contradictions, devoid of color yet somehow swirling with all colors at once. There was a hint of forgiveness in his voice as he corrected his companion, "Do not fret over the mistakes of one who could not possibly know a mistake had been made." Then he turned his attention to the giant and continued, "Maomnosett Bom, son of Bok, grandson of Ott, what consequences have brought you to plan with men against your own kin?"

"I am not a spy," Bom blurted. He quickly added, "I did not agree with my father's campaign to take this land from men or to take the dwarves' land from them, and I do not agree with my grandfather's desire to continue that campaign. We have vast swaths of land, beautiful and untamed. I want nothing more than to return, but I cannot do that in good conscience without helping these souls protect their land."

"What about your god's command?" Moshat asked. "Neither your father nor your grandfather embarked on this mission of conquest without a command from their god, your god, the great and terrible Brerto. He would rightfully consider your actions blasphemous."

"He would. He already told me as much before he fled Cialia's might. Do you fear that loose Dragon as much as he?" Bom did his best to remain defiant before the god despite the sudden pain in his chest.

"I respect the bravery it took for you to stand up to your grandfather. I pity you for believing it wise to stand up to your god. That was foolish. Do not make the same mistake with me. I have not come to punish. However, I will not stand for disrespect. Kneel. I will forgive your transgression and make the pain stop. Stand, and that pain will steadily grow as your new friends watch you suffer and die before them," the god remained disturbingly aloof as he cast his gaze to each set of wide eyes staring back at him in disbelief.

Bom was back on his knees within a second of Moshat's command reaching his ears. Battling a god for the sake of nothing more than ego would be foolish at best. As soon as his knees touched brick, the pain ceased and Moshat had moved on to other things.

The god nodded to Hagen, and the old healer spoke, "Mighty Moshat, the great bear who stalks the north woods honors us with his grace. Havenstahl has been brought low, and our great protector has come to bless us, promising to aid in the rebuilding of our great city. And he brings good news of assistance from all the great cities of men. A massive force approaches from the southeast. We should see our ranks replenished, doubled, and doubled again within the month."

After watching how Bom, a mighty giant was effortlessly brought low by the god, every bit of common sense Daritus had shouted from the back of his mind to hold his tongue. Unfortunately, his tongue had other ideas. "You have remained absent for some time, old friend. Now you return as herald of the great bear. How is it you come to serve in such an intimate capacity?" Before Hagen could consider answering, the fiery general turned his attention to Moshat, "And where have you been? I suppose there is no need for me to remind you how many thousands of your loyal servants have flittered off to the Lake. Havenstahl boasted the mightiest army in all Ouloos. What remains would struggle mightily to sack a village. You promise to help us rebuild? I would challenge you to punish those who brought violence and death upon us. Destroy the invaders from across the Great Sea and take back Alhouim for our friends from whom it was stolen."

"Alhouim is no more," the god remained emotionless. "Maomnosett has been born again from its ashes. I cannot interfere in the affairs of men."

"It would seem your contemporaries share no such restrictions," Daritus spat. "It was not giants who tore this great city down or trampled innocent lives beneath massive paws and broken towers. They were gods like you. They interfered in the affairs of men."

"Those gods are vile and no more honorable than the foul things who worship them," Hagen added.

Daritus raised his arms out to his sides as he cast an angry glance at the walls surrounding him, "Small consolation."

"Enough," Moshat's booming voice echoed through the chamber. "You have seen more challenges than any man should. I will forgive your tantrum but know this, no man sits in judgement of any god. If you have finished your time in the physical, please continue. If you have more to do, repent in your heart and know you are forgiven."

It took Daritus a few moments to calm himself. He did have more to do. Luckily, Moshat was willing to give him another chance to do it. Once he had regained as much of his composure as he likely would, he looked at Hagen and continued, "Old friend, you have been gone for quite some time with only vague reports of where you were or what you were up to. It was quite a shock to see you return with a god at your side. In fact, the idea is only now sinking into my thick skull, and I am suddenly quite afraid. Have any of our lost returned with you?"

"Most should have reported back periodically over the past few weeks. My best estimate of the total number is around five-thousand men and dwarves. I pray none of the latter continued on to Alhouim," Hagen mustered as warm a smile as he could considering the grim report he delivered. "We found far too many who had already departed for the Lake, and even more who had yet to make the journey but were still well beyond my help. I pray there are more still living we have yet to find."

"The search continues?" Daritus asked.

"It does," the old healer nodded. "One hundred men continue the search. I left them to it as I felt you deserved a report of our progress and sensed I may be needed here."

"You are wise," the general decided. Then he looked to Moshat and said, "Forgive my hubris, my lord. I lost control of my tongue. I am a mere man with limited understanding. However, I do struggle with your restraint. How can we defeat our enemies when their gods show no such restraint?"

"Have faith in your god, Daritus. Though our friendship is young, please heed my counsel. I have lived with those who worship the great tiger, even worshipped him as a faithful servant myself. Be thankful you follow one more honorable. My kind are mad with desire for conquest and control. They emulate their god. This exacerbates their wicked ways. I much prefer the company I have found in this place," Bom piped up.

"You would be wise to listen to your new friend," Moshat added. "His heart is earnest and his words true. I am here to fill you with strength of heart, but flesh is flesh."

Daritus turned his frown toward the floor. The god's words were logical enough. If he could unleash the power of a god on his enemies, it would be an act even more wretched than those his enemies wrought against his own. As difficult as it seemed standing in a crumbling hall getting updates about how many had died, he needed to rise above it all if he were going to lead what was left.

"I do have more heartening news," Moshat continued. "The riders of Druindahl boast many new recruits. Their ranks burst with hearty young men eager to serve and protect Dragons and all Ouloos. Your fair wife has once again taken the throne of that city. That seat is where she belongs."

A sparkle made its way to Daritus' eye, "That is more heartening news. The people of Druindahl love her. She has always been just and fair. I pray to see her again someday."

"My brother, Kaldumahn, the great silver lion who stalks the sky, is with her. She is safe in her city," the god replied. "Now, let us get to work on rebuilding this fair city. Havenstahl and Druindahl will serve as beacons for all men, just examples in a crumbling world. Then, you will take that city back from the giants who stole it."

A genuine smile finally made it to Daritus' lips. Rebuild and then destroy. Perhaps the god would not or could not engage his enemies directly. However, having a god back a campaign certainly would not hurt.

# CHAPTER 44
## THE CONQUERING KING

Thick smoke blocked out the glaring desert sun until it was nothing more than a weak, pink pinhole of light struggling through a dark, gray haze. Flames roared like hungry beasts devouring huts of dry twine and casting ash to the wind. Random voices full of fear, pain, and terror screamed out from amid the smoke and ash. Some came from men. They were hoarse and throaty, but far too many came from women or children. Those were high-pitched. They stabbed Maelich the deepest as he looked upon the carnage his Shaiwah had wrought upon their enemies.

A groaning man limped out of the smoke. Covered from hair to sandal in heavy ash, he looked like a gray ghost except for his eyes. Those were wide, white, and streaked with red. He did not resemble the wild and violent beasts Maulom had described. He looked old, weak, tired, and most of all, terrified.

Maelich's first instinct was to rush to the man, cradle him in his arms, and pour water into his dry lips to ease his burning throat. Before the urge became so great he had cause to consider whether to act on the instinct or stay his feet, a spear punched through the man's chest. Somehow, those wide and terrified eyes grew even bigger. It could have been Maelich's imagination, but those eyes seemed to both accuse and beg at the same time, at once pleading and damning. A heaviness grew in Maelich's chest as he watched the life leave those eyes. It felt like sadness but worse.

When the man finally slid off the spear which had impaled him to flop lifeless onto the ash-covered ground and Ding's smiling face appeared where those eyes had been pleading and accusing, Maelich finally understood what that weight had been. It was heartbreak. The peaceful innocence Maelich had seen glimmering in Ding's eyes when first they met was gone. It had been replaced with a vengeful bloodlust. Maelich had turned that peaceful soul into a warrior. That warrior planted his foot victoriously on his vanquished foe's back, held his spear high above his head, ripped through the smoky air with a hellish war cry, and then he was gone, disappearing back into the smoke to slay some more.

"The Shaiwah won their first battle," Ymitoth's voice kept the tear from forming on Maelich's eyelid. "That marks your first victory as their king."

"This does not feel like a victory," Maelich's voice was quiet.

"I ain't the best with numbers, but I only count three injured among us and one dead. I call that a victory," the old soldier shrugged.

"But what have they lost?" Maelich asked as he walked toward a smoldering hut.

Ymitoth followed beside him and replied, "Their fear. These men and women weren't no warriors when we came to them. They'd been afraid their whole lives of these beasts. They ain't scared no more. We gave them that gift."

Maelich's reply died at the back of his throat as he noticed the bloody corpse of a woman clinging to the charred corpse of a small child. The sight was jarring, but not only for the horror of it. Innocence, helpless and slaughtered, was what brought the tear he had been fighting over his eyelid to slip down his cheek, but what was truly jarring was the familiarity of it. He had no idea why the scene seemed so familiar, but it sparked something in him. It was something about mother, an inkling more than an idea or even a feeling. He chased the…thing deep into his mind. It was elusive, shifty, slipping around corners and hiding. What about his own mother?

Ymitoth's voice pulled him away from the search, "It is a shame, but they'd be doing the same to us given the chance. Ain't no sense in shedding tears for our enemies."

"That is a mother clinging to her dead child's body. She selflessly gave of herself in a vain attempt at protecting her defenseless child even in death," Maelich nearly shouted. "What do we have to fear from her? How is she our enemy?"

A roar like a furious beast belching out a territorial warning erupted from the smoky air behind the dead woman. Maelich could not see the monster making the sound, but it was immediate enough that he instinctively drew his sword. The mystery was short lived as a beast of a man leapt over the corpses which had troubled Maelich so.

The man was big—a full head taller than Maelich and half a man heavier—but he moved with the grace of a man half his size. His hair was black waves streaked with ash. His swollen arms and chest were also covered in ash, but it was smeared with blood. Some was obviously his own. One of his eyes was missing. Blood poured from the empty socket. The other was wide and wild with revenge. Veins bulged all over him.

It was not fear motivating Maelich. Nor was it anger or hate. Instinct guided the soldier's hand as he slashed smoothly through the charging man's neck. It was no battle. One moment, the man was charging with ill intent, and the next, his head was arcing toward the flames of a burning hut while his body dropped in a heap next to the dead woman clinging to her dead baby. Was it his wife and child lying there in the dirt? Did it matter? What had any of them done to deserve the terror Maelich and his Shaiwah brought to the small village?

"That is what makes them our enemy," Ymitoth's tone had an annoying I told you so quality. "That mountain of a man would be crushing your head if you gave him half a chance."

"Of course, he would," Maelich shouted. "Look around you. Would you not do the same if it were your family gutted on the ground with your home burning around them. We are the invaders here. They did not come to attack us."

Ymitoth grabbed Maelich by the shoulder and spun him so they were face to face, "Ain't a one of our men raised a spear until one of these monsters attacked, sneaking like a coward out of the brush."

"With a sharpened stick," Maelich complained.

"A weapon is a weapon no matter what that weapon might be," Ymitoth contended.

Maelich stared speechless into Ymitoth's black, dead eyes. What did he hope to find in those lifeless pits, remorse, a soul? Though he was not completely certain what he sought, he was sure he did not find it.

"All dead," Ding called out as he emerged from a smoldering hut. Though the young warrior's voice was a welcomed distraction from

Ymitoth's horrible and empty eyes, the words it carried were not. "Shaiwah win. Shaiwah strong," he added, kneeling before Maelich and holding up a small wooden chest.

Maelich took the thing and opened it, a mixture of shiny coins and assorted gemstones. "What is this?" he asked.

"Treasure," Ding smiled up at him.

"Spoils of war," Ymitoth agreed.

Maelich had not noticed the looting. Ding's proclamation that all were dead should have been a clue. Of course, Ymitoth was right. To the victor go the spoils. The chest Maelich held in his hands felt far heavier than its meager contents. He handed the thing to Ymitoth and quietly said, "Form them up."

Maelich had walked far past the smoldering huts, past the random limbs drying in the desert air, even beyond the stiffening corpses of poor souls who had tried to flee. A few hundred yards were the most the fastest of them made. He looked south along a river. Thick vegetation grew on both banks, stretching a few hundred feet on either side as it cut into a barren and cracked wasteland. Heat rising off the ground looked like vast pools stretching as far as he could see. Above him, the sun had yet to hit its highest point. A few hours were all it took to erase an entire village that no one would miss. Who would sing songs for them? How far until the next village his mighty force of killers would erase?

"Maelich," the sound of Maulom's voice made him cringe. The last thing he wanted to do right at that moment was look upon that wretch in his perfect white clothing with his perfect white hair, neither of which seemed capable of gathering even the smallest speck of dirt.

Despite wanting to dive into the river to wash the filth from himself, he turned toward Maulom and nodded. It would be a waste to jump in the cool water anyway. The dirt on his clothes, in his hair, and coating his flesh could be washed away, but the stink of barbarous death would remain on his soul.

"The Shaiwah are victorious," Maulom continued as he patted Maelich's back earning a puff of dust. "You are a conquering king."

"The Shaiwah are certainly a force to be reckoned with," Maelich agreed before adding, "but these villagers did not pose much of a test. Where are the fierce warriors you described? Where are these horrible, violent monsters trained to kill and bent on destroying the Shaiwah? Are these the Tahnka? Are these peaceful villagers the beasts you taught the Shaiwah to fear?"

"Did you fight in the same battle I witnessed?" Maulom frowned. "I saw blood spurting from Gid's neck when that wicked beast stabbed her throat. Did you miss that?"

Maelich shook his head and sighed. "I saw the attack, and I lament the loss…"

"The first blood drawn in this battle was drawn by our enemy. I am only glad Gid's son was the one to avenge her," the clean, old man interrupted.

"I know they drew first blood. I was there. I fought alongside my men. Given a similar set of circumstances, I would probably have done the same. Still, what is done is done," Maelich's head continued to shake slowly as he paused to gaze across the horizon. After a long silence, he turned back toward Maulom and asked, "When does it end?"

"It ends when you lead your Shaiwah back to the city they were forced from and take your throne," Maulom smiled. "It is true, this village was a small test. However, their opponents will grow increasingly formidable the closer we get to that place."

"King Maelich," Ymitoth's booming voice interrupted the conversation.

The boisterous crowd accompanying the old soldier cheered in response. Before Maelich could even turn to look at them, he was being hefted up amid chants of, "King, king, king…" The joy he saw on each face in the crowd seemed misplaced among the carnage surrounding them. Celebrating the slaughter of unarmed men, women, and even children was something he could not condone. If Maulom's warnings proved correct, he would lead his Shaiwah to war. But this would be the last village his people would sack.

## CHAPTER 45
## THE HIDDEN TOWER

"Havenstahl," Perrin gasped as Dirk and his men led Perrin's small force around a conical peak.

Of course, it was not Havenstahl at all. The buildings, towers, and battlements bared little resemblance to the city where she grew up, but it had the same essence. The massive city stretched toward a lavender sky streaked with sharp yellow clouds. It sat atop a steadily rising hill just like the greatest city of men, but the spires were crooked and constantly shifting. Even the hill it sat upon seemed to lower toward them rather than remaining still while they marched up the incline toward it. The stones—which looked nothing like stones at all—were pink one moment, blue the next, and then orange a moment later. The rays of a green sun reflected off whatever color the stones happened to be until the sun melted into a dull bronze. Nothing seemed constant.

"I have never had the pleasure of looking upon your fair city, highness," Dirk called back, "but I assure you this is not that place."

"Of course it ain't," Glord agreed, "but this place has the same feel as the city I miss during the quiet times when my mind has cause to wander."

Dirk smiled over his shoulder at them, "I would love to see it someday. I wonder if it would leave me feeling the same nostalgia for my city."

"What do you call this place?" Ycharaz asked.

"Home," Dirk replied.

"No," Perrin interjected, "he means, what is this city's name?"

Dirk halted the group and guided his horse up to Perrin. "Home is the only thing I have ever called it. What would you call it?"

Perrin shrugged.

"I know it must seem strange to you, but things here lack elaborate descriptors. This is home for us. That is the only name we need," Dirk smiled.

"Would it not be named for your house like Havenstahl?" Glord asked.

Dirk's eye showed a spark of recognition. "I see. You speak of ownership. We are all one here. No one owns anything. Now that you are here, you may call this home if you would like, be one with us. Everything belongs to everyone, and nothing belongs to anyone."

Glord looked at Perrin, and they both shook their heads.

This forced a dry chuckle from their guide. "Come," he said. "Our queen is far wiser than I. There is no doubt she will have answers you find less queer."

The city remained mysterious. Roads shifted from bricks to dirt to grass to glass to substances none of the small group from Havenstahl had ever seen. These same roads were equally inconsistent in their direction. At one moment they traveled steadily upward, while in the next they descended without a noticeable change in the road itself. At times they even seemed to be upside down, hanging from rather than standing upon the surface beneath them—the back of the group looking up at the front of the group, while the front of the group looked down upon the tail. Walls and buildings behaved similarly. The group would round the bent walls of a building only to see it standing yards before them.

By the time Dirk halted Perrin's group before a tall gate that had looked to be constructed of metal bars right up until they stood immediately before it, the rest of his group had taken other paths. Only he remained with the small contingent from Havenstahl. "Here we are," Dirk smiled at them.

Perrin reached out to touch one of the gate's bars—which appeared flimsy like some kind of cloth—only to touch the solid wood of a door. It did not appear to be painted, stained, or treated with any type of coating, but it cast a golden glow. It vibrated beneath her hand as it shifted from what looked and felt like wood to pitted stone before vanishing completely.

Dirk led the group into a vast, dark chamber stretching out from the opening where first a gate and then a door had been. Ganodin shot a look at Perrin and shook his head as he gripped his axe tighter. Halogren wore a similar look. As Perrin glanced around at the rest of her group, it seemed none of them much liked what they were walking into. She felt no different about it, but the hope she might learn something which would get her closer to Geillan sparkled far brighter in her heart than any trepidation about walking into a dark castle hall on horseback following a man none of them knew.

The dark room filled Perrin with an odd sense of familiarity. Its floors and walls were smooth brick. Unlike the rest of the city, these did not shift or change but remained constant. The vast hall was empty aside from one chair which also remained constant. The paintings along the wall were the same. When she focused on the image of a fallon at the front of the room, it finally occurred to her why the place seemed so familiar. She was standing in the throne room at Havenstahl. She was not really, of course, but the hall resembled her home so completely she may as well have been.

A woman materialized on the throne. She wore no crown on her head and only a simple gray frock to cover her form, but there was something regal about her countenance. Perrin could not help but stare as there was something about the woman that was at least as familiar as the room surrounding her.

The woman suddenly rose and bent to one knee, "Perrin, queen of Havenstahl, welcome to my home. I pray this room makes you feel comfortable and welcome."

Perrin's eyes narrowed. "This place is so far from any of the known world. How could you possibly know who I am or from where I came?" she asked.

"This is some kind of trickery," Glord scowled as he shifted uneasily in his saddle. "This one must be some kind of witch."

"Are you a witch?" Perrin asked.

The woman stood and offered a warm smile as she replied, "I am no witch, nor am I any form of magician. Of course, I have been called both those things by folks who hail from similar lands as you. It no doubt will not surprise you to learn I have even been called far worse. Some of the monikers men from the land beyond the Lake have blessed me with are earned. Some are unfair designations born of simple minds. I am merely a soul seeking knowledge, nothing more and nothing less. You may call me Antopy if you wish. If you do not wish to call me by name, feel free to call me witch or magician or monster, or anything else. Regardless of what I am called, I still am."

"Glord is right," Darg piped up. "She's a witch. We should go."

Antopy's smile remained unfettered, "You are free to leave at any time. No one will hinder you. However, I think it would be wise if you remained for at least a short time. Rest. Eat. Gain back your strength. You have journeyed a great distance, but the road before you remains vast."

"You still have not answered my question," Perrin complained. "How do you know of me, my city, or my journey? Whether witch, magician, or monster, I would still like to know from where you gain this great knowledge."

"There is no simple answer to that question. Knowing is not something one learns. It simply is. For example, take your newfound skill at swinging around that sword and killing things. That is something you learned. At this point in your training, you are a novice, an apprentice to Glord perhaps, but you could someday be an expert. Your body would respond more by instinct than cognizant thought. Knowing is not like that at all. When my essence leaves this physical form, I will still be as much the pupil as when first I arrived in this place. I will never be an expert," the woman's expression was so kind and welcoming, it bordered on frustrating as she said a whole lot of nothing as far as Perrin was concerned.

"Fine," Perrin shook her head. "I may someday be an expert with my sword, and you will always be a pupil of a witch. I would still like to know how you know all these things."

Antopy ignored the slight seeming to float above simple things like frustration and insults as she continued, "The knowledge of everything is accessible to all. One need only open themselves up to receive it. I am no wiser than any of you. I simply allow the glory of Coeptus to exist within me. As individual and unique as we all may be, we all are one. I know you, your story, as well as I know my own. You could know these things too, but that is not your path. You will fight your enemies, battling against what you do not want rather than simply allowing and inviting the outcome you seek. You are common in that regard, but your path leads only to sadness."

Ycharaz leapt down from his horse and approached Antopy. He had only been half paying attention to her story as he examined the room surrounding him. He dipped to one knee in front of her and said,

"Please forgive us, fair queen of this place we only know as home since it has no name, but we are all crude soldiers, warriors on a quest to free an innocent soul imprisoned by a wicked force with power so vast it is beyond our understanding. Though my queen feigns patience, she seeks to be back to the trail with the benefit of whatever knowledge of our adversary and these foreign lands we travel you can provide. If it is not too much to ask, would you please speak plainly to us?"

"A diplomat with a sword," Antopy chuckled. "Please forgive me. I fear I have spent so much time detached from the concerns and yearnings of the physical, I have forgotten what it is like to live under the rules you impose on yourselves on the other side of Ouloos. This place is different than the place you call home. There you are bound by rules crafted by gods to bring order. Things must be how they must be, or they cannot be. I just cannot imagine how. Here, anything is possible. The rules which guide and shape your lives simply do not exist here. Of course, the same way darkness remains in the form of shadows despite the blazing sun, order can exist in this place. This rooms resembles the throne room in Havenstahl because I willed it so. I hoped it would make you feel more comfortable after traveling through the inconsistency of this place. I know it must be troubling for all of you, this lack of order. We do not find it troubling it all. We celebrate the infinite possibilities. Here, anyone can be or do anything simply by wanting it to be. The same was once possible in the lands in which you dwell. They called it magic, twisting and bending the rules to suit your will. That is opposite to what we do here. Here we apply rules to bend the chaos to our will."

Perrin's head spun as she listed to Antopy drone on. Some of it sounded like things Maelich had said, but even more of it made little enough sense she thought the old witch might be insane. Regardless of the woman's level of sanity, Perrin did not have time to talk in circles with her. "Ycharaz has a silver tongue. I lack that quality. My son has been stolen by Kallum. I do not know how that is possible, as my husband destroyed the beast and scattered him to the wind. It seems he managed to pull himself together, as my child's abductors were definitely his priests. The place where he resides exists somewhere in this horribly inconsistent place of which you seem to know so much. Can you help me find my son or not?"

"It was not Kallum who stole your precious Geillan," Antopy replied as she motioned for Ycharaz to rise. "Ijilv, the great hawk, holds him. I am afraid I cannot explain why he did such a thing. He has never actively engaged in the dramas between his siblings. In this act, he has certainly engaged. However, I do not know his desired result."

"Ijilv?" Perrin gasped. "That's impossible. He helped Maelich destroy Kallum."

"The gods pretend to be complicated, even wish they really were," Antopy shook her head, "but they are so very simple. Each of them— good or bad depending on where on Ouloos you were born into the physical—seek only to be worshipped. They thrive on it, even gain strength from it. That was what made Kallum so much more powerful than his kin. Most of the world where you live worshipped the tyrant. Brerto bent his knee living under the illusion the two were equals, Kaldumahn and Moshat hid from his wrath working like spies in the night to oppose him, while Ijilv and," she paused, "there seemed another, but I cannot recall. No matter, the rest hid away, completely refusing to engage until Ijilv aided the lad of the Lake in destroying Kallum."

"Another?" Perrin's head cocked to the side. "I know the names of all the gods. There are and have ever been only five."

"I know the same, but somehow it seems inaccurate," Antopy replied. "Nevertheless, that will remain a mystery unsolved, a story for another time. Based on your eagerness to put foot to trail, we have no time to explore this feeling. For now, we should focus on your son. I fear your path will not lead where you hope, but I know you will not be swayed. Ijilv holds him in a tower that once sat at the edge of time and was ruled by a powerful wizard named Merkhal. He is the one who broke my fair brother, Hagen. Again, a story for another time. Since taking your son, he has hidden the tower away. I can tell you where it once was, but I do not know where it has gone."

"Hagen is your brother?" Perrin's jaw hung slack. It made sense. She had not realized it until just then but speaking with Antopy did bear a striking resemblance to speaking with the old healer she had grown so fond of throughout her life. "Is he a witch too?"

"If you consider me a witch, then yes," Antopy laughed. "We were born in a small village outside of Havenstahl. Our father was a sculptor, and our mother was an adept in the mysteries of Coeptus. They both taught us the beauty in knowledge and our connection to all things. Nobody called us witches then, nor did anyone call the act of allowing miraculous things to take place in the physical world magic. We simply allowed knowledge to come to us. We allowed things to be. Merkhal changed that. He was wicked, bending the rules to benefit himself and hurt others, and Kallum used him to terrorize those he felt did not worship him with enough vigor. My brother opposed Merkhal. The battle nearly destroyed him. When Kallum proclaimed there would be no more magic on Ouloos, Hagen was all too eager to heed the command. As you can see, I was not."

Perrin's brow dipped toward her nose as she considered these ideas. "Hagen is so old. How could he be your brother? And magic? I have seen him concoct healing elixirs out of plants and herbs, but I would not consider any of it to be unnatural."

"He does look old now, does he not? And I appear young enough to be your contemporary," the witch replied. "I assure you I am far older than you. In fact, I am Hagen's elder by five summers. As old as he may appear to you, believe me, he is far older. Both of us have haunted this place for hundreds of summers. My brother has submitted to the rules of that place where you live. It was his battle with Merkhal when he broke. Prior to that, he appeared as youthful as I. Now he probably looks like a beaten old man."

"Impossible," Perrin scoffed.

Antopy shrugged, "Knowledge is knowledge. Whether you believe it or not, you now have it."

The idea of debating this woman who knew so much about so many things seemed fruitless. Whether or not Perrin believed the things she said, she had no way to disprove them. There was no way the kind old man she grew up admiring and even learning from was hundreds of summers old, but she had no evidence to the contrary. What did it matter? The more time she spent away from the only thing on Ouloos which mattered to her, the less things like proving her point meant. Finding Geillan was all she cared about anymore. Hagen could be hundreds of years old, or Antopy could be lying through her teeth. Either way, Geillan would still be lost.

"Fine," she finally said. "Will you take me to this tower at the edge of time?"

"Not even if I could find it," Antopy's smile was no less friendly than it had been as she declined Perrin's request. "The mission offers little for me to learn. Your journey is your own. Dirk will accompany you. He has not been with us long and has never stood at the edge of

Ouloos to stare off into the great expanse. There is much he can learn. You will remain here as long as you like and depart when you are ready."

Before the queen of Havenstahl could offer up complaint, Antopy vanished the same way she had arrived. One moment she was there and the next she was not. "Well, that was little help," Perrin sighed.

"On the contrary, you have learned much," Dirk piped up.

"Nothing useful," Darg countered. "A map, or at least directions, to that tower would have been helpful. Knowing who owns it now or who owned it then does nothing to help us find it."

"Aye," Glord agreed. "And I've known Hagen for most of my life. Knowing how old he may or may not be makes no difference."

"You are all men of action," Dirk smiled. "That fact is helpful in the lands from whence you came. It will be less useful here. My hope is traveling through this place will open your minds to the endless possibility this physical existence presents."

There was so much more Perrin wished to say, but none of it seemed relevant. Dirk would be helpful on their journey. At least he knew the lands they would travel as much as anyone could know a place so inconsistent. Darg's idea of a map suddenly seemed very silly. What would that map look like? Mountains and rivers and skies flipped and flopped. Roads appeared and disappeared at random, sometimes shifting before her very eyes. Any map would need to be equally fluid, and thus completely useless.

"Three days," she said quietly. "We will remain here for three days, rest, and gather our strength. Then Dirk will guide us through this queer place."

CHAPTER 46
# THE GIRL WHO KNOWS EVERYTHING

The world around Cialia seemed unfinished. Half trees covered in grass or weeds—or anything but leaves—grew out of fields of actual leaves not littered about but growing out of the ground where grass might be. A waterfall hundreds of feet high poured deeply until the water ran out, and then it poured back up from the pool it had emptied into. A scarra walked by on two legs smiling as he tugged at the collar of a bright red jacket and puffed at a pipe. Somehow, the strangest thing about it had been the smile. A scarra might slobber, howl, or growl, but she had never seen one smile.

A bird flittered by on one wing. The animal did not appear damaged in the least. Nor did the lack of one wing seem to have any impact on its ability to gain lift from the winds which seemed to swirl too strongly for how light they were. Despite the impossibility of it all, that one winged bird soared to such great heights it was merely a spec in the bright sky when it expanded into a half cloud.

Other shapes zipped by, scurrying along the ground, floating along flowing waters, or soaring among the tops of those unfinished trees. Some looked like things Cialia had seen before. Others were completely foreign. All of them seemed unfinished, like incomplete ideas waiting to be born into something meaningful and real.

A frog hopped out of a river of milk which had not been there a moment earlier and said, "Someday, I will..." in a voice that sounded like a man.

"Someday you will what?" Cialia asked, but the thing turned into a rock, its features quickly smoothing until all the details which made it look like a frog had vanished. "Someday you will nothing, apparently," she quietly added as she passed by the stone.

The world around her remained like that as she travelled. Shapes would emerge from nothing, form into something, and either vanish or soar up into the air. Day became night and night became day so many times she had lost count, and she just kept walking along. She never tired, nor did she sleep or take any kind of nourishment.

A mountain stood in the distance stretching up from the flat land surrounding it like a beacon; the center of the world with everything else stretching out from that one singular point. Though she had no way to determine why the place had meaning, she immediately knew it to be her destination.

Day turned to night and night to day three more times before the path Cialia followed began a steady incline toward the top of the mountain. There were no trees, but grass and wildflowers grew haphazardly on either side of the trail she followed. The colors were impossibly vibrant. The grass was the deepest, richest green she had ever seen, and the flowers were every color she could imagine in more shades than seemed possible. It remained consistent like that except for the very top of the mountain. That seemed too round for a mountaintop, and the grass there seemed too long, too thin, and an odd, yellowish color that stood in stark contrast to the vibrance of everything surrounding it.

It was not until Cialia reached the end of the trail she realized the mountain was completely hollow, and what she had thought was its peak was a separate structure entirely. It looked like a massive statue of a head held up by four giant stone pillars right up until it moved, shifting only slightly.

"Cialia," the giant head spoke in a voice that sounded like her own. "You have travelled a great distance. It is impossible you have found me."

In that moment, Cialia had an incredible realization. "Why do you have my face?" she asked.

"Of course, I do not have your face," the massive head replied. "I am looking at your face at this very moment. If I had your face, you would not have one."

"Fine. You have your face, and I have mine. Why do they look the same?" Cialia rolled her eyes. Overly particular people were irritating.

The face smiled, "You already know the answer to that question. You simply have not thought enough about it. Those swords of yours cannot solve every problem. What if you did not have them? Then what would you do?"

As the question reached Cialia's ear, she instinctively reached for her swords. They were gone. "More tricks," she complained. "I am tired of riddles and games. Can anyone just speak plainly?"

"Some things can be told to us, but some things must be learned," the face continued smiling. "You need to wake up. You will never reach your destination until you do. Those things I can tell you. However, I cannot tell you how to do that."

"You are the second individual I have met on this journey who has told me to wake up while I am already awake. This journey has been a waste of time. The prince is trapped at the top of a mountain of fire, and I am the only who can save him. Can you tell me where is this mountain of fire? Are you the girl who knows everything? If not, can you point me in the direction of where I might find this wise creature?" irritation seeped into Cialia's tone.

"You already know where to find the girl who knows everything," the face replied.

"I do not know anything anymore," Cialia sighed.

"As long as you believe you will not reach your destination, it will remain unfound," the massive face closed her eyes.

"The hawk told me I needed to speak with the girl who knows everything," she complained. "She is supposed to guide me to the mountain of fire. That is all I know."

The head remained silent.

"This cannot be my life," Cialia shouted as she kicked a stone. When it became apparent her outburst would not earn a response from the irritating head, she flopped onto the ground, and let her own head drop onto her bent knees.

She sat like that for a good long while, lifting her head occasionally to look at the massive face in the hopes it might have something else to add. It did not. It just sat there propped up on those pillars. Was it really sleeping, or did it just not want to speak with her anymore? What did it matter? What did anything matter? The prince was probably dead already. She stretched out where she was and closed her eyes. Maybe some sleep would help.

Hours, days, or mere moments? Cialia had no idea how much time had passed while she slumbered. She may have slept the rest of her life away had that familiar voice not asked, "Is this where your story ends?"

What she saw when her eyes snapped open surprised her. The mountainous head in the crater she had fallen asleep upon was gone. She was in a room again. It resembled the room where she had fought the warrior who resembled her so much, but it was different. As she glanced around the room in confusion, "How?" was all she came up with.

The old man who had convinced her to veer off course and search for some girl who allegedly knows everything stood before her. His eyes were just as beautiful and troubling as the first time she saw them. Those horrible, wonderful things stared down at her as he said, "You ask a lot of questions. Sadly, you never seem to ask the correct questions, and you provide very few answers."

Cialia rolled her eyes and laid her head back down on her folded arms, "I am tired of your games. I sought the girl who knows everything and found a giant head who had nothing useful to offer."

"I am disappointed," the old man frowned. "I expected much more from you."

"No more disappointed than I," Cialia countered. "I have failed my mission."

"You have failed nothing. The only thing standing in your way is you," the man vanished, and Cialia was alone again.

Despite how large the circular room was, it seemed the walls were closing in. She had gained nothing on her journey and was no closer to her goal. How could the imbecile suggest she had not failed? The stone walls staring back at her were starkly different than a mountain of fire. "I wish father were here," she whispered to no one as she dropped her head in her hands and allowed tears to overtake her.

She had barely worked her way up to a healthy cry when she heard father's voice above her sobbing and sniveling. "What on Ouloos are you crying about?" he asked.

"Father, I have…" her words trailed off as she raised her head. The man staring back at her was not the man she had cried over in the forest. Nor was he the man who forged her mighty blades and raised her to be a warrior. Despite that, the man sitting cross-legged in front of her somehow was her father. She recognized his dark flowing hair and equally dark eyes. She cocked her head to the side and said, "You are not Agrimon."

"Agrimon the titan? No, I am not. He died years ago. I never knew him, but I did love the stories they told of him," he smiled. "You loved those stories too. I remember I told you the story of how he forged those blades you wield so expertly from a mountain fallen from the heavens."

Recognition sparkled in Cialia's eyes as she tapped the hilts of her swords, "You are Daritus. You gave me these blades, Vengeance and Mercy, when I was very small."

"Have you grown so old you no longer refer to me as father?" he frowned. "I know we share no blood, but you have always been my daughter."

"You taught me to swing these blades," her gaze drifted off toward nothing in particular. "Agrimon was not my father."

"You do share blood with the legend, but no, he was not your father," Daritus agreed.

"You are not really here, are you?" Cialia smiled back at him.

"Only you know the answer to that," he replied and then was gone.

"I am the girl who knows everything in this place, because this place is within me," she added, looking at the spot where her father had been. "I am done with this mission."

The room darkened as the lines around her softened. Bricks broke apart as bright light slipped through the cracks. She floated above it all as it melted away until nothing remained but darkness. Though she could see no visual cues to gauge the rate at which she travelled, the sensation of rapid movement was undeniable. She raced toward something.

Then a dim light sparkled in the distance. It looked little more than a pin prick but added a point of reference to the speed at which she traveled. She raced across a great, black void faster than any horse could hope to run. Milliseconds passed and she could make out a shape. A heartbeat later, she recognized the shape. It was Brerto, his tightly closed eyes snapped open, black voids impossibly swirling with all colors known and unknown. Rage twisted up his face for a moment until fear chased it away.

Cialia's eyes snapped open, and the god was gone. Free from his spell, she saw everything. His garden, so peaceful and perfect, surrounded her, but she saw through the illusion. A snow-covered, barren waste devoid of life sprawled out in all directions. The difference between a lush garden and snow-covered waste mattered little. The door which suddenly stood before her, that was what mattered. It was not a door in the physical sense, no passage between one location and another. It was a passage between the physical reality to which she was accustomed and a spiritual reality she had barely glimpsed while she had split time. Now she saw it clearly. In a thought, she was gone.

Once again, she stood before the god. His eyes widened at the sight of her. His lips moved to speak, but no words came. Cialia simply shook her head and sealed the god's mouth shut. "Brerto, deceiver, false god, I have judged you," her tone was flat and emotionless. "Say your peace before I destroy you."

Brerto's mouth had remained sealed until Cialia allowed him to open it. Rage bubbled deep in his voice as he shouted, "Who are you to judge me? I am eternal. You are but a blink, barely a heartbeat in time. You know nothing."

"And yet, I am your judgement," Cialia's tone remained calm as flames swirled about her. "The next words which leave your vile mouth will be your last. I would not waste them damning another, but do as you see fit."

"Petulant child," the god fumed as his staff glowed brighter than the sun.

Cialia shook her head again and the staff quickly dimmed until no light remained. "All creatures of Ouloos are free from your terror," she whispered.

The moment Cialia spoke those words, Brerto's flesh began to sizzle. Fear once again chased the rage from his face while his body trembled with effort. Spittle formed at the corners of his mouth as his eyes first went wide and then slammed shut. Flames formed out of the air licking his flesh that smoked and smoldered for the briefest of moments until the god exploded in a flash of brilliant light, all colors existing at once in equal saturation. And he was gone.

Cialia fell to her knees. The effort it took to vaporize a god was oddly minimal. It seemed she had grown stronger with each passing moment since finding her flame in the forest outside Druindahl. However, the entire duel had sapped her strength. She had grown weary trapped in his illusion. Something held her attention briefly, something primal. Was it a smell or a taste, or was it just an odd awareness? She could not know. Sleep came far too quickly, and the sensation was gone.

# CHAPTER 47
## FEED THE GODS

Ijilv hid in darkness only partially existing in the realm, like dipping one toe into the water. Despite being equally split between two places, he was acutely aware of everything happening in both. Part of him looked lovingly on the sleeping boy who would one day wake to be his Dragon, his destroyer of worlds, precious Geillan. An equal part of him rested on his brother Brerto's throne, a whisper outside the visible spectrum of light.

He felt his brother's fear and Cialia's odd lack of rage. He expected a fury from her so strong it had flavor. Yet, she remained calm, even aloof. Killing the gods, his brothers, was not malice or revenge. She truly believed it her duty.

"You are pathetic," Kallum's voice was a distraction not quite strong enough to pull him completely away from experiencing the battle going on before him.

"Why?" he asked.

"You admire this weak thing. She is pathetic, a child with a strength she could not possibly understand," Kallum scoffed.

"And yet, she wields it with a mastery none of my brothers could boast. Like most things, you were and still are wrong about her. She is the Dragon. All of you bumbling fools were so worried about Maelich and all your false prophecies. I wonder if you would have been destroyed had you let the lad of the Lake be," Ijilv remained dazzled by the control Cialia held over Brerto as he disregarded Kallum's attempts to denigrate her name.

"Given the chance, she would kill you as well," Kallum continued.

"Yes, she would, and she may still," Ijilv agreed.

A bright flash ended the conversation as Brerto exploded into bits before them. Ijilv inhaled deeply sucking shimmering pieces of his scattered brother into his mouth and nose, his jaw and nostrils expanding to inhale each precious bit. None were spared.

By the time he had finished, Cialia lay sleeping. Ijilv materialized there in the room before her sleeping form. "Look at her," he said. "She is perfect, the most powerful being on Ouloos…for now."

A moment later, he was standing outside Kallum's cell looking down at two of his brothers. Kallum was exactly where he had left him, but now Brerto sat chained next to him. Brerto's head slumped down onto Kallum's shoulder. Not one to allow any creature even the smallest comfort, Kallum shrugged his brother off.

"Welcome, brother," Ijilv boomed. "It has been too long, my friend. Well," he paused long enough to get Brerto's full attention, "at least it seems that way for you. By now, you must know I was your accomplice in the destruction of Havenstahl."

Brerto struggled momentarily against his bonds. Never one to tip his hand, the fear that momentarily flashed in his eyes fled before completely settling in. After a deep breath he replied, "I know all."

"Of course, you do," he laughed at his new prisoner. "I am certain you have an elaborate plan in which I am but a pawn."

Kallum glared at Brerto as he chided him, "You had no plan. If you were as aware of all things as you fancy yourself to be, perhaps it would have been you collecting my scattered parts to restore me to my former glory. Instead, you helped this deceiver take everything away from us both. You have always believed yourself to be the wisest among us, but you were never more than a scrod happy to sniff around at my feet."

"Mind your tongue, brother. I went along with your schemes because we shared a common goal. I never intended to bow before you or allow you to rule this place on your own. Now that all has been revealed, I can tell you that you were the one being used. You have always been the strongest and most prideful of us. That made you an easy pawn. However, where I failed was believing you could control the lad of the Lake," Brerto paused as he glanced around the small cell. "I will defeat this illusion. There will be a reckoning, and I will bring all my brothers to heel."

Kallum laughed in Brerto's face as Ijilv smiled and said, "You are already trying. I can feel it. Please be assured, the effort would be a waste. You are both within me, and soon all of us brothers will be as one."

He left them alone to argue amongst themselves. There was work to do. Two gods remained free to terrorize Ouloos. One Dragon remained lost in an illusion sprouted from a broken psyche, while another charged along on her mission to kill the gods. And his destroyer lay sleeping, growing stronger every day. Everything was going according to plan.

## The End

# ABOUT THE AUTHOR

E. Michael Mettille is the author of To Kill the Dragon (Lake of Dragons Book 1), Kallum's Fury (Lake of Dragons Book 2), and Hell and the Hunger (as Mike Reynolds). He has also written numerous short stories and poems. Mike has spent the last twenty years in direct marketing, print, and communication. He is fascinated by history, belief systems, the human condition and how all of those things work together to define who we are as a people. The world is a wonder and, based on the history of us, it is a wonder we have a world left to wonder about. Mike lives in Milwaukee, WI with his wife, Shelia.